THE
JACKBOOT

THE
JACKBOOT

A novel inspired by true events

**The Incredible Story of The
Greatest Gold Heist in History**

PETER & BILL WELLS

TEEPEE
HOLDINGS, LLC

Published by TeePee Holdings LLC
Lakewood Ranch, FL

www.thejackboot.com

The Jackboot

Cover and Interior Design: Indigo Design, Inc.
designbyindigo.com

ISBN 978-0-578-74293-9

Printed in the U.S.A.

DEDICATION

For Sybil Ann Wells (1932 – 2020)
Wife, Mother, Grandmother, Sister, Aunt and Friend

"I bare you on eagles' wings and brought you unto myself."
Exodus

ACKNOWLEDGEMENTS

Many thanks to Taryn for her patience, guidance,
encouragement and unwavering love and support
in helping complete The Jackboot.
Additional thanks to Cora, Lynda, and Sid,
plus our entire family for their thoughtful comments
and profound enthusiasm.

"It used to be called plundering.
But today things have become more humane.
In spite of that, I intend to plunder and to do it thoroughly."

Hermann Goering
Reich Marshall

Gold — what can it not do, and undo?

William Shakespeare

CONTENTS

BOOK II

Preface

Penmon Beach, Anglesey, Wales

Present Day

It was a crystal-clear day but still bitterly cold following the storm that had raged across the Island of Anglesey the previous night. Kieran McCarthy pulled his black beanie further down over his receding hairline as the cold wind gusted across the golden sands of Penmon Beach. It was one of a handful of secluded beaches that bordered the Menai Straits. These fast-moving waters were some of the most treacherous on earth. When the tide turns, the mighty Irish Sea is forced through the narrow gap between Anglesey and the Welsh mainland. The storm surge that had barreled through the Menai Straits just hours before had pushed the water level mark to the highest that Kieran had ever seen during his twenty plus years of living on the island.

He watched his two border collies, aptly named Gale and Breeze frantically chase each other back and forth on the sand about fifty yards ahead of him. Suddenly, the dogs ventured off towards the rocky bank where the storm surge had eroded a large area causing the land above it to slide down onto the beach. A large, dead tree had toppled over, revealing an old decaying tangled root ball.

Gale was pulling on a long black object while Breeze wagged her tail and watched her sister tug on it to free it from the root ball. Finally, Gale pulled it free and Breeze immediately pounced on the other end and the two began one of their favorite games, tug of war. Tails wagging and playfully growling, the two evenly matched sisters went back and forth scattering wet sand in all directions.

Kieran was concerned that what they were playing with might not be safe so he yelled, "Leave it!" Both dogs instantly obeyed and simultaneously laid down the object and sat with their tails wagging in perfect synchronization fanning the sand. They looked at their master intensely, ears cocked against the wind, waiting for his next command.

Kieran walked up to them and looked at the object. He immediately recognized it as an extremely weathered black leather boot. "Huh?" he exclaimed to himself as he bent down to pick it up for a better look. Could this be what he thought it was? A German jackboot from World War II! A wave of excitement instantly rippled through his body.

The boot had clearly been in the elements for a long time. Kieran knew by its condition that it must have been just above the tide level all these years and had only been revealed by the destruction that last night's massive tide had wrought on the bank. Although it was caked in mud and sand, he could see and feel that the thick black leather that would cover the calf and shin was still in remarkable shape as was the sole and heel.

The two dogs continued to watch Kieran's every move intensely. He walked a couple of steps over to a rock pool to wash off some of the mud and now he could make out the rusted metal that made up a protective horseshoe that followed the edge of the heel. Another quick rinse revealed the rusted remains of a similar metal cleat that protected the underside of the toe. He then turned it over to examine the outside of the boot.

At the top of the boot Kieran saw something that literally took his breath away. "Wow!" he gasped. There in front of him, gleaming in the bright sunshine, attached to the top of the boot on the outside of the leather rim was a small gold badge. The badge was a Nazi eagle, over a swastika and below it he could make out the initials MvS. His hands began to shake. He wasn't sure if it was from the cold or from the sheer excitement now running through his body.

Kieran, a retired Royal Navy Captain had researched and purchased enough military memorabilia to know that what he had in front of him was the real deal. This was a Nazi jackboot worn by an officer. He had never seen anything like the badge before, but it was gold for sure. Whoever MvS was, he must have had considerable wealth and clout. The Nazis were fanatical about their uniforms and how they reflected their rigid discipline and order. For someone to deviate from the strict military dress code, they must have been well up the Nazi food chain.

Instinctively, he looked around. The beach was still deserted, "Finders keepers!" he said to the dogs. They had now got to their feet with tales wagging madly, and a sense that they had done something to please their master. After all, that was the sole purpose of their lives.

"Come on!" he yelled to the dogs. "Let's go home." The dogs took off in a flash towards the footpath where he had parked his Range Rover. As he followed behind, ecstatic at his surprise find, he began to ponder. Who the hell was MvS? And how did a Nazi jackboot end up here on the Island of Anglesey and on the shores of Penmon Beach? What follows is the incredible story of the mysterious man with the initials MvS and his gold adorned jackboot.

BOOK I

— ◆ —

THE LONG ROAD TO PARYS MOUNTAIN

Chapter 1

MAX VON SEECKT

Aberystwyth, Wales

1912

Karl von Seeckt understood the precious metals market better than any man on earth. It seemed as though everything he touched turned to gold, the most precious of all metals. Von Seeckt was so good that he had earned the nickname Midas-the man with the golden touch. Hailing from a wealthy family with ancient roots in Brandenburg, Germany, Karl von Seeckt was destined to lead a charmed life.

Having been educated at Eton and Cambridge, after graduation Karl von Seeckt had gone to work in Berlin for Otto Haus, one of the largest precious metal brokers in the world. He had enjoyed a rapid rise to success with his uncanny ability to read the market. He kept his high roller clientele well ahead of the curve with his sound advice. The profits he earned them were astronomical and his stellar reputation soon spread beyond Berlin to London and New York.

Karl von Seeckt's Rolodex was an impressive Who's Who of Europe's ultrawealthy. He was constantly invited to attend their lavish parties as each tried to outdo the other with their own shows of excessive decadence. Everyone wanted to do business with Midas, and Midas was more than happy to oblige them. With his handsome good looks and piercing blue eyes, von Seeckt was also quite the ladies' man.

It was at one of these parties in the beautiful city of Monte Carlo that he met Cari Owens. She was the only daughter of Dylan Owens, the Welsh copper tycoon whose family had made their fortune smelting copper in the city of Swansea for generations.

Cari had been born and raised in Aberystwyth, Wales but educated in the finest boarding schools for girls in England. With a near genius IQ, she spoke fluent English, Welsh, and Latin. Midas as usual, was in the right place at the right time.

Cari was still heartbroken after the man she thought she was going to spend the rest of her life with turned out to be a conman, with a wife and three children living in Essex. She had been alone in her room for weeks. The bubbling vibrant daughter that Dylan adored was reduced to a mere shell of her former self. Pained beyond belief at his daughter's grief, he tried repeatedly to get her out of the house, constantly coaching her that she still had her whole life ahead of her.

Finally, Cari reluctantly agreed to be persuaded by her father to attend a small cocktail party where much to her surprise she was delighted to meet the dashing Midas. He was the antithesis of the boring stuffy men in tuxedos that usually attended such events.

Midas was different. He was young, full of life and energy, with a seemingly perfect balance of self-confidence and somber humility. Most importantly, he had a sense of humor that was identical to her own. For the first time in weeks, Dylan Owens watched as Karl von Seeckt aka Midas, in less than three hours gave him back the daughter he thought he had lost. From that moment on, Midas could do no wrong. It was love at first sight for both of them. They were immediately inseparable and six months later to Dylan Owens' sheer delight, they were married in a lavish wedding at Swansea Cathedral in Wales.

Midas continued to work his magic while at the same time building a substantial portfolio for himself. He invested wisely and purchased homes in Aberystwyth, Kent, Berne, and Berlin. Life was as good as it gets for the von Seeckt's and they were both over the moon when Cari announced she was pregnant. Eight months later, on a bitterly cold Aberystwyth night in a waning 1912, she gave birth to a healthy son, who they proudly named Max von Seeckt, after Karl's father.

The young family spent most of their time living in Berlin and Aberystwyth. During their time in Wales, Cari would insist on talking to Max exclusively in Welsh and was delighted with the ease the little boy mastered the complex ancient Welsh language.

The Welsh people were fiercely proud of their nation and heritage. Despite the best efforts of England, the Welsh language was still very much alive and well. For Max to be able to adapt and thrive, he needed to speak the native tongue, which he did, along with English and German.

Karl, a proud old Etonian had registered Max with Eton the day he was born. He had made many large donations to the iconic school, assuring Max of his future place swatting alongside England's elite in the school's primordial classrooms. Life for the von Seeckt family was purring away nicely. The future looked bright, but the dark clouds of war were already starting to gather. By 1914, the world erupted in flames as the First World War brought the good times to a screeching halt. Despite excellent contacts in London, in the month of August all of Karl von Seeckt's assets were either frozen or seized by the British government.

Karl von Seeckt had seen the cataclysm coming long before most. He had spent the last year investing heavily in gold which sat securely in multiple bank vaults in Switzerland. With careful and meticulous management by Karl, Cari and their young son Max remained blissfully unaware of the complex financial web Karl had to weave, for the family to maintain the standard of living they were accustomed to. The family weathered the war to end all wars, essentially without missing a beat.

After the war was over, Karl's assets were returned and when Dylan Owen died unexpectedly, Karl assumed the mantle of running the family smelting business, which surprisingly he found to be more enjoyable than the world of high finance. Max had grown to be a wise young man with an astute awareness of the world around him. He had watched his father's pain when Germany had surrendered, and he was acutely aware of both his German and Welsh heritage. Many of his friends were Welsh nationalists with an acute dislike of the English that went back centuries. They mirrored the dislike his German friends also had of the English. Two groups of people he knew and understood better than most and both had one historical enemy...the English. Against this backdrop it took a stern tongue lashing from Karl to convince Max that despite his tearful objections that attending Eton was the best and only path forward for him.

And so, it was on a sunny Berkshire day that Max sat in the back of the family's Mercedes Benz 320 with his father sitting next to him, coaching and encouraging him as it cruised through the winding country roads on its way to opening day at Eton.

Had their chauffeur checked his rear-view mirror, he would have seen the stately profile of a Rolls Royce Silver Ghost following a short distance behind. It too had a proud old Etonian father sitting in the back seat, quietly coaching his own apprehensive son on the virtues of Eton. His son's name was Peter Francis Legh.

Chapter 2

PETER FRANCIS LEGH

Eton College, England

1923

Peter Francis Legh was born with a silver spoon in his mouth. He was the only son of Sir Francis Legh of Addington and his wife, the elegant and beautiful Lady Sybil Ann Legh. Born in England, Lady Sybil had spent most of her life in America. She was the sole heiress of a family owned produce empire that covered thousands of acres in California.

Peter was already a well-traveled young man. He had crossed the Atlantic several times with his parents, followed by the long railroad trip to the West Coast. The family simultaneously juggled its business interests on both sides of the globe. For recreation, the Legh family had enjoyed long vacations cruising the Mediterranean. The young man was given a glimpse of life outside the luxuries of his ancestral home of Addington Abbey in the Cheshire countryside.

His mother made sure that Peter understood the value of money from an early age. She loathed the British class system and never really cared for the title of Lady. It was a testament to her diplomatic skills that she was able to charm Sir Francis, who in so many ways epitomized the system into seeing her often unorthodox American point of view. The result was a well-balanced young man who understood his privilege along with the value and benefit of hard work. He respected people from all walks of life. He was just as at ease when cleaning out the family stables with the Addington Abbey stable boys as he was sitting in the saddle hunting with Sir Francis and his well-connected friends.

One thing Lady Sybil had fully supported was Sir Francis' desire for Peter to attend Eton. Eton was the traditional school for Legh men going back hundreds of years. As ritual required, Sir Francis had registered Peter at the exclusive school on the day of his birth. Lady Sybil was a huge proponent of education and she knew there wasn't a boy's school anywhere in the United States that could hold a candle to Eton.

She also knew the value of being well-connected and the contacts he would make during his time at Eton. They would benefit him long after he graduated from the iconic school. She had drilled into Peter's head the importance of the Old Etonian network that had been so valuable to Sir Francis. And so, as the Rolls Royce hummed along flawlessly, the young man in the stiff new suit with his top hat sitting on his lap was as groomed as he could possibly be for the challenges and opportunities that now lay before him.

Chapter 3

THE WELSH GOLD

Eton College, England
November 1928

There was no doubt that Anthony Godfrey Moorehouse was master of his own universe. There was no other place on earth that he would rather be than in the main chemistry laboratory at Eton.

Moorehouse, who all the boys referred to as The Beak because of his long pointed nose, was totally in his element. His brilliant mind had taken him from his beloved Eton to Oxford, immediately followed by a stellar career in research with Lucas Electric. Several patents had made him wealthy beyond his wildest dreams. He had returned to Eton several years ago to pursue his one and only real passion to teach the wonders of chemistry to the eager young minds at the world-renowned school.

Always immaculately dressed and an absolute stickler for detail, Moorehouse paraded up and down the aisles between the long ancient tables that ran the width of the chemistry lab, with an almost military like precision. His favorite cane, affectionately named Old Woody was tucked tightly under his right arm, with his thumb and index finger lightly holding the curved handle.

His charcoal gray suit was expertly pressed, and his heavily starched collar fit perfectly around his pencil thin, smoothly shaved neck. The last graying remnants of what had once been a fine head of thick black hair was now closely cropped and formed a two-inch stripe across the back of his head. His square-neck haircut formed a perfect parallel line with the razor edge of his white shirt collar. His wire rimmed reading glasses neatly cradled his droopy brown eyes and his impeccably trimmed and waxed moustache added to his air of mastery.

Peter hated chemistry. Other than the occasional experiments that they were allowed to conduct under the strict supervision of Moorehouse, he found the endless formulas and tables that he had to memorize to be quite mind numbing and not at all what he had imagined chemistry would be.

Peter found today's lecture on the earth's metals and minerals to be quite nauseating. The whole lesson had been one long grind. Peter leaned forward over his table with his right hand forming a peak over his brow and his elbow resting on the well-worn surface. He gazed down at the textbook in front of him, all in an effort to convince Moorehouse of his interest in the subject.

In the background, Moorehouse continued droning on about the marvels of bronze. Eventually, Peter looked up from his book, gazed out of the window and began to daydream. His thoughts inevitably drifted to California, where he was sitting in the rear seat of the family crop duster as it flew at low altitudes over the Legh family orchards. Peter felt that he could almost reach out and grab a handful of leaves.

"Mr. Legh!"

Moorehouse's voice snapped him back to the reality of the fume filled chemistry lab at Eton, no blue sky or freedom here.

"Sir?" Peter replied.

"Iron Sir, the symbol is?" queried Moorehouse.

"Fe Sir," Peter responded without hesitation.

Although he hated chemistry, Peter was smart enough to realize that some things at Eton were simply impossible to bypass. The chemical formulas in Moorehouse's class were one of those things. The final chapter that Peter had read in his room last night before lights out was the list of chemical symbols. He knew that Moorehouse expected each of his students to memorize them. Gifted with a steel trap mind, once he learned something he rarely forgot it.

"Good, good," said Moorehouse, his voice rising an octave or two in an involuntary reaction to the delight that his students seemed to be as enthralled with the chemical symbols table as he was.

"Fe Iron, good, good," he continued. He snapped to the right on his immaculately polished, black leather shoes that took him behind Peter's bench. Each mechanical click of his leather sole caused the antiquated plank floors to creak, as he slowly, methodically, paced between the rows of benches.

He stopped in front of a pupil with thick brown curly hair and freckles who nervously tapped his bottom lip with his index finger and realized he was next.

"Mr. Griffith, how about my favorite metal…Gold?"

Robert Griffith tapped on his lips a couple of more times as a thin smile spread across them. Griffith was one of Peter's cricket teammates. The two had agreed that Moorehouse was more than likely to spring the symbols test on them and he too had studied until lights out.

"Gold Sir, the symbol for Gold is Au!" answered Griffith.

Griffith was clearly delighted that he had scored a win. His fist clenched in victory, he now lightly tapped the bench and acknowledged the wink from Peter with a curt nod of his head.

"Excellent! Excellent! Gold…Au!" boomed Moorehouse. "Outstanding gentlemen, outstanding!"

The class breathed a collective sigh of relief that Moorehouse was enjoying himself. They had all been on the receiving end of Moorehouse's red hot temper in the past. They had witnessed Old Woody in action, and it was an experience that none of them cared to repeat.

"Gold, the most magical and valuable of all God's earthly creations. Gold gentlemen has adorned Warriors, Kings and Noblemen throughout the ages. It's still the most prized and sought after metal on earth. Gold gentleman, at the end of the day is still the standard by which civilized countries and men are measured."

"Gold! is what it takes to make sure that the sun never sets on the British Empire, that and of course…His Majesty's Royal Navy!" he added, eliciting a roll of light, polite laughter from the class. Delighting in the spotlight, Moorehouse continued, always eager to try to get the simple realities of life into the boys' heads at any opportunity.

"Gold makes the world go around gentlemen. Your fathers have wisely invested some of their gold to ensure that you boys receive the best education in England that money can buy!" Another roll of laughter. Moorehouse pulled his pocket watch from his fitted waist coat and flipped open the cover to check the time.

"Time for just one more bonus question," he continued. He snapped the watch closed and returned it to his pocket.

"And unless I hear an objection, let us stay on gold, my favorite metal, shall we? I'm a reasonable man so I will throw this one out to the whole class."

Moorehouse gazed out of the old double hung windows at the gray overcast Berkshire sky, involuntarily stroking his moustache, as he pondered his next question.

"Tell me then gentlemen, where is the purest gold on planet earth found?" he asked turning away from the window and walking at the same methodical pace to his lectern at the center of the lab, in front of the black board.

The class shuffled nervously and each boy tried his utmost to appear to be pondering Moorehouse's question. Moorehouse, now at the lectern, his seat of power, statue like, surveyed each boy. His beady eyes scanned the rows of nervous schoolboys. Moorehouse, delighted in the awkward silence, was confident that he had stumped the class. Oh, how he loved these moments.

"Any offers? Gentleman?"

Silence.

"Oh dear, no one?" he stroked his moustache again.

Moorehouse looked out at a sea of bewildered faces, none of whom dared to make eye contact with him. Most stared at the textbooks in front of them. Several gazed out of the windows at the darkening sky, seemingly waiting for a divine intervention.

"No one?"

Moorehouse shook his head, incredulous at what had seemed such a reasonable question that had now apparently stumped the class. He waited a little while longer before slipping Old Woody from under his arm. Then he waved him slowly and deliberately from left to right and back again until he finally stopped in the middle. The tip of Old Woody now pointed squarely at his seemingly random victim.

"Ah! Mr. Bridge, care to take a stab?"

Barrington Bridge cursed his luck. He had almost made it through unscathed only to be singled out in the final minutes of the class. Why me?

"Where is the purest gold on earth found, Sir?" Bridge responded, repeating the question to buy more time.

"Correct, Mr. Bridge! Where is the purest gold found? That is the question boy," replied Moorehouse. Old Woody was still pointing directly between the dark blue eyes of Barrington Bridge.

"South America, Sir?" bleated Bridge, knowing the answer was incorrect.

"South America is a big place Bridge, be more specific," said Moorehouse, as he lowered Mr. Woody and placed him on the lectern.

"Err...Mexico, Sir?" answered Bridge, relieved that his shot in the dark, despite incredible odds, may have hit the target.

"Mexico? How on earth did you arrive at that conclusion boy?" asked Moorehouse, genuinely curious at Bridge's thought process.

"Well Sir, I'm familiar with the Aztec culture and gold played a major role in their civilization. It seemed as good a place as any."

"Ah, excellent logic Mr. Bridge. You will one day make a decent barrister! Of that there is no doubt. However, in this case Sir your guess is incorrect but a jolly good effort! Come on now gentlemen, I would hate to have to order punishment lines for all of you to write. Now anyone?"

Total silence.

"Disappointing gentlemen, very disappointing," moaned Moorehouse as he turned to face the black board picking up the chalk. He prepared to write the punishment lines out.

The class was now collectively doomed to a dose of the legendary Moorehouse punishment lines. The situation was made even more difficult as Moorehouse delighted in substituting chemical equations in place of sentences, much to the chagrin of the boys.

"Wales Sir, the world's purest gold actually comes from Wales." Seemingly out of nowhere, from the back of the class the perfect baritone voice of Max von Seeckt broke the silence.

Moorehouse paused, returned the chalk to its shelf, clapped his hands gently to remove the small amount of chalk dust and turned to face the class. In particular, he turned to face Max von Seeckt.

"Wales! Correct, Mr. von Seeckt! Nicely done, Sir!" beamed Moorehouse. "Wales, right here in this United Kingdom gentlemen, is where the purest gold on earth can be found! It's a fair distance from our good friend Mr. Bridge's Mexico."

The class roared with laughter, clearly delighted that von Seeckt had saved them all from writing out endless lines. Moorehouse's demeanor had changed in an instant back to the kind amicable professor they had originally been introduced to almost five years ago, on the first day of term.

"Excellent, von Seeckt excellent! And your source, Sir?" inquired Moorehouse.

"My mother, Sir. She is Welsh and she comes from a long ancient line of Welsh nobility. She told me of the legendary Welsh gold and its purity when I was a small boy. My father was in the precious metals business for years. He has a rare collection in the family vault in Zurich. My mother also told me that because of its purity, it is the only gold used by the British Royal family to make their wedding bands, Sir," answered von Seeckt, as he began to casually pack up his books.

"Outstanding boy! Yes, that's also correct, well done sir. It's very rare now, most of it was mined centuries ago. The Druids were rumored to have had massive amounts stashed on their spiritual home of Anglesey. It's believed to be the real reason that the Romans, against all odds and expectations invaded Anglesey. There is still a great debate amongst historians. It's believed that the Romans were incensed by the Druids acting very rudely, namely collectively showing their posteriors and various other parts of their anatomy to the Roman Legions. They believed the Romans would never attempt to cross the treacherous Menai Straits.

Unfortunately, they misjudged the Emperor's sense of humor. The Romans crossed the Straits and the Druids were massacred. It is believed that word of the Druids' secret stash of gold had long been discussed in a cash strapped Rome, so perhaps that was the deciding factor. As I said earlier gentlemen, gold is the stuff that empires are built on. Gold gentleman makes the world go around! And the purest gold on earth can be found where...?"

"In Wales, Sir!" bellowed the class in unison.

"So, something other than sheep have actually come out of Wales Sir!" yelled out Peter over the laughter.

The class exploded again.

"Quite right, Sir!" responded Moorehouse, heartily laughing at the joke. The whole class roared in approval, not that Legh's joke was that funny, but that Moorehouse thought it was. The boys knew from past dealings that a happy Professor Moorehouse was always a reason to celebrate.

The whole class was amused, that is except Max von Seeckt. He sat still and stone-faced, glaring at the back of Peter Legh. He and Legh had disliked each other from the moment they first met. They had clashed on the first day over the merits of Mercedes versus Rolls Royce. Max had also teased Peter relentlessly about his last name. Max claimed that Legh had been misspelled and that everyone knew Legh was spelled Leigh. Peter was infuriated. The Legh family name was an ancient one, his ancestry went back to King John of Magna Carta fame and beyond. For someone who had German roots to question it rubbed Peter the wrong way. The mutual dislike had been simmering away for several years now. Both boys knew that a clash was inevitable.

Peter's simple wise crack had inadvertently ignited a fuse in von Seeckt that would slowly burn with a deep-seated hatred. It would ultimately explode a decade from now in a dramatic face off, with consequences that neither he nor Legh could ever begin to imagine.

Chapter 4

FIRST FIGHT

Eton College, England
November 1928

The sound of the chapel bell ringing signaled the end of the class. The boys made a rapid bee line for the exit before Moorehouse could issue the homework assignment.

As the class exited, Max made a point of filing in directly behind Peter. Making their way into the main corridor, he closed in on him until they finally made contact. Peter started to turn as he felt the presence of another body too close behind him, just as Max unleashed a vicious knee right into the middle of his thigh. Peter yelped in pain as he dropped to his knees. Suddenly, Max was on him pinning him to the wall. "You insulted my Mother, my heritage. You'll pay for that Legh, you dog!" he hissed in Peter's ear. The burning pain in Peter's thigh gave way to anger when he realized that he had been ambushed by Max von Seeckt. "You cad! That was uncalled for!" groaned Peter, clutching his thigh, "Have you no morals man?"

"Like I said, you're a dog Legh, pure and simple," he continued. "Your problem is..." he was cut off as Peter smashed him with a head butt that caught him square under the chin. Von Seeckt was taken by surprise and fell backwards. In a flash, Peter side mounted him before he could regroup, quickly applying a headlock. Von Seeckt tried to pry his way out but Peter had the lock on too tight. His legs were now spread eagled. His full body weight crushed against von Seeckt's rib cage, making it impossible for the German to move. The more pressure Peter applied, the more difficult it was for him to breathe.

"My problem is that your German father seeded a Welsh whore, who's spawn somehow found its way into Eton in a piece of junk called a Mercedes. That same spawn now sneaks up and knees a man from behind. It is hardly what one would call cricket, eh von Seeckt?" growled Peter, as he tightened his grip. Peter was in excellent physical shape. Max was surprised by his strength.

Peter was aware of the rapidly growing group of boys that now surrounded their fracas. He knew it was only a short matter of time before Moorehouse would be coming down the corridor. Fighting on Eton grounds was simply not tolerated, that is with the exception of just one place, The Wall.

"You'll pay for this Legh, I swear to God, you'll pay!" grunted Max. Blood now trickled from the corner of his mouth.

"Really? I'll pay? I don't think so. Unlike you, I sir, am a gentleman. I'll beat you fair and square. The Wall this afternoon!" he increased the tension further on the head lock.

"The Wall it is, Legh!" growled Max. "This afternoon!"

"Beak! The Beak is coming!" yelled someone. It was the signal that everyone, including the two combatants knew. It meant that Moorehouse was about to appear.

Peter released his grip and both boys stood up quickly, each eyeballing the other for a possible cheap shot. Max pulled his handkerchief out and dabbed his bloody mouth. Peter brushed off his pants and jacket just as Moorehouse entered the corridor to see what all the fuss was about. Max turned and was gone. Peter, supported by Griffith and Bridge followed closely behind, leaving Moorehouse totally unaware of the clash that had just taken place.

The two boys fought later in the day at the legendary Wall at Eton, where most disputes were honorably settled. The fight was particularly brutal with both boys having to go to the school infirmary for treatment. Max had a deep laceration on his cheek from a vicious elbow landed by Peter that would scar his perfect looks for life. But he had scored his own damage, stamping on and breaking Peter's middle finger so badly that it was always slightly crooked. The fight was deemed most un-gentlemanly by all who witnessed it and determined to be a draw. They never spoke again, but both felt strongly that the business was unfinished. The hatred would continue to burn.

No one in that chemistry class on that dreary morning could possibly know that all the dreams that Professor Moorehouse had for them would sadly never materialize. Their dreams would all go up in smoke, along with many of their lives and the lives of millions more of their generation in the all-consuming flames of the war that would engulf the entire world.

Chapter 5

LAST DAY AT ETON

Eton College, England
July 1929

It was yet another dull, overcast day at Eton. Peter looked through the sea of parents for his father, Sir Francis Cecil Legh, who at six-foot, two inches tall, usually stood out in a crowd. The last day of term had finally arrived and everyone was in a joyous mood. The grueling last few weeks of exams was finally a distant memory. Boys had said their goodbyes and promised to stay in touch, and for seniors like Peter, this was the last time they would gather underneath the clock tower at the bedrock of the English public-school system.

"Master Legh! Over here!" Peter immediately recognized the voice of the family's long-time chauffeur Giles Humphries, known to the Legh family simply as our man Giles. Giles was dressed in his gray chauffeur's uniform and cap with the Legh coat of arms above the peak. He was immaculately groomed as always. His brown leather boots were polished to a shine.

"Hello Giles!" said Peter, glad to finally see a friendly face from home.

"How are you Master Legh? Glad to have Eton behind you?" asked Giles, as he extended his white gloved hand in welcome.

"Rather," said Peter. "Is Father with you?" he asked. He and Giles picked up the suitcases. "No, I'm afraid not. Your mother is waiting in the car. Please, after you," he said as he gestured towards the packed car park.

"Oh, I see," replied Peter, surprised that his father, a proud Old Etonian would have missed a trip back to his beloved Eton.

Peter dutifully followed Giles and soon picked out his mother's preferred vehicle, the gray Rolls Royce Silver Ghost, amongst a sea of Rolls Royce's and Bentleys, as the elite of Britain descended upon Eton to gather up the future ruling class. Giles opened the rear door. Peter took off his top hat and slid onto the rear seat next to his mother, Lady Sybil. She immediately hugged and kissed him leaving a red lipstick mark on his cheek.

"Please don't, Mother," he said and pretended to try to push her away. The smell of leather, polish and his mother's French perfume simultaneously engulfed him.

"Peter my love, I haven't seen you for months. My only son look at you! You are all grown up! I'm so proud of you!" she lavished praises upon him. Giles had stowed the bags and was now back behind the wheel.

"Ready Mam?" he asked, looking in the rearview mirror. "Yes Giles, to Addington Abbey please. Let's get my grownup son back home!" said a delighted Lady Sybil, without taking her eyes off her pride and joy.

"Addington Abbey it is, Mam," said Giles, as he smoothly pulled the Silver Ghost away from the curb. Neither he nor Lady Sybil noticed the glares being exchanged between Peter and another pupil. A young man with thick blond hair was sitting in the back of a black Mercedes Benz that parked beside them. The two boys had remained sworn enemies since their epic fight at The Wall. They were both delighted to be seeing the last of each other. But the hand of fate was not done with the two Old Etonians. They would fight again years from now on opposing sides when the nations of the world would clash in a cataclysm known as the Second World War.

"Where's Father?" asked Peter.

"He's at Addington darling and extremely busy. There are some things that he needs to attend to regarding the agricultural side of the business in California. In fact, we are leaving for New York next week," she said in a matter of fact tone.

"And then to California?" said Peter, suddenly excited.

"Yes, dear," replied his Mother. We have tickets on the Cunard Line's, Lancastria. We sail out of Liverpool on Friday!"

"Oh, good show!" exclaimed Peter. RMS Lancastria was his favorite ship. The family had crossed the Atlantic on her twice when Peter was young. More recently they had cruised the sunny Mediterranean for three weeks aboard the luxury liner. Peter knew every inch of her, deck by deck and had even been given a tour of her mighty engine room. He had a scale model of RMS Lancastria in his bedroom at Addington Abbey, where it occupied the prime spot on his small writing desk.

"Are you excited?" asked Lady Sybil.

"Rather! It's been a long time since we were out there. It will be nice to see the sunshine again," he said, looking out of the window at the gray clouds over head. "How long are we going for?" he asked.

"Well, that's the one thing we are not sure of. It could be a month, six months, a year, more even. Your father will have a better idea once we get there," she said, looking at the same depressing gray clouds.

"I see, but what about Cambridge?" asked Peter.

"Your Father has made arrangements for you to go to Stanford University instead. It's a wonderful University, on a par with America's finest. I believe the plan is for you to perhaps finish up at Cambridge, but I simply do not know. The whole thing is somewhat in flux right now. As I say, you will have to talk to your father," she replied, hoping that the conversation wouldn't turn negative.

"Stanford? I've never heard of it," said Peter, as he tried to envision the stone towers of a grand school called Stanford somewhere in California. He felt a sudden sense of relief. Although he had been accepted into Cambridge, which was the traditional route enjoyed by the Legh's for countless generations, he really didn't want to go.

Since age eleven he had been in the English public-school system. He had enjoyed the absolute best education a young man could get, but after five years of enduring the strictly regimented life of Eton, along with its brutal enforcement of discipline, he was more than ready for a change of pace.

Cambridge, although nowhere near as regimented as Eton, was going to be more of the same. California's warm sunshine and acres of open space with its laid back inhabitants sounded like a perfect plan to him. He smiled, sat back in the plush leather seat, took off his bow tie, undid his starched collar and watched out the window as the Berkshire countryside flew by. He was leaving Eton forever and heading home to Addington. The world was his oyster, and he knew it.

Chapter 6

CALIFORNIA THE GOLDEN STATE

San Francisco, California
October 1929

It was early October when the Legh's finally arrived at their California home located in Clayton, about thirty miles east of San Francisco. The weather was spectacular and a welcome change from the cold wet English climate. The family owned thousands of acres of walnut trees in the adjacent town known as Walnut Creek. Sybil Legh was the sole heir to the Tomlinson family's walnut business which she had left in the capable hands of Graham Freeman, a gifted businessman and long-time friend of the Legh family.

Freeman had steadily grown the business year by year and expanded into apple orchards and lately into grapes, including a small winery in Clayton. Business was good and the Legh's enjoyed and appreciated their yearly dividend check from across the pond. Then tragically, Freeman drowned on a fishing trip to catch salmon, which ran in great numbers in the Pacific just outside of the Golden Gate Bridge. He had left early in the morning on his beloved fishing boat, the Robyn Mae and had never returned. Freeman's deputy David Kenner had done a reasonable job in filling his shoes but was not the man to keep the business on an upwards trajectory. With so much capital at stake, Sir Francis made the decision to return to California to personally take charge until he could find the right successor to Freeman.

Sir Francis was currently staying at the Legh city home in the Nob Hill area of San Francisco which made it convenient to get to the corporate office on Sansome Street. Peter, along with his mother were staying at the sprawling Clayton ranch home that was a lot closer to Walnut Creek and the newly purchased family winery. More importantly the weather was a lot hotter and drier in Clayton than San Francisco which was an added benefit to Lady Sybil who had long suffered from asthma. The warm dry Clayton air was a perfect tonic.

Peter was delighted to be out in Clayton. He also loved the weather and it was where the company's crop duster aircraft was based along with its colorful character of a pilot, a gnarly tanned local man named Charlie Menatti who flew the aircraft.

Peter adored Charlie. He was in so many ways, the antithesis of the teachers who had been molding him at Eton over the years. Fun loving and easy going, he had been an early pioneer flying in the newly formed United States Army Air Corps. He was an excellent pilot and a loyal employee, a characteristic held in high esteem by the Legh family. Peter had always been fascinated by airplanes and loved to spend time in the hanger where Charlie had patiently taught him the mechanics of the aircraft and how the various systems were interconnected.

On a previous trip, Charlie had given him his own logbook for his tenth birthday and had taken him up for his first ever flight. Sitting in the rear pilot's seat, Peter was totally mesmerized and instantly became addicted to flying. It had only been a short flight spraying some of the fields around Clayton before climbing to six thousand feet in a few short seconds and flying right over the summit of Mount Diablo, which was almost four thousand feet high. The mountain dominated the east bay skyline.

The view was something Peter never forgot. The rolling hills of the Clayton Valley and Mount Diablo directly below him, he could see the neat rows of walnut trees for miles. It made him realize just how much property the Legh family owned and were responsible for. He remembered looking west to the city of San Francisco, San Francisco Bay and the white bank of Pacific Ocean fog that rolled into the city most nights, having retreated during the day as the sun baked the California land. The San Francisco bay area was, without a doubt one of the most beautiful places on earth.

As soon as they touched down and taxied to the hanger, Charlie cut the engine. Peter climbed out of the rear seat and ran to the arms of his anxious Mother who had been nervously watching the small bright yellow aircraft as it had screamed across the acres of walnut trees at an impossibly low altitude. "Mother!" he had yelled. "That was the most incredible ride. I want to be a pilot when I grow up. Charlie said if you gave me permission, he would teach me! So, can I Mother, please, please?"

"Of course, dear!" she had replied. "If that's what you want to be when you grow up."

Now fully grown, he had not forgotten his mother's promise all those years ago. Now, she reluctantly let him take to the clear blue California skies daily with Charlie. By this time, his logbook had hundreds of hours of flight time and Charlie had gladly become the passenger. He loved to watch the young pilot hone his skills as they screamed over the tops of the walnut trees at just a few, breathtaking feet above them. Unbeknownst to Charlie, the flying skills that he had taught Peter would one day save his life and those of hundreds of his fellow service men trapped helplessly on the beaches, in a far-off Hell that was called Dunkirk.

Chapter 7

DISTANT RUMBLINGS

Clayton, California
April 1939

The sun was beating down relentlessly on the Mount Diablo foothills. Charlie and Peter, who was now a licensed pilot, had finished flying for the day. They had just flown their new Stearman crop duster, nicknamed Triple Nickel because of its tail number, N555. It was now safely positioned in the hanger and there was nothing left to do but head to their favorite watering hole, the Clayton Saloon for a cold beer.

Ed, the bartender was pleased to see two of his favorite customers push through the squeaky saloon doors. He already had a couple of cold Budweiser's on the bar before they could take a seat. "Hi guys!" said Ed. "Warm enough out there for you today?"

"Yes, indeed!" said Charlie, placing his pack of Lucky Strikes on the bar. "It's 92 degrees in the hanger!"

"Rather!" said Peter, sliding onto the bar stool next to Charlie.

The two men chinked their Budweiser bottles together. The condensation was already dripping off the cold amber glass. "Cheers!" they said in unison and each took several long gulps. The bar was empty except for two old timers who sat at the end of the bar playing cards. It was a small saloon with sawdust on the bare wood floor, a long wooden bar, and behind it a large, decorated Jack Daniels mirror mounted to the wall. The men could see each other as they drank.

The ceiling was adorned with dozens of pairs of old battered cowboy boots hanging by a string, an old tradition in these parts. When a cowboy or ranch hand passed on, their boots were hung from the ceiling with their name and the date they passed painted on the sole in white paint. There was also a couple of lady's corsets hung up for good measure, but those owners remained discreetly anonymous.

"What's new Ed?" asked Charlie, slipping a cigarette between his lips and lighting up. Ed pushed an ashtray in front of him. "Looks like really bad things are happening over there in Germany. Those fascist bastards in the brown shirts are really getting to be a problem. This Hitler character is bad news, mark my words!"

"So much for the war to end all wars, eh Ed?" said Charlie. He knew Ed had volunteered as a Dough Boy and fought the Germans in France. Like many veterans of the Great War, he had seen so much carnage and had lost a lot of his buddies to poison gas. He would never forgive the Germans, ever. That was just the way it had to be.

"Yeah, that was some crazy time. I guess we just did not hit them hard enough. Looks like the same thing is going on all over again. No doubt our boys will get swept up in it eventually, bailing out our buddies, the Tommies all over again, eh Pete?" he said taking a jab at Peter, who took it with a wink. Englishmen were a rarity out here in rural Clayton. Peter was well known and genuinely liked in the tiny village. He was teased relentlessly about his perfect English accent, which he took in good stride.

"So, do you think it is going to escalate Ed?" asked Peter, taking another swig from his Budweiser.

"Well, it all comes down to leadership. Your man, Neville Chamberlain seems to think that there will not be an escalation, but I'm telling you right now, this Hitler character is dangerous. He fought in the war too, so it's not like he doesn't understand the ramifications. Like I said, we should have hit them harder!" Ed slammed his fist into his palm, emitting a loud smack that got the card players attention. "Mark my words, it's going to get ugly," said Ed shaking his head.

Peter thought about Ed's words. Since coming back to California, he had rarely given England a second thought. While he missed Addington Abbey, he had been so focused on flying that he hadn't paid much attention to the dark storm clouds currently gathering over Europe. He was aware of the troubles with the Brown Shirts and had seen Hitler raging away during a speech last time he was at the movie theater in San Francisco.

Now for the first time he began to think of the very real possibility of war again with the Germans. What if that were to happen? Surely, he would have to go back and fight for England. If push came to shove, it was the right thing to do. He was, after all an Englishman, from an unbroken line of warriors, who had fought for England with honor for thousands of years. He thought of his old Eton classmates. What would they do if war broke out? The thought of them going off to fight for England while he was living the good life in California would be more than he could bare.

He finished his Budweiser, then Charlie ordered two more, but Peter declined. He bid both of his friends a good day and walked back out into the warm California sunshine. The smell of pine needles and eucalyptus hung heavy in the air. He looked up at the cloudless blue sky. The conflict brewing in Europe that seemed a million miles away had suddenly got a lot closer. He resolved to find out more about Adolph Hitler and the Brown Shirts. If he was going to get into the fight, he needed to know exactly who his enemy was. From that day on he was astute at listening to the world news every night.

As the weeks went on, Hitler's rantings and threats continued to escalate. Peter recognized trouble when he saw it. He knew the clock had run out on his freedom in California. It was time for him to step up. If England were to fight, he was going to be in it. Reluctantly he said goodbye to Charlie and Ed and left his mother a letter to avoid her inevitable tears. He booked his train ticket for the long trip back to New York and a berth on the SS Lancastria back to Liverpool.

Chapter 8

BACK IN LIVERPOOL

Liverpool, England
May 1939

There was a light drizzle falling from an overcast sky as the SS Lancastria slid by the Royal Liver Building. With the aid of two powerful tugs, it successfully docked at the Pier Head. Peter disembarked with his suitcases and looked up at the giant clock face that read a little after nine o'clock. It was good to be back in England after the long Atlantic crossing which had been surprisingly smooth. He soon saw the faithful family chauffeur Giles waving at him from the parking lot alongside the Royal Liver Building.

"Hello Giles," said Peter as the two men exchanged a warm handshake.

"Welcome back, Master Legh!" said Giles. He was delighted to see Peter after so long. "You look well, Sir! My goodness that is quite a suntan that you picked up in California. Did you have a good crossing?"

"Thank you, Giles! It's good to be back home," replied Peter. He was amused that the chauffeur who had known him since he was five still referred to him as Master Legh. "The crossing was very smooth, thank you."

"And your Mother and Father are well, I trust?" asked Giles.

"Yes, both are doing well. I haven't seen too much of Father as he spends most of his time in San Francisco these days dealing with the business. He is well and both send their regards. All being well they anticipate returning sometime later next month," Peter answered.

"Excellent, excellent," said Giles.

Giles picked up the cases and the two men walked towards the awaiting Rolls Royce. Giles opened the rear door for Peter, who stopped before getting into the car and reached into his briefcase. "Here's a small present from Mother," he said. He handed Giles a bag full of assorted California walnuts, almonds and pecans.

"Why thank you, Master Legh!" said Giles. "I shall enjoy these with a pint of ale later tonight!"

Peter settled into the back of the Rolls while Giles secured his luggage before getting behind the wheel. He fired up the engine, put the car into first gear and pulled away.

"Straight to Addington Abbey, Sir?" asked Giles as he looked at Peter in the rearview mirror.

"Yes, please Giles, take me home," answered Peter.

"I have a copy of the Liverpool Echo here if you care to read," said Giles.

"Please," said Peter. Giles passed the folded newspaper back to him.

Peter opened the paper and read the headline, "Hitler Threatens Austria. War Imminent".

"Good lord!" said Peter. "This doesn't look good. What do you think of what is happening over there in Germany?"

"It's not good. I'm afraid Hitler has desires on other countries. There's talk of all-out war being inevitable if he makes a move. Prime Minister Chamberlain is trying to negotiate with him, but I get the feeling it's only a matter of time till the balloon goes up. Hitler was a Corporal in the First World War, you know, very bitter at Germany's defeat and the Versailles Treaty. The whole thing looks very precarious. The general consensus is that we will be at war before year's end. It's very sad, especially after the last time. It seems like we never seem to learn," said Giles, an air of genuine sadness in his voice.

"Yes, I'm inclined to agree," replied Peter.

"Did you finish your education at Stanford, Master Legh?" asked Giles, eager to change the conversation.

"Yes, thank goodness! I graduated with honors last summer. I'm so glad to have school finally behind me. Guess what else I've been doing over there?" Peter asked.

"With honors, good show!" replied Giles. "No idea Sir, what did you get up to?" asked Giles, looking in the rearview mirror at the healthy tanned face sitting behind him.

"I learned to fly!" said Peter with a sense of pride.

"You can fly? You mean in an airplane?" asked Giles.

"Yes, quite. In an airplane! I have a private pilot's license," replied Peter, delighted in seeing Giles surprised at his announcement.

"Oh, good show Master Legh! Good show, a pilot! That is impressive!" repeated Giles.

"Thanks Giles!" said Peter. "It's the most exciting thing I have ever done. Actually, that's why I returned early. My parents don't know it yet but I'm joining the Royal Air Force. I'm going to be a fighter pilot!" said Peter, relieved at finally being able to share the news with someone else. Outside of Charlie and Ed, he had kept his decision to himself. He knew his father would not approve of him joining the RAF. The Legh's were soldiers not air men, and his mother would be naturally terrified at the thought of her only son flying combat missions in the skies over Europe.

"The RAF! A fighter pilot, good lord!" said Giles. "That is exciting! Congratulations Master Legh. When do you start?" he asked.

"Next week, I have to report to Adastral House in London next Monday. I trust you can take me?" asked Peter.

"Yes Sir. Absolutely, the RAF. Good show, Sir!" replied Giles. He pressed the accelerator and the Rolls gently lurched forward and sped quietly down the East Lancashire Road towards Addington Abbey.

Chapter 9

PETER JOINS THE RAF

London, England
May 1939

Giles waited patiently in the Rolls Royce parked outside Adastral House, the home of the Air Ministry located on busy Kingsway in the heart of London. The steady drizzle that had been falling for most of the day had finally subsided, leaving the streets and pavement soaked. It gave the whole area a surreal newly varnished appearance. He watched as the businessmen in their drab suits and umbrellas walk by on their way to yet another meeting. They were the tiny cogs in the enormous machine that powered an empire so vast that the sun could never set on it. He also observed several Royal Air Force officers looking sharp in their blue uniforms coming and going from the same entry that Peter had gone through.

Giles checked his watch and Peter had been inside now for well over an hour. He considered that to be a good sign. He was confident that his young master's flying skills would be more than enough for him to pass the selection board and gain entry into the RAF as a fighter pilot. He knew that Peter's mind was already made up. The events unfolding in Germany, coupled with the ranting and threats of Adolph Hitler towards his neighbors on a daily basis, had simply reaffirmed his decision.

He glanced up again at the entryway of Adastral House just as Peter emerged. His broad smile indicated that things had gone well. Giles quickly exited the driver door and opened the rear door as Peter handed him a note as he said, "That went well! They want me to go for a medical exam right away. Here's the address, it's just a short distance away."

"Good show, Master Legh. We are on our way!" said Giles, as he started the Rolls and slid smoothly out into the London traffic. Peter relayed the directions to him and in less than five minutes he pulled up in front of a small non-descript gray stone building, a sign over the door read Highfield Clinic.

Peter exited the Rolls and went quickly inside for his medical exam as Giles parked the car. Figuring Peter would be at least another hour and noticing that the sun was now beginning to break through the rapidly diminishing clouds, Giles gambled that the rain had now finally stopped. He opened the trunk, retrieved a chamois leather and began to methodically wipe down the exterior of the Rolls Royce.

It was quite literally gleaming in the sunshine when Peter finally emerged. "Everything well Sir?" asked Giles as Peter slipped by him into the back seat. "Absolutely! Now I'll just have to wait. Apparently, they notify applicants by mail. We are all done here Giles, let's head back to Addington."

"Yes, Sir!" said Giles. He fired up the engine and headed North. Peter rolled down the window, the warm spring air felt good blowing in his hair. It reminded him of California.

He checked his watch. Dawn would be breaking on the west coast of America right about now. Almost certainly the first rays of sunshine would be cascading over Mount Diablo, marking the beginning of another beautiful day in the Diablo Valley. No doubt the flying conditions would be perfect. He thought about his friends Charlie and Ed and a broad smile crept across his face. If he made it into the RAF, he would send them a portrait of himself dressed in his blue dress uniform. He would include a set of pilot's wings to hang behind the bar at the Clayton Saloon.

He knew it might be awhile before he returned to California, and he was fine with that. Right now, his focus was on getting into the RAF and being able to make a difference if Mr. Chamberlain failed in his efforts to persuade Adolph Hitler to pursue a more peaceful path. If war were to come, Peter Legh, like all the Legh's before him was determined to be in the thick of it.

Ten days later a letter arrived for him at Addington Abbey congratulating him on being accepted into the Royal Air Force. He was requested to report for duty the following week to the No. 7

Elementary Flying School located in Desford Leicestershire. With a youthful folly, he had made it over the first hurdle and was now on a fast track to the very forefront of an epic and deadly clash that would soon come to be known around the world as the Battle of Britain.

Chapter 10

MAX JOINS THE BRANDENBURGERS

Berlin, Germany
May 1939

Per his father's wishes, Max went on from Eton to attend the prestigious Friedrich Wilhelm University of Berlin. After his graduation, Max was introduced to Captain Theodor von Hippel at a Nazi fund-raising event sponsored by his father. Von Hippel was a charismatic officer who had served in Africa under the legendary Paul von Lettow-Vorbeck, known as The Lion of Africa during the First World War. Von Hippel had been inspired by the success that von Lettow-Vorbeck's guerilla tactics had achieved, tying down tens of thousands of British soldiers with a relatively few well-trained men.

Von Hippel, working for Department Two of the Abwehr under Admiral Canaris had formed the Brandenburgers, a small group of highly skilled individuals who were made up of foreign nationals supportive of the Nazi doctrine. The Brandenburgers took their name from their original meeting place in Brandenburg, Germany, the von Seeckt family's ancestral hometown. The Brandenburgers were extremely intelligent, often considered outsiders and misfits that spoke multiple languages fluently and were generally in superb physical shape. Max was fascinated by von Hippel and his stories of daring and valor and was totally mesmerized by von Hippel's most prestigious award, the Iron Cross First Class.

At that meeting, Max von Seeckt knew exactly what he wanted to do with his life and with the full support of his proud father, he signed up for the Brandenburgers the next day. Von Hippel was delighted. He knew talent when he saw it and Max in his opinion, from what he had seen of the young man so far, was the perfect recruit.

Another young man also signed up for the Brandenburgers at the same time. He was of German Irish decent and spoke fluent Gaelic. His name was Fritz Hott. He and Max were the same age and instantly bonded. While Hott couldn't compete with Max physically, he was a tough individual with a razor-sharp whit and mind. Hott knew a good deal when he saw one and made the sound decision to ride on Max's coat tails for as far as the ride would take him. He had no idea just how wild a ride it would turn out to be.

Max spent seven months in intensive training with the Brandenburgers. One of his fellow recruits was a massive man named Bruno Schmidt, but everyone just referred to him by his nickname, the Beast. Max immediately recognized his enormous strength and fearsome appearance as a great asset and the Beast was delighted to become the third wheel. He loyally followed Max and Hott, the threesome was a tight knit unit. Max was totally in his element and graduated at the very top of his class. Von Hippel had a rising star on his hands. As the drum beat of war grew ever louder, it looked more and more likely that Max, already promoted to Second Lieutenant would get his chance to be at the absolute tip of the spear when the invasion of Poland began.

Von Hippel was so impressed with Max that during a routine inspection he introduced him personally to Admiral Canaris, the head of the Abwehr. Canaris liked what he saw. While he had doubts initially about von Hippel's unorthodox methods, he had grown to be a supporter of the tight knit group. He was particularly impressed with the high level of talent from other countries that von Hippel was able to attract. If the Brandenburgers were able to achieve the results von Hippel claimed, their effect on the invasion's outcome could well be significant. The acid test was about to come with Operation White, Hitler's plan for the invasion of Poland.

Preceding Operation White, the Brandenburgers would first carry out Operation Himmler. Frustrated after months of failing to provoke the Poles into a border incident, Hitler decided to pursue other more devious methods. Bored by the old school generals and the painfully slow speed that they operated, he decided to pursue a different path. For help, he turned to his trusted ally and master of such matters, Heinrich Himmler. He implored Himmler to come up with a false flag operation to ignite the conflict and justify an invasion. Himmler plunged himself into the project and soon came up with a diabolical plan specifically designed to kick start the Second World War.

Dozens of prisoners were rounded up and dressed in Polish Army uniforms. They were murdered by lethal injection then shot at various points on their corpses to make it look as if they had been an attacking force. For good measure, they all conveniently received sufficient facial trauma to make identification impossible. The bodies were left behind at specific targets of the Brandenburgers to bolster their claims that the Germans were defending themselves against Polish aggression.

Just before midnight on the night before the invasion, Max led a small group of heavily armed Brandenburgers dressed as Polish troops where they seized a radio station in the border town of Gleiwitz. Accompanying them was a heavily drugged German civilian named Wolfgang Schlitz also dressed in a Polish uniform. Known to be sympathetic towards the Poles, Himmler's Gestapo had arrested him the previous day. The Brandenburgers muscled their way into the radio station and seized the microphone and broadcasted an anti-German message they had prepared. Then Max coldly shot Schlitz in the face at point blank range and left his corpse on the radio station steps. Photographs were quickly taken and sent back to Dr. Goebbels, the Minister of Propaganda to be used to help bolster the Nazis bogus claims. Fittingly, in his callous act Max von Seeckt almost certainly drew the first blood of the Second World War for Germany.

Similar acts of deception took place simultaneously at over a dozen targets located along the German Polish border. Strategic objectives were quickly captured to allow the main invasion to follow. The Brandenburgers gave their Fuhrer more than enough reasons to light the fuse. The Brandenburgers went on to outperform even von Hippel's expectations. Admiral Canaris was delighted that his Brandenburgers were the first special operations force to engage in combat officially sparking the Second World War. Now a Lieutenant, Max von Seeckt was riding the crest of the wave that would wash over Europe with devastating and bloody consequences. Firmly at the very tip of the spear, there was nowhere else he would rather be.

Von Hippel was a victim of his own success. Once Canaris realized the success that the Brandenburgers had achieved with glowing accolades from the chief-of-staff of the High Command of the German armed forces Wilhelm Keitel, von Hippel was quickly reassigned to other duties. Canaris personally took command of the elite fighting force. Its exploits and brutality had already become legendary. When Hitler was presented with Iron Cross recommendations for over seventy percent of the small band of elite warriors who had performed so heroically, it was no surprise that Lieutenant Max von Seeckt was among the recipients. Already a favorite of Canaris, and anxious to keep the rising star firmly in his corner, he took the unprecedented action of personally promoting Max to Captain.

But the winds of war can blow erratically. Canaris was oblivious that a paranoid Hitler had already made plans for the future of the Brandenburgers and they did not include Admiral Canaris as the leader. That coveted position was going to be given to his rival, the man who had orchestrated Operation Himmler and was responsible for successfully unleashing the Nazis into Poland, Reich Fuhrer Heinrich Himmler, the feared head of the SS.

Chapter 11

BRITAIN GOES TO WAR

RAF Croydon, England
September 1939

Peter made excellent progress through flying school. His previous piloting experience was a huge plus and initially it put him at a considerable advantage over his classmates. He had learned humility from his mother, he was never brash, and he used his experience to help his classmates whenever possible. Besides, he had his own plate full. He still had to master gunnery school, navigation, and communications as well as the unique RAF way of doing things. He loved the camaraderie of his fellow trainee pilots. The bonds he developed with several of them were as deep as those he had forged with his classmates back at Eton, that now seemed an eternity ago.

Things all changed dramatically for everybody on the first day of September 1939 when the Nazis, spearheaded by the Brandenburgers invaded Poland. Two days later, on an overcast morning, the squadron huddled around the hut's radio in silence sipping hot cocoa or tea and smoking cigarettes. They listened to Prime Minister Neville Chamberlin declare in a monotone voice, "We are at war with Germany." The reality of the situation suddenly hit home. Britain was once again at war.

His old friend, Ed the bartender back in California had been right. Germany would need to be fought all over again and the fighter pilots of the Royal Air Force would be at the very forefront. From that point on, the training took on a whole different attitude and the pace was quickly accelerated to now fill the country's desperate need for trained fighter pilots.

A couple of weeks later, amongst much fanfare the British Expeditionary Force confidently crossed over the channel into France to join the French Army and march on to defend the Belgian border. Here they dug in, smoked cigarettes, brewed tea and waited. Neither side made any major moves in what soon became known as the Phony War.

Chapter 12

HIMMLER SWEATS IT OUT

The Berghof, Bavaria

October 1939

The steel cables whined as the electric winches that were expertly hidden within the gigantic walls slowly lowered the massive panoramic window until it completely vanished from sight. Bormann, who had designed it, regularly bragged that it was the largest operable window in the world. The great room instantly filled with the smell of fresh pine that emanated from the surrounding baking pine forest. It was an unusually hot Bavarian autumn day. The panoramic view of the Bavarian Alps was simply breathtaking.

"Better?" asked Heinz Linge, Hitler's personal valet as a resounding thud reverberated through the floorboards, indicating that the gigantic window was now fully lowered.

"Much better!" replied Hitler. He looked out at the magnificent spectacle before him and slowly folded his arms.

"Good, is there anything else you require, Mein Fuhrer?" asked Linge.

"No. Thank you, Heinz. Go ahead and show Reich Fuhrer Himmler in now but interrupt us in twenty minutes. I don't want to go any longer than that with Herr Himmler on such a pleasant day," answered Hitler.

"Very well, Mein Fuhrer," replied Linge, and with a knowing smile and quick bow he left.

Hitler had deliberately kept Himmler waiting for well over an hour, all part of his never-ending mind games that he loved to play on almost any of his innermost circle. It was always good to keep them guessing. Hitler was constantly pitting his henchmen against each other. While he was the undisputed lead dog, he wanted to keep the intense competition for his attention as ferocious as possible.

He was particularly coy of Admiral Canaris, the Head of the Abwehr. He knew Canaris had a long and powerful reach. His built-in sense of self-preservation told him that Canaris in charge of a powerful elite force such as the Brandenburgers, was simply too big of a potential threat. He had therefore decided that Himmler should be in charge. It would be a much safer bet. Himmler was also a lot easier to control than the ever cunning Canaris. Having already relieved Canaris of command of the Brandenburgers, he had sent for Himmler to give him the news himself. This would further cement Himmler's loyalty in the process. It was good to be the lead sled dog he mused, as all the other dogs get the exact same view.

Hitler continued to soak up the stunning views as he heard the door hinges creak behind him. The huge wooden door opened and the familiar voice of Linge announced, "Reich Fuhrer Himmler, Mein Fuhrer!" Hitler heard the jackboots of Himmler clomp rhythmically across the polished hardwood floor and then come silently to a stop behind him. He heard his heels snap to attention and knew at that moment that Himmler had shot him a Nazi salute. Still he gazed out at the view, his back to Himmler, static, enjoying the pressure that he knew Himmler was beginning to feel. He was tempted to turn around but knew he could milk it for a few more seconds, why not? It was a fabulous day, so he did, before slowly turning around.

"Ah! Heinrich! Good to see you!" said the Fuhrer with a smile as he casually returned a salute to a relieved Himmler.

"You too, Mein Fuhrer. Thank you!" said Himmler, standing ram rod straight in his immaculate SS uniform.

"At ease Heinrich. Can you believe how beautiful it is today?" asked Hitler as he turned around again and gestured with a sweep of his arm at the magnificent panorama before them. Himmler quickly scurried alongside his master, ecstatic to be alone in his company. "Yes, Mein Fuhrer, it's an incredible day. I believe you have the most spectacular view of it compared to anyone else on the planet!" answered Himmler.

"I believe you are right, Heinrich. This is as good as it gets!" replied Hitler.

"Only befitting for the leader of the Third Reich," said Himmler, shamelessly groveling with a bow of his head.

"Agreed!" said the Fuhrer. "Let's go on the patio and enjoy the sunshine, shall we?"

"Absolutely! That's a splendid idea," replied Himmler, as he followed the Fuhrer outside onto a small private limestone patio facing west and a totally different view of the majestic Alps. There were several sun loungers and two small round wooden tables and chairs. Each table had its own bright red and orange striped sun umbrella that gave the area a distinct resort look. An armed SS guard, well out of ear shot walked slowly around the perimeter of the patio.

"Here, this one will work," said Hitler as he walked towards one of the tables. A quick glance at the sun told him which seat to take. Naturally, he took the one in the shade while directing Himmler to take the one in the bright sunshine. Himmler reluctantly obeyed as he glanced up at the bright afternoon sun. "Perfect!" he lied. He sat down in his thick black SS uniform.

"Not too hot?" asked Hitler.

"Oh, no!" lied Himmler again. "It's good to be outside in the sunshine. I spend way too much time in the office these days."

"Good!" said Hitler. "I'm limited on time today, so let's get down to business."

"Of course, Mein Fuhrer. How may I be of assistance today?" replied Himmler, dragging his seat in a little closer. The shade was still just out of reach.

"As you know, Canaris had incredible success with his Brandenburgers going in ahead of the main thrust into Poland. Your Operation Himmler was a great achievement. The advanced work they did in confusing and disrupting the enemy was invaluable. After that they went on to show enormous courage against great odds. I have recommendations in my office for dozens of Iron Crosses," explained Hitler, leaning back in the shade. He was delighted that he had opted for a light tan double breasted suit on such a hot day. He knew that Himmler in his all black SS uniform was literally cooking.

"Yes, I was aware of the Brandenburgers' success. They are a shining example to all of our armed forces. I have the utmost admiration for the brave work they do for the Reich," replied Himmler.

"Agreed!" said Hitler. "Unfortunately, as you are also aware, we did not do a good job of securing the Polish gold. In fact, we did a piss poor job! We basically ended up with peanuts, actually peanut shells would be more accurate! You know how expensive military hardware is these days, Heinrich. I was counting on securing Poland's gold to keep the bankers happy but by the time we got there, the cupboard was bare, so to speak. We were too focused on hoisting the Swastika flag over Warsaw, while the Poles were smuggling out their gold reserves. Our priorities were all wrong. I realize that now, so things will change when we invade Norway. We won't be making the same mistakes," said Hitler. Himmler could see the look of concern on his master's face but wisely chose to remain silent.

"I think Canaris is on the right track. There is no question that small teams of specially trained elite forces, if used correctly can cause havoc and tie up entire brigades for weeks, if not months. I just think some of their efforts need to be redirected into specific areas so they can be even more effective," said Hitler as he looked directly at Himmler.

"I see, redirected? How? What did you have in mind?" asked Himmler, his eyes subconsciously narrowing behind his glasses.

"Canaris has a lot on his plate as head of the Abwehr, especially since we took over Czechoslovakia and now Poland," answered Hitler. He noticed Himmler's forehead was already turning pink under the bright Bavarian sunshine.

"Yes, I'm sure he does. The workload on our own Gestapo has ballooned also, so I can only imagine what Canaris is dealing with," said a genuinely sympathetic Himmler.

"Exactly. So, I have decided to make a few changes for our upcoming invasion of Norway. Changes that will help Canaris with his workload and more importantly help the Reich secure the Norwegian gold. I have decided to place a select number, let us say around six hundred of the Brandenburgers under your direct command. Then I want you to personally hand select a small crack team to go into Oslo ahead of the main invasion force and secure that Norwegian gold."

"I see!" said Himmler. "Of course, I'd be honored to command any of the Brandenburgers. They are a unique group of individuals with some very distinctive talents," said Himmler with a thin smile and a squint of his eyes.

"Good! Yes, I agree, some very distinctive talents. However, the only talent I need is for them to get into the Bank of Norge and secure the gold. Then they must hold it until we can muster sufficient forces to bring it safely back here to the Reichsbank," answered Hitler, now getting a little distraught. He considered the little men in their drab suits who had no concept of life in the military world just sitting around their boardroom tables smoking their dammed cigars. They continued to hound him about the dwindling amount of gold left in the Reichsbank's coffers. He loathed them because there was no way of getting around the simple fact that at the end of the day, they were correct. To wage war, the Third Reich needed more gold.

"I understand completely, Mein Fuhrer. I've seen some of the expenses, colossal simply colossal," replied Himmler. He was now squinting into the bright sunlight as small beads of sweat appeared on his forehead and around the edge of his stiff white shirt collar.

"Yes, those little pricks have no idea of the costs involved. Look at iron ore for God's sake! The price just keeps getting higher and higher! Wait till we occupy Scandinavia. Then we will see some relief! Then they will be all smiles, those Bastards!" he said, waving his hand as if swatting a fly away.

"Agreed," said Himmler. "What about Canaris? Have you spoken to him?"

"Yes, he was not happy initially, but he came around to my way of thinking. He knew how upset I was at not getting the Polish gold. He offered the Brandenburgers with their incredibly unique talents as a possible solution. He is immensely proud of the Brandenburgers and the unorthodox way they operate. But as I said earlier, he has his plate full and it is just going to get worse, but he also understands economics. In addition, securing gold does not fit under his umbrella by any stretch of the imagination. It would be way too much exposure for the Abwehr, his real pride and joy.

Canaris likes to operate in the shadows. That is where he is most effective, and he knows I need just a few select men. He pretty much washed his hands of it when I told him that they would be specifically going in to grab the gold, a pinpoint mission, so to speak. Canaris is very old school! And it smacked way too much of a gold heist for him to want to risk soiling his stellar reputation. Now you, Heinrich…well, let us just say, you and I think more alike. We are a little more committed to the cause! As I see it, to the victor goes the spoils. It is as simple as that," laughed Hitler.

"Absolutely!" replied Himmler, delighted that he and the Fuhrer were on the same page.

"Good! Then it's settled. Give Canaris a call, he will be expecting you. Let us keep this civil. Have him send you the personnel files so you can begin your selection. But I want to be crystal clear Heinrich, I need that damned gold from the Norwegians! Understood?" spat the Leader of the Third Reich. He glared from under the cool shade of the umbrella at the now profusely sweating and very red-faced Himmler.

"Yes, Mein Fuhrer! It will be an honor!" replied Himmler. Suddenly, Linge appeared out of nowhere at the side of the table.

"Excuse me Mein Fuhrer, your two thirty appointment is here!" he barked.

Hitler looked at his watch as if surprised. "Where does the time go Heinrich?" he said with a smile. "That will be all. Congratulations on your new command, good luck!" The Fuhrer got up and shook the sweaty hand of the Head of the SS, and one of the most feared men on the planet. "Ah, looks like you caught a little sun today, my friend. That is good for you!" he said as he pressed his thumb squarely in the middle of Himmler's deep red forehead, leaving a distinct white mark, much to his delight. It was a terrific day at the Berghof.

Chapter 13

OPERATION GWILYM

SS Headquarters, Berlin
October 1939

Max was delighted that his unit of Brandenburgers had been reassigned under the direct command of Himmler and was now officially part of the SS. The Fuhrer, giddy from his success in Austria and Poland was already planning several steps ahead of his generals. Hitler knew there was no question that the toughest nut to crack in his conquest of Europe would be the stubborn British on their own Island. It was Himmler who had pointed out that Chamberlain was the weak link in the chain. The Fuhrer sensed blood. With his newly heightened killer instinct, he was anxious to make another quick kill.

He knew that time was of the essence. After the success of Operation Himmler, Hitler had every confidence that Himmler could repeat the process. Without even consulting his generals, he had decided to work directly with Himmler to look at alternative options to invade Britain utilizing the SS. Himmler was sworn to secrecy to avoid rocking the boat with the top Wehrmacht generals.

At the explicit command of the Fuhrer, under his top-secret directive, Himmler had assembled his brightest minds to begin to cultivate plans for the future invasion of Britain. Von Seeckt was the sole Brandenburger representative and the lowest ranking member involved at the secret meeting. Having been raised in Wales and educated at Eton, he had a unique perspective on the British. Himmler found his input invaluable. In a few short weeks Max had become a firm favorite of Heinrich Himmler.

It was on a cold windy night in Berlin at the SS headquarters that Captain Max von Seeckt took the plunge. He was standing before the Reich Fuhrer himself, preparing to present his brainchild for a most unconventional invasion of Britain. He had meticulously planned and researched his idea for months. His was the last plan to be submitted.

"You have fifteen minutes, Captain. I'd suggest you use them wisely," said Himmler as he removed his thick leather belt and handed it to his personal valet. "You said you had an exciting new invasion concept for capturing the British Isles. Go ahead, let me hear it. But please, only the short version. I have neither the time nor the patience to listen to a lot of numbers! It's been an exceptionally long day."

Himmler sat his small frame in the ornate armchair that rested behind an antique writing desk in his private office. He held his left leg up for his valet to remove the first of two black polished jackboots that he had been wearing all day. "Arrrr! So much better! Thank you, Bruno," said Himmler. He flexed his cramped toes and then dismissed his valet with a wave of his hand.

Next, he unbuttoned the top buttons of his tunic, then finally lit a cigar. He inhaled and fixed his attention on Captain Max von Seeckt, clearly the brightest rising star among his newly acquired Brandenburger elite warriors. He already knew that von Seeckt had been nominated for the Iron Cross but until it was officially approved, he did not want to jump the gun. It was also the main reason he was even affording von Seeckt an audience. While he was elated that von Seeckt had taken the time to submit his idea, all he really wanted to do was sleep.

"Thank you, Reich Fuhrer. I'll be as brief as possible," replied von Seeckt, standing rigidly at attention while holding a bulging black leather attaché case.

"Be seated," said Himmler, gesturing for von Seeckt to be seated opposite him.

Von Seeckt obeyed. He sat down and removed a thick manila file from his attaché case. He placed the file on the desk. The cover of the file read Operation Gwilym Top Secret. Himmler noticed the name Gwilym.

"Gwilym? What kind of an operation name is that?" asked Himmler, smiling.

"It's Welsh for William, Sir. The last successful invader of Britain was William the Conqueror in 1066! I believe you will see the connection once my presentation is complete," replied von Seeckt. Himmler nodded his approval then said, "Proceed Captain."

He opened the file and removed several papers from its interior and placed them to one side. The papers contained the numbers that Himmler had just made clear he had no time for. Then he pulled out a map and carefully unfolded it before placing it in front of his bespectacled leader. The map showed the British Isles and the coast of Northern France.

There were three red arrows pointing across the English Channel from France to the south coast of England. Himmler tugged on his cigar and looked at the map. It was similar to dozens of other maps he had reviewed over the last few weeks since the Fuhrer had ordered him to gather ideas for the invasion of Britain. Many ideas had come from those who would be at the very tip of the spear. They were the ones that would do the dirty work of confronting the stubborn British on their home turf. The Brandenburgers were odds on favorite to play a leading role, almost certainly landing ahead of the main assault.

Southampton, Dover, and Plymouth were all obvious targets for the across-the-channel invasion. Each was located at the tip of the red arrows shown on the map. "These are the obvious points of invasion that we are no doubt considering to get a foothold in England, correct?" asked von Seeckt as he pointed at the map before them.

"Yes," said Himmler. "With Dover being the current favorite," he tapped at Dover with his nicotine stained finger. A small amount of ash fell from the end of his cigar directly on to the coastal town of Felixstowe, effectively obliterating it from view.

"Good," replied von Seeckt. "The problem is I'm sure Prime Minister Chamberlain is thinking along the exact same lines, particularly Dover. It is the shortest and most obvious crossing." He casually flicked Himmler's ash from the map, folded it precisely and returned it to the file. Then he pulled out an identical map and unfolded it before placing it in front of the Reich Fuhrer. "But, Reich Fuhrer, have you ever considered this?" asked von Seeckt as he now pointed at one solitary red arrow.

Himmler leaned forward and examined the map with its single arrow. He remained silent and again took another long drag off his cigar before exhaling a thick cloud of blue smoke. "Dublin? Dublin to let's see...Holyhead, Anglesey! Now that is a first Captain, I will give you that!" said Himmler, shaking his head. He looked at the arrow heading from Dublin across the Irish Sea with the point going directly into the port of Holyhead, Anglesey, an island off the coast of North Wales.

He looked up at von Seeckt. There was a hint of anger in the beady eyes behind the lenses. "You can't be serious Captain? You do understand that Ireland is a neutral country?" asked Himmler.

"Of course, Sir. However, it is also home to the Irish Republican Army who detest the British and I believe they would make an excellent ally. We could easily work with them outside of the knowledge of the Irish Government," replied von Seeckt.

"I'm familiar with the IRA Captain and agree that they hate and have even declared war on the British. Even if they were to cooperate with us and we manage to launch an operation from Dublin, why would you land on Anglesey of all places? Isn't it just a rural island with no real strategic value?" replied Himmler.

"Because Sir, that rural island is also home to two Royal Air Force bases named RAF Valley and RAF Mona. My plan calls for a small elite force of Brandenburgers, aided by the IRA to get onto Anglesey by way of the Dublin-Holyhead ferry. Then take over the airfields and hold them long enough to allow us to land paratroopers in sufficient numbers to take over the island, including the deep-water port of Holyhead.

We come in through the back door while all of England's forces are concentrated here in the south looking the wrong way!" said von Seeckt as he pointed towards the south coast of England and the narrow English Channel. "We use stealth and surprise! We do the unexpected. We use Holyhead's deep water docks for a full-scale landing. By the time the British realize what has hit them, it will be too late. Our Panzers will be crushing Liverpool and once we capture it, we control access to the Atlantic!" exclaimed an excited von Seeckt.

"I see, interesting Captain, very interesting," said Himmler. He pondered von Seeckt's radical invasion plan with a renewed enthusiasm. For some reason neither he, nor the dozen or so other experts who had presented plans to him had considered anything quite so revolutionary and bold. All the other plans had included a cross channel invasion from France. Himmler was shrewd enough to know von Seeckt was right about one thing. The British would be looking the wrong way for sure. If they could get a foothold on Anglesey, the British could never turn their forces around fast enough to come to the rescue of Liverpool. The brilliant young Captain was on to something.

"Thank you, Sir," replied von Seeckt. "If I may continue…" The intercom buzzed on the Reich Fuhrer's desk. "Reich Fuhrer, will you be having dinner in your office or will you…" Himmler cut off his assistant in mid-sentence. "No! Hold everything, including my calls. I don't want to be disturbed by anybody until further notice, understand?"

"Yes, Mein Reich Fuhrer," replied the assistant, and the intercom went dead.

"Now Captain, you have my undivided attention. Now show me the crap you have in that pile and tell me what the perceived obstacles are," said Himmler, extinguishing his cigar and sitting back in his chair.

Almost two hours later Himmler concluded the meeting. Von Seeckt had produced an incredible plan. It was well thought out and a totally different concept to the obvious Dover crossings that had dominated the planning since the Fuhrer had first thrown out the challenge.

The biggest problem with von Seeckt's plan, besides relying on the Irish Republican Army was the redesign required of the existing troop-carrying planes that the Luftwaffe currently had available. They simply could not carry the number of troops required to rapidly secure the airfields. But Himmler was reasonably well in with Goering. He was also aware that the need for larger troop-carrying planes was already one of many projects currently on Goering's plate. Through his excellent intelligence network, he already knew that the prototype of a giant aircraft being developed by Messerschmitt was called The Giant. He knew the Giant was close to final testing. Himmler, a master at organizing understood the politics at the highest level of the Third Reich. He would get

Goering on board by appealing to his considerable ego. He would inflate his ego by praising the Giant as a huge leap forward for the Luftwaffe. Then with Goering on board they would have a real shot at bending the Fuhrer's ear.

Himmler pressed the button on his intercom. "Yes, Reich Fuhrer?" replied his assistant.

"Track down Herr Goering for me, immediately!" barked Himmler.

"Yes Sir, right away!" answered the assistant.

Himmler sat back as he carefully observed the bright young Captain beaming before him. "OK Captain, I like it enough to give it a shot. Let's see what Goering has to say, shall we? I will be in touch, leave the file with me. Also, this conversation goes no further beyond this office. Stealth is paramount for your plan to have any chance of success and that stealth starts right now. Am I clear?" he asked with a menacing look.

"Thank you, Mein Reich Fuhrer. You won't regret it," replied an elated von Seeckt as he handed the file to his commander. Himmler accepted the file. "I like the operation name, Gwilym. Now I see the connection. It's a nod to your proud Welsh ancestry Captain, nothing wrong with that. That will be all," said Himmler. He stood up indicating the meeting was concluded.

Von Seeckt had passed his first obstacle. It was up to Himmler to get Goering on board and von Seeckt was confident that his new commander would close the deal. He stood up, snapped the Nazi salute and was gone.

Himmler listened to the steel cleated jackboots clatter down the stone corridor until they finally faded as von Seeckt left the building. He pulled the file towards him and gazed at it as he reached into his cigar box for another cigar, but he was out. "Dammit!" he cursed. Then he put his feet up on the desk and leaned his head back. He took several deep breaths, closed his eyes and was sound asleep in seconds.

Chapter 14

HIMMLER MAKES A DEAL

Reich Chancellery, Berlin, Germany
November 1939

Heinrich Himmler was beginning to second guess his decision to request an audience with the Fuhrer. He had been eager to share with him what he deemed to be the most brilliant and unorthodox plan to invade Britain that he had reviewed in the last three weeks. Since his recent success with Operation Himmler had earned him plenty of bargaining chips with the Fuhrer, he figured now was as good a time as any to roll the dice handed to him by von Seeckt.

It had only been a few minutes since Himmler made his closing argument to the Fuhrer, but it seemed like an eternity. Adolph Hitler, Fuhrer of the Third Reich, stared at the file in front of him in utter silence.

Himmler was well aware of the perils of rubbing the Fuhrer the wrong way. He had to dig deep, very deep, to hold his tongue and not break the unbearable silence. A shrewd negotiator, he was also aware that after fully presenting a case and waiting for a favorable answer, that the first person to speak and break the silence inevitably loses. This knowledge of the art of negotiating had held him in good stead during his rapid rise to Reich Fuhrer. But previous similar situations had usually pitted his considerable intellect against his peers, or even easier, his underlings.

On this occasion, the most powerful man in Europe was sitting directly across from him in a dark gray business suit. It was a totally different kettle of fish. Himmler, unable to bare the tension any longer drew a breath to speak. Then surprisingly, Hitler made a move. With a slightly trembling right hand, he slowly removed his reading glasses and set them on the desk. Himmler was massively relieved that he had not spoken. He waited for the Fuhrer to break the silence.

Hitler carefully stroked his moustache with his thumb and index finger, while he flicked through the pages of the file in front of him. He stopped on a page that had a map of Great Britain with the English Channel and parts of Northern France.

He opened his desk drawer and pulled out a magnifying glass with an ornate deer antler handle and focused on the map. Himmler watched as Hitler put his finger on the Isle of Anglesey. Then he moved it east to the Port of Liverpool where he stopped and tapped it a few times. Still silent, he slid it across further east to Manchester, then to the east coast and up to the city of Newcastle. He paused and tapped his finger again before moving it back to Carlisle on the northwest coast of England.

Then he took out a ruler and a red pencil and carefully and deliberately drew a bold red line across England from Carlisle to Newcastle. He stared at it for a moment and then finally looked up at Himmler. "Heinrich," he said, making direct eye contact. "This is quite simply the most radical and brilliant plan to invade Britain that I have seen. Brilliant, simply brilliant!"

"Thank you, Mein Fuhrer!" replied a now delighted Himmler. "I had hoped that you would agree. It certainly goes against the grain of conventional wisdom, but it is brilliantly simple. Bold in the extreme, but so logical given that Tommy, still licking his wounds, will be watching across the channel. He will be waiting for what he knows will be the final battle for him in the rolling fields of Kent. While he watches and waits for us to cross the English Channel, we will come in silently through the back door that has been left... wide open."

"Brilliant!" repeated Hitler.

"After we capture the two airfields on Anglesey, we will have sufficient forces to hold the island against any counterattack from the British. There are only two ways onto the island, the Britannia railroad bridge and the Menai road bridge. We will hold both within four hours of landing. That will allow us time to bring in sufficient resources to move with lightning speed on Liverpool. Once we capture Liverpool, we control access to the Atlantic. Liverpool is the main seaport for the British. It is where 90 percent of food and arms come in from America. If the British do not surrender, we can simply starve them to death, Mein Fuhrer," explained Himmler, now leaning forward with a cynical smile spreading below his small, groomed moustache.

"The back door! Tommy forgot to guard the back door! A glaring error, eh Heinrich? On a par with the French and their so called impenetrable Maginot Line! I see history repeating itself, do you Heinrich?" asked Hitler, now clearly excited. He looked down again at the file. "Then Phase Two, we take Manchester?" asked Hitler.

"Yes, Mein Fuhrer. Manchester is a short distance from Liverpool, less than forty miles. Then we control the two biggest cities in Northern England," answered Himmler.

"Ah! Manchester! Home to Manchester Cathedral, one of the greatest examples of gothic architecture in Europe!" said Hitler. "Be sure those Panzers do not damage it Heinrich!"

"Of course, Mein Fuhrer," said Himmler. Then we take Newcastle on the east coast. A smaller group will move north from Liverpool to Carlisle. We expect very little resistance at that point. We draw a line right across England, annexing the Scots, who we have no desires on. Effectively, we will have cut England in two, North and South," beamed Himmler.

"Excellent!" said Hitler. "Let's rename Hadrian's Wall built by the Romans as Himmler's Wall!" Hitler laughed out loud.

"I'm honored, Mein Fuhrer!" said Himmler, now clearly delighted and relieved at how well the meeting was going.

"And Phase Three?" asked Hitler, preferring to listen to Himmler instead of reading. "I assume we take control of Birmingham and the Midlands."

"Yes, Mein Fuhrer! In Phase Three, we roll south to the industrial cities of Sheffield, Birmingham and Coventry. Once they fall, we will own the north of England and the industrial Midlands. Tommy will be stuck in the south of England, sandwiched between our forces in France and our Panzers in the north. It will be futile for him to fight on. At that point he can either surrender or starve, or stay in London, which will be reduced to ashes!" Himmler slammed his clenched fist into his open hand to emphasize the point.

"Good, good!" said Hitler, his eyes wide open. He stood up and walked over to the large picture window that adorned his office. He looked out across the mountains of Bavaria, a thin snow cap still visible on the highest peaks. Finally, he turned back to Himmler and then returned to his desk.

"Obviously, this will take significant manpower and resources. What, if any are the perceived obstacles?' asked the Fuhrer.

"There is actually only one obstacle to overcome so far," said Himmler reaching into his briefcase and pulling out a file marked Top Secret-The Giant. He opened it and placed it in front of Hitler. "In order for the operation to succeed, we need to produce bigger transport planes. They must be capable of carrying over 100 armed paratroopers. Our current Dornier aircraft are simply not big enough to pull this off," said Himmler.

"One hundred paratroopers!" exclaimed Hitler. "That's a big plane, and a big ask Heinrich!" said Hitler. A look of disappointment crept over the Fuhrer's face.

"Yes, Mein Fuhrer, it is," answered Himmler.

"I took the liberty of running it by Goering to see if it was even feasible. He felt confident that the current Messerschmitt ME320 could be built with modifications to meet the 100-paratrooper requirement and an outside shot at getting as many as 120 armed paratroopers on board. They already have several prototypes under construction, and they will be ready to start test flying as soon as we give them the green light."

"I see," said Hitler, visibly perking up. "So, what did the man in the fancy fur coat have to say about your plan, Heinrich?' asked Hitler. He always enjoyed giving his Head of the Luftwaffe a little dig.

"He, like you and I, thought the idea was brilliant. He was highly confident that the aircraft could be built to land sufficient paratroopers with enough equipment to capture the two airfields on Anglesey," said Himmler. "Once we capture these two airfields, Goering assured me that he could get enough aircraft on the ground to destroy any counterattack from the RAF. Of this he was supremely confident, Mein Fuhrer," answered Himmler.

Hitler was thumbing through the pages of the report that showed various blueprints along with photographs of planes and what looked like engines and engine parts. He studied it carefully for several minutes before looking back at Himmler. "It looks like there are several challenges. The biggest challenge seems to be bringing the plane to a halt before it runs out of runway because it is so heavy. That's a big challenge, Heinrich," said Hitler.

"That is my understanding Mein Fuhrer, but its beyond my field of knowledge. Tanks yes, airplanes no!" joked Himmler.

"You and me both, Heinrich!" laughed the Fuhrer. "We Army men are better to leave these challenges to those magnificent men in their flying machines, no?" smirked Hitler.

"Yes, Mein Fuhrer agreed!" said Himmler.

"So, where do we stand currently? The idea is brilliant. I'm glad you got the fat one involved, for surely he knows how these things must work for us to have success," stated the Fuhrer.

"As I mentioned, Goering is confident that the Giant is almost ready for a test flight. There are also many other aircraft projects that are being worked on, each claiming its own priority. It will take a direct order from you to push this to the head of the line. I just need your approval and we will move forward rapidly," said Himmler.

"I see," said the Fuhrer. He pushed the Giant file aside and returned his gaze to the map of Great Britain. "It's simply too good to not give it a shot. I will approve it. We move forward with it!"

"Excellent call, Mein Fuhrer! Thank you!" said Himmler.

The two men stood up and Hitler extended his hand. "Outstanding Heinrich, outstanding!" said Hitler. "If more of my leaders had your vision Heinrich, the Reich would already control Europe. When did you conceive of this?"

"I didn't Mein Fuhrer," replied Himmler.

"Oh?" said Hitler, looking puzzled. "Who did?"

"One of my young Captains. He has a brilliant tactical mind, almost on par with mine!" joked Himmler then he continued. "He responded to the challenge that we put out, for ideas on invading England. He came over with the Brandenburgers and he's currently in intensive training with the team. He will be leading the team into Norway to capture King Haakon and his gold reserves. He is fearless, the best of his generation, in fact. I believe you will meet him when he returns from training. You are due to present him with the Iron Cross in Berlin. He will be recognized for his heroics in Poland at the ceremony that Dr. Goebbels will be filming, so we can share our glory with the entire Fatherland."

"Excellent!" said the Fuhrer, clenching his fists and smiling. He loved that Himmler was honest enough to give credit where it was due. Unlike many of the leaders in the Army, Himmler idolized his men and they in turn remained loyal to him. It was an effective chemistry. Himmler knew that if he credited his men for their commitment to the cause and didn't steal the glory for himself that they in turn would make him the leader that he was.

"What's his name?" asked Hitler.

"Captain Max von Seeckt, Mein Fuhrer. His father is Karl von Seeckt, the millionaire stockbroker who has made many considerable financial donations to our party. Captain von Seeckt has an incredible intellect. He was educated at Eton, no less," replied Himmler.

Hitler made a note of his name on the open cover of the file and then double underlined it.

"Von Seeckt! I like him. Be sure to remind me at the ceremony, Heinrich. I'm always interested in the next wave of great leaders for our Reich."

"Yes, Mein Fuhrer!" Having achieved his goal, Himmler knew when to retreat. He snapped his jackboot heels together, saluted and yelled, "Heil Hitler!" He collected his briefcase, cap and left.

Chapter 15

Goebbels Gets His Man

SS Headquarters, Berlin, Germany
December 1939

The four Brandenburger officers stood ram rod straight in full military dress uniform as the Fuhrer was introduced to each man by Reich Fuhrer Heinrich Himmler. Hitler saluted each one before personally pinning the Iron Cross on their tunic. Then he shook their hand and gave the Nazi salute. Behind him was a film crew under the direction of Dr. Joseph Goebbels that silently went about their work of documenting the event.

The Invasion of Poland was over. The world had never witnessed anything like the speed that the Nazis had swept the Polish Army aside. Now was a time for celebration and a golden opportunity for the Minister of Propaganda to hone his considerable skills.

The last recipient to be introduced was a tall, strikingly handsome man with cropped blond hair. Just visible below his cap were piercing blue eyes, and to Goebbels' sheer delight, a vivid scar on the side of his face.

"Captain Max von Seeckt, Mein Fuhrer, of whom we talked recently," said Himmler.

"Ah, yes!" beamed Hitler.

"It is truly an honor Captain von Seeckt. The Reich Fuhrer here is a big fan of your work, as I might add, am I," said Hitler.

"Mein Fuhrer!" snapped Max, "The honor is mine, Sir!"

"It seems that you have a unique way of figuring out how we can defeat the British. I'm impressed with your proposal that the Reich Fuhrer here showed me last week," said Hitler as he presented Max with his much-coveted Iron Cross.

"Thank you, Mein Fuhrer!" replied Max.

Goebbels had signaled for the film crew to get a close-up of Max and the Fuhrer chatting, making sure to zoom in on Max's scarred cheek. Aware of the camera, Hitler politely stepped back and let them focus on the fearless warrior standing at attention in front of him, adorned with his new Iron Cross.

"Ah! Dr. Goebbels!" said Hitler feigning surprise.

"Mein Fuhrer!" yelled Goebbels, snapping a quick salute.

"This is the warrior that I talked to you about, as a possible candidate for your newest project. May I present Captain von Seeckt."

"Ah, of course," said Goebbels. He squinted his beady eyes in the bright Berlin sunshine to get a better look at the textbook Aryan specimen before him. It did not take more than a second for him to conclude that he had finally found his perfect poster boy. "Perfect!" was all he said, as he looked Max up and down. Getting closer to Max's face, he looked admiringly at the scar and then the piercing blue eyes, along with the blond hair, square jaw, ample height, and almost flawless athletic build. "Perfect!" he repeated, then turning to Hitler he said, "Mein Fuhrer, I believe we have our man."

"I agree. Get to work Joseph," said the Fuhrer.

Max looked on, standing at attention. He wasn't sure exactly what Goebbels meant, but he really didn't care. Here he was aged twenty-eight, receiving one of Germany's highest awards from the Fuhrer himself. And he was being filmed by Dr. Goebbels for the whole nation to embrace. For Captain Max von Seeckt of the Brandenburgers, this was as good as it gets.

Hitler turned to Himmler and said, "Reich Fuhrer, get together with Dr. Goebbels. He has some important work he needs to complete, and I believe Captain von Seeckt can help him with his quest. Let's make this a priority, am I clear?"

"Yes, Mein Fuhrer!" barked Himmler, totally baffled at the Fuhrer's request and always suspicious of the hovering Dr. Goebbels, who he despised.

"Good," said Hitler. He saluted, turned, climbed into his awaiting Mercedes and left.

"Captain von Seeckt, please join Minister Goebbels and I for some coffee over here in the refreshment tent. Apparently, he has an important assignment he would like to discuss with you," said Himmler to the beaming Captain.

"Yes, Sir!" answered von Seeckt. He walked alongside his bewildered commander to the white refreshment tent with Goebbels shuffling along enthusiastically behind them. He had been searching for weeks for the perfect Nazi to feature in his next propaganda piece. The Fuhrer himself had just handed him one of Himmler's finest Brandenburgers. A gift that he knew would grate on Himmler. That made it even sweeter.

Chapter 16

THE GIANT

Celle Airbase, Germany
December 1939

It had been several months since Hitler had approved the radical operation known as Operation Gwilym. Sitting in the back of his gray Mercedes Benz, Reich Marshall Goering was already beginning to sweat. He wasn't sure if it was caused by his latest elaborate pure white uniform or the relentless pressure from Hitler. His most recent responsibility was to get the massive planes for Operation Gwilym from prototype to fully functioning aircraft. Either way he was glad that they had finally arrived at Celle Airbase for what he hoped would be a final successful test flight.

The armed sentry snapped a salute as the Mercedes and its accompanying motorcade passed through the upraised barrier arm and headed straight for the main Celle runway. The cars came to a stop alongside a small group standing by the runway. Behind them at some distance sat an enormous aircraft with three massive propellers under each wing. The plane had affectionately been dubbed the Giant. With a wingspan of over 160 feet it was by far the largest aircraft in the world.

Goering immediately recognized his good friend and the Luftwaffe's top test pilot, Captain Erik Dietz. Dietz, already an Ace was as good as it gets as a fighter pilot. Already, he had been highly decorated and was looking to add Crossed Swords to his Knights Cross of The Iron Cross with Oak Leaves, when he reluctantly succumbed to Goering's personal request to head up test flying the Giant.

An immaculately dressed Luftwaffe guard quickly stepped forward and opened the rear door for the huge unmistakable figure of the Reich Marshall. Goering eased his legs out onto the warm concrete runway and lifted himself out of the car with the aid of a specially strengthened hand strap. His dazzling white uniform caused most in the reception group to squint as the bright sunlight reflected off his considerable frame.

"Hello Erik, I see you have laid on the sunshine. We have the perfect weather for a test flight!" said Goering. He smiled and extended his white gloved hand to Dietz. "Assuming that is, you're ready?"

"Especially for you Reich Marshall, it's good to see you again. And absolutely we are ready!" said Dietz. He first saluted and then accepted Goering's handshake.

"Good answer, Captain. The Fuhrer is very anxious for success today," replied Goering, as he playfully tapped his gold tipped baton several times on Dietz's chest.

"As are all of us here, Reich Marshall. Please let me introduce you to the team that has worked extremely hard the last few months to meet this deadline today," said Dietz.

Goering was introduced to the line of officials by Dietz. He deliberately took a moment to have a few words with each one, including Director Rudolph Kemp, the Head of the Giant project.

"Very impressive, Herr Director," said Goering, as he walked towards the aircraft. "And I am told that you exceeded our goal of carrying 100 armed paratroopers. Is that correct?"

"Thank you, Herr Reich Marshall. It all comes down to weight at the end of the day. We are still finalizing a few things, but either way we will be at least at 100 and hope to push it to 120 when all is said and done. Everyone we can squeeze in after that will be a bonus. Even at the low end of 100 troops, it's still miles ahead of any of our enemies, that's for sure," said a confident Director Kemp as they arrived at the aircraft.

Goering handed his baton and cap to his batman. He laboriously climbed the aircraft steps, finally heaving his huge frame through the narrow doorway.

"Would you care to start with the cockpit?" enquired Dietz.

"No, I think I have a good idea of how it flies," said Goering, glancing at the two-man cockpit. "I am more interested in looking at what constitutes the seating arrangements for the paratroopers.

After all, this aircraft has dual purposes. As I understand it, the final design enables 100 plus paratroopers to land with their light weapons in a conventional manner or, alternatively, they can drop in their usual way. Is that correct Captain?"

"Correct," answered Dietz. He opened the curtain with a swish to reveal the spartan interior. It exposed two long benches running the length of the windowless fuselage with three trap doors built into the aisle and a door either side at the rear near the tail.

Goering slowly walked down the aisle, testing the floor with his weight, and pressing the padded benches with his hands remarking, "Pretty basic, don't you think Major? Even for a paratrooper!"

"Yes, Reich Marshall, everything has been designed to save weight and even the wooden benches are likely to be replaced with aluminum. We are working on a few other things to lighten the plane. Every kilo saved in the plane will help lift-off and ensure that the glider behind it takes off as smoothly as possible."

"Good!" said Goering, shuffling to the rear of the aisle. "Now, let me see the towing gear."

The Reich Marshall and Dietz squeezed through a small door at the rear of the plane to see a large steel trip hook. Attached to it was the small ring of a steel hawser which in turn ran out through a heavily greased hole below the tail fin. Alongside the hook, Goering could see a sledgehammer. Dietz picked it up and explained to Goering that if anything went wrong during takeoff or in flight, one of the crewmen could hit the hook release arm and the cable would rush through the hole.

Satisfied, Goering left the stuffy cramped fuselage and rejoined the others waiting on the runway. "Is there anything else you would like to see, Herr Reich Marshall? Perhaps you would like to inspect the glider?" asked Director Kemp.

"No, I have seen plenty of gliders when they were being built so I am satisfied that their design is excellent. I think I have seen enough for now. Let's see how well this Giant will fly, shall we?" said Goering as he stood back and again marveled at the colossal aircraft.

"Excellent!" said Dietz. "We are fueled up and ready to go."

Dietz nodded to his co-pilot and the two of them climbed quickly into the cockpit.

"Would you prefer to watch from the ground or the control tower, Herr Reich Marshall?" asked Director Kemp.

"The tower," said Goering, as he climbed back into his Mercedes for the short trip to the control tower.

Goering was now visibly wheezing by the time he had climbed the steep stairs up to the tower cab. He entered the cab and caught his breath as he briefly wished the controllers a good morning before gratefully taking a specially provided seat next to the tower chief.

"Have you any questions, Herr Reich Marshall before we clear Captain Dietz for takeoff?" asked the tower chief.

"No, go ahead with the takeoff. Please proceed," responded Goering, taking in large breaths of air as he dabbed his sweating forehead with his folded white gloves. His collar was feeling way too tight. He made a mental note to inform his tailor to increase his collar size yet again on his next elaborate outfit.

After a brief exchange of technical instructions, the tower chief gave the order for the takeoff procedure to commence. Slowly, the chocks were removed from the plane and then from the glider wheels. The ground crew ran to their assigned posts and the leader gave Dietz the thumbs up.

Goering heard Dietz check off the various items from his pre-flight checklist. Then the plane edged slowly forward, and the towing hawser began to lift off the concrete and take the strain. The tower chief informed Dietz that the hawser appeared taut and the aircraft was first in the queue for takeoff. Dietz reported back that all systems were go, and they were ready for takeoff.

The tower chief took one final look around, then issued the order, "Cleared for takeoff!"

The anxiety in the tower was palpable as the colossal plane rumbled down the runway, slowly gathering speed with its glider in tow. Goering leaned forward in his seat. It seemed the enormous plane might just run out of runway before it had gained enough speed to get airborne. "Come on Dietz, come on!" he whispered under his breath.

Everyone in the tower strained their necks towards the glass panels, almost willing the Giant to become airborne. Finally, to everyone's relief they saw the nose of the plane slowly begin to lift off. The glider followed and they both climbed slowly, ever so slowly into the clear blue Celle sky.

The audience was elated. A spontaneous cheer and round of applause rang out in the tower and the Head of the Luftwaffe turned to a visibly relieved Director Kemp and said, "Congratulations, gentlemen! A job well done! It is magnificent to see your efforts finally come to fruition. I assure you, the Fuhrer will be delighted!"

"Thank you, Herr Reich Marshall, thank you!" said Director Kemp.

"After seeing how long it took to lift off, I was a bit worried that Dietz would run out of runway! But I knew he would pull it off. When it comes to flying, there isn't anything that man cannot do!" replied an elated Goering.

"Agreed, we couldn't be happier Herr Reich Marshall!" responded a beaming Kemp.

"Excellent! So, tell me Director, what remains to be done now?" asked Goering as he struggled to get out of the creaking chair.

"We just have some interior configurations to work out as we discussed. Other than that, we should be ready for a final test with a full complement of men and their equipment. I will be happy to get back to you with a date. We would love to have you return here to Celle for the final test flight. It is always an honor and a great moral boost to our workers when you grace us with your presence," answered Kemp.

"Count on it, Herr Director. I'll be here," replied a smiling Goering as he looked at his diamond encrusted Cartier wristwatch. It was time to leave. He then straightened out his tunic and tucked his baton under his arm. He turned towards the door and headed down the steel staircase accompanied by his entourage. Their combined steel heeled jackboots made such a racket on the metal steps that Goering couldn't even hear the raucous applause still emanating from the massively relieved group up in the tower.

By the time the Mercedes passed back through the guarded gate, all thoughts of the Giant had vanished from his mind. Goering was focused instead on the cocktail party that he would be hosting later that evening to preview his latest plundered works of art, including a very rare Van Gogh.

As Goering considered what attire he should wear for the evening's event, he was oblivious to the fact that although the takeoff was a success and Dietz had successfully released the glider, the veteran test pilot had to use every skill in his considerable repertoire to land the aircraft and bring it to a stop. In fact, the aircraft was traveling so fast when it landed that it ran out of runway, smashing through the wooden barricades at the end before finally coming to rest in the soft, muddy fields that surrounded the airfield.

Chapter 17

THE END OF THE GIANT

Celle Airbase, Germany
March 1940

A light breeze was in the air and the sky was perfectly clear with excellent visibility. The conditions were ideal for Dr. Goebbels and his film crew to record the official maiden flight of the Giant, the largest military aircraft on earth. This was to be a proud moment for the entire nation, again showing off Nazi superiority. However, in truth the aircraft did not have a good track record. Three of the Luftwaffe's top pilots had perished during recent test flights. The consensus was that the plane was simply too big and heavy. While Messerschmitt had been successful in developing the engines to produce enough power to get the plane and its payload in the air, the problem still remained in slowing the aircraft down once it landed. Messerschmitt had developed a triple parachute system that deployed from the tail when the aircraft touched down. After several failures, the last two flights finally had been successful, much to the engineer's relief.

Messerschmitt had asked for more time to develop the chute release system, but the pressure from Goering to produce a finished product and go into production had been relentless. Today, the Luftwaffe's top test pilot and Goering favorite, Captain Erik Dietz was at the controls of the Giant. It was assigned the call name Silverfox.

Goering himself was back in the control tower along with the top directors of Messerschmitt. Goering knew that today's test flight had to succeed. The Fuhrer could not have been more explicit. He had run out of patience and expected Goering to deliver good news today or the consequences would be grave.

Based on Goering's assurances of success, Hitler had dispatched Dr. Goebbels to film the event so the German people could see the massive plane in action. It was yet another shining example of the superior Aryan brain and exceptional German manufacturing.

Goebbels, always the innovator had placed cameras at various positions along the runway. They would all take different angle shots of the Giant as it took off. Then he would later splice the best sequences together to provide the finest possible footage for the Fuhrer to review. Perhaps more importantly, the cameras would also capture his latest genius idea to achieve the money shot. He had mounted a camera in his open top Mercedes. He would be in the back seat directing the cameraman as the Mercedes sped along the runway following the Giant. He intended to get as close as possible to the Giant as it took off and when it landed.

All went according to plan and he was filming it as it finally took off with its full pay load and a loaded glider in tow. The sun was shining off its raw aluminum wings as it took to the air delighting Goebbels. He knew how pleased the Fuhrer would be when he played the film for him later that day. They continued filming as the Giant grew smaller, gaining altitude and leaving six exhaust trails in the sky, until it faded from view. Now he directed the driver to go back down the length of the runway to where it started, so they could film the same scene as the Giant came back in to land. Here they waited, squinting into the sunshine anxious for the Giant to return.

Goering was in his full-dress sky-blue uniform waiting nervously along with the Messerschmitt directors for the Giant to reappear. He tapped his baton slowly into his leather gloved hand, waiting. Then the radio crackled back to life and the calm voice of Dietz came through loud and clear.

"Celle Tower, this is Silverfox, five miles east, inbound for landing, over."

Dietz, having successfully deployed his glider was now ready to return to the airport. He knew the most difficult part of the test flight would be the landing. He had needed every inch of the main runway to be able to finally get airborne. After releasing the glider, the Giant was performing as expected. Dietz knew the real test was about to begin. His approach needed to be perfect in order to utilize every inch of the runway. He had already overrun the end of the runway previously and that was without the added weight of the paratroopers and their gear.

"Silverfox, this is Celle Tower, make straight in approach to Runway three zero, winds three two zero at one five, altimeter three zero one two, over."

On previous test flights when at slow speeds, Dietz noted that without explanation the wings tended to dip abruptly and take the plane into a steep left turning spiral. To prevent a stall, he would have to keep his speed up during final approach and maintain power throughout the landing. The parachute braking system would need to execute flawlessly to slow the plane down or they would surely run out of runway. There was absolutely no room for error, Dietz knew he had to get it dead right. He quickly finished his landing checklist and began to slowly throttle back on the six massive engines just enough to slow the aircraft down but keeping it well above the stall speed.

"Celle Tower, this is Silverfox on final approach, ready to land, over," Dietz' voice was dead calm.

"Silverfox, cleared to land, wind three three zero at two zero," replied the controller.

"Roger, cleared to land." Dietz subconsciously tightened his seat belt, flexed his fingers, silently said a quick prayer, and began what he hoped would be the highlight of his glorious Luftwaffe career. He, Erik Dietz would safely bring in the monster aircraft.

Dietz heard the wind report and wasn't happy that the windspeed had increased and shifted to more of a crosswind than before. Not ideal, but not beyond his skills either. He adjusted his altimeter to the latest setting and lowered the flaps fifteen degrees.

"This is it. We are going in," yelled Dietz to his copilot. "Have them brace for landing."

The copilot pulled back the curtain that separated the cockpit from the paratroopers that were crammed into the fuselage behind them. He gave the Sergeant the signal to prepare for landing.

"Here we go," said Dietz. As he throttled back on the power, he felt the huge wings take a dip. Dietz increased the power slightly, but the wings continued to dip, and he could feel the aircraft pulling to the left. Dietz fought with all his might, but this time the Giant did not respond. "More power!" he yelled as the engines screamed. Dietz' mind raced. He watched the altimeter spinning as they careened towards the runway. Too late, he realized they were not going to make it. "Abort! Abort!" he screamed.

Suddenly, the tower controller's eyes widened as he watched the Giant flash past the runway threshold. "Too fast, too fast! He's going way too fast!" The tower chief turned to Goering. A look of sheer panic could be seen on the normally stolid face. It was evident that the airplane was crossing the runway threshold well above the normal speed. Goering was now out of his seat as he bolted towards the door that led to the tower's outside catwalk. He flung it open and ran to the rail, gripping it with both hands. He braced for the crash that must surely come. He could see Goebbels in the back of the Mercedes already racing down the runway in anticipation of the great plane touching down, blissfully unaware of the peril he was in.

Traveling much too fast, the landing gear grazed the runway while Dietz desperately tried to lift the nose. He made a valiant effort to abort the landing and go around, but it was too late. The nose ballooned up and at the same time, three huge parachutes deployed from the rear of the aircraft. Dietz desperately fought the controls, but the Giant was rapidly reaching the point of no return.

To everyone's horror, the parachutes suddenly snapped away tearing off a large piece of the tail. The metal winch that was still attached to the parachutes bounced down the runway in a shower of sparks. Then the massive plane smashed down into the concrete with a colossal force, crushing the landing gear instantly and sending out a cascade of sparks and flames. The right wing dropped and was instantaneously sheared off, splitting the fuel tanks, and releasing hundreds of gallons of fuel.

Immediately, a massive fire ball erupted incinerating Dietz, his copilot and 120 paratroopers in seconds. Goering, his mouth agape looked on in disbelief from the catwalk at the horror unfolding in front of him.

Goebbels and the film crew, already doing close to 80 miles per hour and dangerously close to the point of impact, felt the concussion and blast of heat from the gargantuan plane exploding in an enormous ball of fire.

The cameraman, seemingly isolated from what was happening by his camera lens, continued to film. He had captured the entire crash. The driver instinctively applied the brakes, causing the Mercedes to fish tail wildly on the runway, smoke pouring from its tires. Goebbels had ducked when the plane exploded and fallen to the floor as the driver hit the brakes. The driver managed to get control of the car and brought it to a screeching halt.

Now Goebbels pulled himself back up on the seat and watched what was left of the fuselage still being consumed by flames as it continued careening down the runway. Burning pieces of the wreckage and mangled bodies that were thrown hundreds of feet in the air by the explosion began to fall all around them. A massive plume of black smoke from the main wreckage filled the warm Celle air.

"My God!" said Goebbels at the apocalyptic scene surrounding him. The smell of aviation fuel and burning rubber filled the air. The smoke was choking. Goebbels looked at the cameraman who incredibly continued to look through the lens and film the catastrophe seemingly oblivious to the peril they were in.

"Back up! Back up!!" screamed Goebbels. The driver didn't need to be told twice. He slammed the Mercedes into reverse and punched the accelerator. The tires spun noisily on the concrete runway before getting traction and sending the Mercedes backwards away from the burning wreckage. Goebbels finally yelled, "Stop! This is good, get this! Make sure you get all of this!" His eyes were wide in terror at what he had just witnessed. The cameraman signaled thumbs up and continued to view the scene through the lens. The first emergency vehicle raced past them in a futile attempt to try to fight the blaze.

Goebbels turned and looked up at the tower. There he was the massive, unmistakable figure of Hermann Goering. He was clearly visible in his sky-blue uniform standing alone on the catwalk, both hands covering his face. Goering realized he had just watched the end of Operation Gwilym and final flight of the Giant.

Goebbels tapped the cameraman on his shoulder, who looked up from the camera for the first time. He was jerked back to reality of how close they had just come to their own peril. His young face instantly turned an ashen white as he looked at Goebbels for some kind of guidance. "Goering!" he yelled, "Pan to Goering! Now! Now!"

Obediently, the cameraman turned the camera away from the wreckage towards the tower. He focused on the beaten Head of the Luftwaffe still covering his eyes in a vain attempt to shut out the horror of the burning carnage now littering the runway.

"We are done here," said Goebbels. "Back to the studio now!" The cameraman disconnected the camera from the tripod and handed it to Goebbels, who placed it beside himself on the floor in the rear. He then collapsed the tripod, nodded to the driver, and took his seat next to him as the Mercedes made a U-turn. With its tires screaming, it roared away from the burning debris covered airstrip.

Goebbels nervously lit a cigarette, his hands shaking visibly. He glanced over his shoulder one last time at the black smoke rising from the catastrophe that he had just witnessed and caught live on camera. A twisted smile crept across his evil face as he inhaled the smoke gratefully. He sat back in the plush leather seat and thought about the wrath that Goering would endure when the Fuhrer viewed his film later that day in the private viewing room at the Berghof.

Chapter 18

THE SILVER SCREEN

The Berghof, Bavaria
March 1940

"I'm sorry Joseph, the Fuhrer is not to be disturbed, no exceptions, period!" said Martin Bormann. He was delighted in the utter disappointment on Goebbels' face. "Our Leader was up all night with stomach cramps and is in a foul mood. Rest assured, I'll have the theater set up for him to review your film as soon as possible," he said poker faced. Unflinching, he held out his hand to accept the film canister.

Goebbels thought for a moment, then reluctantly handed over the film. He absolutely despised Bormann, all of Hitler's henchmen did. Nobody had more power over access to the Fuhrer than Bormann. His word on access was final and Goebbels knew it. "Thank you, Martin, and please give him my regards for a speedy recovery. I'm sure he will want to talk to me after he views it. You have a good day, Sir!" said the Propaganda Minister. He flipped the Nazi salute and left.

Goebbels deliberately decided not to bother telling Bormann about the catastrophe that had unfolded that morning at Celle. Why should he? Bormann had been short with him and never asked. His film would have even more impact, he rightly surmised, when Hitler viewed it on his private silver screen, unaware of the disastrous end he would witness.

The cameraman had surpassed even Goebbels' wildest dreams. The final shot of Goering with his face buried in his hands was simply priceless. To Goebbels, the failure of the Giant was almost irrelevant. Landing a knockout punch on his archrival Goering was far more important. In the continual battle to gain the attention and confidence of the leader of the Third Reich, nothing was off limits. No blow was considered too low.

It was much later in the day before Hitler finally entered his private theater, accompanied by Himmler and of course Bormann. The men sat down in the plush leather seats. The Fuhrer, still tired, irritable and in a horrible mood sat in the center. His seat was wider and taller than the others with the German eagle and swastika embossed in gold leaf on the leather headrest.

Once the Fuhrer was settled, he nodded to Bormann, who simultaneously raised his hand. The SS guard at the door turned off the lights and the projectionist switched on the projector. The noisy hum of its fan immediately filled the room. A series of numbers appeared on the screen followed by written warnings about viewing restrictions. Next, the screen was filled with the swastika flag, superimposed over it were the words THE GIANT.

The film began with a wide shot of the Messerschmitt factory. The swastika flag was flying proudly from the corporate office, followed by footage of workers enthusiastically working on the production lines. Then the film went on to show the massive aircraft in its hanger and a team shot of hundreds of workers standing in front of what was about to be unveiled. It was the world's largest troop-carrying plane.

The aircraft was then pulled out slowly by a tender onto the runway as the team looked on. Next comes footage of Goering arriving in his Mercedes, a decorated Luftwaffe officer welcoming him as he gets out of the rear of the car. A group of aircraft executives is assembled in a line, which Goering inspects as he walks past them. Occasionally, he stops to talk to one or two of the anxious executives. Then Goering is filmed heading to the control tower, dutifully followed by his entourage and several of the men in suits.

The camera then zooms to the cockpit showing the pilot who smiles and gives the thumbs up.

"Ah! Dietz is the pilot today. That's good, Dietz knows what he's doing," said the Fuhrer. He instantly recognized the man that he had recently added Oak Leaves to his Knights Cross of the Iron Cross medal at a private ceremony with Goering at the Berghof.

The next shot shows the three huge engines on each wing starting. Smoke and flames belch out of the exhaust system as the engines sputter to life and the massive propellers begin to turn. The plane with its glider in tow, taxis out to the runway. The sun is shining off its aluminum skin as it turns around to line up with the center of the main runway. A massive swastika is proudly painted on the tail.

The pilot applies full power and the huge machine begins to rumble down the runway, gathering speed. The camera pans back to the aircraft workers all now waiving small swastika flags and smiling in the bright sunshine. Then it returns to the plane as it speeds past a flanking open top Mercedes racing along the runway with a camera crew filming the actual take off. Hitler can clearly pick out Goebbels at the rear of the Mercedes in his tan jacket, the wind blowing his hair, frantically directing the cameraman.

Himmler obviously noticed the same thing. "Is that Dr. Goebbels in the back of the Mercedes? Surely not!" he asked.

"Yes! That's Joseph, what that man will do to get the best shot. I've never seen such a thing. He never ceases to amaze me!" beamed Hitler as he shook his head in feint disapproval.

"It's probably not a good decision on his part, Mein Fuhrer. The Minister of Propaganda should never be exposed to such unnecessary risk. Don't you think it's a little extreme for one who holds such a vital position?" asked Himmler. His beady eyes narrowing behind his round wire rimmed glasses.

Hitler considered it for a moment and realized Himmler had a point. Goebbels was a vital part of the success the Nazis were now enjoying. Nobody understood the power of the media, in particular the film industry better than Goebbels. Hitler knew Goebbels was a rare gift and Himmler was right. The last thing he should be doing is standing up in the back of a convertible, perilously speeding alongside a huge aircraft towing a glider. "You're right Heinrich, it's ridiculous. I will put a stop to it when I see him. He needs to think these things through."

"Of course, Mein Fuhrer," replied Himmler, the slightest trace of a grin crept across his thin lips as he reveled in the fact that he had just blocked Goebbels from doing one of the things that he clearly enjoyed. The film returns to the plane now getting close to the end of the runway as it finally slowly, lifts off.

"Yes! Bravo Dietz!" exclaimed the Fuhrer, clearly relieved to see the Giant airborne at last. "I was worried it would never get off the ground! But I knew Dietz would get it done!" Both men either side of him feigned a laugh. The cameraman followed the plane as it slowly gained altitude, six trails of blackish gray exhaust followed it through the blue sky. The glider was still in tow as it gradually faded from view.

The screen is filled with the workers clapping wildly and waiving their swastika flags to shield their eyes against the bright sun. Hitler is clearly pleased. "This is a great moment, Mein Fuhrer!" said Himmler. The image of the screen reflected in his glasses as he looked at the Fuhrer who smiled but didn't comment. The Fuhrer's eyes stayed fixed on the screen.

The next shot is of the ground crew checking their watches and looking through binoculars, anxiously awaiting the return of the aircraft. Finally, one of them is seen pointing into the distance. Then the cameraman picks up a tiny speck and stays focused on it. It grows rapidly in size and begins to lose altitude while coming in for its final approach.

Now the dot is clearly visible as a large aircraft. More details are evident every second it continues its descent. It appears to Hitler to be traveling very fast as it speeds towards the runway. Then it seems at the last moment that Dietz tries to raise the nose but it's too close to the ground. A cloud of smoke appears when the wheels touch the runway. Dietz looks to be increasing the power to presumably abort the landing.

"Come on, Dietz! Come on!" said the Fuhrer under his breath. Suddenly, a triple parachute is deployed and opens. Then to the men's horror, it seems to detach from the aircraft ripping the winch out of the rear of the plane and tearing away a huge chunk of the tail, including the vertical stabilizer. The Fuhrer leaned further forward in his seat and watched the Giant, now clearly doomed, slam hard into the runway. The landing gear disintegrated immediately, and the aircraft bounces once then hits again. Himmler and Bormann now lean further forward as they look on in horror to see the wing get sheared off. Finally, there is a massive explosion and the aircraft is instantly engulphed in a colossal fire ball.

"Mother of God!" gasped Himmler. He watched in shock as the disaster unfolded before him on the screen. Hitler watched the flaming wreckage bounce along the runway. Bormann covered his mouth with his hands and gazed at the screen in silent disbelief.

"Mother of God!" repeated Himmler. "Mother of God! What the hell just happened?!" said the head of the SS, his mouth agape. Hitler looked on in shock and utter silence. He was unable to look away from the catastrophe playing out before him.

Then the camera panned from the burning fuselage to the tower where it zoomed in. There was the unmistakable figure of Reich Marshall Hermann Goering, Head of the Luftwaffe in his sky-blue uniform. He was standing fifty feet in the air on the catwalk, motionless with his hands covering his face.

Hitler erupted in anger and screamed. He lurched at the screen, punching a hole straight through the thin canvas and tearing at it as it fell from its tripod. The solitary figure of Goering continued to play out on the white plaster wall behind the screen. The silhouette of Hitler, giant sized, manic, in the bright light of the projector, his fists shaking in the air, exploded. "Bastard! Bastard! Bastard!" he screamed. "Out! Out! Everybody get out!! Now!! Out! Out! Out!"

The projectionist was first to get to the door. He was followed by Himmler and Bormann, who turned to look back as Hitler began tearing at the canvas of the screen. His eyes were wide open, and spittle was flying from his mouth as he screamed. "Get me that fat Bastard! Get him here now!!" his feet stamping on the remains of the crumpled tripod.

"Right away, Mein Fuhrer!" bleated Bormann. He exited, leaving the Fuhrer to stamp on the remnants of the screen before finally stopping and standing in silence. Hitler drew deep breaths, his hair stuck out at an absurd angle. His face was a deep red and sweat covered his forehead. He clenched his jaw tightly and his eyes were wide with rage as his chest heaved beneath his pinstriped business suit. He kicked the tripod stand a final time, sending it flying into the wall with a crash. Finally, he smoothed back his hair and stormed out.

In the empty theater the film ran its course and finished, leaving the reel spinning rapidly. The tail end of the film made a rhythmic flapping sound as it hit against the projector casing. Its bright projection light shining on the wall where the now mangled screen had previously been.

Chapter 19

OPERATION GWILYM CANCELLED

Berlin, Germany
April 1940

The intercom on Reich Fuhrer Himmler's desk buzzed. "The Fuhrer, line one, Reich Fuhrer!" said the male voice. Himmler was surprised at a call from the Fuhrer himself. He straightened up in his chair, reached for his pen and turned to a fresh page on his blotter and picked up line one.

"Mein Fuhrer!" snapped Himmler into the handset.

"It's Bormann," said the gravelly voice on the other end of the phone. "Hold please and I'll put you through." There was a brief pause then the Fuhrer came on the line. "Reich Fuhrer Himmler," said Hitler.

"Mein Fuhrer!" repeated Himmler.

"I'll be brief. I wanted you to be the first to know that Operation Gwilym has been cancelled by my orders, effective immediately," said the Fuhrer in a matter of fact tone, as if cancelling an appointment with his barber.

"Mein Fuhrer? Operation Gwilym has been cancelled? Surely this can't be?" Himmler was astonished at what he had just heard.

"Yes, cancelled. Suspend all aspects concerning this operation. Those are my direct orders," said Hitler in the same monotone voice.

"Cancelled? Mein Fuhrer, we have everything in place, ready to roll. We are just waiting for the Me 323 Giant to be combat ready..." said Himmler, still reeling. He had assumed that the secret alliance he had originally formed with Hitler to circumvent the old school generals was rock solid. Getting Goering on board to develop the massive aircraft had been a game changer. He knew the catastrophe they had watched on the screen of the Giant exploding in a fireball was a considerable set back but nothing more than that. Now it seemed the whole operation was being scrapped.

"Yes, cancelled," answered Hitler, still not indicating why.

"Mein Fuhrer, may I ask why?" asked Himmler, fully aware that he was pushing his luck.

"Yes Heinrich, you may ask. And on this occasion, I believe you are entitled to know," replied Hitler.

"Thank you, Mein Fuhrer," replied a relieved Himmler.

"After the disaster that you and I witnessed on film, I took personal command of the situation. It appears that reports were doctored and issues with the aircraft were swept under the rug. Too many engineers buried their heads in the sand, but the reality is it will never be ready. The aircraft is simply too big and too heavy to land. Given the size of the landing fields on Anglesey, we will never be able to land the amount of assault troops needed for Gwilym to succeed. The facts are the facts, Reich Fuhrer," replied Hitler.

"No! I talked to Goering himself just last week. He assured me that despite the crash they would be ready to go into full production, that they had ironed out the problems, he..." Hitler cut him off in mid-sentence.

"Yes Heinrich, he gave me the same assurances. But the reality is Goering has failed you, me and the German people. It is unfortunate but we cannot afford to lose resources chasing a Goering pipe dream. I know how much time and effort you have put into your end. The Reich appreciates it. However, at the end of the day, if we cannot get your men on the ground in the numbers we need, then the operation is doomed to fail. Therefore, I'm cancelling it effective immediately, understood?" asked the Fuhrer.

Himmler knew the Fuhrer was right. The success hinged one hundred percent on getting sufficient numbers on the ground fast enough to secure the airfields and without that, the attempt would be suicidal. He knew it was over.

Himmler took a deep breath, "Understood, Mein Fuhrer," he conceded.

"Good," said Hitler. "I know this will be a crushing blow to the young von Seeckt. His plan was quite brilliant, regardless of

Goering's failure to deliver. Let him know that I appreciate his dedication. He is a rising star amongst your men. I have high hopes for him. Now I must get going. Heil!"

"Heil," replied Himmler. The line went dead. Himmler hung up and shook his head. Months of hard work and meticulous planning had just gone up in smoke, as surely as the Giant had done on the landing strip at Celle.

Himmler lit a cigar, inhaled deeply, and sat back in his chair. "Goering, such a fool!" he said out loud. Then he thought for a moment as he took another drag off his cigar. He disliked Goering and his flamboyant ways. He was more of a circus clown than a military leader, he always had been. The fragile bond they had formed over Operation Gwilym was now over. Goering would go back on his hit list, along with Goebbels, Canaris and Bormann. All of whom he considered as his main competitors for the Fuhrer's attention on a daily basis.

Then a smile crept across his face. He thought about the beating that Goering would surely have taken from Hitler. He leaned forward, tapped his cigar in the ash tray and considered his options. He would hold off on informing von Seeckt about the cancellation of Operation Gwilym until he returned from the invasion of Norway. The Fuhrer could not have been more explicit about the Norway mission. During Operation Weserübung, the Brandenburgers needed to seize the Norwegian gold from the vault at the Norges Bank in Oslo. It was estimated to be in the region of 50 tons, more than enough to fund the Nazi war machine. There was no point in distracting von Seeckt from his mission.

Chapter 20

HIMMLER'S NIGHTMARE

SS Headquarters, Berlin
April 1940

Himmler was now aware of his arched rival, Doctor Joseph Goebbels' intense interest in his new protégé, Captain von Seeckt. He knew from his extensive intelligence network that Goebbels was under massive pressure to produce a propaganda victory over the British. Goebbels was about to try to sell Hitler on the idea of creating the perfect Nazi poster boy using von Seeckt to fill the role. Himmler thought he had beaten Goebbels to the punch. He had already informed Hitler that Captain von Seeckt would personally lead a small Brandenburger strike team to seize the Norwegian gold. Hitler was delighted to hear the news and fully supported his decision.

However, Hitler unpredictable as always, reversed course less than a week later. He had broken the news to Himmler when they had afternoon tea with Goebbels at the Berghof. Hitler had approved the selection of von Seeckt as the Nazi poster boy and his decision was final. Himmler could still see the smirk on Goebbels face as Hitler delivered the awful news.

Himmler was seething that of all the perfect Aryan officers in the SS, Goebbels insisted on choosing his favorite, von Seeckt. The argument between himself and Goebbels was so heated at one point that the Fuhrer himself had to step in and demand calm. Hitler let it go on for several minutes as he reveled in the vicious back and forth between the two. In the end Hitler ordered a compromise. Goebbels would be allowed access to some of the special training undertaken by the strike force so that he could film von Seeckt in various combat situations. But he was to be strictly hands off and could not disrupt the rigid training schedule in any way.

The night before the strike force was due to deploy to Norway as part of Operation Weserübung, Himmler summoned von Seeckt to his headquarters. Himmler wanted to reassure himself that von Seeckt understood where his loyalty lies, namely to the SS. Himmler had watched von Seeckt walk the razor edge of diplomacy. He was impressed at von Seeckt's calm demeanor and steel focus even when under pressure. Himmler had seen him successfully navigate between himself and the Minister of Propaganda in the presence of the Fuhrer, remaining ice cool. There was no doubt in Himmler's mind that von Seeckt was destined for greatness within the Third Reich. It was a greatness that Himmler alone would take credit for, not the clubfooted cripple who lived in a Hollywood fantasy land.

In order to further cement the relationship, Himmler wanted to do something very special for von Seeckt. Himmler's personal jeweler determined that a rare gold medallion belonging to the Mayor of a pillaged Czech city was cast from the purest gold that he had ever seen. In his opinion it was almost certainly pure Welsh gold.

Delighted, Himmler had ordered him immediately to melt it down and recast it into a design that he had personally conceived and drawn out. It would be a badge that featured the German eagle over the swastika and below the swastika the initials MvS. Himmler insisted that the badge have as rugged a finish as possible. He wanted it to replicate the type of gold badge or medallion that had adorned the ancient warriors of yesteryear.

The jeweler exceeded Himmler's expectations. Himmler loved gold, unlike the Fuhrer who did not care one iota for it. It was just a means for him to buy the resources to build the Nazi war machine. Hitler, like Goering preferred actual works of art but Himmler was simply smitten with the alure of gold. To him it was almost mystical. There was more to it than its value as a currency. History was riddled with stories such as The Golden Chalice, The Arc of the Covenant, and The Golden Fleece. Things he had marveled and fantasized about since boyhood now seemed as though they had, by the hand of fate, been put into his reach. Quite fitting he thought for the second most powerful man of the Master Race.

Himmler had been charged by the Fuhrer with seizing the entire gold reserves of the Kingdom of Norway. Convinced that von Seeckt and the strike team of sixteen highly trained individuals would deliver for the Fuhrer, he wanted to present the custom golden Nazi badge to him for good luck before he left for Norway.

Von Seeckt and his fellow Brandenburgers were due to board the ship, Blücher the next day. The Blücher was the latest addition to the Kriegsmarine. It was an impressive vessel that could transport around 1000 armed troops in her belly. Besides von Seeckt and his Brandenburgers strike team, there were also numerous men from the Gestapo and SS heading into Oslo to set up headquarters in the City Hall. They were to begin the immediate process of identifying undesirables to be instantly rounded up, interrogated, and shot.

The Blücher was to be the flag ship of Group Five. She was to lead the naval attack by sailing right up the narrow Oslo Fjord and depositing her lethal cargo of crack troops and their equipment right into the Norwegian capital. Blücher was equipped with three catapult launched sea planes. The plan called for them to fly ahead of Blücher once they entered the fjord and identify any potential threats. The Blücher would then neutralize the threats with her impressive arsenal of eight, eight-inch guns.

The new Kriegsmarine was all about speed. The brand-new Admiral Hipper class Heavy Cruiser Blücher epitomized the speed doctrine with an impressive top speed of 32 knots. Typically, in a seaborne invasion, the Blücher and other naval ships would have to slow down considerably in order to escort the slower moving troop carriers and cargo vessels. Obviously, this negated their huge speed advantage.

In a sweeping change of tactic, the Germans decided to forgo the normal procedure of moving troops by slow moving troopships and instead cram them aboard their Navy vessels opting for speed and surprise. At the same time, an airborne assault would be launched against Oslo Airport. It was the first time that paratroopers would be used in an airborne assault in World War II.

There were many firsts for Operation Weserübung, too many. Enough to cause Himmler numerous sleepless nights. He knew that the element of speed and surprise were essential. His stress levels were elevated close to the breaking point. Last night was the worst so far. Still, hours later in the day as he stared at the burning logs in his fireplace, he was haunted by his latest nightmare. Thankfully, a foggy mist shrouded most of it, but one clear apocalyptic vision was still fresh in his mind and had been all day. In the nightmare, he seemed to be flying, effortlessly like a bird. He was over an ink blue ocean looking down from an elevated position, a clear voice was reading out loud. It was one of his favorite poems, Tennyson's The Charge of the Light Brigade. He knew the poem well. The words came through, precise, soothing, calm, and clear. Now he seemed to be skimming over the surface of the water before effortlessly landing softly. The voice was familiar, reassuring.

> *Half a league, half a league,*
> *Half a league onward,*
> *All in the valley of Death*
> *Rode the six hundred.*
> *Forward, the Light Brigade!*
> *Charge for the guns!*
> *Into the valley of Death*
> *Rode the six hundred.*

For a while it seemed like he was back at school and not in the sea. The voice was clearer now. He recognized it as one of his high school teachers but couldn't place the face. Now he was back in the water again, floating effortlessly. He could see a great navy battleship coming forward out of the mist and the wake caused by its massive bow. He could see its mighty guns and super structure. He could feel the power of its engines as it surged through the water. The words were louder now.

> *Theirs not to make reply,*
> *Theirs not to reason why,*
> *Theirs but to do and die.*
> *Into the valley of Death*
> *Rode the six hundred.*

The bow was getting closer to him. He needed to go back to his classroom, this was not safe! But he couldn't pull himself away from gazing at the ever-increasing gray steel bow. The voice was getting louder and louder as the ship got closer and closer to him. He could sense the vibration of the huge propellers running through his body. He wanted to fly again, to get out of the way of the ship, but he couldn't move. He was mesmerized by the bow as it came closer and closer.

Cannon to right of them,
Cannon to left of them,
Cannon in front of them
Volleyed and thundered;
Stormed at with shot and shell,
Boldly they rode and well,
Into the jaws of Death,
Into the mouth of hell
Rode the six hundred.

Still riveted and transfixed on the massive ship now bearing down upon him, he closed his eyes and waited for his inevitable death. Suddenly, he was flying like a bird again. The sky was blue and vast. He could feel the warm welcoming rays of the sun. The voice had gone. He could still see the mighty ship below. He marveled at its sleek lines, its white foamy wake trailing behind it as it sailed effortlessly through the dark blue water.

It was a magnificent sight. Then quite suddenly the ship was rocked by a series of massive explosions. It lurched out of the water from the impact and was consumed in a massive orange fire ball. Horrified, he looked on, then suddenly he realized he was high in the air and not in his classroom. Now he was falling from an incredible height, screaming through the air at a colossal speed. He tumbled head over heels heading straight into the flaming ship. He was screaming "God No!!!" Then he had been woken up by his wife Margarete. He was home, safe in his bed. His pajamas were soaked in sweat. It was all just a horrible nightmare. Thank God.

Himmler was still gazing into the flames of his fireplace when his thoughts were suddenly interrupted by the phone buzzing on his desk. "Captain von Seeckt is here to see you Herr Reich Fuhrer," said the female voice. He wasn't sure how long he had been replaying the nightmare in his mind, but it was still very vivid. It had put him in an almost trance like state and caused him now to be sweating quite profusely.

"Excellent! Show him in," replied Himmler. He pulled his monogrammed white linen handkerchief out of his pocket, removed his glasses, and quickly dabbed his forehead.

Chapter 21

THE GOLDEN BADGE

SS Headquarters, Berlin
April 1940

Von Seeckt's men had trained hard for the mission. Himmler had been unable to watch any of the training due to his jam-packed schedule. He had received reports that Goebbels had spent a great deal of time filming the dashing young Captain and his team as they powered their way through seemingly impenetrable obstacles. He needed to feel von Seeckt out, to be assured that his loyalty was still to himself and the SS.

The door opened and the imposing figure of Brandenburger Captain Max von Seeckt entered. He clicked his polished jackboot heels and gave the Nazi salute that Himmler promptly returned. The two men then warmly shook hands. Himmler wanted to make sure that von Seeckt made good eye contact, which he did.

"Captain von Seeckt. Welcome back! What a pleasure, please come in and be at ease," said Himmler. He kindly beckoned von Seeckt towards the roaring fireplace that dominated Himmler's private office. Even though it was late spring, a cold front had moved in and there was a definite chill in the air. "Will you join me in a glass of Cognac, Max?" asked Himmler. He used von Seeckt's first name in order for him to feel more relaxed. The consumption of alcohol was generally prohibited at SS headquarters, but this was different. It was more of a social occasion. Besides, he was Heinrich Himmler. Those rules didn't apply to him.

"The pleasure is mine Reich Fuhrer and yes, I would be honored," replied von Seeckt.

"Good!" said Himmler. He turned to the crystal decanter on top of a silver tray displayed on the antique sideboard and poured two generous measures. A massive picture of Adolph Hitler looked down menacingly at the two men from above the sideboard. Himmler handed von Seeckt a glass then turned to the portrait and said, "To our Fuhrer!"

"To our Fuhrer!" repeated von Seeckt and the two men each downed their shot. Himmler retrieved von Seeckt's glass and refilled them both. He handed Max his glass and gestured for him to take a seat opposite his own in front of the fire.

"Please relax. I just wanted to get together with you briefly before you leave for your mission," said Himmler.

"Thank you, Herr Reich Fuhrer," said von Seeckt. He sat down and removed his cap and placed it on the coffee table between them.

"So, how was the training? I was unable to get by to evaluate things myself, but I was kept apprised of your progress. The reports I received indicated things went very well. Was that the case?" asked Himmler.

"It went well, Reich Fuhrer. The amphibious training was particularly beneficial. It took us a while to get our sea legs so to speak but we worked with the Kreigsmarine crews. In the end, we were a well-oiled machine. I feel very good about our chances once we leave the safety of the Blücher. I have come to the conclusion that war, whether fought on sea or land comes down to two elements, speed and surprise. The Norwegian's will not know what hit them. My men are more than ready to take over the Bank at Oslo," replied von Seeckt with a genuine air of confidence.

"Good, good," said Himmler. "And you will remember to stay focused on the bank Max? Don't get distracted!"

"Yes Sir, the bank is our only objective. We will remove anyone who stands in our way, quickly and efficiently. Once we are in the bank, the gold is ours. No one, and I repeat no one will be allowed anywhere close to it until our main force arrives to transport it safely back to the Reichsbank under the protection of myself and the team," explained von Seeckt as he sipped his Cognac.

"That's it. The bank, that's the only objective. We must get that gold, Max. I cannot begin to tell you the importance of securing the gold. If the Reich is to expand, it simply must have gold to fund the effort. The situation may become quite desperate if we do not replace the coffers. We have already burned through most of our funds just financing our expansion into Czechoslovakia. Then with the actions we've taken in Poland, the expenses are enormous," lamented Himmler. He swirled his Cognac in the bottom of his glass while staring into the warm flames of the fire. He was relieved that the vision from hell had vanished, at least for now.

"Yes Sir, believe me I get it. I grew up around money and wealth. My father was a master at finance. He was always a huge fan of gold. He always told me how there was a finite amount of gold in the earth and that gold, unlike currency had never been worth zero. It has survived for centuries and has always been the safe haven in troubled times, such as the ones we find ourselves in currently. So, I totally understand why we must make this a priority," assured von Seeckt, sensing Himmler was genuinely concerned.

"Good Max! Your father is a very smart man. Did he ever tell you the golden rule?" asked Himmler.

"Yes, he is very smart, a genius actually. The golden rule? No...I don't recall him ever discussing the golden rule," answered von Seeckt.

"Ah!" said Himmler. He stopped swirling his Cognac and took another hefty gulp. "Then let me explain the golden rule to you Max," he continued. He leaned a little closer to von Seeckt who leaned forward, eager to hear the words of wisdom that Himmler was about to reveal.

Himmler stared directly into von Seeckt's eyes and said, "Are you ready, Max?" He deliberately lowered his voice while looking over his shoulder for an imaginary figure lurking in the shadows.

"I'm ready Reich Fuhrer," said von Seeckt. He was eager for the knowledge that Himmler was about to share but also ready for a one liner that he sensed was coming.

"The golden rule is, he who has the gold, makes the rules!" Himmler laughed out loud as he watched von Seeckt's reaction. Von Seeckt had heard the line years before at Eton. He feigned laughter, much to the delight of the leader of the SS. The two men laughed together. It wasn't the first time. Himmler had an extremely dry and dark sense of humor that von Seeckt had tapped into on their first face to face meeting. He also had a slight inferiority complex when he was in the presence of true warriors like Max von Seeckt.

He often successfully used humor with them in order to help break down his own insecurities.

Himmler desperately wanted to be a warrior. He had missed out on the First World War but always imagined that he would have been fearless if tested. He loved being in uniform and being in the company of men like von Seeckt, especially when they were smart enough to use humor as a means of getting closer to him. Von Seeckt had noticed this on their first meeting and had subsequently made Himmler laugh several times previously when they had been alone together.

His mother had instilled in him the importance of humor. She taught him that when used correctly, it could be a considerable benefit in cementing lifelong relationships. "Max," she would say, "There are two ways to make sure someone will always remember you. Either piss them off or make them howl with laughter. Both will work but laughter my dear boy is by far the preferred path." So far, the advice had served him well, especially with the leader of the SS.

"That's a great rule!" said von Seeckt. They finished laughing and drained their Cognac.

"The best!" said a still beaming Himmler. "So, the training Max, I assume my friend Dr. Hollywood showed up with his movie crew?" he asked as the smile vanished from his face. Himmler and Goebbels had been locked in a vicious personal battle of late. Himmler was concerned that Goebbels was getting way too close to the Fuhrer at his expense. Von Seeckt had become an unwitting pawn in the power struggle between the two high ranking Nazis. Himmler was determined to prevail when it came down to where von Seeckt's loyalty lay.

"Yes Sir, he did," answered von Seeckt.

"I understand. He was respectful, kept his distance, and didn't meddle or get in the way. I need you to tell me if he did," said Himmler, hoping von Seeckt would complain.

"Yes Sir, he kept his distance. Well more specifically, the film crew kept their distance, especially once they realized all of the exercises were conducted using live rounds!" laughed von Seeckt.

"Oh, perfect!" replied Himmler. He imagined Goebbels and his film crew cowering for cover.

"Yes, we had one close call early on when a ricocheting bullet smashed the windshield of one of their vehicles. That was more than enough to convince them not to get too close. It takes a certain breed of men to work under those conditions. I seriously doubt whether any of Goebbels' cameramen have the metal for it. Overall, they were not a factor. I assure you my men and I were more than focused on the job at hand. Live rounds zipping over your head will get your attention every time."

"Excellent!" replied Himmler. "My men are warriors, not cowboys dancing around on a set with cap guns!" He drank the last of his Cognac. Without asking, he took von Seeckt's glass and refilled it along with his own. As the warm glow of the first few shots passed through his body, he was feeling good about his meeting with von Seeckt. He was sure that Goebbels had not tried to permanently woo away one of his finest SS officers into his seedy world. He still wanted to be sure though. He needed to know. "Did you get time to meet with him, Goebbels I mean?" he asked as he handed von Seeckt another generous measure of Cognac.

"Yes, just once," answered von Seeckt.

"Oh? When was that?" asked Himmler. His eyes narrowed slightly as he gazed at von Seeckt through his glasses.

"It was a couple of days ago when we were all done training for the day. We noticed the film crew had set up a large reception tent by the river. It turned out to be for an award ceremony for The Attack newspaper. They were there to film it as Goebbels was due to make the keynote speech. A beautiful young lady handed me an envelope with a personal invitation to attend the award ceremony as his guest. So naturally I attended," answered von Seeckt.

"Oh, I see. And did he say anything to you?" asked Himmler. He took another swig of Cognac that now seemed much smoother.

"Nothing of any consequence. It was loud and there were a lot of people in the tent. Lots of pretty girls! Dr. Goebbels made a rousing speech. There is no doubt he is a very good public speaker. Everybody wanted to shake his hand and take pictures. We just talked briefly. He said he wanted to talk to me about doing promotional work for the Reich when I get back from the mission, nothing specific.

"I see and how do you feel about that Max?" asked Himmler.

"Well, he added that the Fuhrer was anxious for him to complete the promotion. So naturally I agreed to talk with him on my return. If it helps the Fuhrer, then count me in."

"Of course, the Fuhrer must always come first," replied Himmler.

"Of course," repeated Max. "And naturally I will always keep you well apprised of anything I hear that could be of interest or a benefit to you, Reich Fuhrer," he added with a wink.

That was it! That was all Himmler needed to see and hear. He really should never have doubted where von Seeckt's loyalty laid. He just needed some reassurance that he was loyal to the core. Himmler concealed his delight and simply added, "Good Max, I know I can trust you." Himmler put his glass on the table and picked up a small silver bell that he rang a couple of times. In seconds, Himmler's batman appeared. He politely saluted and held out a small silver tray for Himmler. Sitting on the tray was a black gift box of the type that might contain a medal or award. Alongside it was what appeared to be a metal punch. Himmler ignored him and instead stood up motioning for von Seeckt to do the same. The two men now stood facing each other in front of the fireplace.

"I wanted to show my appreciation for the way you have handled your meteoric rise through the ranks of the SS and now through the Special Strike Force. You are a special individual Max, with a very bright future in the SS. I have the utmost confidence that you and your team will successfully capture the Norwegian gold. With that said I am promoting you to Major, effective immediately," said Himmler with a smile.

Max was stunned. "Thank you, Reich Fuhrer. Thank you!" was all he could muster.

"You've earned it, Max. Congratulations." Himmler extended his hand and the two men exchanged a firm grip. Then he continued, "I also have a small gift for you. This will mark the occasion, so you will always remember it." He turned to the batman, picked up the small box from the tray and handed it to a surprised von Seeckt.

"Mein Reich Fuhrer, I don't know what to say," said von Seeckt clearly surprised by Himmler's gesture.

"Thank you, will be fine Max!" laughed Himmler as Max opened the box. He smiled as he gazed at the golden badge laying on the black velvet cushion in the box. "It's incredible, and with my initials! I've never seen anything like it," said von Seeckt. He removed the badge from the box and gazed at its magical luster. It was heavy and weighed close to an ounce and had been cast in one piece. It was truly one of a kind. "Thank you, Sir. I am speechless. Thank you."

"Excellent! I'm glad you like it," replied Himmler. "My jeweler assures me that it is Welsh gold Max, nothing but the best for an SS leader, eh?"

"Welsh gold! My mother would approve. She has a good eye for these types of things," answered von Seeckt. He rubbed his thumb over the smooth gold finish. "Your Mother has good taste. Now, Bruno please do the honors!" said Himmler turning to his batman who bent down and taking his punch, pierced a hole at the top of von Seeckt's left jackboot with an audible pop. He positioned the hole on the outside of the jackboot about an inch from the top. Then he looked up at von Seeckt and held out his hand, "Badge." Von Seeckt handed him the gold badge. Bruno removed the clasp, forced the pin through the hole in the boot and replaced the clasp. He then straightened the badge, pressing it into the boot. Finally, he patted down von Seeckt's pant leg and stood back up.

"Excellent!" said Himmler as he leaned sideways to admire the gleaming gold badge attached to von Seeckt's black polished jackboot. "That will be all, thank you Bruno!" The batman gave Himmler the Nazi salute, smiled at von Seeckt and left the two men alone in front of the fireplace.

"Good, I'm glad you like it Max. It's completely custom, one of a kind, just like its wearer! I know it's been a long day for you and tomorrow you will embark on a great operation. I wanted to see you before you went and wish you and your men the very best of luck! One more toast for the road?"

"Absolutely!" replied von Seeckt. Himmler poured them each another shot.

"To a successful gold heist!" said Himmler. The two men drained their glasses and simultaneously threw them in the roaring fire. "Good luck Max," said Himmler.

"Thank you, Herr Reich Fuhrer! For everything," replied von Seeckt. He looked down at the gleaming golden eagle, swastika and the initials MvS neatly attached to the outside of his boot. He slowly shook his head from side to side, almost unable to believe his good fortune. He had received an immediate promotion to Major along with a custom gold badge from the head of the SS himself. He retrieved his cap from the coffee table, placed it on his head, and pulled the peak down. Then snapping to a ramrod straight posture, he saluted and was gone.

Alone, Himmler stood by the fireplace gazing into the dancing flames. While the promotion to Major was more of a jab at Canaris, he was glad that the golden badge had worked out so well. He knew that if Max had that unique gift on his jackboot, his loyalty to him, the Brandenburgers, and the SS was absolute.

His thoughts now turned back to the Norwegian gold. He tried to imagine the stacks of gold bars neatly sitting in the vault of the Bank of Norway with Major Max von Seeckt and his band of Brandenburgers fearlessly standing guard. But as he gazed into the flames, the nightmare of the burning ship returned. He endured the terror for a moment. Then he shuddered and snapped himself back from the dark abyss. Perhaps he had just drunk a little too much Cognac.

Chapter 22

THE INVASION OF NORWAY

Oslo, Norway
April 1940

While the invasion of Norway was a success for the Nazis, it was an unmitigated disaster for Major von Seeckt and his crack Brandenburger strike team whose specific mission was to secure Norway's gold reserves.

Initially, things went smoothly for the invasion fleet. The sea was covered in a thick fog and it seemed to be the perfect cover until they were spotted by the Norwegian patrol boat Poll III that fired off warning flares. The German Motor Torpedo boat Albatross immediately broke away from the fleet to engage her. The Poll III, which was a converted fishing trawler was hopelessly outgunned. Perhaps in a hint of things to come, the Captain, Leif Welding Olsen in an act of defiance, heroically rammed his small ship directly into the Albatross. The Albatross raked the Poll III with anti-aircraft fire setting her ablaze and gravely wounding her brave Captain. The crew abandoned ship but one of the lifeboats overturned, pitching the men into the icy water. By this time, Welding Olsen had lost too much blood and was unable to hold on. He became the first casualty of the invasion of Norway.

The flag ship Blücher, under the command of Admiral Kummetz continued into the mouth of the Oslo Fjord, past the Oscarsborg Fortress. Suddenly, she was illuminated by searchlights from the fortress. The ancient eleven-inch cannons ironically made in Germany, were named Moses and Aron and they roared at Blücher's port side from less than 2,000 yards. The first 600-pound shell destroyed the battle station located high above the bridge, killing the commander of the anti-aircraft batteries. The second shell hit and set fire to one of the Blücher's three sea planes. The fire spread rapidly to the other planes in the hanger and then ignited the fuel that was stored on board for the 163rd Infantry Division's land assault.

The Blücher's crew fought the flames valiantly but as she continued past the fortress, two torpedoes from a land-based battery hit her in the side. The Blücher's sister ship Lutzow was also hit and seeing the fate of Blücher, turned around with the rest of the fleet. This left the Blücher to face her inevitable doom alone.

One of the torpedoes ruptured the ship's fuel supply, which now caught fire spilling burning fuel into the water. Unable to steer, the ship began to list. The fire was now raging out of control and ultimately reached the ship's own ordinance, resulting in a colossal explosion.

Admiral Kummetz realized the situation was now impossible and gave the order to abandon ship. In a desperate situation of every man for himself, von Seeckt was forced to draw his weapon to hold back the frantic troops. He made sure that his team was aboard the last available lifeboat that was lowered into the burning sea. They were able to row safely to shore where to their horror they witnessed the mighty Blücher roll over and sink. The Blücher took hundreds of men with her to the bottom of the Oslo Fjord. The screams of the men left in the burning water rang in their ears as they headed to the rocky beaches that lined the fjord. Himmler's nightmare had become von Seeckt's terrifying reality.

While von Seeckt and his men had survived, much of their equipment went down with the Blücher. The key element of surprise had completely vanished. By the time they had regrouped and finally made it into Oslo, the bank vault at the Norge Bank was empty. An epic two-month pursuit led by von Seeckt had begun with the Brandenburgers chasing the gold from Oslo to the extreme northern port of Tomso in appalling weather conditions. Despite the best efforts of the Luftwaffe to halt their progress, the brave Norwegians were always one step ahead. It ended with von Seeckt and his exhausted team having to watch helplessly as the gold, along with the Norwegian Royal Family and their entourage sail to the safety of England aboard the British Royal Navy ship HMS Devonshire.

Summoned back to Berlin by Himmler, a defeated Max von Seeckt prepared himself for a possible early grave. His dreams of glory and of capturing the gold for the Fuhrer and the Fatherland were now left in tatters.

Chapter 23

GERMANY NEEDS GOLD

SS Headquarters, Berlin
May 1940

The Fuhrer was in a pleasant mood. For the first time in weeks he wasn't suffering from debilitating stomach cramps and diarrhea. At the suggestion of Margarete Himmler, the wife of Reich Fuhrer Heinrich Himmler, he had switched from black to chamomile tea. Margarete had explained to him how thousands of years ago, the ancient Egyptians had used tea made from the tiny chamomile flower because of its known ability to calm the stomach. Also, it could be taken at night before going to bed.

Margarete, charming as always, had gifted the Fuhrer a box of the finest chamomile tea, much to his delight. He had followed her advice and now after three days of religiously drinking the chamomile tea and finishing his day with a cup of it, he felt reasonably refreshed for a change. He had slept solidly until early afternoon.

This was all a welcome change for the Fuhrer, as the next meeting on his calendar was one that he particularly detested. It was with Hjalmar Horace Greeley Schacht, who had previously served as the Currency Commissioner and the President of the Reichsbank. He remained in service as a minister without portfolio. While Hitler did not particularly dislike Schacht, it was more the subject matter. He despised discussions about money and the despicable bankers who controlled it.

Hitler walked over to the full-length mirror in his office and checked his appearance. Satisfied, he smoothed down his jacket pockets, puffed out his chest, cleared his throat and checked his wristwatch, any second now...

A loud methodical knock on his office door preceded the appearance of Martin Bormann. "Herr Schacht is here to meet with you, Mein Fuhrer. Will you require my presence or your Secretary's?" asked Bormann.

"No, Martin. Please bring him in and that will be all. If I need anything else, I will let you know," replied Hitler. He crossed his palms smartly in front of his crotch, stuck his chin out and tilted his head slightly back, eyes fixed hypnotically on the doorway. The bespectacled minister without portfolio Schacht entered Hitler's private office.

"Mein Fuhrer," said Schacht, bowing slightly and extending his hand.

"Horace! It's been a while," replied Hitler, feigning delight as he shook Schacht's hand. "Please, be seated," he continued, gesturing with his hand to one of four chairs in front of his large oval desk.

"Thank you," said Schacht. He waited for the Fuhrer to retake his seat before sitting himself.

"May I offer you a cup of tea, Horace?" asked the Fuhrer.

"Yes please, that sounds wonderful," answered Schacht, pleasantly surprised at Hitler's friendly demeanor. He and the Fuhrer had clashed many times but had always resolved their differences. After all, Hitler knew that Schacht was at the very top of his game in his world, that of banking and international finance. His worldwide financial connections were still second to none. Schacht was widely credited with being at the center of Germany's economic recovery after the disaster of the 1914-1918 Great War. He was the only man anywhere near Hitler's inner circle who refused to wear the Nazi uniform or even a swastika arm band. This was a true testament to the power of a man who wore his immaculate business suits with pride. It was a signal to his powerful and influential friends throughout the world that he had not slipped over to the dark side, a fact the Fuhrer was acutely aware of. It was Schacht's fearless independence that the Fuhrer most admired, as long as the relationship enabled the Nazi war machine to continue its expansion.

"Black or with cream?" asked Hitler. He was careful to avoid offering up any of his now precious chamomile tea.

"Black, please," replied Schacht.

"Excellent," said the Fuhrer. He pressed a small buzzer on his desk.

Martin Bormann appeared instantly at the door.

"Yes, Mein Fuhrer?" asked Bormann.

"Tea, black, for the Minister, and I'll take a chamomile," said Hitler.

"I'll have it sent in, right away, Sir," replied Bormann. He closed the door behind him.

"Good," replied Hitler, turning his attention to Schacht, who stared back at him from behind his wire rimmed glasses. "It's been a while since we last met. Is everything alright, Horace?"

"Yes, thank you, as well as can be expected, other than my constant rows with your comrade, Herr Goering. But you of all people know how difficult he can be," said Schacht. He was well aware of Hitler's own run ins with the flamboyant head of the Luftwaffe.

"Yes, indeed," replied Hitler, a slight smile appearing on his face.

"Such a stubborn man, we are basically at a standoff. I take no notice of him on financial matters and he takes no notice of me on what the role of his beloved Luftwaffe needs to be. It seems to work, I suppose," said Schacht, with an air of resignation.

"No matter, you are the minister without portfolio with a very wide brief. So, I want to tap into your banking knowledge that you gained when you were Currency Commissioner and Reichsbank President," said the Fuhrer.

"Ah, as you well remember those interesting, if not happy days, Mein Fuhrer. Looking back, a simpler world in many ways. It's so much more complicated these days," sighed Schacht.

"You and your colleagues managed to do an incredible job to continue to run our economy without adequate gold reserves to back up the currency. Horace, I need to know, do you think it could be done again today?" asked Hitler.

Schacht slowly shook his head.

"I doubt it, the economic conditions are poles apart. In the thirties, we got the economy off its knees by huge financial injections into our infrastructure and rearmament. We were encouraged by our people to do so. We needed to relieve the massive unemployment and suffering at that time. Powerful countries accepted that we would repay what essentially were…IOU's."

"So, what about today?" asked Hitler. Leaning further towards him, his hands placed flat on the desk, he eyed Schacht closely.

"Today, my Leader we have conquered several countries at great cost in lives and resources amounting to many millions. My banking friends and those at the Treasury think that we need to draw a deep breath and endeavor to replenish our coffers as quickly as possible. Therefore, I am afraid that at the moment, hard currency rules the day," replied Schacht.

"You mean gold?" asked the Fuhrer.

"Yes, particularly gold, but silver and other precious metals together with certain types of securities and assets. For instance, the Mona Lisa is not just paint and canvas. If we acquired it and sold it on the open specialized market, if we could do such a thing, then you would be able to buy quite a few gold bars with the proceeds, I'm sure," said Schacht, growing in confidence and gesturing with his hands.

"Ah yes, Horace, you have not lost your ability to simplify difficult complex situations, even when you knew at times I would not like the answers," said Hitler.

Herr Schacht shuffled his feet on the carpet and stroked his carefully centrally parted head of thick hair as he recalled several recent run ins with the leader of the Third Reich. Then to his relief, Hitler asked another question. "Apart from the neutral countries who may help us, do you think that it is still possible to buy gold and physically move it to Berlin?"

"That would be almost impossible. The majority of physical gold is held in New York and London. That is well beyond our reach, even though some of it belongs to the nations we now occupy. Some gold movement should still be possible through Berne in Switzerland, but I am not currently up to date on that situation," replied Schacht.

"Martin informed me that we managed to confiscate much of Czechoslovakia's gold and take it to our Treasury in Berlin quite recently. The Bankers all seemed incredibly happy about that. Not a mention of how we acquired it, almost as if the gold just appeared out of nowhere, out of thin air...poof!" said the Fuhrer as he clicked his fingers and eyed up Schacht.

"Mein Fuhrer, it is quite a while since I was directly involved in the Reichsbank so I cannot answer that question as I do not know. However, I do know that such a transfer would not have been possible without the approval of my friends in the Bank of England that I did business with for many years," said Schacht, relieved that the conversation was now heading back into a more comfortable area for him.

"Your friends? Which friends are those?" queried Hitler.

"Oh, there are many. I have known Montague Norman of the Bank of England for many years. Before they declared war on us, we were close friends and he helped Germany a great deal when others would not. We were on the Board of Internal Settlements together. He is a good friend of mine and I think a friend of Germany too, but we haven't spoken in a long time. Norman is a very influential figure and second only to the Americans in terms of banking clout," answered Schacht.

He knew Hitler loved it that he was well-connected in the financial world, probably better than anyone else in the Fatherland. His connections alone more than justified his avoidance of wearing the swastika arm band. Hitler was smart enough to know that Schacht operated in an entirely different world than his, a world of business suits, cigars and cocktail parties where the military and partisan politics were not welcome.

"Were the English asleep when we took the gold from the Czechs? Surely they knew that we had it?" asked Hitler genuinely curious.

"I don't know but the gold could not have been transferred to Berlin if they had objected. It is my guess that it was a case of wheels, within wheels, in internal banking where the 'old boy network' reigned supreme, especially if you were educated at Eton, as Montague Norman was. The Old Etonians are by far the best-connected group of men anywhere on earth. There aren't too many levers of financial power that do not have an Old Etonian's grip on them," responded Schacht.

"But you studied political science and economics in Berlin not at Eton and then became a Freemason if I recall correctly," said Hitler, who had made a point of having Schacht thoroughly investigated long ago.

"Correct, Mein Fuhrer but the Eton old boys are everywhere. They are highly organized, much more than any Freemasonry. Like it or not, at the end of the day in the financial world the old school tie still rules supreme."

"Difficult to argue with that Horace, I agree. But putting the old boy network aside, you still have your finger on our nation's economic pulse. What do your banker friends, the ones at the very top, think about the current state of our economy? What are they saying? I need you to be truthful Horace," asked Hitler.

Before Schacht could answer, Martin Bormann knocked on the door and opened it. An elderly maid entered carrying a tray with two cups full of tea and a small plate of plain biscuits. She carefully placed the tray in front of Hitler, before curtseying politely and leaving. Bormann closed the door and the two men were alone again. Hitler passed Schacht his tea and offered him a biscuit, which he politely declined.

"Please proceed," said Hitler, eager to get the answer to his last question.

Schacht took a sip of his tea, placed the cup carefully back on the saucer and stroked his moustache that he had carefully trimmed to mimic the Fuhrers. "They are simply astounded at your achievements but very concerned about the drain on our national resources as you can imagine," said Schacht. He was about to continue but Hitler spoke first.

"Yes, I agree with that concern. Our nation was not blessed with the abundance that other countries have beneath their feet, which is exactly why we need to expand our borders so we will have the necessary resources. Believe me Horace, I have a plan to address our national short comings. You have already seen the speed that our panzers have swept aside any opposition and now that we have Norway under our jackboot, we will be bringing a lot more iron ore into our factories, I can assure you of that," said Hitler wafting his hand in the air several times and becoming just a little more animated.

"Excellent, Mein Fuhrer and congratulations. As I said, they are astounded by your achievements," interjected Schacht. "On the subject of Norway, I know they hold significant reserves of gold. I am sure that will go a long way to help ease any concerns. New gold entering the Reichsbank will always help in that area," he added, picking up his cup and smiling at the Fuhrer. He knew immediately that he had strayed onto thin ice. Hitler's expression changed in an instant. He sat silently for a while before taking several deep breaths, then he spoke, quietly, causing Schacht to lean forward slightly in order to hear him.

"Unfortunately, we failed to secure their gold," said Hitler, staring downwards at the desk in front of him. He placed both of his hands on his blotter and adjusted it slightly out of square with the edge of the desk. Then he moved it back again, buying a few seconds of silence that Schacht could barely stand. "Oh, I see," said Schacht awkwardly. Then he quickly added, "That is most unfortunate."

"Yes, very unfortunate, especially as our two main objectives were to capture or kill the King and to seize his gold reserves. We failed on both accounts," said Hitler, as he began to rhythmically tap his fingers on the desk.

Schacht sat nervously waiting, now not sure how to respond or what to say. In the end, he opted to play for time by reaching for his tea, then Hitler spoke. "We missed capturing them at the Royal Palace by less than a few hours. We chased them for months, from Oslo all the way up north to Tromso, where they were finally rescued by the British. The Norwegians had the advantage of knowing the terrain. They were able to stay one step ahead of us, despite the best efforts of the Brandenburgers and the Luftwaffe. They escaped back to the safety of Britain with all of their gold aboard the HMS Devonshire. No doubt it is sitting in your friend Mr. Montague Norman's vault as we speak," Hitler said, slowly shaking his head still in disbelief. A frown covered the now reddening face.

"Good Lord, I had no idea. I assumed that once our brave soldiers were in Norway that they would have secured the gold. I cannot imagine how the Norwegians could move so much gold at such short notice, a most amazing fete in itself. I would not have thought that it was even possible. Gold is not exactly a light metal, Mein Fuhrer," replied Schacht.

"The Norwegians are a determined lot. We learned later through our inquiries that they escaped with 53 tons of gold and gold coins. The bullion alone weighed 49 tons," lamented the Fuhrer.

"Good Lord!" repeated Schacht, reaching into his pocket and pulling out a small leather note pad and pencil. He began scribbling a calculation while muttering silently to himself as his mind whirled.

"Are you trying to calculate its value Horace?" asked Hitler, watching Schacht wrestle with an obvious equation.

Schacht caught up in the moment, paused and looked up, "Yes, Mein Fuhrer, I wanted to get an idea of how..."

"No need. Martin already calculated its value for me," said Hitler cutting Schacht off in mid-sentence.

"Oh, I see," replied Schacht, eyeing the Fuhrer over the top of his wire rim glasses. "How much?" he asked.

The Fuhrer took another deep breath and rolled his eyes up towards the ceiling.

"One hundred and twenty million Krone," replied the leader of the Third Reich in a barely audible whisper.

"My God!" gasped Schacht. He removed his glasses and placed his face into his open palmed hands. He remained motionless for a moment before removing his hands and looking back at a solemn faced Hitler.

"One hundred and twenty million Krone," he repeated. The Fuhrer nodded slowly in silence.

"I had no idea the Norwegians had that much gold! How could they possibly move that weight, especially given the snow and ice in the north? That is incredible, simply incredible," said Schacht.

"Yes, as I said, a determined lot. They used over twenty lorries of all varieties to transport it and we still couldn't catch them!" Hitler's voice rose to a yell and he slammed his fist onto the desktop causing both cups of tea to jump simultaneously on their saucers. Schacht braced himself for an outburst, but surprisingly Hitler jerked his head slightly a couple of times as a fighter might do to keep the sweat out of his eyes. He then took another series of deep breaths, ran his hand across his greasy hair at the side of his head, then finally reached for his tea and drank in silence. Schacht, confused but relieved, followed the Fuhrer's lead and did the same.

"Still, no point in crying over spilt milk, as they say Horace. But 53 tons of gold would more than help pay for our recent hard-fought victories, don't you agree?" asked the Fuhrer.

"Agreed, that's a huge amount of gold. It would have gone a long way to keeping my aforementioned friends in the banking business from being overly concerned about the nation's coffers, that's for sure," replied Schacht, still thankful that following his fist slam on the desk, the Fuhrer had not thrown one of his renowned tirades and now seemed surprisingly quite calm.

"Yes, but it's over now. We need to learn and move forward. We will not make those mistakes again. I have already mandated that in the future the first order of the day when we conquer a nation is to secure their gold reserves immediately! Then it must be transferred at once to the vaults of the Reichsbank. No ifs, ands, or buts about it!" said Hitler.

"Excellent!" replied Schacht. "To the victor, surely must go the spoils!"

"My sentiments exactly," said Hitler. "So, we agree. Let us get back to the bankers. What are their other big concerns?"

"Currently, the biggest concern is that our other trading partners may follow Portugal, demanding gold upfront to underwrite any trade. No one likes uncertainty and in troubled times such as these, gold is always the safest bet. It never loses its luster, so to speak. The bottom line here is unescapable. One way or another you need to get more gold, Mein Fuhrer."

"I know you speak the truth Horace, that's why I seek your counsel. So, how would you go about replenishing our gold reserves? It seems as though everyone comes into my office with the problem, but no one ever comes up with the solution," lamented Hitler.

"Mein Fuhrer, in this case there may not be a solution, short of conquering Britain and emptying the vaults at the Bank of England. But going back to what we discussed earlier, my advice would be that you should find out how it was possible to get Czechoslovakia's gold into our Treasury or the Reichsbank's vaults in Berlin and see if that route is still possible. Perhaps with a little persuasion we could buy gold in Berne from other neutral countries willing to help our cause.

The Swiss are very discreet, and I still have excellent contacts there. The last time I worried about such matters there was only about ten percent of the world's gold that was not controlled either directly or indirectly by New York and London. So, that might be a good place to start, with respect Mein Fuhrer," said Schacht as he drained the last of his tea.

"You know my views on bankers Horace, excepting present company of course. What I would like to do to them for manipulating the price we paid after 1918. Who would I talk to in order to take this further? Unless you would like to take on such a task, eh Horace?" asked the Fuhrer while offering up a playful wink of his eye.

"Lord no, Mein Fuhrer, my banking days are long over. There are a few people who might be able to discreetly take on this task for you. Let me see if I can get a recommendation of someone who could handle such a task, someone who would be up to date with the current gold situation on the international market and would jump at such an opportunity to serve you, Mein Fuhrer," said Schacht.

"Good. Do you think we could be successful if we used Switzerland?" asked Hitler, looking for any lifeline.

"You have no choice. Your assets and those of the countries you now occupy are frozen stiff in both New York and London," replied Schacht, shaking his head.

"Is it even worth a try in your opinion, with all your banking knowledge and experience?" asked the Fuhrer.

"Yes, I think you have nothing to lose at this point, but I think the odds are stacked against you. So, be prepared to use alternatives if they exist. These are very turbulent times. Opportunities may be out there. You have to recognize them when they are presented to you even if they may seem a little, how should I say...unorthodox perhaps?" answered Schacht. This time it was he who winked at the Fuhrer.

"Yes, quite. Unorthodox opportunities, I'll remember that. Thank you, Horace," said Hitler. He glanced at his wristwatch, signaling to Schacht that the meeting was about to conclude.

"It's always a pleasure, Horace. I thank you for your advice today which I shall take to good heed," said Hitler. He stood up and extended his hand to Schacht.

"Before you go, I wanted you to know that Martin said if you changed your hair from a center part to a side part, with that moustache and the wire rimmed glasses you could easily pass for my double...would you be interested in that position instead?" laughed Hitler. He and Schacht shook hands.

"Lord! No thank you, Mein Fuhrer. I'd rather go back to banking!" laughed Schacht. He left the office a relieved man.

Hitler returned to his desk, opened his notebook and wrote a solitary word in bold capital letters, GOLD. Then he underlined it twice.

Chapter 24

THE BATTLE OF FRANCE

RAF Biggin Hill, England
May 1940

It was early spring when Peter Legh finally received his coveted flight wings. He was immediately posted to the RAF 92nd Squadron based at Tangmere, flying the Bristol Beau fighter under the command of the legendary Roger Bushell. Peter finally posed for his official portrait in his blue RAF uniform complete with its pilot's wings. On the same day, he mailed one of the photos to the Clayton Saloon in California with a note to place it behind the bar until his return. The war that he had feared was coming for so long was finally here. It was time for him to step up and do his part and test his metal.

On the ground in France, things became much worse for the British Expeditionary Force along with the French and Belgian Army. In early April, the phony war came to an abrupt end. The Germans unleashed a form of warfare that the world had never seen before known as Blitzkrieg.

The Germans simply bypassed the impenetrable Maginot line pushing at rapid speed through the Ardennes forest. In a few short weeks by early May they had occupied Holland, Belgium, and Luxembourg. The British and their allies had collapsed and were in full retreat. Finally, looking for a desperate rescue from across the English Channel they became trapped without shelter in a pocket on the beaches of the French coastal town of Dunkirk.

At the same time, momentous events took place within the British Government. Chamberlain was forced to resign for his failure to secure peace and the country elected a new fire brand leader, the former Lord of the Admiralty, Winston Spencer Churchill.

In May, the squadron had been posted to RAF Croydon and had received its first shipment of a brand-new fighter, the game changing Supermarine Spitfire Mk1. Peter instantly fell in love with the new aircraft. Its slick lines and aerodynamic shape shamelessly flirted its thoroughbred speed, still clearly apparent even when the fighter was securely tethered to the ground.

Its performance, power and agility were unlike anything he or his mates had ever experienced before. He literally felt like he had become a part of the aircraft whenever he flew it. It was a truly exhilarating experience and he, like his fellow pilots felt a special bond with this manmade flying machine that none of them could ever quite explain.

While things in the air remained relatively quiet, on 23rd of May the squadron flew its first real combat mission over France. Peter was both terrified and exhilarated at the same time. They also experienced the loss of their beloved leader, Squadron Leader Roger Bushell. He was seen crash landing his heavily damaged Spitfire close to Calais, but not before he had inflicted heavy damage on a pair of Messerschmitt 110's.

The deadly reality and terror of aerial combat came crashing down on the young fighter pilots like a ton of bricks. "If it can happen to Roger, what chance do I have?" was the sad but silent question on everyone's mind when they finally returned to the safety of their base at Croydon.

Despite the loss of Bushell, the 92nd did the best they could during the month of May to defend the vulnerable troops that were huddled on the cold sandy beaches of Dunkirk with no protection. The 92nd now flying out of Biggin Hill, fought valiantly and often but they were hopelessly outnumbered. The distance they had to fly to protect the beleaguered troops only allowed them a precious few minutes over enemy territory before they had to return to England to refuel and rearm. This contributed to the anger and dismay of the men trapped on the beaches waiting to be picked off by the Luftwaffe. They would never know the gallantry and sacrifice of the men of the 92nd Squadron. These men and their Spitfires savagely engaged the Luftwaffe high in the French skies, miles away from the beaches of Dunkirk and unobserved by the troops huddled on the sand.

There was also a growing concern about the number of aircraft losses that were piling up. It soon became apparent that the new Prime Minister, on the advice of Air Chief Marshall Sir Hugh Dowding, was not willing to risk his precious fighters on what was rapidly becoming a lost cause in France. Churchill knew that he would need every one of them if he was to have any chance of defending his island against the might of the Luftwaffe.

A few days later, Churchill addressed a packed House of Parliament and a nervous population huddled around their radio sets throughout the Kingdom. Churchill said, in a solemn speech to the nation, that the Battle of France was over, and the Battle of Britain was about to begin.

Chapter 25

THE KING AND LADY LUCK

Buckingham Palace, London
May 1940

"The Prime Minister, your Majesty," announced the King's personal butler.

Churchill stepped into the King's luxurious, private office for his weekly Tuesday luncheon to update King George VI on the war effort.

"Your Majesty," said Churchill as he gracefully bowed before his King.

"Please," motioned the King. He pointed to the leather chair situated dead center in front of his desk. Churchill obeyed and watched the King as he simultaneously lit a cigarette, inhaled deeply, and sat down opposite him. The King adjusted his cuffs before fixing his gaze squarely on Churchill, whom he still disliked. He would have so much preferred to deal with Lord Halifax. He found Churchill to be quite belligerent at times and was also concerned at the amount of alcohol that he was known to consume every day.

"Congratulations on your speech to the British people, Prime Minister. It was excellent and has rallied our people to the cause once again," said the King. Churchill had recently delivered his, Blood, Toil, Tears and Sweat speech to Parliament and the British Nation.

"Thank you, your Majesty," replied Churchill.

The King cleared his throat and as usual immediately got down to business. "Today I would like an update on the final movement of the Nation's gold, Prime Minister. Its code name is Operation Fish, as I recall. Where do we stand currently, with Operation Fish?"

By now, Churchill was used to the King's style. They rarely exchanged pleasantries at the onset of their meetings. That tended to come later, if at all, during luncheon served in the King's office. That is only if the early session went without any glitches.

Under Neville Chamberlain, the British government had long been wary of another war with Germany. In a remarkable act of sagacity, it had steadily moved the nation's gold reserves and securities from the Bank of England to the safety of Canada, shipping it in top-secret via the Royal Navy. The King's recent enormously successful tour of Canada and the USA had also been used as a partial cover for the accompanying Royal Navy warships, secretly loaded with gold bullion destined for Fort Knox. The King had intervened at the last minute before departing England, causing a well-coordinated plan to divide the gold equally amongst the war ships, to be scrapped and reconfigured. Now, with the fall of France, the effort had been rapidly accelerated and simplified. The remaining gold still lying in the Bank of England's vault would be moved in three colossal shipments. In total, it was the single greatest movement of wealth in history. The operation had been ambiguously named Operation Fish.

"Well, as you are aware, the need for absolute secrecy has been paramount which has obviously slowed down the process. It has been a long and difficult operation. Now that we have some of the earlier problems worked out, I would have to say that things are going well, your Majesty, very well," replied Churchill. He was careful to avoid unnecessary detail until he could get to the root of the King's enquiry. Churchill continued, "We are on schedule. I met briefly with Montague Norman last week and he assured me that Martins Bank in Liverpool was ready to receive the final shipments. The first train is scheduled to leave for Lime Street Station very soon I believe."

"And how many t...t...t...trains will it take?"

Churchill noticed the King had started to stammer, an affliction that had bothered him since childhood. It usually preceded a probing question, "Three, your Majesty," Churchill replied.

"Three, I see. And this will make up the final convoy to Halifax, Canada? This will be the last and by far the largest shipment, correct?"

"Yes, your Majesty, that's correct."

"Splendid, splendid. D...d...d...d...do you believe in Lady Luck...P...P...Prime Minister?"

Churchill thought for a moment before answering. It was, to say the least an unusual question. He drew a deep breath, paused, then said, "I believe we make our own luck, your Majesty."

"Quite, we make our own luck," repeated the King. "Very good Prime Minister, we make our own luck, very good. Do you remember the ship Laurentic?"

"Yes, sadly your Majesty, a horrible tragedy. It was a loss of both precious life and treasure, an awful business all around."

"Do you remember the cause?"

"If memory serves me right, a German U-boat sank her with mines off the coast of Ireland, your Majesty."

"Yes, you are correct, Prime Minister. Do you know how many poor souls were lost?" The King took several large drags on his cigarette and placed it on the lip of the ashtray.

"I'm sorry your Majesty, the number escapes me, but it was in the hundreds. Many froze to death in their lifeboats. The crew was never able to get off a distress call, it was a dreadful loss."

"354 Prime Minister, 354 of our citizens perished."

"Dreadful, your Majesty. May they rest in peace."

"Quite. May they rest in peace. And the gold bullion Prime Minister, do you know how much was lost?" asked the King, retrieving his cigarette and taking several more drags off it.

Churchill searched his memory. He had known roughly the initial loss, but he was aware that the Laurentic had gone down in a relatively shallow water of about 130 feet. After the war, the Royal Navy had launched a massive salvage operation to recover the gold bullion. They had a great deal of success, but the exact amount retrieved escaped him. "I'm sorry your Majesty, I don't."

"43 t...t...t...tons of gold bullion worth m...m...millions of pounds went to the bottom. Fortunately, a heroic effort by our Navy divers recovered all but 25 of the gold bars. Quite remarkable, don't you agree?"

"Quite remarkable, yes your Majesty," answered Churchill, still not sure where the King was heading.

"And quite an incredible stroke of luck that the waters in which she was sunk were shallow enough to be able to conduct a successful salvage operation, don't you agree?" The King took several more pulls off the cigarette before again returning it to the ashtray.

"Agreed, your Majesty."

"So far, we have not lost a single ship. We have had several close calls with weather and mechanical problems, but to date every ounce of gold has made it to Halifax and is safely in the hands of our Canadian cousins. Considering how many crossings we have already made, I'd say we have had a remarkable run of good luck, don't you Prime Minister?"

"Yes, your Majesty. Given how many Atlantic crossings that we have made successfully despite the U-boat threat then I would whole heartedly agree. Lady Luck has been more than kind to us," answered Churchill.

"Good, then we agree?" said the King staring at his ashtray.

"Agree? On what, your Majesty?" asked Churchill, genuinely baffled by the King's comment.

The King closed his eyes as if searching for words that would not come. He leaned back and breathed in the stuffy, warm smoke-filled air of his office before opening them again and looking directly at Churchill.

"Lady Luck, Prime Minister."

Churchill sensed something was coming his direction and stiffened up in his chair. At the same time, he instinctively reached into his inside pocket and removed his cigar case. "Lady Luck? I don't quite understand. May I request clarity, your Majesty?" asked Churchill. He placed the cigar in his mouth and fished his lighter out of his trouser pocket.

"Hmmm," muttered the King, as he half-heartedly stubbed out the cigarette in the ashtray. He was beginning to get a little agitated, "I thought I was being very clear, Prime Minister. Let us just say I am a trifle concerned about such an enormous amount of gold crossing the Atlantic. With the undeniable threat of the enemy U-boats, as you have correctly pointed out. One well-placed t...t...

torpedo or a mine and the wealth that our country has accumulated over the centuries will be lost forever at the bottom of the ocean. I very much doubt we would be dealing with the same depth that we were when the Laurentic met her fate. Once out in the Atlantic, the ocean's depths are way b...b...beyond the grasp of any salvage operation. This troubles me deeply, Prime Minister. Lady Luck, as we agreed, has been good to us so far, b...b...b...b...but one can only rely on her for so long. Would you agree, Prime Minister?"

Churchill did not respond. He focused instead on lighting his cigar, emitting massive clouds of blue smoke that easily engulfed the last of the smoke emanating from the King's cigarette butt slowly petering out in the ash tray.

"Yes, your Majesty, I agree. But we also discussed at great lengths the consequences of not sending our gold to Canada. There is no bank vault in your Kingdom that can keep out the Nazis. This is the best solution, your Majesty. Should the worst come to the worst and the Nazis do actually invade, we will relocate the entire war cabinet, along with the Royal Family to Canada where our gold reserves are already secured. We can continue to pay America to supply us with the arms that we require to carry on waging war against the Nazis. At the end of the day, we really do not have another option, your Majesty."

Churchill paused as he watched the King light up another cigarette.

"There is one option that we never discussed," said the King. He ran his fingers over his hair while looking out of the massive double hung windows behind Churchill. The sky was a rare deep blue and cloudless.

Churchill waited for a moment, wondering if the King was seeking inspiration from outside of his windows, but no further words were spoken. Churchill took another tug off his cigar and broke the silence.

"Another option? Your Majesty, I don't recall..." The King raised his palm to cut Churchill off in mid-sentence.

"Yes. Another option might be to simply hide it, hide it somewhere here in the Kingdom."

"Hide it, your Majesty?" asked Churchill, his eyebrow raised.

"Yes, Prime Minister. Find a place that we can safely hide it. Find a place that the Nazis would never find it if they looked for a thousand years, similar to what we have done already to protect the nation's works of art." answered the King.

The King was aware that the nation's art collection, along with thousands of priceless artifacts had been secretly removed from the National Gallery and hidden in an abandoned slate quarry under Manod Mountain, in rural North Wales. The British public were clueless, as lorries commandeered by the War Department from Cadbury's Chocolate Company and the Royal Mail, rumbled through their great cities. The familiar lorries were not filled with their favorite chocolate bars or sacks of mail. They were instead loaded to the gills with massive irreplaceable paintings by the world's great masters. Churchill himself had personally intervened knowing that unlike gold, any of the priceless paintings would be ruined if they were exposed to the cold salty water of the Atlantic. He had boldly declared, "Hide them in caves and cellars. Not a single painting shall leave this island!"

"Your Majesty, the sheer size of the bullion itself would make hiding it somewhere totally impractical. If such a hiding place existed, the logistics of such an operation would make it impossible to keep its location a secret..."

"Not all of it!" interrupted the King. "Just a percentage enough for us to be able to continue to conduct our business and carry on as usual. Sometimes one needs to look at an alternate view Prime Minister, don't you agree?"

"Alternate view?" queried Churchill, examining his cigar to avoid the Kings gaze. The first small beads of sweat appeared on his deeply furrowed brow.

"Yes, an alternate view to being invaded, Prime Minister. Our brave RAF pilots are ready and eager for the showdown with the Luftwaffe that we surely face ahead. Our people are resolute, and the Royal Navy is still the mightiest sea force on earth. Our factories are now producing aircraft and munitions in record numbers. The English Channel is a formidable barrier. Every able-bodied man I'm sure, when called on to protect his homeland and family, will give his full measure. As you are well-aware Prime Minister, Herr Hitler is no fool. I personally feel strongly that such an assault on our shores is getting less and less likely. I personally do not believe we will ever hear the sound of Nazi jackboots marching down Whitehall. Unless he can control the air, he cannot launch a ground attack. I have every confidence in the RAF to fend off Goering's Luftwaffe, don't you Prime Minister?" the King stopped, put the cigarette between his lips, his hand shaking slightly and waited for Churchill's response.

Churchill absorbed the King's words. They were remarkable in that they were spoken with a passion and belief that Churchill had not heard in a long time. Even more remarkable was that they were delivered flawlessly, without pause, and without a single stammer.

Churchill took the cigar out of his mouth and boomed, "Bravo! Your Majesty! Bravo! Very well said!" A broad smile spread across the King's face and for the first time, the two men made eye contact and connected on an entirely different level, their mutual love for their country. "I agree whole heartedly your Majesty with every word you have just spoken. But that said, the wheels are already turning on Operation Fish. Even if such a location were to be found, it would be a logistical nightmare to alter the plans now..."

"I agree, Prime Minister but I want to emphasize, I'm only asking for a percentage to remain here hidden, not the entire shipment. It is a matter of prudence," said the King, dragging again on his cigarette before returning it to the ashtray.

"How big a percentage, your Majesty?" asked Churchill, seeing a potential compromise.

"Naturally, I have given this some considerable thought. I believe 50 tons would be just about adequate," replied the King, who had clearly been preparing for the exchange.

"Fifty tons!!" blurted out Churchill. "Your Majesty, that's an enormous amount of gold!"

"Yes, Prime Minister, I am aware of that, but it's roughly the same amount that King Haakon of Norway was able to escape with. It is also just a tad over what was aboard the Laurentic. Let us just say one might consider it an afront to Lady Luck to tempt fate a second time around by shipping the same amount twice... so to speak. Fifty tons of gold is the weight I am requesting that we hide here on our island. We must find a safe hiding place until such a day comes when the Nazi threat is over, and we can return it safely to the vault of the Bank of England."

"But 50 tons your Majesty, I can't even begin to conceive of where we could hide such an enormous amount, I can only..." Churchill did not get to finish his sentence before the King again cut him off.

"Prime Minister, I'm not asking you to conceive anything. I am asking you to convey my request directly to whomever you designate to find the perfect hiding place. You have at your disposal the finest minds in Great Britain, Prime Minister. Surely, we can come up with something?"

Churchill realized that the King had made up his mind and as irrational as the suggestion had initially seemed, it did have some value. It was true, there were many things in their favor. During the initial skirmishes over France, the RAF had already inflicted heavy losses on the Luftwaffe that would be difficult for Goering to sustain over time. More importantly, the people's resolution to a man was absolutely unshakable. He had experienced this time and time again while mixing with the public. The cheers and heartfelt well wishes from people who had already lost so much, was intensely real to him. He felt their solidarity, their desire to carry on, to never quit, to never surrender, to win. They all wanted the same thing, to go back over there and sort out Jerry once and for all. Then when the job was finally done, they would come home and live in peace.

God willing, if things could swing England's way there would be no need to relocate the Royal Family or the War Cabinet to Canada. They would remain here in London, in the nation's capital where they belonged. If that were to be the case, it was true that the country would certainly need plenty of gold to be able to continue to conduct business while awaiting the return of the remaining gold back from Canada.

The most important thing would be to continue to carry on seamlessly. It would be disastrous for national morale if word got out that the country's entire gold reserves and securities had been shipped off to Canada, along with the Royal Family and top government officials. It would be perfect fodder for Goebbels. That simply could not be allowed to happen. The King's idea, although outlandish, was beginning to have some merit. Not least of all, it was the only sure way to hedge their bet with Lady Luck.

Churchill considered his options, then spoke, "Your Majesty, please rest assured that I will give your idea serious thought and consideration and report back to you soon with my findings."

"Excellent Prime Minister, excellent. Now will you join me for lunch?" asked the King as he pressed the small buzzer on his desk.

"I'd be honored, your Majesty," replied Churchill. His mind buzzed trying to figure out where on earth he could secretly hide 50 tons of the nation's gold reserves.

Chapter 26

PARYS MOUNTAIN

The War Room, Whitehall, England
May 1940

"Yes!" barked Churchill into the intercom. "Major General Joseph Scholes and The Minister of Transport John Reith are here to see you, Sir," replied the voice through the intercom.

"Good Lord, it's eleven o'clock already?" he asked pulling out his gold pocket watch even though he already knew the answer. Churchill had been below ground in the War Room for five days straight. With no windows or natural light, it was becoming more difficult to discern night from day.

"Yes, Sir," answered the voice again.

"Alright, send them in," he grunted, as he sat back in his leather chair while simultaneously reaching for his cigar box. He removed a perfectly rolled King Edwards and skillfully snipped off the tip. Then, he sucked on the end a few times and expertly rolled it between his thumb and forefinger. Finally, he examined it and then suitably pleased, he fired it up, emitting plumes of thick blue smoke.

The door opened and a young, immaculately dressed secretary introduced the two men, "Major General Joseph Scholes and the Minister of Transport, Sir."

Churchill continued to work on his cigar without looking up, fully aware that the Major General had snapped a salute and remained ram rod straight awaiting his at ease command. Minister Reith stood at attention alongside him, holding his small attaché case in front of his crotch with both hands. His eyes were transfixed on the worn tartan carpet beneath his polished oxblood shoes.

Suitably impressed with his ignition, Churchill took another massive draw and placed the cigar carefully onto his ashtray before finally looking at the two men standing in front of him.

"Gentlemen," he said, and with a gesture from his hand he invited them to sit in the two green leather armchairs in front of his desk. "What have you chaps been able to come up with in relation to safely stashing a portion of the country's gold?"

The Minister glanced at the Major General who took his cue to begin.

"Well Prime Minister, it's been a challenge to say the least," said the Major General. He simultaneously flipped open his briefcase and handed a manila file marked Top Secret to Churchill. Surprisingly without opening it, the Prime Minister placed it on the leather blotter in front of him. "Challenge, eh Major General? Imagine that," he sneered, picking up the cigar and taking another drag. "So, a challenge that you were able to overcome, I assume?"

"Yes, Prime Minister. I believe that after a considerable process of elimination we have come up with what we believe is the perfect location."

"Good," said Churchill, "As I recall, I had given you total flexibility in your quest with only two absolute requirements. One, is that the location be as remote as possible and two, that it had an operable railroad spur. So, given those requirements gentlemen, where is this perfect location?"

The Major General looked at the Minister of Transport and nodded to him to proceed. The Minister nervously fingered his Windsor tie knot, cleared his throat and in a quiet voice said, "Parys Mountain, Sir."

Churchill frowned, "Which mountain?"

"Parys Sir, Parys Mountain." replied the Minister

"I've traveled our beloved island from John O'Groats to Land's End and I've never heard of a mountain called what? Paris? You said?" asked Churchill, peering over the top of his glasses.

"Parys Sir, P-A-R-Y-S Mountain, and...well, it's not exactly a mountain, Sir," answered the Minister.

"Parys Mountain? Yet it's not a mountain?" asked Churchill, raising his voice. He was already beginning to lose patience with the Minister who now shuffled nervously in his seat. Tiny beads of sweat began to appear across the bridge of his nose.

"Well Prime Minister, you had also asked for stealth. What better stealth, one might ask, than to select a location that is named Parys Mountain where there is no actual mountain Sir, if you follow my drift...so to speak...How can one begin to look for a mountain that doesn't actually exist? We all thought that it was quite brilliant, actually, Prime Minister...Sir."

Churchill began to visibly turn red. He was getting quite exasperated.

"If I may, Sir?" interrupted the Major General, realizing the Minister was beginning to flounder in the opening round. "Parys Mountain is in fact a vast copper mine located on the Island of Anglesey. I believe it's named after a John Parys, probably a Welshman, Sir."

"Ah!" said Churchill, satisfied with the Major General's intervention. "Wales! Then that might explain it, carry on Major General."

"Thank you, Sir. Parys Mountain is more or less the name given to an entire area. If you'd like to open the file Sir, the exact location is on the second page."

Churchill pulled on the cigar and blew a thick cloud directly at the Minister before retiring it to the ashtray and then he finally opened the file. He quickly noticed the operation name, Operation Minnow. He flicked to the second page and looked down at a detailed map of Anglesey. A large area in the northeast corner of the island was outlined by a thin red ink line. The tiny fishing village of Amlwch was the only notable landmark.

"It certainly hits the remote requirement, that's for sure. The whole island, with the exception of Holyhead would probably qualify though. So, why Parys Mountain? Tell me more," asked Churchill without taking his gaze off the page in front of him.

"Quite Sir. Its origins go back to Roman times. They discovered gold there. Consequently, they enslaved the surviving Druids to move massive amounts of earth and shipped the tiny gold nuggets back to Rome. Later, copper was discovered in vast quantities and Parys Mountain became the largest supplier of copper on earth. Back then, copper was primarily used to protect the keels and hulls of the wooden ships, so the demand was significant. It enabled the Royal Navy ships to sail faster and turn on a sixpence. It was the difference that allowed Britannia to rule the waves. Amlwch is the small village that is closest to Parys Mountain and it became a major ship building center.

Much of this is ancient history, but the mines continued to produce copper up through the industrial age. With the arrival of the rail system and the Britannia railroad bridge, which links the island to the mainland, the copper was exclusively shipped out by rail. The ship building industry had long declined so the railroad was and still is the way the copper was transported from the mines to Swansea for smelting. The mine itself suspended operations indefinitely when the war broke out and all the local chaps signed up or were drafted.

Your request for the chosen area to have access to rail was the biggest challenge. While there are many remote areas throughout the land that met all the other criteria, they are by their very nature of being remote simply not accessible by rail. We found this area by complete chance. One of our chaps on the location search team was a captain in the Welsh Guards. He grew up in Amlwch and was familiar with Parys Mountain and the railroad that still operates. If it hadn't been for him joining the dots, we would be I'm afraid, completely out of options."

"Good, good, Major General. What about the locals still in the area? I'm sure there are shepherds and farmers everywhere on Anglesey. How will we keep them in the dark?"

"Quite, Sir. We have a couple of good solutions that we have come up with to make sure no one, including the men ordered to guard the gold, are aware of anything being hidden there. We have some good naturally occurring phenomena at Parys Mountain that we can tweak to work in our favor. If you would turn to page three, Sir."

Churchill, now intrigued, duly turned to the next page. The Major General continued, "The land at Parys is extremely toxic because of the amount of toxins naturally occurring in the rocks and soil. There is a tremendous amount of pollution in the ground and the ground water. Nothing grows there other than the hardiest of heather. There is no wildlife. It really is a barren, inhospitable place. Other than the railroad, there is just one single road into the area. There is nothing there for literally miles around the mines. Neither man nor beast venture to Parys Mountain, Sir. It is as remote and desolate a place as you could possibly find anywhere in Britain."

"Excellent! It sounds like what we were looking for Major General, do carry on," said Churchill as he continued to study the pages in front of him.

"Because of the value of the gold, we also wanted to take a few extra precautions to make sure that no one will venture into the area. We have decided to create a local toxic scare, if you will, to make sure that no one will want to come within a few miles of the mines themselves. We can easily cordon off the entrance area with barbed wire. As I said, there is only the one road in and out of Parys Mountain. We plan on circulating flyers in all the local villages that there has been a toxic runoff that has poisoned the ground water and consequently the surrounding fields and that the mine has been closed by the government until further notice. We feel a few strategically placed rotting sheep carcasses, along with Government warning signs will be more than enough to dissuade any curiosity seekers. We plan on closing the only road through the area by placing a manned roadblock here, on the B5111 Sir," said the Major General, leaning forward over Churchill's desk and indicating with his index finger the one road that ran by the entrance to the area.

"Excellent, good, good," continued Churchill. He thumbed quickly through the rest of the report. "The abandoned windmill building as the location to actually hide the gold Major General, that's interesting, are you sure about that?" he asked without taking his gaze off the paper.

"Yes Sir, I'd be happy to explain our thoughts. Parys Mountain itself, as the Minister has pointed out, does not exactly exist. While the whole area is elevated, there is no mountain there. Parys Canyon or Parys Abyss would be a much better name. Because of the importance of the situation, after the recommendation, the Minister and I traveled up there to see it with our own eyes.

It was quite an extraordinary experience. The location, as you can see from the aerial photograph is incredibly remote. The area itself is vast and goes deep into the earth. It is riddled with tunnels that have been dug out by hand over the centuries. It's an incredible feat of human endurance. The problem is accessibility to the mines or tunnels. It is extremely difficult to get to the tunnel entrances especially given the weight of the gold. You can see from the photographs that the walls of the canyon are extremely steep, and the rock is very unstable..."

"Yes," said Churchill, interrupting the Major General, "I see that. How on earth did they move so much rock before steam power?" he asked genuinely inquisitive.

"By hand, Sir. Literally a bucket at a time. They would build wooden platforms that hung over the edge of the canyon and they would lower and raise a bucket full one at a time. It was very hazardous. Hundreds fell to their deaths or were killed by falling rock. It must have been a god-awful place to toil."

"Nothing but elbow grease," said Churchill, pulling again on his King Edward, "Quite extraordinary. Carry on."

"Yes, Sir. They had a simple hand crank system that was literally man powered. It continued that way until the addition of the windmill. That was used until modern industrial times. We considered bringing in some heavy equipment to try to help get access to the tunnels but that simply was not feasible, especially as we did not want to bring attention to the area. Moving in such specialized equipment would no doubt be noticed, which would not be good.

Then we realized that the solution was standing right there in front of us, the old windmill itself, Sir. It's of adequate size, we just need to have a steel floor installed and a suitable racking system. We can fill it to the top, much like a grain silo, Sir. I already have a report back from the Royal Engineers. They said 48 hours would be ample for the work, including a temporary lift to load the crates of gold onto the racks. This makes it easy to unload the gold and stack it in the windmill.

If you look at the map, we have marked in red where the road will be closed. We will put up a small guard hut there with armed guards to prevent anyone from entering the entire Parys Mountain area. We won't need to make any other changes to the area whatsoever. We have run and rerun all possible scenarios and firmly believe that Parys Mountain is our best bet to safely hide the nation's gold for the duration of the war. Once we have achieved victory, we can reload it on the train and have it back in the Bank of England vault within 24 hours, Sir. No one will ever know it was gone. And short of a steel floor and a steel door installed in an abandoned windmill, as far as Parys Mountain goes, it will be as though nothing ever happened, like we were never even there, Sir." Satisfied with his summary, the Major General sat motionless and awaited Churchill's response.

Churchill continued to analyze the report in silence for several minutes, occasionally muttering an approval while nodding his head. The Major General and Minister sat silently in a cloud of thick blue smoke while trying to decipher Churchill's body language. Eventually he sat back and smiled, "Gentlemen, I like it. You have served our Nation well, Parys Mountain it is!" He picked up his pen and turning to the last page, signed and dated his name and handed it to the Major General.

"Well done," he said. "You have exceeded my expectations! You have my authorization to move forward immediately, we don't have a second to waste. This needs to be priority number one." He extended a handshake to both of them.

Thank you, Sir!" they replied in unison. And with that the Major General saluted, turned on his heels and marched briskly towards the door with the Minister following suit.

After they left, Churchill was left alone to enjoy a rare quiet moment with his cigar. "Parys, the mountain that never was. Perfect, just perfect!" he chuckled to himself. "Figure that one out Adolph." Then he pressed the button on his intercom and said, "Get Montague Norman, Governor of The Bank of England on my calendar at the first available opening. Thank you!"

Chapter 27

MARTINS BANK

Liverpool, England
May 1940

Eamon Dylan knew his boss was furious by the sound that his metal cleats on his Clark's shoes made as he moved across the enormous marble floor of Martins Bank. Simon Henry Akroyd, Chief Inspector for Martins Bank in Liverpool was marching at double time for sure. Dylan literately ran the last few steps to open the massive ornate bronze doors ahead of his boss.

The sky was heavily overcast and the rain was almost horizontal as the cold wind blew off the River Mersey and howled its way up Water Street, "Taxi!" Dylan yelled. The first "fast black" taxi pulled up in front of the bank. Dylan obediently opened the door for Akroyd to step into the back of the cab and immediately followed him into the rear. "Where ya goin, Mate?" asked the taxi driver in a thick Scouse accent. "Lime Street, as fast as you can, please," said Dylan. He slid the glass window closed that was between him and the driver. The driver turned off his For-Hire sign and sped off towards Lime Street train station.

"So, as I'm sure you gathered during my telephone conversation with Montague Norman that Operation Fish has finally been given the go ahead. This means that life, as you and I know it Eamon will effectively be over until further notice I'm afraid." He lit a cigarette and wiped the condensation off the inside of the window with his cuff and peered out at the sea of drab wet overcoats, cloth caps, and umbrellas. Summer in England, what a joke he thought to himself while they sped past a soaked St. George's Hall.

"I see. Do we know when to expect the first shipment?" asked Dylan, in his soft Irish accent as he lowered his window a crack. To his relief, the blue smoke instantly vented. "Not yet, but you know how the machine works, Eamon. It could be any time. The security is as tight as you can get. They will only let us know once the gold has actually left London. I'd be remiss not to get ahead of the curve on this one." His mind began to briefly drift. The prospect of the Bank of England's entire gold reserves being loaded aboard special trains, protected by heavily armed guards, and heading directly non-stop to Lime Street Station, and then on to Martins bank was a daunting one, to say the least. The fact that once it arrived at Lime Street, it was officially in his custody until it was safe in Martins bank vault, was simply terrifying.

In reality, what was even more terrifying was that the man that Akroyd entrusted with the most confidential banking information that he was involved in, was actually a mole for the Irish Republican Army. Eamon Dylan had a deep-seated hatred of the English after his father was shot by the British at the North King Street massacre during the Easter uprising. Dylan had attended Liverpool University studying Mathematics, where he had met Sean O'Reilly, heir to the O'Reilly Meat Company of Dublin. O'Reilly was the largest exporter of Irish beef into Britain. He was also a high-level commander in the IRA and after a thorough screening, he recruited the enthusiastic Dylan to be the organization's eyes and ears within the top levels of British Banking.

The ride to Lime Street Station took about five minutes. The taxi pulled up in front of the heavily sandbagged main entrance. Men dressed in all the different uniforms of the British armed forces were milling about everywhere. Dylan paid the taxi driver and scurried after his boss, who was already pacing towards the main office in his attempt to make the acquaintance of the Station Master. He would let him know that very soon he would be receiving a very special delivery of fish. This would require a Government mandated major change of station operating policy in order for the fish to safely reach their destination.

Chapter 28

THE IRA MOLE

Liverpool, England
May 1940

Dylan heard Akroyd hang up the phone. He was already out of his seat and heading into his boss's office before he heard him shout, "Dylan, come in here for a minute, would you?"

"Yes, Sir!" said Dylan. The door was permanently open, so he quickly entered the inspector's office. Akroyd preferred it that way. He trusted Dylan implicitly and knew he could not have a better personal assistant. Dylan had a remarkable knack of being in exactly the right place at exactly the right time.

By good fortune, Akroyd had inherited Dylan from his predecessor with nothing more than a handwritten note that Dylan had presented to him on his first day in the position. It basically said that Dylan was a decent chap, loyal, a fast learner, and that he (Akroyd) would do well to keep him aboard. They were now in their third year of working together. Akroyd was impressed with Dylan's intellect and his general knowledge of banking and finance, especially on the larger scale. Dylan had attended numerous top-level finance meetings alongside Akroyd, with bankers from all over the world. Dylan was naturally humble and able to easily tackle complex situations, always making Akroyd shine.

"You will need to contact the Station Manager at Lime Street and let them know that Operation Fish is on. The fish will be arriving at midnight tonight at Platform Number Eight. It's still early enough for you to go home and get some shut eye. It's going to be a long night. Just meet me at Lime Street on Platform Eight, say eleven thirty," said Akroyd. He grabbed several manila folders from his desk and shoved them in his briefcase. "Yes, Sir. Is there anything else that needs tying up today?" asked Dylan. "Go ahead and cancel my nine-o clock meeting tomorrow morning, I'm going to head home too. Lord knows when I'll see the old bed again," he said as he walked out of his spacious office and sped by Dylan's desk. He stopped at the coat stand, put on his bowler hat, picked up his umbrella and walked out of the outer office door, gently closing it behind him.

Dylan was all alone. He waited a few minutes, then stepped behind Akroyd's desk eyeing up the two identical telephones that sat on the massive teak wood desk. One was black, and the one Akroyd had just hung up was red. It had recently been installed as a secure line for all communication regarding Operation Fish. He sat in the oversized chair, scooted forward closer to the desk, and picked up the black handset. "Outside line please," Dylan said when the receptionist came on the line. He waited for the dial tone. Then placing his finger in the rotary dial, he entered a series of numbers and waited. The phone rang exactly three times, then a male voice answered, "O'Reilly residence."

"Good morning, this is Mr. Dylan calling for Mr. O'Reilly," said Dylan.

"Yes, one moment please," said the voice. Dylan waited a few seconds. There was a click and then the unmistakable voice of Sean O'Reilly came on the line. "Top of the morning to you, Mr. Dylan. How are things today?"

Dylan smiled, "Top of the morning to you, good Sir! I was calling to let you know that the first shipment of fish you were interested in is due into Lime Street Station tonight at midnight."

"Oh, that's excellent news, Mr. Dylan. Keep me posted on how things develop if you would be so kind," said O'Reilly.

"Yes Sir, I will do that," replied Dylan.

"Have a good day, Mr. Dylan," responded O'Reilly, bringing the brief call to an end.

"You too, Mr. O'Reilly," replied Dylan.

Then the line went dead.

Dylan sat back. He was mightily relieved that his initial report to O'Reilly about the potential movement of gold had finally panned out. It had been a long time, but Dylan was well aware that his IRA commander had been anxiously waiting for confirmation that

Operation Fish was actually under way. He finally felt that he was contributing to the cause. He didn't know exactly what he was contributing, but as long as Sean O'Reilly was happy, he knew that he was contributing something. He grinned, pushed back the chair, and picked up the Financial Times that Akroyd had already read. He tucked it under his arm, closed and locked the office door, and headed home to his seedy flat in Bootle to try to get some sleep.

Chapter 29

OPERATION FISH

Liverpool, England

May 1940

"Sorry mate, it looks like they've got the whole road closed up ahead. I'm not sure what the hell is going on. I can try and get around the long way if you like," said the taxi driver.

"That's alright," said Dylan. "I'll go ahead and walk from here, thanks." He paid the cabbie and stepped out onto the wet cobblestones of Lime Street and walked past the line of cars to the roadblock. People were getting out of their vehicles and talking to each other trying to figure out what was going on. The familiar smell of fresh horse manure filled Dylan's nostrils. It reminded him of happier days back in Ireland when life was simple, before the Easter Uprising.

A line of soldiers accompanied by local police on horseback had formed a line across the street and were directing traffic back to the city center away from Lime Street. Dylan walked up to a soldier with Sergeant stripes on his sleeve and a clip board. "Good evening, Sir," said Dylan as he pulled out his identification. "I should be on your admittance list."

"Evening, Sir," replied the Sergeant, checking his identification and briefly shining his torch in Dylan's face. "Just a minute, please," he said, shining the torch on his clip board. Finding Dylan's name, he checked him off. "Thank you, Sir, you are cleared to pass."

"Thank you," said Dylan. He slipped his papers back into his jacket pocket and headed into the station. The loudspeaker was blaring out a final warning for all non-authorized personnel to evacuate the station. He walked across the massive station, counting off the platforms. He noticed a line of heavy-duty carts, each accompanied by a team of soldiers. At Platform Eight, there was another security check before Dylan was finally allowed onto the actual platform. He could see Akroyd standing with two other gentlemen in suits and an Army Major.

At least a hundred soldiers, all sworn to secrecy, were lined up, at ease, evidently waiting for the arrival of the mysterious midnight train. Akroyd saw Dylan walking towards him and excused himself from the group.

"Good evening, Eamon," Akroyd said, delighted to see his trusty right-hand man. They shook hands.

"Good evening, Sir," said Dylan. "Everything going according to plan, Sir?"

"Yes," replied Akroyd. "The train is right on time. Everything is in place. Did you see the lorry convoy?"

"No, I missed it," Dylan responded. "They must be parked on the other side. I came in through the main entrance. It was pretty hectic outside. They have the whole of Lime Street blocked off. The security out there is very tight. People are not too happy about it."

"Yes, they are lined up on Skelhorne Street. There is a line of them as far as you can see, very impressive. When we pull out, I will be in the lead vehicle with the Major and Montague Norman, that is if he decides to come with us. I'm afraid you will be in a military scout vehicle with some heavily armed squaddies bringing up the rear. They have cordoned off all the streets around Water Street, starting at Dale Street. We will get escorted all the way into the bank," said Akroyd, as he nervously checked his watch again.

"Yes Sir, understood!" said Dylan.

Akroyd pulled out his cigarettes and lit up. Dylan could see the stress on his boss' face. He noticed his hand was shaking as he lit his cigarette. Dylan actually liked Akroyd. He knew that Akroyd was a decent and good family man who was fiercely loyal to Martins Bank. It was what Akroyd represented, the British financial system led by the good old boys from Eton and Harrow, that he despised.

"Did you get any sleep, Sir?" asked Dylan, feeling the need to get a conversation going. "No, unfortunately not. I gave it the old school try but no matter how hard I tried, I couldn't get any of this off my mind, not for a moment," lamented Akroyd.

"Specifically, Sir?" asked Dylan.

"The scale of what we are doing...at times it seems like I'm living in an Enid Blyton adventure story, that it's not actually real," said Akroyd, trailing off as he deeply inhaled the cigarette smoke. "Well Sir, it is a little unorthodox, you'd have to admit," replied Dylan. "I mean, how often have you been at Lime Street Station at midnight on official banking business?" he smiled at Akroyd. "Yes, unorthodox, quite," said Akroyd, relieved that his trusted number two was here. He managed to return a thin smile. "And there is a war on!" added Dylan, hammering home his point. "Yes, the bloody war," lamented Akroyd.

The loudspeaker interrupted their conversation, announcing that the train bound for Platform Eight would arrive in five minutes. The Major nodded to his Sergeant, who in turn barked out, "Right Lads! Ten Hut!!" The soldiers snapped to attention in a perfect line.

Akroyd took a final drag on his cigarette, stubbed it out on the concrete floor and moved closer to the edge of the platform. He stared down the shiny steel rails that disappeared into the blackness of a Liverpool night. Squinting into the distance, he looked for a sign of the train, waiting, waiting, any minute now.

First, they heard it, the massive steam engine rumbling in the distance. It was the sound of bellowing steam, the classic chuff, chuff sound that every schoolboy in England had mastered from their earliest childhood days. Then finally it appeared out of the darkness. The platform shook as the powerful steam engine slowly rumbled by. The engineer nodded at Akroyd and the Major as he crawled by, then it came to a dead stop. The engine let out an enormous blast of steam that engulfed the platform, announcing that the first train of Operation Fish loaded with solid gold bullion had made it safely to Lime Street.

The doors of the carriage immediately behind the tender swung open. Several high-ranking military officers exited the train. The Major walked towards them and introduced himself. Then a tall solitary figure emerged from the train, sporting a panama hat, tilted at the perfect angle, nicely accentuating his height. It seemed as though everyone on the platform stopped what they were doing and gazed at him as he stood on the step of the railway carriage and surveyed the scene. He wore a dark gray cape, starched white shirt, gray bow tie, gray pin striped trousers and carried an ornate walking stick. He had a perfect D'Artagnan moustache and beard. Montague Collett Norman, Governor of the Bank of England had arrived.

A smaller man with thick spectacles, in a slightly worn dark gray suit and bowler hat, stood close behind him. He carried a bulging leather briefcase. Norman eyed the platform and seeing Akroyd, waived his stick in his direction, stepped down from the carriage and paced towards him. The smaller man shuffled along behind him with the briefcase clutched closely to his chest.

"Akroyd, Old Chap! How are you?" asked Norman. He extended a hand and the monogrammed cuff of his shirt sleeve pulled back briefly to reveal a solid gold Rolex. "Good, Montague!" replied Akroyd. "And you?" He shook Norman's outstretched hand.

"Splendid! I have a large delivery of fish for you!" beamed Norman. Then his cold gray eyes fixed on Dylan. "Mr. Dylan, always a pleasure, still keeping Martins Bank in the black?" asked Norman, giving Akroyd a deliberate shot.

Norman had met Dylan on several occasions at various high-level financial meetings that he had attended alongside Akroyd, especially since Britain had declared war on Germany. Norman had an eye for talent, and he was acutely aware of Dylan's ability to grasp complex situations a good deal faster than most. He had watched him several times anticipate problems and suggest solutions to his boss that even Norman himself had overlooked.

He had seriously considered poaching Dylan for his own personal assistant but then once the decision was made to move the country's gold to Martins Bank in Liverpool, he thought it prudent to leave Dylan at Martins, at least until the top-secret shipments were complete. "Good to see you, Sir." said Dylan, bowing slightly, while deliberately ignoring his compliment, or jab at his boss.

"This is Mr. Jeffries. He will be handling all the paperwork with you," said Norman, gesturing towards his assistant. Jeffries nodded but did not extend a hand, choosing instead to hug the briefcase a little tighter to his chest, his eyes fixed on the concrete platform floor.

"Dismount! At the double!" bellowed the Sergeant. His voice echoed from the high arched ceiling that covered Lime Street's platforms. There was a clatter of activity as dozens of armed soldiers climbed out of the various train carriages and stepped past their waiting counterparts, forming a line behind them. They spread out at arm's length, each holding a rifle at the ready, statue like. "Right! Lads! It's not going to unload itself! Now move!!" screamed the Sergeant.

The first line of men jumped into action. They unlatched the carriage doors and slid them back. Akroyd and Dylan looked inside. There it was the wealth of the nation. Solid gold bars were neatly stacked in wooden crates, each precisely numbered.

There was a racket of steel wheels on concrete as the men wheeled in the steel dollies and lined them up alongside the rail carriages. Two soldiers jumped into each carriage and between them began to lift the 130-pound crates out of the carriage and into the arms of their mates, who loaded them onto the dollies. Their armed comrades watched over the proceedings.

"Will you be coming the rest of the way with us?" asked Akroyd.

"Good God, no! It's your responsibility from now on Old Chap! Mine was to get it as far as Liverpool. I am on the next train back to London. I have another meeting with the Prime Minister later today. It seems like it's almost every other day these days that he wants to meet. Still, as long as Herr Hitler is sitting on our doorstep, I'm afraid this will be the new business as usual, until something happens, I suppose. Jeffries here will get your signature once everything is safely in your vault. Good luck, Old Chap!" he smiled and tapped the rim of his hat with his cane and was gone.

And so, the back-breaking work of unloading tons of gold bullion began. It was 5:00 AM when the last of the crates slid down the specially made ramp and were safely stacked in Martins Bank vault. An exhausted Akroyd finally signed off on Jeffries' paperwork, confirming that the first shipment of fish had arrived safely with no losses or incidents to report. He then headed home and slept solidly for twelve hours straight.

Dylan, loyal as ever, was back at the bank later that morning in time for opening. He had already reported back to O'Reilly all the pertinent details of the first top-secret shipment of gold. He efficiently cleared Akroyd's schedule when it was apparent that his boss was not going to make it in on time. He easily dealt with the flood of mundane reports that passed over Akroyd's desk every day, placing them in one neat pile in order of priority. Some required his signature. Many would never be read. Akroyd was confident that Dylan would mention anything of relevance that he needed to know. And right now, the only thing relevant to Eamon Dylan was would there be another shipment of gold? And if there was, when would it be?

He found out it was to be forty-eight hours later when he and Akroyd repeated the exact same exercise again, flawlessly.

Chapter 30

THE LAST SHIPMENT OF FISH

Liverpool, England
May 1940

Things ran so smoothly with the second gold shipment that Akroyd was beginning to think, perhaps this wasn't going to be as bad as he feared. The police now had a much better handle on blocking and redirecting traffic. The Army lads all performed with a lot more precision the second time around. The bank staff were outstanding, efficiently working as a team with Dylan to log every single box, along with its exact location in the massive underground vault at Martins Bank.

Figuring the shipments would be coming every other day until told otherwise, he and Dylan were relieved to have the weekend off before the next shipment would come in on the following Monday. Both were a little disappointed that day when the red phone never rang. Nothing happened the next day or the entire week. Here it was Friday again, a week since the arrival of the first gold, and nothing else had happened. Perhaps that was it? Akroyd was relieved that his responsibility for getting two train loads of the country's gold bullion securely from Lime Street to Martins vault was over. As they had not heard anything else for over a week, he figured his part in Operation Fish had played out. That was until the red phone on his desk suddenly rang. It was Montague Norman.

"Akroyd old chap, I hope I didn't disturb your nap," joked Norman.

"Governor Norman, always a pleasure," said Akroyd, not interested in taking Norman's bait.

"I wanted to let you know that we will be bringing another shipment of fish tonight at midnight, Platform Eight again."

"Very good Governor, I'll be here to accept it."

"Good show...there is, however, one small change," Norman paused, waiting for Akroyd to respond.

"I see, and what would that be?" queried Akroyd.

"Well, you will remember the business with Churchill and His Majesty, wanting to leave a small stash of gold behind, hidden somewhere in the Kingdom, no?"

"Yes, I recall. But the last time I was involved, they were still trying to find such a place. They were having great difficulty was my understanding."

"Yes, quite. Well, apparently, they finally found the perfect hiding place. It appears as though some modifications had to be made, but it looks like the Royal Engineers have it cracked now. So, the operation is officially back on."

"I see," said Akroyd, waiting for more information. He could hear paper rustling in the background.

"Yes, here it is. It even has an official operation name," said Norman.

"And that is?" asked Akroyd.

"Operation Minnow!" answered Norman.

"Operation Minnow, very clever, excellent Sir," repeated Akroyd as he wrote it on his blotter.

"Exactly," said Norman.

"And how much gold did his Majesty decide should remain hidden?" asked Akroyd.

"Hmmm...let's see," said Norman, again Akroyd could hear the rustling of papers. "Ah! Here it is, 50."

"50 gold bars!" gasped Akroyd.

"No, tons old boy. 50 tons will go to the secret location," replied Norman, nonchalantly.

"Good Lord!" cried Akroyd. "50 tons! That is an enormous amount of gold! I don't think that's a good idea at all! Have you considered..." Norman instantly cut him off.

"I couldn't agree more. But these decisions are made at an extremely high level," said Norman.

"But...50 tons of gold!" opined Akroyd.

"Oh, trust me old chap, you have no idea, but that was the number that the King and the Prime Minister finally agreed on. At the end of the day, yours is not to reason why, eh? Akroyd, surely, you know the drill by now," replied Norman.

"Yes Sir, and how exactly does this affect things here, on Martins end?" asked Akroyd.

"Well that's what I wanted to talk to you about. I am sorry for the late notice Akroyd, but you know how things are. There is a war on. The construction work at the secret location took much longer than planned. This shipment was supposed to leave last Monday. Things are well behind schedule. The Prime Minister is furious. We will all need to pull together to make this happen.

So, the plan is that at Crewe Station, the last two rail cars will be separated from the rest of the train, along with their own armed guards. These two rail cars will then be pulled by another engine to the top-secret destination. The rest of the train will then continue on up to Lime Street into your safe hands," said Norman.

"I see, so we will be two cars less tonight, that's not a problem," replied Akroyd as he rapidly scribbled himself a note.

"No, I agree, it shouldn't be a problem at all...however, there is a bit of a sticky wicket that you will need to overcome," said Norman.

"I see, a sticky wicket and what exactly is that?" asked Akroyd.

"Well, you will need to be at Lime Street to meet the train, but you will also need to have someone at Crewe to board the Operation Minnow train to sign off when they reach the secret destination. Unless physics have changed, I don't see how you can be in two places at once," replied Norman.

"Do you know the destination after Crewe?" asked Akroyd.

"Lord, no!" said Norman. "That's a secret!" Then he howled at his own humor.

"I'm not sure how this is Martins responsibility?" said Akroyd unamused.

"Well, technically it's not, but I have to tell you Simon, everyone down here is so impressed with the job that you and your staff at Martins have done. We are asking that you or someone in your charge accompany the shipment to its final destination. Then you will sign off that it all has been accounted for and secured and get the documentation back to us as soon as possible. Your help is appreciated by King and Country," said Norman, effectively closing the deal.

"Of course, Sir," answered Akroyd, subconsciously straightening up and puffing out his chest. "You can always count on Martins Bank."

"Thank you, Simon. I appreciate it," said Norman, for once he sounded sincere.

"So, do you have anyone in mind to accompany the gold to its secret destination, Sir?" asked Akroyd. He was sure what Norman would say in response, which is why he asked the question.

"Well, given the short notice, and the resulting unfortunate predicament you've been placed in, I can't think of anyone more capable than your man...Dylan," answered Norman.

"Mr. Dylan, my thoughts exactly, Sir. I'll brief him and send him on his way to Crewe. He will need to get going," said Akroyd, glancing at his watch.

"Yes, absolutely! I will have Jefferies telegraph you the box numbers that Dylan will be taking to the secret destination as soon as I hang up. Also, I will be staying up in Liverpool for a couple of days this time. Perhaps we could go to dinner at the Adelphi Hotel where I will be staying, tomorrow night?"

"Yes, that would be splendid. Thank you, Montague." Akroyd almost gagged. The prospect of listening to Montague Norman drone on over dinner for hours on a Saturday night appalled him.

"Good show, Akroyd. I'll see you in a few hours," Norman hung up without saying goodbye.

"Dylan!" yelled Akroyd.

"Yes, Sir!" said Dylan who instantaneously appeared at the door.

"Pack your night bag! We have a special delivery of fish that you will need to meet in Crewe," said Akroyd as he slipped a cigarette between his lips.

"Crewe, Sir?" enquired Dylan feigning curiosity.

"Sit down, I'll fill you in," said Akroyd as he lit his cigarette.

It really wasn't necessary. As usual Dylan had listened to every word Akroyd had said. He knew exactly what he was getting into. More importantly, he now had some intriguing information to call his commander, Sean O'Reilly about...a top-secret operation, code named Operation Minnow. There would be a special shipment of 50 tons of gold, not bound for the safety of Martins Bank vault as per usual but diverted at Crewe to a top-secret location. A top-secret location that he, Eamon Dylan would learn, very soon.

Chapter 31

OPERATION MINNOW

Parys Mountain, Anglesey

May 1940

Dylan was met at Crewe Station by a young Brigadier from the Royal Lancashire Regiment. The coupling took place on a side spur that was out of the way from public view. In less than a half hour Dylan, along with 50 tons of gold and the armed soldiers headed off to an unknown destination. The third and final shipment of Operation Fish headed on to Lime Street where it was met by Akroyd and seamlessly secured in Martins Bank vault.

Dylan was in a small cabin along with the Brigadier. After a couple of hours, the Brigadier was fast asleep, mouth agape, snoring loudly. Dylan got up and walked up and down the railroad carriage. Most of the soldiers had also nodded off or were playing cards. The air was thick with cigarette smoke and sweat. Dylan was glad that he was at least in a cabin with a fellow nonsmoker.

The train had reduced speed significantly the last half hour or so. One time it came to a complete stop. The Brigadier, as a matter of caution called the men to attention and just in case, had his own Browning drawn at the ready. Soon the train lurched forward again, and he ordered the men to stand down.

Dylan dropped the window of the carriage door and peered out into the blackness. He felt sure that they were heading West and he could tell by the smell of salt in the air that they were close to the sea. If his sense of direction was right, they must be far into North Wales by now. Dylan figured the secret destination would have to be somewhat remote and except for the Scottish Highlands, one would have to go some to beat North Wales when it came to remoteness. Satisfied that he had a rough idea of where they were, Dylan returned to his cabin to try to get a little sleep.

Hours later he was awakened by the sound of loud voices out in the carriage. He was alone and checked his watch to see that it was close to 3:00 AM. Dylan stepped out of the cabin and as he did, he noticed that the rhythmic sound of the train that had so effectively lulled him to sleep had just changed. The soldiers were pushing each other and clowning around to get a better view out of the window. "What is it?" he asked a young soldier next to him. "The Britannia Bridge, we are crossing over the Menai Straits. We're going to bloody Anglesey!" replied the soldier, as he slowly shook his head in disbelief.

Dylan allowed himself a wry smile, Anglesey, the Mother of Wales. He knew O'Reilly and the IRA had deep roots and acres of property in Anglesey. Through his charm and natural charisma, O'Reilly had established a working relationship with the Welsh Nationalists on the island who had long viewed Anglesey as their natural ancestral homeland. He was delighted to find that they also hated the English as much as the Irish did.

The train rumbled on. The first cracks of dawn were starting to appear in the East, but the countryside was still cloaked in darkness. Dylan waited in line for the toilet and then returned to his cabin. Sitting back down, he pulled out yesterday's Financial Times and checked the latest price of gold.

After about a half hour, there was just enough daylight to make out field after field shrouded in early morning mist. The dark outlines of the hedgerows and stone walls, and the larger trees, were in contrast against the pale mist. Now, Dylan could also begin to make out the shape of cows huddled together. He knew that the main train line ran to the Port of Holyhead, which must be their final destination. It was the last outcrop of the island before dropping into the Irish Sea.

From the sunrise, he determined that they were heading in that direction. Then he began to make out the blackness of the Irish Sea. Soon they would be in Holyhead, he assured himself. He was ready to get off the train as were the young squaddies who now jostled for position in the long queue for the toilet. Dylan was glad that he had gone when he had.

Then the train began to slow and gradually curve away from the Irish Sea and head inland. Dylan was puzzled. No one else on the train seemed in the least bit interested. The sun was up now, and the sky was a clear blue. It was going to be a hot day on Anglesey. Dylan settled back down and watched miles and miles of lush green pastures dotted with sheep and cows pass by his window. Other than the occasional stone farmhouse and one tiny church, Dylan saw no sign of any humans. Eventually, he noticed that the green fields gradually turned to a brown, coppery colored rocky landscape. The hedgerows had vanished as had the trees. They passed through what looked like man-made piles of shale rock and boulders. There was no sign of any of the green pastures and livestock, no sign of any life at all.

Dylan noticed that the soldiers had stopped talking and baiting each other. They were silently looking out of the window at a landscape that none of them had ever seen before. All seemed to be asking themselves the same question as Dylan, "Where the hell are we?"

The train began to slowly climb and take a long curve. Dylan was terrified at how close to the edge he was of what appeared to be a massive void dug into the earth. The sides of it were made up of the same rocky material that seemed to be everywhere, except that some of the pieces of rock were gigantic. He could see several entrances to caves burrowed deep in the stone walls with tiny passages hewed into the rock. Presumably, the passages were there to gain access to the caves. Dylan shuddered, he hated heights. Then he started to run terrifying scenarios in his mind. Surely, they were not considering putting the gold in one of the caves. He couldn't possibly climb down to those entrances, that would be insanity. The train seemed suddenly very hot and stuffy. He felt the first beads of sweat running down his back and armpits.

Then the Brigadier popped his head back in the cabin. "Just a heads up Mr. Dylan, I've been given the five-minute warning, we are five minutes out!" Then he was gone to organize his men. "Thanks," said Dylan. He packed the Times back in his briefcase, straightened his tie, checked his hair in the reflection of the window, fastened his shoelaces, and stepped out of the cabin. He looked around once to make sure he had gathered everything and then headed to the carriage door to be the first off the train.

He lowered the window. A gust of warm air greeted him along with a metallic smell that was harsh on his nostrils, Sulphur perhaps? He could see several ponds, surely man made, that seemed to contain green brackish water, toxic for sure. He also noticed a dirt road that ran parallel to the tracks. The soldiers were scrambling to get their uniforms on correctly, some checked their weapons. All, along with Dylan were more than anxious to get off the train.

Finally, the train slowly pulled to a complete stop. Dylan stepped out and was floored by what he saw. In front of him about fifty yards from the train was an ancient, abandoned stone tower. There was scaffolding around the single doorway and what Dylan assumed were engineers swarming all over the place with a variety of tools and equipment. There was a road that lead from the tracks to the tower and then circled around it. Dylan could see at least three Army Matador lorries amongst a variety of vehicles. The whole area was a barren rocky wasteland, covered in the sharp shale rock that Dylan now found underfoot.

The sun was already higher in the sky and he noticed a cloud of copper colored dust fly up with every crunching step he took. His polished black shoes were instantly covered in a layer of reddish-brown dust. He turned around full circle. They were elevated for sure, but the landscape was the same as far as he could see. It was the same dry, awful inhospitable scene. He suddenly felt thirsty. "Where the hell are we?" he said out loud. The answer came immediately, "Mr. Dylan?" asked an older Major coming towards him, hand extended. "Welcome to Parys Mountain!" he continued, "The most God-awful place on Earth!" Dylan noticed the Royal Engineers' badge on his shoulder.

"No kidding," said Dylan, "Not exactly prime dairy land, now is it?" he joked as he shook the Major's hand.

"Major Peer Hunt. Let me show you around," said the Major. "That would be very kind of you, Sir," replied Dylan, following behind the Major. "May I interest you in a spot of tea first?" asked the Major.

"God Bless you, I thought you would never ask. I'm parched," laughed Dylan.

"Over here, we have a mess tent set up." The Major pointed to one of two large khaki colored army tents that had been erected at the site and headed towards it.

When they arrived, the Major pulled back the tent flap and gestured to Dylan to enter ahead of him. "After you," he said. Dylan entered the tent. It was equipped with a field kitchen. Several soldiers were sitting on benches eating scrambled eggs with toast.

"Morning, Major Hunt," said the Army chef.

"Morning, two teas please. Are you hungry, Mr. Dylan?" asked the Major.

"I'm absolutely famished," said Dylan.

"And a breakfast for Mr. Dylan," snapped the Major.

Two teas appeared in Army metal field mugs and scrambled eggs on top of toast with a slice of spam in a mess tin.

"This way," said the Major. "Let's sit here." They sat on a bench at a table a little further away from the soldiers. Dylan tucked into his breakfast. The eggs were powdered, and the toast was cold, the spam was, well spam, but he was grateful to get something in his stomach. The tea was surprisingly good. After several big mouthfuls, Dylan finally asked the question, "So, where am I, and what the hell is this place?"

"You, Sir are on Parys Mountain or Mynydd Parys, which is the Welsh pronunciation," he said with a smile. "Yes, we knew we had crossed over the Menai Straits on the Britannia Bridge, so I knew we were somewhere on Anglesey. But this place, I've never seen anything like it in my life. It's more like being on the moon I'd say than the Island of Anglesey," said Dylan. "Yes, it's a strange environment for sure, but actually it's an ancient copper mine," said the Major. "That would explain a lot of the color that I see in the rocks," said Dylan.

"Exactly, copper, iron, and believe it or not even gold! Over the centuries they have pretty much pulled everything out of here," said the Major as he drank his tea. "Gold, no kidding?" said Dylan. "Yes, considerable amounts of pure Welsh gold," answered the Major. "But I'm afraid that was a long, long time ago. The Romans took the bloody lot!" he laughed.

"That's fascinating," said Dylan. "What about the old stone tower outside?"

"That used to be a windmill. It was the first time they built anything up here that could generate power. Believe me, it gets pretty windy up here. That's the Irish Sea," answered the Major. He pointed to the dark blue waters that met the horizon off in the distance. It was visible through the open flap of the tent.

"Of course, what did they do before windmill power?" asked Dylan genuinely interested. He swallowed the last of his toast. "By hand old chap, one bucket at a time!" said the Major as he finished his tea.

The first group of hungry soldiers from the train had lined up outside the mess tent. "Come on," said the Major, "I'll show you around. Then we shall unload your crates of fish," he said with a broad smile. Dylan finished his tea and followed the Major out into the hot summer sun.

The Major walked at a brisk pace past the windmill and followed the gravel road as it started to loop around. He followed a small rocky foot path toward the canyon rim. Dylan dutifully followed at his heels. Soon they came to the edge of a huge ravine. "Don't get too close to the edge but take a look down here," said the Major as he gingerly peered over the edge. Dylan edged a little closer, just enough to be able to peer past the rocky rim. He could see it was a straight drop off of at least two hundred feet. "Good lord!" gasped Dylan. Then stepping back, he said, "I don't like heights, absolutely not my cup of tea."

"Me neither!" said the Major. That's why I went in the Army. You won't get me in a bloody Spitfire!" Both men laughed and walked back towards the windmill.

The Major continued, "Anyway, that's the story of this place in a nutshell. So, when the powers that be selected this location because of its remoteness, they originally intended to hide the gold in some of the caves that you saw way down in the pit. But it was simply too difficult and dangerous to get down to the caves, especially if you were carrying a 130-pound crate of fish, so to speak," grinned the Major again. This time he knowingly tapped the side of his nostril.

"I couldn't agree more," said Dylan, again replaying the horror of going over the edge. He shuddered. "Then they realized that the answer was in front of them the whole time...Voila!" yelled the Major as he spun 180 degrees while holding his arms aloft at the abandoned stone windmill in front of them.

"The windmill!" exclaimed Dylan. "Brilliant and thank God."

"Exactly!" said the Major. "The only problem was that the old wooden floor would never be able to take the weight. So, we had to come in and do a little bracing work, here follow me!" he said. They walked around the windmill away from the scaffolded main entrance to a side door that led down into what appeared to be the basement. It was refreshingly cool inside. Dylan could clearly see the work that the Major's team of engineers had accomplished. Dozens of round steel columns supported a web of steel I-beams that in turn supported a floor of one-inch steel plates. All were neatly welded together to provide a flat steel floor to stack the crates of gold on.

"Do you think this will do the job, Mr. Dylan?" asked the Major, lightly slapping one of the steel columns. "I do, it's more than adequate," said Dylan impressed by what he saw.

"Jolly good show!" said the Major. "Let's go upstairs, shall we?" he turned and walked back out into the dusty heat.

They walked under the scaffolding and through the main entrance and onto the new steel floor. Steel racks had been laid out in straight rows to allow the boxes to be neatly stacked. Also added was a small portable cable lift to reach the higher shelves. The Royal Engineers had clearly done themselves proud.

"We had a few challenges with the door, but we have that all figured out now. Once your work is done, this place will be permanently sealed until further notice!" said the Major with an air of accomplishment.

"Excellent!" said Dylan, "A lot better than climbing down to those caves!"

"Agreed," said the Major. "Well I suppose we had better get on with it."

As the two men left the windmill, the Major explained how they had overcome the problem of trying to hinge the arched door by permanently anchoring it to the structure. Once they realized there would be no reason to reenter the windmill until the invasion threat was over, the Major received permission to seal it in place until it was time to return the gold to the safety of the Bank of England's vault.

The soldiers were now in better spirits after their breakfast and were ready to knuckle down and get the task done. With the Brigadier's permission, they had all stripped down to their trousers and vest. The sun was now directly overhead, and the temperature was soaring. Other than the grunts and heaves of the men, Parys Mountain was silent. There were no birds, no sheep, no cows, nothing was alive on Parys Mountain except the sweating soldiers, and an intrigued IRA mole. The brutal radiant heat bouncing off the rocky shale added to their misery. They labored, crate by crate for hours until Dylan finally ticked off his bill of lading for the last time.

The Royal Engineers, with the aid of a field crane lifted the heavy steel door into place and the welders went to work to secure it. Fifty tons of Britain's gold reserves had been successfully hidden in an abandoned windmill in the middle of nowhere. The King's request had been honored. Dylan was well satisfied. He thanked the Major and his men for their service and content that Operation Minnow was successfully completed, he boarded the now empty train along with the tired troops for the long ride back to Crewe. He was delighted to bid farewell to what the Major had most accurately described to him on his arrival…as the most god-awful place on earth.

Chapter 32

THE MOLE DELIVERS

Liverpool, England
May 1940

Dylan waited until he got back safely to Lime Street to call O'Reilly. Given the nature of what he knew, he made the decision to call from a public phone box at the station. He dropped his coins in the slot, pushed button A and proceeded to dial. After a short delay, he heard the ring tone and then heard a familiar voice, "O'Reilly residence," answered O'Reilly's personal butler. "Mr. Dylan calling for Mr. O'Reilly," said Dylan.

"One moment, Mr. Dylan," said the Butler as he transferred the call to Sean O'Reilly who was relaxing with a fine cigar in his smoking room.

"Mr. Dylan, a little late for you to be up isn't it?" asked O'Reilly.

"It is indeed, but I had a very long day and night, if you will," said Dylan.

"Excellent, Eamon and you have some news for me?" asked O'Reilly.

"Indeed, I do but it's a little more than I'd like to talk about on the phone, if you get my drift," said Dylan.

"Is it regarding the fish again?" asked O'Reilly, a grin crept across his face. He stood up from his chair and walked towards the antique drink trolley nestled below an enormous, stained glass window.

"Yes, as a matter of fact it is. There have been some very interesting developments," said Dylan. He could hear the chink of fine crystal in the background.

"Really?" said O'Reilly as he poured himself an extra-large Irish Whiskey. "Interesting enough to have my man Richard stop by for a chin wag with your good self?" asked O'Reilly.

"I think that would be a very good idea. It is always a pleasure to see Richard," answered Dylan.

"Alrighty then, why don't we say six o clock tomorrow, in Liverpool. How about under the Liver Bird, would that work for you Eamon?" asked O'Reilly.

"That will work just fine, I'll be there!" answered Dylan.

"Consider it done, lad!" said O'Reilly.

"Thank you, Sir," replied Dylan.

"No, on the contrary, thank you, Eamon. Your long hours are much appreciated. Good night and God bless you, lad." O'Reilly hung up. He rang a small bell and seconds later a man in a black tuxedo appeared. "Thomas," he said to his butler, "Call Richard and have him meet Eamon Dylan, six o'clock tomorrow night, underneath the Liver Bird."

Richard Tully and Sean O'Reilly had grown up together. Both of their fathers were high ranking members of the Irish Republican Army. The only time they had ever been apart was when O'Reilly opted for Liverpool University to earn his degree. Richard chose to stay on Irish soil and had attended Trinity College in Dublin. He had worked for O'Reilly ever since his graduation. He was firmly the number two man for Sean O'Reilly, both at O'Reilly Meats and over the men that O'Reilly commanded in the outlawed IRA. His loyalty was absolute, and he was well rewarded. He had a unique gift of being able to see opportunity when others saw obstacles. O'Reilly claimed it was almost as though Richard had an ability to see around corners. O'Reilly always counseled his old friend before he ever made any major business or IRA moves, a habit that had so far served him well.

"Yes sir!" replied Thomas.

Dylan hung up too. He was flushed with pride that his commander appreciated his time. He left the station and walked the short distance to his bus stop. The bus arrived within a few minutes. Dylan climbed on board and slumped in a vacant seat and closed his eyes. He was blissfully unaware of the lady seated opposite him. She frowned at the state of his pants and shoes.

They were still covered in a thick coppery colored layer of dust from his surreal experience of hiding 50 tons of British gold in an abandoned windmill at Parys Mountain.

Chapter 33

UNDER THE LIVER BIRDS

Liverpool, England
May 1940

Richard arrived early. Looking up at the massive, twenty-five-foot diameter clock face of the Royal Liver Building, he could see it was exactly five minutes to six. Mariners traveling up and down the River Mersey had been setting their time pieces to it since 1911. It was one of the first buildings in the world to be constructed using reinforced concrete and was the first real skyscraper in Europe. He moved his line of sight up higher above the clock, following the square pillars that supported a round turret like structure. It was capped with a massive patina copper dome, and there she was, 300 feet above him, the mythical Liver Bird. Its wings were spread, looking out across the River Mersey and beyond to the Irish Sea.

The Liver Bird has long been the symbol of the great city of Liverpool. There was an identical one, over a near identical clock tower on the other side of the building that looked over the city. The legend was if either of the birds ever flew away, then the banks of the River Mersey would break, and the city of Liverpool would cease to exist. Fat chance thought Richard, looking up at the steel chains that anchored the bird securely down.

They even had their individual names, Bertie and Bella. Although they were identical, Richard knew that Bella looked out to Sea and Bertie guarded the City. He never forgot which was which after a friend of his who was born and raised in Liverpool told him, "It's simple Richard, Bertie is watching the city to see when the pubs are going to open, while Bella is looking out to sea, waiting for a handsome sailor to come and rescue her."

To his right was the famous Cunard Building, of Cunard Line fame and to the right of that was the Port of Liverpool Building. The three buildings that made up the world-famous Liverpool waterfront were affectionately known as The Three Graces by the local people, or Scousers as they proudly called themselves.

Turning away from the buildings, Richard leaned on the thick worn teak top rail of the railing that ran along the Pier Head. He watched as the Royal Daffodil ferry boat, packed with tired office workers returning home, cast off its mooring ropes and headed off across the Mersey to the town of Wallasey. Wallasey was on the land peninsula known as the Wirral, directly across from Liverpool. Richard could see the outline of the Wallasey Town Hall and the neighboring docks of Seacombe and Birkenhead. The seagulls dove down noisily and swooped behind the Royal Daffodil as she churned up the brown waters of the Mersey and made her way quickly across the fast-moving span.

"Hello Richard," said Dylan.

"Eamon, it's been a while. You look well!" said Richard as the two men shook hands.

"Yes, I'm doing great!" agreed Dylan. "It's been a while for sure, how have you been?"

"Good!" said Richard. "Busy! But good! So, the boss said he would pick up our tab tonight. Shall we go to Shenanigans Pub for a few scoops to start? I assume we will be on the Higsons Bitter tonight?" Higsons was the local beer brewed by Scousers in Liverpool since 1780. It was the only beer that the Irish really enjoyed instead of Guinness. It was a lighter ale and pulled directly out of the barrel. On a good night Richard could easily drink eight pints or a gallon and still maintain his faculties. Dylan could match him pint for pint. Beyond that, or one over the eight as the saying goes, there were no guarantees.

"Sounds like a great plan mate, after you!" replied Dylan. The two men walked off in the direction of their preferred Irish pub where Richard sat spell bound, not only at Dylan's story, but the meticulous details he had both observed and recollected.

In fact, Richard was so impressed with what Dylan revealed to him, six hours later as the same Royal Liver Building clock struck midnight, he caught the last ferry from Liverpool back to Dublin that same night. "Goodbye, Bella my love! Till we meet again!" said Richard. He took a half bottle of Irish Whiskey from his coat pocket and toasted the giant Liver Bird, eerily silhouetted against a perfect full moon. "Wait till the boss hears this one!" he said to himself for the umpteenth time. He took another good swig before disappearing into the passenger area to find himself a vacant bench, and god forbid perhaps even get a little shut eye. He was, after all one over the eight.

Chapter 34

RICHARD THE ENLIGHTENED ONE

Graystones, Ireland

May 1940

"Mother of Mary, Richard that's quite a story!" exclaimed O'Reilly. He stood up from behind his desk and headed to the small built-in bar in the corner of his spacious, private office. "Aye, that it is," replied Richard, rubbing his stubbly chin. He had talked continuously for over two hours. O'Reilly had rarely interrupted him but as usual had made copious notes. Richard had relayed Dylan's extraordinary tale remembering every detail and it now filled the pages of the notepad in front of him.

O'Reilly poured two large Irish Whiskey's and handed one to Richard. "Here's to our man Eamon Dylan. Sounds like he's done us all proud!" said O'Reilly. "Aye, that he has. To Eamon Dylan, proud soldier of the IRA!," replied Richard. The two men toasted the absent Dylan and placed the empty, antique crystal glasses simultaneously onto the worn surface of O'Reilly's desk. O'Reilly returned to his chair, opened his silver cigarette box, and slid it silently to Richard. With a nod, he gratefully accepted the offer of a smoke. O'Reilly flipped open the matching silver lighter and leaned forward to light Richard's cigarette, now clenched between his thin lips. He leaned back, lit his own and inhaled deeply, closing the lid of the box with a metallic click. He placed the lighter on top of it, pushing it to one side.

"So, you know I value your opinion Richard," started O'Reilly. "I'm sure you've thought things over on the ferry. Given what we know and the assets we currently have available at Rhosybol, do you think it's worth taking a crack at it? Or are we getting in over our heads?" He focused intently on his trusted friend now sitting opposite him contently smoking his cigarette, as he gazed out of the window.

"Well Sean, my mother used to say never look a gift horse in the mouth. I ask you what are the chances of the Brits deciding to hide 50 tons of their gold in our very own back yard? Our army needs guns and ammo to fight the Bastards. We know they don't come cheap these days. Think of the impact we could have with that kind of a haul. It would be fun to watch our mates in Boston scrambling to fulfill our order!" laughed Richard.

"Aye, it would for sure," said O'Reilly, smiling and always one to enjoy a laugh with his trusted old friend. He picked up the telephone on his desk and mockingly said, "Yes Declan, you heard me, that's 20,000 tommy guns, with 500,000 rounds of ammo for the initial order! Oh! And we could use some hand grenades too. Throw in 10,000 of your finest grenades!" The two men laughed as he hung up the phone. "Oh, to be a fly on the wall!" he continued as he took another drag from his cigarette and casually flicked the ash into his crystal ash tray. Then he thought for a few minutes, as did Richard. Both men sat silently, processing the incredible events that Dylan had reported.

Richard spoke first, "I think we should take a crack at it, boss. I really do," he said, nodding his head slowly. He continued to gaze out of the office window at the lush rolling green fields that surrounded O'Reilly's mansion. "We've talked before, you and I, off and on and for some time now, about possibly knocking over a bank to finance our own war efforts against the British. So, what's the bloody difference? One is a bank robbery. An old-fashioned stick 'em up raid is a risky business and could get very messy, very fast. The alternative to a stick up would be breaking into the bank after hours. That is never going to be easy. Then you would have to get into the vault, which would be very difficult. The other is an abandoned windmill on Anglesey in the middle of bloody nowhere! Like I said, never look a gift horse in the mouth, ever."

"Agreed. Irish eyes are smiling, no doubt. Comparatively speaking, the windmill should be a cinch, especially in our own back yard. I mean, what are the chances of that?" O'Reilly continued to eyeball Richard, who, in turn, continued to stare out of the window. Finally, he switched his gaze back to O'Reilly. "Oh, they are smiling on us alright! I have already run a few scenarios in my head. With a few modifications to our fleet and with a well-executed plan, I think we could pull it off. I really do," said Richard, an impish grin lit up his tired face. "That's my boy!" replied O'Reilly. "Talk to me, my son," he said, leaning across his desk. Listening intently, his green eyes shone in the morning sun that was now streaming through the blue smokey haze that had filled the room.

"Ok, here you go. In a nutshell, here are the genius thoughts of Richard the Enlightened One! The hardest part would be the logistics of the whole thing. Basically, we already have that covered. We simply replace the bags of flour we bring back from Spillers Mill with the crates of gold. If we load the crates of gold correctly in the lorries, we should have enough room on top of the crates to lay one layer of our usual sacks of grain. That way if anyone takes a close look at the load, all they would see are sacks of grain.

We simply add an extra run as though all twelve lorries are going to the Guinness brewery. Naturally, we will have to increase our payment to our friends down at the docks to make sure it all passes through without a hitch. We will need to beef up the suspension on all the lorries. All the equipment we need to do that is already out at Rhosybol so that's a piece of cake. Other than that, I don't see any problem. We run convoys of up to a dozen lorries all the time, so nothing unusual there. There is one ferry that we should return to Dublin on. It's the very first one on Monday morning that leaves Holyhead at 4:30 AM, it's always deserted," said Richard.

"Ok, it sounds doable to me so far. So, what about the armed squaddies guarding the roadblock?" asked O'Reilly.

"That will be a synch. Nothing I'd like better than to slice up a few of those Bastards. It's out in the middle of nowhere, no one will hear their screams," answered Richard coldly.

"Fine with me. How do we get into the windmill?" asked O'Reilly.

"Well, the actual break in would be the easy part. We have the Murphy brothers on our side. Those two men can cut their way through anything, period. The biggest problem, believe it or not, would be getting rid of the gold once we get it back here to Ireland. As an organization, it's of no use to us. Our friends in Boston will only take dollars for arms. What the hell are we going to do with a windmill full of gold bars, for god's sake?"

"You have a point there, lad. What's the plan?" asked O'Reilly.

"Well, we just need to look at it from a different angle. We know the gold is no good to our Irish brothers in America. They want hard cash. And it is no good to us, we want arms. So, on this deal we may need to look to a new arms supplier, so to speak," said Richard, winking at his boss.

"Carry on, my son," replied O'Reilly, with a wink back of his own. Richard took another drag on his cigarette. "So, who hates the British? Who can trade in gold even if it is stolen and who's also got lots of guns and ammo?" he asked looking directly at O'Reilly.

O'Reilly thought for a second, then a broad smile spread across his face, "The Nazis! Richard, you're a bloody genius lad!"

Richard smiled. "Aye, I know it," he replied with a grin, dusting some imaginary dandruff of his shoulder. "We currently have an official alliance with them. So why not do some mutually beneficial business together. We trade the gold for arms with Mr. Hitler. He gets the gold that he needs to finance his war effort. Then we get the weapons we need to finally be able to effectively fight for our freedom against a common enemy. It's a win, win all around, don't you think?" he asked, looking closely into O'Reilly's eyes.

"Yes, I do. We win and the British lose. That's always a great deal. I'll start the ball rolling. Let's see what our German friends have to say. Our Chief of Staff is very well-connected in Germany. I know that we have already worked with the Abwehr on a couple of operations so far. I'm just not familiar with the details. I'll get in touch with him as soon as we are done here. He is definitely going to want to be involved," answered O'Reilly, as he continued to write on his pad.

"What about manpower? Do we have sufficient? That's an awful lot of gold to move. It's not exactly lightweight stuff you know Richard," he pointed out.

"Well, the way I see it, is we have about half the force we will need. So, if we do business as partners, they will need to kick in some manpower also. They'll need their own tackle, obviously," replied Richard, puffing away on his cigarette and returning his gaze to the cattle peacefully grazing in the warm Irish sunshine.

"How much manpower do they need to kick in?" asked O' Reilly, his pen poised above his notepad.

"I'd say around a dozen ought to do it. All heavily armed of course," answered Richard nonchalantly, as if ordering his breakfast. O'Reilly, equally as nonchalantly, wrote the number 12, then "Armed" on his note pad.

"The number might change depending on how well guarded the windmill is, naturally. Although I'd like to kill the guards myself, it would be wiser to have the Nazis do that. No point in fouling our own nest with murdered British soldiers. We don't need that kind of heat. After it's all over, the Nazis will be back in Germany. We still have to do business in Anglesey, right boss?" asked Richard.

"Exactly. The last thing we need is our fingerprints on dead British squaddies," replied O'Reilly.

"I'll need to do a little recon work first. Our man on Anglesey is Hugh Moran. He knows that area like the back of his hand. I'll have him show me everything I need to see and report back to you. Then we can fine tune the details. If it still looks good, let's see what our friends the Nazis have to say," said Richard. He took the last drag on his cigarette before extinguishing it in the ash tray.

"Ok, what about timing? When would be the soonest we could make a move?" asked O'Reilly.

"Well it needs to be carried out at nighttime, obviously. It's pitch black out in the Anglesey countryside and the British have black out restrictions. The lorries are fitted with shaded head lights, but they are not much help. So, when we pick the date, make sure it's a full moon so we can see as well as possible," answered Richard.

Sean O'Reilly thought for a moment, then reviewed the notes on his pad. "Alright Richard, I'm on board so far. With a little Irish luck, we might just pull this thing off. Why don't you rest up here for a while? I want you on the Holyhead ferry tonight. Get together with Hugh and let's see how well guarded it is. We need to strike while the iron is still hot!" he said reaching for the bell on his desk. His butler, Thomas appeared almost immediately.

"Sir?" Thomas enquired as he entered through the office door.

"Run a bath for Richard here and put him in the Emerald Room. And set up a meeting with the Chief of Staff for me as soon as possible. Let him know that I have something in the works that will need the cooperation of our friends in Germany, and I know that he is the man to make that happen. Thank you, Thomas," said O'Reilly, as he stubbed out his cigarette butt.

"Yes sir!" replied Thomas. He bowed and swiftly left the office.

"God Bless you, Sean," said Richard, sniffing his armpits. "I could use a hot bath."

"No kidding," replied O'Reilly, as he wafted his hand in front of his nose, laughing. "You did well, my son! Another Whiskey before your bath? Oh, Enlightened One," asked a clearly delighted Sean O'Reilly.

"I thought you'd never ask," laughed Richard.

Chapter 35

THE LORIENT MYSTERY

10 Downing Street, London
May 1940

"The Director General of MI5, David Petrie and the Admiral of the Fleet, Dudley Pound, Sir," announced Mary Shearburn Thompson, the Prime Minister's private secretary, as she walked into Winston Churchill's private office. Behind her were the two men, one dressed in a dark gray business suit and the other in an Admirals uniform. "Will you need me to take notes, Sir?" she asked, pad and pencil at the ready.

"No, I believe this will be short and sweet. I'll buzz you if I need anything, thank you," said Churchill, as he rose from his desk to greet the two men.

"Very well, Sir," replied Mary. She turned and left his office, gently closing the door behind her.

"Gentlemen," said Churchill, shaking each of their hands, "always a pleasure, please sit down."

Petrie put down his briefcase on the lush, thick carpet and sat down in one of two small armchairs located in front of Churchill's desk. Admiral Pound did the same but winced in pain as he bent to sit down. Churchill immediately picked up on it, "The hip bothering you again, Admiral?" asked Churchill.

"Yes, I'm afraid so. It's pretty much all the time these days, especially when I sit or climb the stairs, but I'll be alright," said Pound, who did not look at all well.

"I'm sorry to hear that Dudley. Perhaps a shot of Scotch might help?" asked Churchill, concerned about the pasty appearance of the First Sea Lord.

"Yes, that might help, thank you," said the Admiral.

"Excellent! And you Director General? Care to join us?" asked Churchill.

"No, thank you Prime Minister, not while I'm on duty," replied Petrie with a smile. He was always amazed at Churchill's ability to drink vast amounts of Scotch, Brandy, wine and Champagne at any time, without impairing his faculties. He had never heard Churchill slur his words.

"Good Show!" said Churchill, as he poured himself and the Admiral a stiff shot and returned to his seat behind the desk where his smoldering cigar was perched on the ashtray.

"Well, now to business I suppose. We all have our respective plates full. I have asked you both here today to discuss a resolution to the unusual amount of construction underway at the Port of Lorient in France. After much discussion with Dudley and his advisors, it's obvious that we cannot mount a successful campaign against the U-boat threat until we know their numbers and where they are based. Lorient is clearly the main hub of activity. The entire area has been cordoned off so the resistance, despite their best efforts, have been unable to determine just how many U-boats, if any are based there," said Churchill. He opened the file in front of him and glanced at a grainy, aerial shot of the Port of Lorient.

He went on, "Judging by the aerial shots provided by the RAF, the Germans are up to something big under those colossal camouflage nets and we simply must know what that is. Short of mounting an invasion, which I'm sure you will agree would be a little premature to say the least, I see no option but to get an agent on the ground in Lorient. We need to penetrate their security and find out what the Nazis are up to. This would obviously fall into your lap, David," Churchill nodded to the head of MI5.

"May I take a quick look at the photograph you have there, Prime Minister?" asked Petrie, as he pulled a small magnifying glass out of his inside jacket pocket. Churchill handed him the photo.

"Thank you," said Petrie.

"You're welcome, Sherlock Holmes," quipped Churchill.

Petrie ignored the shot while looking intensely through his magnifying glass at the photograph. After a few minutes, he handed the photo back to Churchill and retrieved his small pocketbook and pencil. He wrote several notes before looking up at Churchill and in a sober tone said, "It's not going to be easy. Hard to tell from the photograph but it looks like a double barbed wire fence and security towers every hundred yards or so."

Petrie continued, "Almost certainly, there will be armed guards patrolling between the two fences, probably with dogs. Getting into the secure area would be tough enough but having time to gather the intelligence you require and then being able to extricate oneself from the area without detection, would be an extreme challenge Prime Minister, to say the least."

"Which would therefore require an equally extreme MI5 agent. Surely you have such a chap, David?" asked Churchill, taking an enormous pull on his cigar.

"Sadly, I'm in agreement with you Prime Minister. I do not see any other option. In view of the tonnage of ships being lost to the U-boats crossing the Atlantic, if we do not get a handle on the threat level then it's going to continue to get worse and our people will face the very real threat of starvation. So, with that in mind, I do have an outstanding individual who is currently available. If anyone can get in there and return with the goods, he's our man," said a reluctant Petrie.

"Excellent, Director! I know it's a big ask. Thank you," boomed Churchill. He exhaled a massive cloud of smoke that obscured his vision of Petrie as he wrote in his notebook the name John Ashley. Then he drew an arrow pointing directly down and wrote Lorient.

"Thank you, Director. I will eagerly await your findings. The entire Royal Navy will be indebted to your chap, and may God watch over him," said the Admiral with sincerity, as he shook hands with Petrie.

"Thank you, Admiral. He will need all of God's help. There is no doubt about that. Will that be all, Prime Minister?" asked Petrie.

"Yes, that was the main thing. Thank you, Director. We will need that intelligence as soon as possible, so anything you can do to expedite it would be very much appreciated! Good man," said Churchill. He got to his feet and shook the hand of Petrie who seemed to tower above him. Petrie picked up his briefcase, nodded to the Admiral and was gone.

"He's a good man, that Petrie," said Churchill.

"Yes, he is. A very difficult job, in difficult times," agreed the Admiral.

"Yes, indeed. Another Scotch Admiral? For the hip of course," asked Churchill.

"Yes, I'll take another. I think it's helping," replied the Admiral.

"Splendid," said Churchill, as he picked up the two empty glasses and headed to the drink cabinet.

Chapter 36

GOEBBELS IN HIS ZONE

The Berghof, Bavaria
June 1940

Goebbels was nervous waiting in the plush reception area at the Berghof to be summoned to meet with his Fuhrer. He had not slept well. Bormann, as usual had offered no specifics other than the Fuhrer had requested his presence immediately. He had waited for over two hours and it was now close to four o clock, which had done little to quell his anxiety.

Finally, the door opened. It was Bormann, stone faced as usual, "Dr. Goebbels, I'm sorry for the delay," he lied. "The Fuhrer will see you now. Please," he said indicating for Goebbels to exit the reception area. "Thank you, Martin," replied Goebbels as he saluted. "I trust everything is going well?"

Bormann acknowledged the salute but skillfully ignored his question. Goebbels knew it was futile to press Bormann who was already out the door. "We are in the main dining room today," he said as they walked down the long wooden paneled corridor. Goebbels shuffled quickly behind Bormann. Bormann knew of Goebbels disability, so he deliberately picked up the pace. Several armed SS guards stood at attention outside the various doors that adjoined the corridor. Each flipped the Nazi salute as the pair went by. Bormann stopped outside the dining room door. The SS guard stood aside, clicked his jackboot heals, and opened the door. Bormann entered first. He politely bowed his head and announced Goebbels, "Dr. Goebbels, Mein Fuhrer." The nervous Goebbels entered, stood to attention and snapped his best Nazi salute, "Heil Hitler," he shouted while rapidly scanning the room.

Hitler was sitting behind a round mahogany table. It was set in a viewing turret that was built into the dining room exterior wall. It had five tall double hung windows that offered a panoramic view of the main terrace, with the Alps providing a breathtaking backdrop. The Fuhrer was dressed in a white shirt, black tie and a dark brown double-breasted suit with a swastika band around his arm. Next to him was Himmler, dressed in full black SS uniform. His cap sat on the table next to a small stack of files. At the side of the table was a man he did not recognize in civilian clothes who had a tape recorder and several other pieces of electronic equipment in front of him. There was a maze of wires that ran from the table to an electrical socket on the wall behind him.

'Ah! Joseph! My Minister of Propaganda! Please come in," said Hitler, rising to his feet and walking towards Goebbels, returning his salute. Goebbels was relieved that the Fuhrer seemed cordial at least and extended his hand which the Fuhrer accepted. At the same time, Hitler patted him warmly on the shoulder. Himmler stood up and followed his master's lead. "Joseph," said Himmler, feigning politeness and shaking Goebbels's hand. "Heinrich," replied Goebbels. He was aware of the smirk on Himmler's face clearly delighted to be sitting next to the boss. Nothing new there, so far so good.

"Please have a seat," said Hitler, gesturing to a spot opposite him and Himmler and next to Bormann who was already returning to what was clearly his seat. "I apologize for the delay. May I offer you some tea?" asked Hitler. "I'm fine, thank you. I had some a short time ago in the waiting area but thank you," answered Goebbels. He took a seat next to Bormann and placed his leather attaché case on the table.

The Fuhrer poured himself a glass of water and took a few sips before leaning forward and focusing on Goebbels, who nervously ran his fingers over his greased hair. "Joseph, I believe we have a problem that your department may be able to assist us with," said the Fuhrer, as he simultaneously nodded at Himmler, who in turn nodded back in agreement.

"Of course, Mein Fuhrer, how can I help?" replied Goebbels. He felt a little more comfortable that he had already survived the initial opening round of banter unscathed at least.

"The new leader of the British, that drunk Winston Churchill has delivered a rousing speech to his Nation. Heinrich, Martin and I are very concerned. After much analysis and discussion, short of assassinating him, which would prove to be very difficult, we believe it falls more in line with your expertise. We should fight fire with fire so to speak, if you follow my drift," answered the Fuhrer.

"Of course, Mein Fuhrer, when was the speech?" replied Goebbels as he removed a small notepad from his attaché case.

"He delivered it very recently, have you not heard it yet?" asked Hitler.

"No, I'm sorry Mein Fuhrer, I've been traveling since early this week. I'd be happy to contact my office to get an update if you like," said Goebbels. Now he was more confident that he was not going to be on the receiving end of a verbal beating, or worse.

"No need. Martin has taken the necessary steps. We can play it for you if you like," said the Fuhrer. Goebbels turned to Bormann next to him, who smiled sarcastically at the Minister of Propaganda, then turned and nodded to the civilian at the end of the table. The civilian went to work on the battery of electronic equipment in front of him. Then as if by magic, following a little static, the haunting, unmistakable voice of Winston Churchill, the Prime Minister of Great Britain, filled the room.

"We shall go on to the end, we shall fight in France,
We shall fight on the seas and oceans,
We shall fight with growing confidence and growing strength in the air,
We shall defend our Island, whatever the cost may be,
We shall fight on the beaches,
We shall fight on the landing grounds,
We shall fight in the fields and in the streets,
We shall fight in the hills;
We shall never surrender, and even if, which I do not for a moment believe, this Island or a large part of it were subjugated and starving, then our Empire beyond the seas, armed and guarded by the British Fleet, would carry on the struggle, until, in God's good time, the New World, with all its power and might, steps forth to the rescue and the liberation of the old."

The recording finished and Bormann nodded at the civilian who flipped several switches. Having done so he then sat back, his eyes wisely transfixed on the table before him.

"Comments?" asked Hitler, glaring directly at Goebbels and now visibly seething at the sound of Churchill's voice, whom he had always despised. Goebbels raised an eyebrow and tightened his tie knot. He thought for a second, then spoke, "Powerful, very powerful," said Goebbels, massively impressed at what he had just heard. He continued, "I had not heard it before. This Churchill is a powerful orator, no doubt. I don't know who wrote it for him or if they are his own words, but it's powerful, and very well spoken."

"Yes, we agree. It is the best delivered speech we have heard coming out of the British so far. That pompous ass is one of a kind, for sure. Damn him! this is the last thing we need. Not good for us Joseph, not good at all. Don't you agree?" asked Hitler, clearly agitated.

"I agree, he is no Chamberlain that's for sure. Peace in our time!" replied Goebbels, waiving an imaginary piece of paper in the air. "Do you have a transcript of the speech by any chance? I'd like to review it, if possible." With another smirk, Bormann slid a sheet of paper in front of him with a typed transcript of what he had just heard. Goebbels slipped on his reading glasses and studied the page in front of him. The room remained silent.

Goebbels focused on the paper intensely. Hitler waited patiently, softly tapping his fingers on the table in front of him to calm himself. Himmler simply glared directly ahead at Goebbels, whom he disliked intensely.

Goebbels now leaned forward, his elbows on the table, avoiding the gaze from the Fuhrer as he stared at the transcript in front of him. Hitler continued to tap his fingers, seemingly content to allow Goebbels whatever time he needed. Himmler deliberately checked his wristwatch, hoping to get the Fuhrers attention, he failed. The Fuhrer's eyes stayed locked on the Propaganda Minister. He was delighted that Goebbels was lost in what he surmised was "The Zone". That was what Goebbels called his state of mind just before producing his finest pieces of work. While the Fuhrer surmised that Goebbels was in his zone, he could take all the time he needed.

Finally, Goebbels sat upright. He removed his pen from his inside jacket pocket and followed the line, "We shall fight them" down the page, pointing to each word before getting to the bottom. Then he paused and circled the last paragraph. He looked up at Hitler and said, "This is quite brilliant, no doubt. He has covered all the bases, beaches, hills, landing grounds, streets, and valleys. It really is an astonishingly well written piece, Mein Fuhrer," said Goebbels before deliberately stopping and enduring the silence that then followed. He desperately tried to hold his tongue from further conversation until hopefully the Fuhrer spoke first, which he did.

"And?" said Hitler, smiling at Goebbels. He had learned how his brilliant Propaganda Minister liked to operate and as he had delivered the goods so far, Hitler was more than happy to now indulge him. Himmler leaned forward, his eyes narrowing behind his wire rimmed glasses, glaring, hoping, and praying that Goebbels was about to flounder. He hated that the Fuhrer always seemed to cut Goebbels additional slack.

Goebbels flipped the pad around and pushed it in front of Hitler. Reaching over the table, he tapped the page on the bottom paragraph that he had circled. The pen left several small wet ink dots at the point of contact. "Here," he said. "Here is the chink in Churchill's armor, Mein Fuhrer."

Hitler reread the paragraph and then looked up at Goebbels. His smile was now warmer. He tilted his head slightly and raised his eyebrow. "Let me have it Joseph, let me have it," said the Fuhrer, anxious to hear more.

Goebbels smiled, turned and looked suspiciously at the civilian, then back at Hitler who picked up the cue and nodded at Bormann. Bormann turned to the civilian and barked, "Leave!" The civilian relieved, got to his feet, pushed his chair back under the table and moved to the door. He nervously bowed several times in the direction of the Fuhrer. The SS guard opened the door and he was gone.

"Joseph," said the Fuhrer, indicating Goebbels had the floor.

Goebbels was clearly in his zone. "May I?" he asked the Fuhrer before spinning the paper back to his side. "The first portion, I can't touch, it's very good. But then I read and re-read the last paragraph, the phrase, 'and even if, which I do not for a moment believe, this

Island or a large part of it were subjugated and starving, then our Empire beyond the seas, armed and guarded by the British Fleet, would carry on the struggle.' This is the weakness in the speech. To me he's telling the British that there is a good chance that they will lose a war with us. He is saying in essence, if they lose the Battle of Britain, the war will be carried on from overseas."

"Carry on Joseph," said the Fuhrer, eager for more. Hitler had risen now from his seat and collected his glass of water. He began to walk around to Goebbels' side of the table, taking the seat next to him. Much to Himmler's dismay, he was now sitting alone opposite the other three. Goebbels looked at the seething tight lipped leader of the SS and sarcastically returned the smirk that Himmler had given him when he had first entered the room. Bormann picked up on it. He disliked Himmler as much as he disliked Goebbels, so he was enjoying watching Himmler squirm while Goebbels looked to be on a roll.

"Look here," said Goebbels. "This phrase...in God's good time... What in the hell does that mean? Talk about a vague time frame, in Gods good time? What is that a week? A month? A year? A decade? A hundred years? A thousand years??"

"A thousand years. Yes, Joseph! A thousand years, a thousand-year Reich! I'll settle for that, eh Heinrich?" Hitler beamed looking at Himmler who immediately feigned a thin smile and nodded, still boiling inside and scowling at Goebbels.

"Anything else?" asked Hitler, hoping his star Minister might have a little more to add.

"Yes," said Goebbels. He looked directly at the now elated Hitler and pointed his pen. "Here also, 'The New World, with all its power and might, steps forth to the rescue and the liberation of the old.' Clearly, he's referring to the Americans. Roosevelt will not like that. The American people have made it clear that they do not want any part of Europe's wars. We can work with that, Mein Fuhrer."

"Excellent, excellent!" said Hitler. His mood now clearly elevated since the meeting with Goebbels had begun.

"One other thing, Mein Fuhrer," continued Goebbels, "This part...'steps forth to the rescue and the liberation'...This is a clear indication that the British would have already lost to us. Otherwise, why would they need to be rescued or liberated?"

"Exactly, he's basically telling the British people that they are going to be invaded and it's up to the Americans to come and save them on a timetable that's up to God almighty!" said the Fuhrer.

"Exactly, Mein Fuhrer," said Goebbels, smiling broadly at his leader. "Does this sound like a reassuring plan to you?"

"No! It sounds like a plan for capitulation!" laughed the Fuhrer.

"My point exactly, Mein Fuhrer," responded Goebbels.

"Joseph, you Sir are a genius!" he slapped Goebbels on his shoulder. Himmler looked on, glaring at Goebbels, who had clearly won another round in the battle to gain the Fuhrer's favor. Hitler stood up and walked over to the wall of windows that lined the dining room and stared out at the spectacular view before him. Without turning around, he said, "So how do we respond? We need to nip this in the bud. After Dunkirk, we need to make sure that we block every attempt Churchill makes to rally the British people."

"Agreed, Mein Fuhrer. Give me some time. I'll work with my team and see what we can come up with," responded Goebbels.

"We don't have much time, Joseph. I need you to come up with something to stop that drunkard in his tracks. We need to drive a wedge between him and the British people. When will you have something for me?" asked Hitler.

"Hmmm," said Goebbels. "It will take a little time, but I'll get to work on it immediately, Mein Fuhrer."

"Excellent. Martin, put Joseph back on my schedule as soon as he has something for me," directed Hitler, turning now towards Bormann. Then he strode forward, extended his hand to Goebbels who clasped it in both of his. Hitler patted him again on the shoulder, with a broad smile beneath his pencil moustache.

"Thank you, Mein Fuhrer," said Goebbels as he gave him the Nazi salute. Then he turned to Bormann, shook his hand and simply said, "Martin, good day." He completely and deliberately ignored the still livid head of the SS, gathered his attaché case and left the room.

Chapter 37

AN IRISH FOX

The Berghof, Bavaria

June 1940

Hitler watched from the top of the steps outside the main entrance to the Berghof. The sky was a deep blue with a few puffy white clouds seemingly balanced on top of the snowcapped peaks of the mighty Alps. The distant hum of BMW motorcycles announced the impending arrival of his next guest. The motorcycle escort arrived first, quickly followed by the dark gray Mercedes of Admiral Wilhelm Franz Canaris, Head of the Abwehr, the dreaded German military intelligence service.

The SS guard stepped forward and opened the rear door as Canaris stepped out into the bright sunlight, bedecked in his full Admiral uniform. He looked up at the top of the imposing granite steps at the figure of Adolph Hitler, dwarfed by the massive structure known as the Berghof or simply the Berg to those in Hitler's inner circle. Hitler was dressed in a light gray double-breasted suit and surprisingly a brown suede Panama hat. It was perched on his head at an angle, efficiently shielding his eyes from the bright summer sunshine. The hat clashed horribly with the suit. It looked out of place, and somewhat comical on the Fuhrer, but today that was the least of Canaris' concerns. To his delight he saw no signs of Hitler's ever-present gatekeeper, Martin Bormann.

Canaris retrieved his briefcase from the rear seat and proceeded up the steps with an agility that defied his age. Hitler smiled at his old friend, "Admiral Canaris, it's good to see you."

"Likewise, Mein Fuhrer," said Canaris, snapping a quick salute. "Perhaps, I'm a little overdressed!" laughed Canaris, gesturing towards Hitler's Panama hat. "Never! It is not every day that I get to meet a real Admiral, in a real uniform with real medals, and an Iron Cross that they actually earned in battle!" said Hitler, as he returned Canaris' salute.

The Fuhrer was well aware of the Admiral's impressive war record and also his daring escape from Chile in 1915. Hitler knew that Wilhelm Canaris was the real deal. The reference to real uniforms was a direct jab aimed at Himmler whom Canaris disliked intensely. Hitler perpetually fed lines to those in the inner circle about their fellow competitors for his undivided attention. Himmler and Goering were the two easiest targets by far. Himmler and the uniform was too easy a shot for the Fuhrer not to take.

"Ah! How is the fearless leader of the SS? Thankfully, our paths do not have to cross very often," retorted Canaris, always more than willing to land a blow on Herr Himmler.

"Oh, Heinrich has his hands full, believe me," replied Hitler. "We can meet outside on the patio or in the lounge, whichever you prefer."

Canaris glanced up at the bright sun again, squinted, thought about it for a second and said, "Normally, I'd take the patio, but as I said, I over dressed for this beautiful day. The lounge would be the best bet, I think," replied Canaris. His response had nothing to do with the weather or even his hot uniform. Canaris knew that the atmosphere on the patio with its breathtaking views and relaxed atmosphere was not the best environment to utilize a one on one audience with the leader of the Third Reich. He also knew from experience that Hitler much preferred the relaxed atmosphere of his private lounge to any of the numerous locations at his disposal in the vast sprawl of the Berghof.

"Excellent!" said the Fuhrer. "Come," Canaris dutifully followed Hitler to his private lounge. The SS guard snapped to attention before opening the door for the two commanders. Hitler headed for his favorite chair and gestured for Canaris to sit on the peach colored velvet couch. Canaris took off his cap and carefully placed it on the couch on top of his briefcase. Almost immediately, there was a gentle knock on the side door and a maid entered and politely curtsied.

"May I offer you tea or coffee, Admiral?" asked Hitler.

"Just water would be fine, with plenty of ice please," replied Canaris.

"Good idea. Do you care for anything to eat, a sandwich perhaps?" asked Hitler.

"No thank you, the iced water will be fine. I could do with losing a few pounds. I'm spending too much time behind my desk these days. I can feel my pants getting way too tight!"

"Good for you, Wilhelm. You should talk to the head of the Luftwaffe about your self-discipline. Now there is someone who could lose a few pounds, believe me!" laughed Hitler, playfully patting his gut. Another cheap shot at one of the other top dogs, which was just fine by Canaris.

"Not Goering, he just orders ever larger uniforms. Did you see the latest sky-blue calamity?" asked Canaris.

"Please, don't get me started. He looked like a buffoon and I'll tell him so next time I see his fat ass!" replied Hitler, and both men laughed simultaneously. Then Hitler turned to his maid and said, "Two waters with plenty of ice." She nodded, curtseyed, and left.

"So, Wilhelm, you managed to piss Bormann off! Not too many are able to maneuver their way around my gatekeeper." said Hitler. "That's why I met you at the steps myself."

"Yes, I noticed your shadow was missing. He will get over it. He needs to learn that when I request a meeting with you to discuss sensitive intelligence, that it is on a need to know basis. There are some things that a gatekeeper does not need to know...and on this occasion, Martin Bormann does not need to know!" said a confident Canaris.

"I'll remind him that you live and operate in a dark and covert world and are not subject to the same degree of scrutiny that others are. I understand your need for discretion and secrecy, my friend," replied Hitler. He leaned forward and picked up his note pad to make a note of Canaris' request.

"Much appreciated, Mein Fuhrer," said Canaris. The lounge setting was already working its early magic. Canaris had just secured a pass directly to the Fuhrer should the need arise in the future. This put him at a distinct advantage over the others in the Fuhrer's inner circle. Even more important, none of the others would even have a clue that he had his own private access to Hitler. The meeting in the lounge had already produced a nice dividend.

There was another knock on the side door and the maid reappeared with a glass jug of ice-cold water along with an ice bucket and two tall glasses each filled to the brim with crystal clear ice cubes. She sat the tray down on the coffee table and expertly poured two glasses full of water. The ice audibly cracked as the condensation immediately began to form on the outside of the glass.

"Am I going to need my secretary to take any notes for my own records?" asked Hitler.

"No, that would be a little premature at this stage," replied Canaris as he leaned forward and picked up the ice-cold glass closest to him."

"That will be all, thank you," he said to the maid, who again curtseyed and left the room. Hitler removed his hat and placed it on the coffee table. He smoothed down his hair and then he too picked up his glass of water.

"Cheers!" said the Fuhrer.

"To Germany!" replied Canaris. Both men touched glasses and drank gratefully before replacing them, now half full, back on the white linen napkin lining the tray.

"So, back to business Wilhelm, what do you have for me today?" asked the Fuhrer.

"Do you recall that some time ago before Operation Gwilym was cancelled that we had cemented a strong alliance with the outlawed Irish Republican Army?" asked Canaris.

"Yes, they had the ability to get our initial SS troops in using the cattle trucks coming from Dublin into Britain. It was an impressive, well thought out operation, especially working together with the IRA. Too bad our fat friend could not deliver on his big plane commitment!" answered Hitler, getting a little perturbed as he recalled the time, effort and money wasted on the aborted operation.

"Yes, agreed. Well, there may be a silver lining in it for us after all," said Canaris as he casually brushed at the perfect crease on his pant leg, removing a small piece of lint.

Hitler's mood instantly lightened up, "A silver lining, that would indeed be a welcome change, tell me more Wilhelm."

"Recently, I had a most interesting meeting with a man by the name of Seamus Kelly," said Canaris.

"Seamus Kelly? The name does not ring a bell with me," said the Fuhrer, his brow furrowed in thought.

"It shouldn't. He's the Chief of Staff of the Irish Republican Army," answered Canaris.

"Wait, the Chief of Staff of the IRA is here in Germany? You can't be serious," asked Hitler, now confused.

"Yes, Mein Fuhrer, he is currently in Berlin," replied Canaris.

"Good God, Wilhelm! What the hell is the Chief of Staff of an outlaw organization doing in Berlin?" asked Hitler.

"We picked him up and fetched him here," answered Canaris in a matter of fact tone, while casually examining his neatly manicured fingernails.

"Fetched him here? How in God's name did you fetch him here? There is a war going on, at least the last time I checked!" Hitler was not sure where Canaris was going, but he knew it would be fascinating. Canaris was a very shrewd operator. He must have something really good up his decorated sleeve to have out trumped Bormann. He leaned forward on the edge of his chair and waited for Canaris to answer.

"We picked him up at a place called Dingle Bay in Ireland," answered Canaris in a casual tone.

"Dingle Bay, Ireland? How?" asked Hitler.

"In one of our U-boats," answered Canaris.

"Our U-boats are landing in Ireland? Are you serious?" asked Hitler. He already knew that Canaris was.

"We don't actually land, Mein Fuhrer. We have a regular rendezvous point in a remote place on the County Kerry coast, called Dingle Bay. We can get in as close as a half mile and then use our dinghies from there. The IRA set it up for us during Operation Gwilym. We move our agents in and out of there on a fairly regular basis. The Royal Navy is doing a poor job of monitoring that particular area of the Irish coastline. They are too busy trying to protect the convoys heading into Liverpool. It works very well," answered the Admiral.

"Good God!" exclaimed Hitler. "I had absolutely no idea."

"Exactly, Mein Fuhrer, and let's keep it that way, shall we?" said Canaris. Now without Hitler realizing it, Canaris was already in control of the meeting, the way it needed to be.

"Of course. Absolutely! Please carry on," said Hitler. He sat upright, stuck his chin out and tilted his head back, as if to remind himself that he, the Fuhrer was above such trivial matters.

"As I was saying, Seamus Kelly is here in Berlin. I have made arrangements for him to travel as a Diplomat during his stay here. He is being well taken care of as a guest of the Abwehr."

"Good, good," said Hitler.

"Mr. Kelly has some interesting intelligence on the British. Interesting enough for me to send a U-boat and bring him here," said Canaris with a smile.

"I hope so, so what does he know?" asked Hitler, unable to contain himself.

"We already know King Haakon of Norway made it to England with their entire gold reserves. It would…" Canaris was cut off in midsentence by Hitler.

"King Haakon! Don't get me started…that lucky Bastard! We chased him from Oslo almost to the north pole! Damn him! I needed that gold to silence those bastard bankers! You have no idea the amount of pressure I'm under from those arseholes in their business suits!" Hitler seethed for a moment, lamenting again about the lost opportunity.

"Well, I showed King Haakon. We flattened Oslo! And Molde! Ha! That place was wiped off the face of the earth! The Luftwaffe firebombed it. Molde is no more! See what King Haakon thinks of that!" Hitler yelled as he violently slashed his upturned hand horizontally across the coffee table, narrowly missing the top of the water jug. His eyes were now wide open. He was still furious. The missed Norwegian gold was still clearly a very sore point.

"Yes, I heard that it was a narrow escape. However, if I may continue, Fuhrer," said Canaris, keen to keep the leader of the Third Reich exactly where he wanted him.

With a slightly trembling hand, Hitler picked up his glass of iced water. The condensation dripped on his gray pants leaving distinct spots as he took several large gulps before returning it to the tray. He wiped his fingers on the napkin and then stroked his moustache several times. Now finally composed, he took several deep breaths and said, "Please, continue Admiral."

"Thank you. It would appear that what happened in Norway may have spooked Churchill. The British decided to secretly move their gold from the Bank of England in London to the safety of Canada, via Martins Bank in Liverpool," said Canaris.

"I see," said the Fuhrer. "A smart move on Churchill's part, damn him. That old drunkard!"

"Yes, all things considered, it was. Churchill is no fool, he knows that wars are expensive and need to be funded and that gold is the only currency that the Americans will take. The British are all alone. They know that sooner or later they will be firmly under our jackboot. It is a logical move if they want to prolong the war. We know they moved the gold last month in secret on special heavily guarded trains by night over a specific period of time," said Canaris.

"Given the circumstances, it's the move I would make if I were in their shoes. Interesting, very interesting, but where is the silver lining? What's in it for me?" asked Hitler with a scowl.

"Agreed," replied Canaris. "So, here is where there is an interesting twist in the tale. Kelly's IRA have a mole highly placed in the British financial system. The mole reported a total of three of these trains were successfully sent to Liverpool, everything went according to plan. Except..." Canaris deliberately stopped, then reached for his glass of water. He leaned forward slightly to avoid dripping on his pressed pants as he had just witnessed the Fuhrer do. Then he gratefully emptied it. Hitler waited patiently, almost relishing the anticipation. He enjoyed that about Canaris, he certainly knew how to tell a good story. Of all his henchmen, no one was better than Canaris at story telling. Hitler was almost spellbound as he waited for Canaris to continue.

"Except...that the last train that left London stopped in a place called Crewe. There, the last two box cars were separated from the rest of the train and with a carriage of armed guards, these two gold laden box cars were diverted to a top-secret location. The rest of the train then continued on to Liverpool per plan," said Canaris, toying with the Fuhrer.

"And the IRA know where the top-secret location is?" asked Hitler, raising an eyebrow at Canaris, hoping the Admiral was about to say yes.

"Yes, Mein Fuhrer, they do," answered Canaris, calmly.

"Yes!!" shouted Hitler as he slapped his thigh. "Wilhelm! You are the best!"

"Thank you, Mein Fuhrer," said Canaris, as he moved his cap and slowly and deliberately retrieved his briefcase, placing it unopened on his lap.

"This man Kelly, has he shared the location with you?" asked the Fuhrer, his gaze fixed firmly on the unopened briefcase.

"Of course! Mein Fuhrer, you didn't think I sent a U-boat all the way to Ireland for nothing did you?" replied Canaris, with a broad smile, as he fingered the clasp on his briefcase.

"Good! And Seamus Kelly, you can trust him?" asked Hitler, now intensely interested.

"Yes, as I said, we are basically working with the same group that we allied with in the past for Operation Gwilym. He is the Chief of Staff. He is risking certain death just by being here with us. The British would hang him in a heartbeat if they could catch him. The IRA is totally committed to their cause of a free united Ireland. Their hatred for the British runs deep, very deep," said Canaris as he slowly opened his briefcase and peered inside.

Hitler involuntarily strained to peek over the top. Canaris saw him out of the corner of his eye and blocked him with his sleeve that was emblazoned with his Admirals stripes. He slowly removed a file. Placing the briefcase back alongside himself, he opened the file pulling out a series of black and white photographs. He looked at the top one for a second and then handed it to an anxiously awaiting Hitler.

Hitler was literally drooling from the corner of his mouth as he looked at the photograph in front of him. It showed some kind of a tower, or possibly from the shape of it an old windmill in the middle of nowhere. There was nothing else but rocks and a huge quarry.

"This is where the English have hidden 50 tons of gold bullion, Mein Fuhrer," said Canaris calmly.

"Good God!" exclaimed Hitler. "50 tons of gold! What is it? A prison tower or an old windmill even?"

"Good observation, Mein Fuhrer. It's the latter. It used to be a windmill," answered Canaris.

"But where are the guards and the barbed wire fences? Where are any people for that matter? You said they hid the gold in there, right?" asked Hitler, gazing back at the photograph. He reached into his pocket and pulled out his glasses. He fumbled to get them on to take a closer look at the gems Canaris had casually pulled out of his briefcase.

"Correct, Mein Fuhrer. There are armed guards, but they are posted several miles away." Canaris peeled off the next black and white image and handed it to Hitler. He noticed that Hitler's hand was now trembling, ever so slightly, but he noticed.

Hitler looked at a grainy photo of a typical guard post or type of roadblock, the kind you would find guarding an entrance to a restricted area. He could just about make out four figures, a small hut, sandbags, a road barricade, but nothing special. It certainly was not adequate to guard a windmill stashed full of gold. "That's it? Why so few men to guard such an enormous amount of gold? That does not make any sense to me. Where is this place? It looks like it is in the middle of nowhere," asked Hitler. He looked back and forth at the two photographs before checking the Admiral's hand. There was still more to come. Good, very good, he thought to himself.

"Exactly, Mein Fuhrer, it is in the middle of nowhere, that's the point," said Canaris. He handed Hitler a small map of Great Britain with a red arrow pointing directly to the Island of Anglesey. You will recall that Anglesey played a pivotal role in Operation Gwilym?"

"Yes, the vulnerable back door!" said Hitler. "So, Anglesey is back in play? I'll be damned. Tell me the gods are smiling on me today for a change, Wilhelm," he asked as Canaris flipped him his final photograph. It was an aerial shot of what looked like a portion of a rocky island surrounded by choppy seas.

"Oh, very much so Mein Fuhrer. This is an aerial shot taken by the Luftwaffe. They take the coastal route when they go on their bombing raids to Liverpool. I've circled the windmill for your reference," said Canaris.

Hitler peered at the aerial shot. He could see the windmill circled in red by Canaris.

"The smaller circle is the location of the only guard post that you saw in the second photograph," continued Canaris. Hitler maintained his focus on the picture that he held in his now clearly trembling hands. He could make out the second circle. It was far enough from the windmill that it was barely in the frame. He could see a roadway that ran near the guard hut and the single road that teed off it. Then it snaked its way back up to the windmill where it wound around it and returned. He could also clearly see railroad tracks that followed the road but ended in an obvious spur at the windmill.

The area itself was vast and appeared to be devoid of any buildings or evidence of civilization except for the windmill and several smaller buildings close by that looked to be in a state of ruin. Filling the photograph was a series of vast open canyons and pits, clearly showing the rings of mother earth as they got deeper and deeper towards the center.

"I don't see any sign of life or civilization. Where is the nearest town or village?" asked Hitler, still fascinated by the aerial photograph in his hands.

"The tiny Port of Amlwch is closest but it's too far away to be in the photograph. That is the point, the British needed somewhere that was remote but also accessible by rail in order to move the gold there efficiently and without suspicion. The area you are looking at is a vast open copper mine known as Parys Mountain. The British came up with a cover story that the ground water was highly toxic. They cordoned off the one road in and out at the roadblock as you can see. The area is rural anyway and very few would go out there, but you would have to get by the guards to get in, which is why they are stationed there. Churchill went for total stealth. No one pays any attention to this part of the country. It's the perfect location to hide 50 tons of gold!" said Canaris, now excited himself. It was the most excited he had been since Seamus Kelly had shared the incredible information with him.

"I can see that. He's as cunning as a fox this Churchill, damn him!" replied Hitler.

"Yes, but on this occasion an Irish Fox is loose in his chicken coop and he has absolutely no idea," chuckled Canaris.

"Excellent! An Irish Fox!" said the Fuhrer. "But why are the Irish sharing the information with us? It's not every day you find 50 tons of hidden gold bullion guarded by just four Tommies, what are they looking for?" asked Hitler, finally looking up from the photograph.

"Well, it's quite a dilemma for them. As you have so correctly pointed out they are an outlaw organization, so the gold is useless to them. They cannot trade it on the open market, it does nothing to help their cause. What they want are small arms, ammunition and explosives, which fortunately we have in abundance.

They want to conduct a joint operation with us. Instead of taking gold, they would trade their share to us for the ordinance they need to wage war against the British. They get their guns to fight the British and we get the gold...and those bastard bankers as you call them, will finally get off your back, Mein Fuhrer. In a nutshell, that is what the IRA would like. It's a win, win situation, Mein Fuhrer," said Canaris.

"I see," said the Fuhrer, his eyes brightening, as he processed what Canaris was telling him. After the catastrophe of the Giant and missing out on the Norwegian gold, this was the best news the Fuhrer had received in weeks.

"How do we get the gold out? How do we make the switch for arms?" asked Hitler.

"The IRA has all that handled. They are responsible for getting the gold, along with our men out by a lorry convoy on the Holyhead to Dublin ferry. We will pick up the gold and our men by U-boat at the same time we deliver their ordinance at our usual rendezvous spot at Dingle Bay."

"Good, can we get that much gold in a U-boat? They are pretty cramped at the best of times," said Hitler, as his mind recalled his brief claustrophobic visit aboard a U-boat at a recent launch. The thought of cramming 50 tons of stolen British gold into the vaults of the Reichsbank made him giddy.

"A normal U-boat no, but we still have two that we modified some time ago for Operation Gwilym. I assure you they will be ready when needed," answered the Admiral.

"Impressive, you seem to have all your ducks in a row as usual, Wilhelm," replied Hitler.

"Thank you, Sir, but really most of the big moveable pieces were already in place from Operation Gwilym. We just refined them a little, downsized the whole operation if you will." Then he paused, observed Hitlers body language and satisfied that the Fuhrer was now totally captivated, he continued, "It went from trying to capture two active heavily protected RAF bases, to seizing 50 tons of gold hidden in the middle of nowhere and guarded by four Tommies. Given the choice, Mein Fuhrer, which operation would you choose?"

"Easy! I will take the gold. Every time!" beamed the Fuhrer.

"So, a silver lining then after all?" asked Canaris.

"Yes, yes indeed! More like a gold lining!" blurted out the Fuhrer, now visibly animated. His mind continued to imagine crates of stolen British gold being loaded aboard his U-boats. "This is exciting news, Wilhelm. So, I am assuming we will supply the military muscle to take care of the guards. How do our men get onto Anglesey to get the gold?" asked Hitler.

"Correct, we will supply the military muscle. We will be taking them in by U-boat, Mein Fuhrer. Look up at the top right of the aerial photograph," replied Canaris. Hitler snatched up the photograph and looked at it again.

"Do you see that large natural bay with the big sandy beaches?" asked Canaris.

"Yes, I see it," answered Hitler. His eyes concentrated on the coastline.

"That's Red Wharf Bay. It is perfect for us to land a small crack team to do the job," replied Canaris. The Irish secret headquarters are less than a half hour from the landing zone.

"I see, Red Wharf Bay, how many men are we talking about?" asked Hitler.

"Very small, probably around a dozen or so," answered Canaris.

"Excellent, that's small enough, very stealth. I like it Wilhelm, I like it!" said Hitler. He nodded his head as he got up from his chair and began to pace up and down the lounge, nervously ringing his hands as he ran various scenarios in his mind. "So, where do we stand currently?" he asked Canaris who was now digging into the file to produce several pages of typed notes and numbers.

"Well, the Irish are ready to roll. They are naturally anxious to strike while the iron is hot. They have all the assets already in place to carry out the mission. It is all there in the report for you to analyze. We do not know if the British might move the gold at any time, which is why time is of the essence. We basically just need to settle on a number that works for us and the IRA. I have run some preliminary numbers for you to look at, but as you know this is not really my field.

Basically, Seamus Kelly is desperate to make a deal, any deal, to get guns and ammunition into the hands of his men to fight the British as soon as possible. It would be best to run the numbers by your bean counter, Bormann first. Once you agree on what works for the Reich, Bormann can meet with Mr. Kelly to finalize the agreement. Then it just needs your sign off. Given its priority, it would be wise to run it all through Himmler and the SS for security reasons. I would imagine that the Brandenburgers, with their unique skill set would be the natural choice. Then, as soon as we are ready, we move on Churchill's gold. It's incredibly simple, really," said Canaris with an air of confidence.

"Almost too simple, Admiral. So, what is the downside?" asked Hitler.

"We lose about a dozen Brandenburgers and worst-case scenario, a U-boat. We could possibly get a few diplomatic feathers ruffled over neutrality issues amongst the men in suits in Dublin. I am not worried about that. I have an ace or two up my sleeve should they start to kick up a fuss," said Canaris, skillfully sucking in the Fuhrer one step closer. Canaris knew how to close a deal.

"An ace that you can share with your Fuhrer, Wilhelm?" asked the Fuhrer, almost woozy with anticipation. Canaris thought for a moment, enjoying the expression on Hitler's face. He used the opportunity to hammer home his case to bypass Bormann in the future.

"Mein Fuhrer, I also learned from our friend Mr. Kelly that the RAF has been illegally flying their sea planes over neutral Irish air space in order to short cut their way to the Atlantic when going after our U-boats," said Canaris.

"I see," said Hitler, "That is intriguing!"

"Again, as you can see, these are critical pieces of information. If used correctly, they have immense value, too much value to be shared with an overreaching gate keeper. You can see the benefit of me being able to discuss this type of material with you directly, with the absolute minimum of people in the loop," said Canaris, closing the deal.

"I agree, it makes complete sense. This type of information in the wrong hands could also have a negative effect on the bigger picture," said Hitler. He wasn't sure exactly what that was, but he was worldly enough to know how issues with neutral countries could rapidly escalate.

"This is why it will remain tucked up my sleeve until we decide to play it. On this occasion, I have total confidence in the Brandenburgers to be able to pull this off. As far as the downside goes, that's it, Mein Fuhrer," said Canaris, having already run the scenario hundreds of times himself and always coming back to the same conclusion.

"That's totally acceptable Admiral, for such a huge financial gain for the Reich," said the Fuhrer.

"My thoughts exactly, Mein Fuhrer," replied Canaris with a subservient bow of his head. He had achieved his objective. It was easy now to be humble.

"I'd like to meet with Seamus Kelly. I need to look him in the eye. Anyone who is an enemy of the British is a friend of Germany," said Hitler.

"Agreed, Mein Fuhrer. Why don't you brief Bormann. Then he can set up a meeting that works for you as soon as possible. Perhaps bring in Himmler, maybe Goebbels up front, he may be a good source on how best to spin it. Get all the main players on the same page. Keep those in the know to an absolute minimum. Speed is the critical factor. Only you can make that happen Mein Fuhrer, thus my request to meet with you directly and not go through Bormann. I hope you see all that now," said Canaris. He gathered up the photographs and notes from the coffee table and placed them neatly in the folder, which he then held close to his heavily decorated chest.

"Bormann will get over it. You did the right thing, Admiral. I am glad you came. From what you have told me today, I will approve the Operation. This is based of course on us being able to work out the numbers with Mr. Kelly," said the Fuhrer.

"Excellent! Thank you, Mein Fuhrer!" said Canaris.

"Do you have any idea for an Operation name, Admiral?" asked Hitler.

"Yes, actually," said Canaris as he handed the file to the leader of the Third Reich. Hitler peered at the cover and read the typed label. Top Secret for the eyes of Adolph Hitler Only - Operation Goldilocks.

"Goldilocks! Just Perfect!" yelled the Fuhrer. "Thank you, Admiral! Please have my secretary track down Bormann and send him in here. Let Mr. Kelly know we will be in touch, very soon!" He extended his hand and the two men shook.

"Mein Fuhrer!" Canaris snapped a salute, picked up his cap and briefcase, and left the lounge. He had not got to the end of the corridor before he could hear the enchanting sounds of Wagner emanating from the lounge. The Fuhrer was convinced that the gods were again smiling on him and that a new golden fleece was suddenly well within his grasp. He determined right then and there that Operation Goldilocks, the ingenious gold heist would be his creation. He would take the glory for this one himself. He would have Himmler offer Major von Seeckt a chance at redemption. Von Seeckt would surely get the gold this time.

Then he recalled the words of Hjalmar Schacht, his Minister Without Portfolio at their last meeting. That he should be aware of unorthodox opportunities and take advantage of them if they present themselves. An alliance with the IRA to pull off the greatest gold heist in history, with Churchill on the losing end of the deal certainly checked off all the boxes. It most certainly qualified as an unorthodox opportunity. His mind was set. From this moment forth it would be his brainchild. When the greatest gold heist in history against Germany's oldest foe was concluded, he wanted to be sure that Churchill knew who was behind it. Even more importantly, he could finally get the relentless bankers off his back. The Fuhrer was suddenly in a very good mood. Alone in his lounge, feeling very much alive, he smiled, clapped his hands together and did what he claimed was an Irish jig. The smooth leather soles of his new shoes slid effortlessly across his priceless, stolen Persian rug.

Chapter 38

GOEBBELS PLAYS HIS HAND

The Berghof, Bavaria
July 1940

"Herr Goebbels, Mein Fuhrer!" said Bormann as he introduced Goebbels to his leader.

"Mein Fuhrer!" said Goebbels. He flipped a Nazi salute and entered the Fuhrer's private parlor. His delight in being summoned ahead of Himmler for his audience with the leader of the Third Reich was evident in his beaming smile. Himmler was left to pout alone in the waiting room.

"Joseph Goebbels, the Master of Deception!" said Hitler, as he returned the salute and extended his hand. A genuine look of delight flickered across the usually pained face.

"Whatever it takes to further your agenda, Mein Fuhrer. The rest, as they say is just merely details!" Goebbels smiled and shuffled towards the velvet couch that the Fuhrer had indicated for him to sit on. Hitler turned to Bormann who was still standing by the open door, "Martin, please join us. Joseph generally thinks on a big scale and that usually requires big money. With our current cash deficiencies, I'd appreciate your council." Hitler knew that Goebbels loathed Bormann and vice versa. He never missed an opportunity to pair the two of them together and watch them try to one up each other for his attention. It was a game the Fuhrer played on a regular basis with all the henchmen who made up his inner circle.

"Yes, Mein Fuhrer! Of course," said Bormann with delight. "Will you be taking tea in here?" he asked.

"Joseph, would you care to join us in a little chamomile tea?" asked the Fuhrer.

"Yes, I'm very fond of chamomile," lied Goebbels who hated the taste of chamomile, as he glared at Bormann.

"Good! Tea for three!" said Hitler to Bormann, who left the room briefly, then returned and sat in the armchair opposite Hitler and Goebbels. An ornate Victorian coffee table with a bowl of fresh fruit on it separated them. Hitler smoothed over his hair and picked up a manila file from the coffee table and placed it on his lap. He turned to Goebbels and said, "So you said you had come up with something very special to get back at Churchill that you wanted to get my opinion on. What do you have for me Joseph?" asked Hitler. He flipped open the file and glanced briefly at its contents before turning his mesmerizing gaze back to Goebbels.

"Did you get a chance to look over the file I sent you, Mein Fuhrer?" asked Goebbels.

"Briefly," said Hitler. He detested lengthy reports, and with men as bright and entertaining as Goebbels, he much preferred to get the information firsthand.

"Give me the short version Joseph," Hitler said as he closed the folder and handed it to Bormann, who opened it and immediately began to read it line by line. His photographic memory soaked up the pertinent details.

"I realized after our last meeting regarding the upcoming Operation Goldilocks, that we have a very unique situation. If spun correctly, it could land a devastating blow on the British. It won't cost any additional funds. If executed properly, it should do enormous damage to the British morale, which as you know is currently extraordinarily strong because of the rantings of the Drunk! As you have so aptly named him," said Goebbels.

"No additional funds! I already like it," beamed Hitler. "Tell me more!"

"When we last met with you and Herr Himmler, we had agreed on making Major von Seeckt our poster child for recruitment and promotion of the Nazi party. As we have all agreed, he is the perfect specimen of Aryan superiority, and his credentials are unsurpassed. The filmed footage of him receiving his Iron Cross from you personally Mein Fuhrer, is priceless. It will inspire a whole new generation of Germans to strive to be the next Major von Seeckt."

"Yes," agreed Hitler. "He is the perfect specimen, we agree on that." A brief flicker of a smile under the thin moustache signaled his delight in discussing his favorite Brandenburger warrior. "We have agreement on that already, so what else are you after Joseph?" asked Hitler, a subconscious frown was forming on his brow. "You know how pissed off Himmler was over that whole business. Let's not be rubbing salt in the wound now, Joseph!"

"Oh no! Mein Fuhrer, not at all. The operation von Seeckt is now about to embark on epitomizes the message we are trying to send. We are bolder than our enemies, bold enough to enter their back door while they are looking the wrong way to steal their wealth. We outsmart the British on their own soil, then we rub their noses in it!" said Goebbels, his face lighting up as he explained his latest brilliant scheme. "We film Major von Seeckt when he returns, telling us how they outwitted the English and emptied their secret piggy bank. Then we film him victoriously holding up two solid gold bars above his head." Goebbels raised two imaginary bars above his head, then he continued.

"We ask the million-dollar question, why were they moving their gold? Where to? We blow the lid right off their Operation Fish! We tell the British that Churchill and the Royals, along with the government and the country's entire gold reserves are planning the coward's exit, to the safety of Canada!"

"Very good Joseph, anything else?" asked Hitler.

Goebbels was pretty confident that he had done enough. While Hitler was still smiling, it was a good time to wrap up his first proposal. "Yes, think of the visual, Mein Fuhrer. The rats escape the sinking ship! Leaving the everyday British people penniless to fall under the jackboot of the mighty forces of the Fuhrer Adolph Hitler, or starve to death!" Goebbels was now sitting on the edge of his seat, hands gesturing wildly. He had set the table nicely for his showpiece.

Hitler watched him perform. It was so much more entertaining than dealing with the stuffy generals. He loved Goebbels' enthusiasm and his ability to see things differently than the way the military saw them. He had the ability to see things that the young men of Hitler's Germany were yearning to see, such as stories of battles, victory, heroism, sacrifice, stealth, cunning, the superior Aryan brain outwitting the enemy on every level, winning every battle by fair or foul, and taking the gold. To the victor goes the spoils! Goebbels, as far as Hitler was concerned, simply got it.

"I like the idea, Joseph! Very much! Martin, your thoughts?" asked Hitler looking at Bormann, who had continued to look through the file while listening to Goebbels.

"I agree, Mein Fuhrer," said Bormann, reluctantly. "I think that would be a very powerful image, enough to nullify any morale boosting that Churchill is trying to glean from his defeat at Dunkirk. Rats fleeing the sinking ship is something I'm sure Dr. Goebbels can develop for maximum impact. I fully support the idea, but I believe there is a little more in the report that I'm sure the good Doctor is about to share with you." Bormann nodded at the beaming Goebbels to proceed, while seething inside that Goebbels was about to hit yet another home run.

"Thank you, Martin. Since we last met, you asked me to come up with something special, to deliver a knockout punch to Churchill. I have one other vision that I cannot get out of my head, Mein Fuhrer. We have some of the latest movie cameras that the Reich has developed. They are surprisingly small, and easy to operate. I would like to propose now that in addition to filming his triumphant return, that we actually film Major von Seeckt and the Brandenburgers stealing the English gold, right there in their homeland.

The fear factor of our warriors on their shores stealing their gold is priceless. We let them know that we can be back anytime in the dead of night, at a time and place of our choosing. The paranoia would be rampant. We terrify the British, while motivating our own people. It is a win, win, Mein Fuhrer! Let my people film the heist as it happens and I'll guarantee you that the film will do more damage to British morale than Goering and his Luftwaffe could do if they firebombed their cities for a thousand nights!" proclaimed Goebbels as he rested his case and sat back awaiting a response from the leader he idolized.

Hitler thought in silence for a moment. He looked at Bormann, who grudgingly nodded his approval, then he spoke. "Thank you, Joseph. Your idea is radical, but it makes perfect sense to me. The impact of filming our own raid on the British gold and then rubbing their noses in it would be significant. We need to drive a wedge between Churchill the drunk and his people. He is a brilliant orator. We cannot let him get too established. We need to act swiftly, cut him off at the knees with a scandal that he can't recover from." Hitler swiped at the air with his hand for emphasis, then continued, "It's brilliant Joseph, quite brilliant. You never cease to amaze me. You have my full authorization to move forward!"

"Thank you, Mein Fuhrer! Time is going to be of the essence. I can have the camera and two operators sent over to Himmler immediately, that's not a problem. The issue is getting the film back here as soon as possible to process and then immediately go into production. Every day lost is another opportunity for Churchill to rally his people. We can't allow him to recover as you have just so brilliantly stated," said Goebbels as he enthusiastically rubbed his sweaty palms together.

"Martin, any idea on the time frame? The operation is still on for August 17th correct?" asked Hitler who had now stood up and was pacing up and down behind the couch, intensely ringing his hands together, deep in thought, much to the delight of Goebbels.

"Correct, Mein Fuhrer," said Bormann. "Then there is the added time of crossing to Ireland, making the exchange at Dingle Bay and finally funneling it back to Germany by U-boat. That will naturally take some time," he continued.

"Joseph is right, every day lost is another day Churchill can rally his people. He is a lot more dangerous than that old fool Chamberlain. We cannot afford too many more 'We shall fight them on the beaches!' speeches, now can we Joseph? Martin, I do not want to wait for the exchange. Every day is critical to me. What is the fastest way to get that film safely back to Joseph so he can grace us all with it by showing it on the...what's the American expression? the Silver Screen!" said Hitler, now visibly excited. Goebbels had scored again.

"Well, the fastest way is obviously by air, but I can't see the RAF Spitfire's allowing that to happen regardless of what Goering will claim. The safest bet would be by U-boat. Why not have von Seeckt himself bring it directly back to Joseph on U38 via Lorient as soon as they have finished filming the gold heist? Lieutenant Hott is more than capable of taking over the safe transfer of the gold out of Holyhead. We could save a couple of days right there. That would be the best bet in my opinion, Mein Fuhrer," said Bormann.

"That sounds good to me. Joseph, do you agree?" replied Hitler.

"It's perfect, Mein Fuhrer, have the Major bring it directly to me," purred Goebbels.

"Good, then it's settled. I need that film released to the world as soon as possible gentlemen, no excuses," said Hitler.

"Understood, I can have the changes typed up in a few minutes if you would like to sign them. It's not complicated. Shall I summon Reich Fuhrer Himmler now? We will need to notify him of the change in plan," said Bormann. He closed the file, avoiding eye contact with the beaming Goebbels. He immediately began scheming how to get even with the Minister of Propaganda who clearly needed bringing down a peg or two. He was confident that Himmler would be more than happy to assist him in that respect.

"Excellent! Yes, bring in Heinrich. We all need to be on the same page," said the Fuhrer. He clapped his hands together, delighted with his Master of Deception for another bold and brilliant idea. "Now, let's have some tea. Shall we?"

There was a knock at the door. An SS guard entered, followed by a maid holding a silver tray with chamomile tea and sliced apples. Bormann left to retrieve Himmler, who was still fuming alone in the reception area, his paranoia mounting with every passing minute.

Chapter 39

OPERATION MOTHER'S MILK

The Berghof, Bavaria
July 1940

Bormann announced Himmler's arrival and they enthusiastically joined the group for tea. Himmler ignored Goebbels. He could tell by his smarmy grin that the Minister of Propaganda had been weaving his usual glittering web. The Fuhrer began the dialog. He explained Goebbels' idea to film the Brandenburgers and von Seeckt actually stealing the British gold. Himmler bristled at first at the idea, but once he realized the value of such a propaganda film it was difficult to muster any real objection, especially given the glorious publicity it would ultimately bring to his Brandenburgers. Himmler considered it a case of losing the battle to win the war.

It was only when Hitler explained that von Seeckt would be returning by U38 with the film directly to Lorient, leaving Lieutenant Hott to escort the gold to Dublin, that Himmler decided to play his ace in the hole. Himmler had been at the meeting with Hitler and Bormann when Bormann had returned from his meeting with Seamus Kelly, the Chief of Staff of the Irish Republican Army. While the overall details of the plan to steal the gold were agreed to by both parties, the problem had been settling on the split of the gold. Hitler had insisted on the Reich receiving the lion's share of 60 percent, but Kelly was not having any of it. He declared that it was a joint operation and therefore, the IRA would not settle for anything less than 50 percent.

Hitler was furious, but also powerless as he needed the IRA's connections to get the gold safely into Ireland and aboard the Nazi U-boats. Finally, the Fuhrer succumbed when Kelly threatened to cancel the alliance altogether. Hitler simply was not willing to risk losing the shot at securing so much gold, especially as it belonged to his mortal enemies, Winston Churchill and the British. He cancelled his face to face meeting with Kelly but approved the 50/50 split of the gold.

It was later when Himmler poured over the details of the planned heist that he had spotted a chink in the Irish armor. A shrewd negotiator, Himmler had been waiting for his chance to share his findings with the Fuhrer to elevate his standing within the inner circle. The grin on the face of his archrival Goebbels and the fact that he had managed to successfully insert his propaganda department into a covert Brandenburger operation, was the last straw.

"Mein Fuhrer," said Himmler as he returned his china cup to its saucer. "I have something that I have found in Operation Goldilocks that I believe we should take another look at."

"Oh, what is it Heinrich?" asked Hitler.

"A serious weakness that the Irish have overlooked, that I believe we can capitalize on," replied Himmler, as he glanced at Goebbels who was still grinning at him. Goebbels knew that Himmler was going to have to pull a rabbit out of his hat to top his own brilliant performance. He confidently sat back, crossed his legs and waited for Himmler to give it his best shot.

"What kind of weakness?" asked Hitler. He sipped his tea and looked directly at the Head of the SS.

"So, in the plan it is agreed that after the heist is completed, we return to the Irish headquarters at Rhosybol. Here my men will turn their weapons and ammunition over to the Irish. This way they will easily pass through customs disguised as unarmed Irish lorry drivers," said Himmler.

"That is correct, it makes sense to me. We will not need our arms after we have secured the gold. The IRA will meet us at Dublin and escort the lorry convoy to Dingle Bay to make the exchange. Then our men will board the U-boats and return to the Fatherland with the gold. They don't need to be armed in order to do any of that Heinrich," replied Hitler.

"Agreed, it makes sense. Then it occurred to me, what if Major von Seeckt held on to his side arm? It would be easy to hide a Luger in his greatcoat. Once the ferry is far enough out to sea, suppose von Seeckt backed up by sufficient muscle, forced the Captain at gunpoint to sail to a different port?" asked Himmler, eyeing the Fuhrer intensely.

"A different port?" asked Hitler, cocking his head at an angle, while simultaneously raising an eyebrow and looking directly at Himmler. He returned his cup to its saucer and sat back in his chair, waiting for the head of the SS to deliver.

"Yes, a different port, La Rochelle in France would be my personal choice," replied Himmler, who was clearly well prepared. He looked at Goebbels as he said it. Goebbels' smile was now replaced with the beginnings of a frown.

"La Rochelle? France? How on earth does that work for the Irish?" asked Hitler.

Himmler shrugged his shoulders and nonchalantly said, "It doesn't, Mein Fuhrer. That's the point."

"Heinrich...let me have it," said Hitler shaking his head in disbelief at what he thought Himmler was suggesting. He needed to be sure.

Himmler knew that the fifty-fifty split that they had settled on with the Nazis was still a sore point with the Fuhrer. It was time to play his hand. "Well, let us look at the big picture. The IRA are really nothing more than a bunch of part time soldiers who hate the British with a passion, but they are a small minority. Their goal of a united Ireland is a lofty one. It is an ancient struggle that I believe will remain unchanged for the foreseeable future. The reality is that even with a huge cache of arms, they will still be like a gnat on an elephant, up against the British Army.

Their vision, in my opinion is nothing more than a pipedream. No matter how determined they are, the British will put down any rebellion, hard and fast. The IRA will be back to square one, writing songs and poetry, dreaming of unity and drinking too much Irish whiskey," replied Himmler as he took another sip of his tea, before continuing. "The Irish would never in a million years consider that we would take over the ferry by force. Once we have control of the bridge, we can bring the ship to La Rochelle. Remember, the Captain and his crew will have no idea that the gold is on board. He will also have no idea that he is carrying a dozen Brandenburgers. We force him at gun point to La Rochelle. We will then have a neutrally flagged merchant ship full of gold in our possession. What we do with it next…is our choice." Himmler's last sentence hung in the stuffy summer air.

"So, the Irish get nothing? We take the whole lot?" asked Hitler, his eyes now open wider.

"Exactly, all 50 tons of gold," replied Himmler.

"The Irish will not take kindly to that," said Hitler.

"Tough! We are at war. The Reich needs that gold. The IRA will have no idea what has happened. They will be waiting at Dublin to escort the lorry convoy to Dingle Bay, but unfortunately, they will have a long wait. By the time they realize we have double crossed them it will be too late. Besides, who are they going to report us to? The Irish Government? The British?

Let us not forget that they are an illegal organization. They have zero recourse, and you, Mein Fuhrer will have 50 tons of gold bullion to do with as you please," Himmler paused to let his words sink in. Confident that they had, he continued, "If I may be so bold, I also have an idea on how to best use the gold, one that doesn't follow the normal line of thinking," said Himmler, finishing up his tea. He kept an eye on Goebbels who sat silent, his mouth now slightly open. There was a look of bewilderment on his face as he digested what Himmler had just proposed.

Hitler looked at Bormann for his reaction. Bormann had watched both Goebbels and Himmler deliver two stunning proposals that bent the arc of traditional warfare to a near breaking point. Bormann simply shrugged his shoulders. The cynical smile on his face was all Hitler needed to see. He looked at Himmler and nodded at him to proceed.

"I realize the bankers are constantly putting you under pressure about the lack of gold in the Reichsbank, but they have no clue about the gold heist we are planning. So, what if we keep it that way. We tell them nothing about the gold. Instead of giving it to those leeches with their fat wallets, we use it for a much greater and nobler cause," said Himmler, his eyes narrowed behind his spotless lenses as he looked intensely at the Fuhrer.

"What kind of cause Heinrich?" asked Hitler.

"A cause that all of us here in this room believe in deeply, our shared destiny, if you like," replied Himmler. Hitler continued to stare at Himmler as he analyzed what he had just said. Himmler paused for a moment, then seeing a blank look on Goebbels' face, he switched his gaze to Bormann who now had a slight smile on his face. Bormann knew what was coming.

"The Fourth Reich," answered Hitler in a barely audible whisper.

"Exactly! Mein Fuhrer, the Fourth Reich, our future. All of our futures," said Himmler.

"Das Muttermilch," replied the Fuhrer quietly. He slowly nodded his head, his eyes now open wide were transfixed on Himmler.

"Yes, the Mother's Milk! Exactly!" replied Himmler, grinning at his leader.

"We use the gold as seed money for the Fourth Reich," said Hitler, now intrigued by Himmler's new plan. "Carry on, Heinrich," he said to the SS leader with a gesture of his hand.

"That's exactly the plan. We will never get an opportunity as clean as this one, especially for such an enormous haul of gold. Here is what I propose. We take over the Irish ferry as soon as we clear the Welsh mainland. Now that I see the importance of Major von Seeckt returning directly to you with the film, I'll have Lieutenant Hott commandeer the ferry instead. We divert her to La Rochelle. Once she docks there, we turn the Captain and his Irish crew over to the nearest neutral embassy. We replace them with Spanish speaking Brandenburgers, then sail the neutrally flagged ship with the gold to Buenos Aires, via friendly fueling stops along the African coast," explained Himmler before shifting his gaze towards Bormann. Then he continued, "My understanding is that Martin already has excellent contacts with several banks in Argentina that are sympathetic to our cause. I'm sure they would be more than happy to store the gold for us for a small fee," said Himmler as he stared directly at Bormann.

Bormann was caught completely off guard. The smile quickly vanished. He was not aware that Himmler knew of his business dealings in South America. Then he silently chastised himself for being too careless. He had underestimated Himmler's reach. Clearly the head of the SS and the dreaded Gestapo had contacts in every dark crevice of The Reich. He would have to be more careful in the future. He felt the Fuhrer's gaze fix on him along with Goebbels. Both knew Himmler had just delivered a rabbit punch to Bormann.

"That would be a fair statement," was all Bormann could muster after nervously clearing his throat.

"What about the film? My intention is to let the world know that Germany has the gold. We need the film above all else," interrupted Goebbels, to the relief of Bormann, still under Hitler's glare.

"You will still get your film as agreed by the fastest route aboard U38," spat Himmler towards Goebbels, before continuing, "You can dazzle the audience with your Hollywood glitter. Major von Seeckt will still be a star and a hero to the German people, I have no issue with that. But the gold, well that will be thousands of miles away, and as I said previously, no one will ever know. We may get a few questions from those at the top of the banking business because of the film but the reality is we can blow them off indefinitely. What are they going to do, send Hjalmar Schact over in his business suit to threaten us? Ha! Good luck with that!" mocked Himmler.

Hitler suddenly saw the funny side and roared laughing at the thought of his favorite banker trying to find out about 50 tons of missing gold, that would be safely locked up in a Nazi favorable bank vault in Buenos Aires. Himmler was right. The men in expensive suits would be no match for the bruising Nazis that surrounded Hitler and his henchmen. Goebbels and Bormann followed suit. All four of the top Nazis laughed together. Himmler had scored a cracker, easily equal to Goebbels and his film. Finally, the laughter stopped, and all three men simultaneously looked at the Fuhrer.

"So, we shaft the Irish. We take their ship and all 50 tons of gold to a safe bank in Argentina to seed the Fourth Reich. We will use it as mother's milk. Other than the Brandenburgers who will do the dirty work, this does not go any further than the four of us in this room. Am I clear?" His menacing eyes fixed on the three men around him. All three replied, "Yes, Mein Fuhrer."

"Good, then it is settled. I had no idea that either of you had such brilliant ideas tucked up your sleeves. Joseph, I firmly believe your propaganda film will do enormous damage to that drunkard

Churchill. It may even drive a wedge between him and the British people. Nobody would be happier than me to see that! You have delivered for the Reich once again.

Heinrich, your ability to stay focused on the future is admirable. All too often these days, we all get consumed with the moment that we are in. Sometimes we need to look to the future. If I am to build a Reich that lasts a thousand years, then the Fourth Reich has to start somewhere. Fifty tons of gold is an impressive statement. I am approving the double cross of the IRA. We take all 50 tons of gold! So, we have Operation Goldilocks to steal the gold and what is the operation name for your little act of piracy, Heinrich?" asked Hitler as he crossed his arms and stuck his chin out victoriously.

"Operation Mother's Milk," announced a delighted Himmler, grinning fron ear to ear.

"Very applicable, Heinrich. Alright, I'm giving you both my approval, move ahead!" announced Hitler as he got to his feet indicating that the meeting was now over.

"Excellent!" said Himmler.

"Thank you, Mein Fuhrer!" yelled Goebbels as he snapped another Nazi salute.

Bormann sat motionless. His mind whirled as he processed what he had just witnessed. He suddenly felt quite nauseous. What else did the beady eyed head of the Gestapo have on him?

Chapter 40

RETURN FROM NORWAY

SS Headquarters Berlin, Germany
July 1940

Max slumped into the back of the staff car utterly and completely gutted. He had been in transit coming back from Norway, when he was notified that his brilliant Operation Gwilym had been cancelled by the Fuhrer following the devastating crash of the Giant. Captain Dietz, plus his copilot and one hundred and twenty paratroopers had been killed. Further, he was ordered to personally report to Reich Fuhrer Himmler immediately upon his return to Berlin.

It was a short ride to Himmler's Headquarters. Max exited the car and saluted to the guards as he entered the swastika adorned reception area. He checked in with the SS officer at the reception desk and was asked to take a seat.

In his office, Heinrich Himmler cursed as he crumbled up yet another sheet of paper and threw it in his wastepaper basket. He readjusted his spectacles and gazed yet again at the stack of blank paper sitting on his desk in front of him. He thought for a moment, took a deep breath and began to write once again. Before he could even finish his first sentence, his intercom sprang to life as Hedwig Potthast, Himmler's private secretary and secret lover, announced softly, "Major Max von Seeckt has arrived. He is a little early, Reich Fuhrer. Do you want to see him now or shall I have him wait for you?"

"Yes, that's fine Hedwig. I'll see him now, thank you," said Himmler checking his wristwatch. "Have my guard show him in as soon as possible." Then he returned to completing the sentence.

Satisfied with it he continued until there was a loud knock on his door.

"Come in," said Himmler, as he continued to write.

The door opened and an armed SS guard entered, "Major von Seeckt, Mein Reich Fuhrer!" he barked. He stepped aside to let the imposing, immaculately dressed figure of Major Max von Seeckt enter the room. Von Seeckt stood at attention, clicked his gleaming jackboots together and shot out the Nazi salute.

Himmler, imitating an annoying habit of the Fuhrer that he had recently picked up on, deliberately ignored him and continued to write on the paper in front of him. Max stood at attention in silence, waiting. Himmler's pen continued to scrawl across the paper for several more sentences before he added a full stop and placed the pen carefully on the paper. Then he finally looked up at Max and simulating surprise said, "Ah, Major von Seeckt, at ease. It's good to see you again." Himmler stood up and extended his hand, "Please have a seat Major."

"Thank you, Mein Reich Fuhrer," replied von Seeckt, shaking Himmler's hand and relieved that the silent treatment was over. He accepted the chair opposite the Reich Fuhrer and placed his leather attaché case flat on the Persian rug that covered the floor of Himmler's office. He then removed his peaked cap and placed it carefully on top of his attaché case.

"Make yourself comfortable, Major. Undo your jacket if you wish. Our uniforms were not designed for comfort but rather to impress and intimidate," said Himmler, smiling at the young Major in front of him.

"I have noticed that. Thank you, but I'm fine," said von Seeckt, politely declining Himmler's offer. Max was all too aware of Himmler's habit of playing cat and mouse with people. Instead, he sat ramrod straight with his chest stuck out, now bedecked with the much-coveted Iron Cross.

Himmler gestured to the unfinished note in front of him. "I was writing, or to be more precise, trying to write a letter when you arrived a little bit ahead of schedule. I simply cannot get it right as you can see from my wastepaper bin," said Himmler looking at the almost full wastepaper basket.

"Sir, I apologize, I was early. I see that you are using a pen so it must be personal. If you wish I can leave until you are finished," offered von Seeckt.

"No, it's not personal, but no copies will be kept either. It's Gestapo business and in our line of work, sometimes it's better not to leave a paper trail," said the SS Chief.

"I understand, I am sure it will come together eventually," said Max.

"Count on it, Major. Count on it!" answered Himmler. "What happened to your face?" he asked, looking at Max's beet red nose and cheeks that emphasized the small white circles around his eyes where his tinted goggles had been for months. It gave him a racoon like appearance.

"Oh, just a slight frost bite, nothing serious. It's cold as hell up in Tromso." Max regretted mentioning Tromso as soon as the words left his lips.

"Ah yes, Tromso!" said Himmler seizing his opportunity. "So, tell me about your little escapade in Norway. I understand from the field reports that the King, along with his gold escaped your clutches by less than an hour, after you chased them doggedly for months. Say it's not so, Major."

"Yes Sir, sadly that was the case. They had a lot of help along the way. It was very difficult as they naturally know the terrain like the back of their hand. Things happened as they do in war that were way beyond our control. Once the cruiser Blücher was sunk, the odds were always stacked against us. We could never make up the delays that her sinking caused, it had a domino effect. By the time we reached the Norwegian Central Bank in Oslo, the alarm had been sounded. They knew we were coming, and the vault was empty.

We chased them from Oslo to Lillehammer, from Lillehammer to Otta, from Otta to Dombas. There we lost their trail and did not catch up with them again until Molde. That is where it got challenging because they took to the water. They could have hidden in any one of a thousand fjords. We lost a lot of time and did not pick up the trail again until we got to a tiny village called Bodo where we learned that they had continued by boat up to Tromso.

We headed after them, but the Royal Navy had laid a mine field which dramatically slowed our progress again. On the way, we watched the Luftwaffe fight it out with some Royal Navy cruisers. We also knew that they were looking for the escaped party from above, but over land the heavily wooded terrain made it almost impossible to spot them from the air.

We were basically on our own. Many of the places that we chased them were only accessible by boat or ferry. They were tiny hamlets in the middle of nowhere. That is where they had the edge. My men will fight and die anywhere for the Fuhrer, but the sea is not our natural theatre. We adapted the best we could, but we simply did not have the assets available to catch them. To make matters worse it began to snow. The weather was appalling. We did not have any foul weather gear. The goggles belonged to a dead Norwegian," he said, pointing to his racoon eyes.

He continued, "By the time we finally made it in to Tromso, we could see HMS Devonshire and her escort through our binoculars. They were too far out to sea for us to try to follow them and it would have been futile, like taking a pea shooter to a Panzer tank. The Kriegsmarine were nowhere to be seen. We watched them simply vanish into the mist. We had been on the move for 48 hours straight to try to catch them before they were finally rescued by the British. It was a bitter pill to swallow as we were so close," lamented von Seeckt. "So very close."

"I'd remind you, close only counts when playing horseshoes or throwing hand grenades, Major. The Reich desperately needed that gold. Waging war is an expensive business. Our Panzer tanks don't run on fresh air!" snapped Himmler, his beady eyes squinting over the top of his glasses directly and menacingly at Max.

"I apologize profusely, Mein Reich Fuhrer. It was largely a case of…" Max didn't get to finish his sentence before Himmler abruptly cut him off.

"I do not need your apology, Major! I know it was a herculean effort put forth by you and your men. I have read the report. Things went sideways from the moment the Blücher was spotted. It was the most advanced war ship of its day with defenses second to none. It even had its own spotter aircraft, yet it got sunk by a couple of antique cannons built by us right here in the Fatherland!!

Once she was hit, the men could not contain the fire. Then when it got to the magazines...poof!" said Himmler, clicking his fingers in front of von Seeckt's nose.

"Hundreds, maybe as many as a thousand brave Germans lost their lives, just like that. Well you cannot hang that on the SS. Where the hell was the Luftwaffe? That is what I want to know! Goering should have blown the Norwegian defenses into rubble long before the ships tried to enter the Oslo Fjord, where was he? That pompous ass! As far as I am concerned, the failure to capture the gold hangs squarely on his shoulders!"

Himmler continued, "The Fuhrer was livid. Fortunately for you Major, he agreed with my assessment as did Admiral Doenitz. I don't know what the Fuhrer said to Goering afterwards, but he's been very quiet lately." An evil smirk appeared on Himmler's face. Then he went on, "Let us just say, errors by others outside of the SS and home field advantage won the day on this occasion, shall we? Either way, as I see it, we had two big failures. One is that they escaped with the gold, and two, the gold will be used to buy arms from the Americans, which will be used against our men. A double-edged sword if ever there was one."

"Thank you, Reich Fuhrer. A double-edged sword is right, straight through my heart and that of my men," said Max, anxious to move on, but Himmler wasn't finished.

"You are still bitter, Major?" asked Himmler.

Max clenched his jaw muscles but thought carefully before he answered Himmler's question.

"Bitter? No, I believe disappointed or frustrated would be a more appropriate choice of words, Mein Reich Fuhrer."

"Disappointed, that you failed the Fuhrer?" asked Himmler, his eyes narrowing menacingly.

"Yes, of course, but I'm even more disappointed that an opportunity was lost to get much needed gold into our banks so that we could fund the German war machine. I realized that once the King and the gold were in the hands of the Royal Navy, that it was on its way to London and the safety of the Bank of England. It can now be used to fund the British war effort against us. So, it was not just losing the gold, that was bad enough. It was that the gold we needed, instead went directly to our enemy, a double blow.

That, Reich Fuhrer, is the biggest disappointment," lamented Max, "The damage caused to the Reich."

"I see, and the frustration?" Himmler continued with his questioning.

"Frustration! That is easy, because there was such a large amount of gold for the taking. It could have had a drastic effect on the direction of the war. To know that I, Major Max von Seeckt of the Brandenburgers had the chance to possibly change the trajectory of the war or even history, and I failed! Therein lies the frustration. Opportunities for one man to be able to change history are few and far between, extremely rare, one could say. A once in a lifetime experience, lost forever. I will never get an opportunity like that again even if I live to be a hundred. It was my destiny and I blew it," said Max, his eyes staring into space as he relived the painful memory of watching the HMS Devonshire and her precious cargo disappear from view into the cold mist of the icy North Sea. Himmler could see the hurt in Max's face. Satisfied that he had toyed with his favorite Brandenburger Officer long enough, he threw von Seeckt a lifeline.

"Never, is a long time Max," said Himmler, a smile appearing on his thin lips.

"Yes, I know the English have an expression, never say never," said Max.

"Yes, they do Major. I am familiar with it and on this occasion... the English would be correct. Never...could in fact be just around the corner!" said Himmler, the smile on his face grew ever wider.

Chapter 41

REDEMPTION

SS Headquarters Berlin, Germany
July 1940

"I'm sorry Sir, I don't understand," said Max, genuinely perplexed.

Himmler continued to grin. Then he leaned across his desk and nodded to Max to also lean in closer. Quietly he said, "There has been an interesting development and an opportunity has surfaced for you to achieve the redemption you so desperately require."

"What kind of development?" asked Max, his tired blue eyes suddenly radiating a new flicker of life.

"All in good time Major, all in good time. Do you recall in your original plan to invade Britain, you brilliantly utilized our allies, the Irish Republican Army? They were to get your initial commandoes onto the Island of Anglesey by way of the Dublin Holyhead ferry using cattle lorries." reminded Himmler.

"Of course, but how does that relate to Norway?" asked Max.

"It's not related to Norway. Get Norway out of your head. Norway is history! This is an entirely new operation," snapped Himmler.

"Yes Sir, I see. Please go on," said Max.

"Well, the contacts we made with the IRA during the early planning stages of Operation Gwilym are still solid. The Abwehr, under Canaris has done an excellent job of forging a strong alliance with the Irish. Recently, they gathered some incredible intelligence, so incredible that the Fuhrer himself has authorized a top-secret joint operation between the Brandenburgers and the IRA."

"To invade England with the help of the IRA! I'm confused," said von Seeckt, moving a little closer to the leader of the SS.

"No, not to invade, but to acquire something the British have Max, something…very, very precious," said Himmler, waiting for Max to respond, which he did immediately.

"Their gold?" asked Max. His mouth subconsciously remained slightly open as the last word passed his lips. His eyes now intensely focused on Himmler's face, looked for a clue.

"Exactly! Their gold," answered Himmler.

Max's jaw dropped completely. His eyes remained transfixed on Himmler. He knew from his contented smile that he was serious. Max pulled back from the center of the desk and sat back, continuing to eye the head of the SS carefully and respectfully. Then he spoke, "Please tell me more, Mein Reich Fuhrer."

"I'll give you a brief outline Major and no more. But only if you feel confident that given the chance, you can redeem yourself and by default Germany and the Fuhrer also," said Himmler, reveling in how well his pitch was going.

"Of course, I'll gladly lay down my life for just a chance at redemption. I won't let you down Mein Reich Fuhrer, I swear," said Max.

"Good, then here is what you need to know. Listen carefully Major, there will be no more mistakes, am I clear?" asked Himmler, his tone was as ice cold as his menacing eyes.

"You have my sworn oath, Reich Fuhrer. I will not let you down!" replied Max.

Finally, now ready, Himmler began his incredible story.

"Here is what we know from our Irish friends. Some time ago, the British, correctly fearing an invasion from across the channel, decided under total secrecy to move the country's securities and gold reserves from the Bank of England in London to a safer location. Churchill was smart enough to know that there was not a vault built anywhere in the world that could keep out the SS. They had made the decision to move the gold out of London and relocate it up north to Liverpool. From there, it is sent to Canada by the Royal Navy.

The main plan is to relocate the Royal Family, the gold, and the key elements of the government to Canada. That would allow the British to continue to wage war from Canada and the rest of their Commonwealth, backed up by the Royal Navy. The gold would allow them to purchase whatever arms they needed from the United States. They could prolong the war for years, decades even," explained Himmler. Then he paused and watched von Seeckt closely for any facial signs. None were forth coming.

"That is amazing, but it makes total sense from the British point of view. I know the British well. They will not surrender, not when it comes to defending their own island. They will fight to the death, but that is only if they believe in their leader Churchill, which they do. He has done a remarkable job of galvanizing the British people. However, if the King and Churchill were to flee to the safety of Canada, leaving the people to fight on by themselves, well that would be, as they say in England, an entirely different kettle of fish," said Max, a knowing smile crept across his chapped lips.

"Good, we agree. Here is where it gets interesting. At the last minute, the King prudently decided that part of the very last gold shipment out of London to Liverpool would be kept back in reserve should the Battle of Britain turn out in their favor, enabling the government to continue the façade of business as usual. The gold was taken to a secret location in a remote area where it still sits today," said Himmler.

"Good God!" said Max. "Do the Irish know where it is?" he asked, hoping, praying.

"Yes!" beamed Himmler, unable now to contain his sheer delight.

"Where?" asked Max, his face mirroring the delighted leader of the SS. Himmler remained silent. He continued to grin and raised his eyebrows as he shook his head rapidly up and down, encouraging Max to take a guess. Without saying a word, he basked in the moment.

Max thought for a milli-second. "No...not there. It couldn't be!" said Max, his face began to feel flush, his tight collar suddenly felt quite hot. Himmler almost childlike, continued to nod frantically. He smiled like a Cheshire cat. He wanted to hear Max say it, say it out loud. Say the word.

"Anglesey!" Max blurted out. His eyes were wide open in excitement.

"Yes!" cried Himmler. "The Mother of Wales is back in play!"

"No!" yelled Max, slapping the desk hard. Both men erupted in hysterical laughter.

Mistaking Himmler's squeals as a scream for help, the SS guard burst into the room. "Is everything alright, Mein Reich Fuhrer?" he yelled as he looked at his commander's bright red face, now with tears running down both cheeks.

"Yes! Everything is fine! Just fine! Leave us! Leave us!" said Himmler with a wave of his arm. The bewildered guard immediately complied.

After a couple of minutes, the two men regained their composure. Himmler took off his glasses and dabbed the tears from his eyes and spoke first. "Can you believe it, Max? Anglesey comes back into play again. What are the chances of that?" asked Himmler.

"It's incredible, simply incredible!" was all Max could say. He had not laughed so hard in years, neither had Himmler. Both men now felt rather euphoric. Eventually, a silence fell upon them. Simultaneously, each took a deep breath. Himmler again spoke first, as he wiped away his tears.

"So, the Fuhrer has signed off on what is now officially his brainchild, known as Operation Goldilocks, and he wants you to lead a raiding party to steal the gold for the Fatherland. Because I was able to lay the blame on Goering for missing the gold in Norway, you have been given a second chance by the Fuhrer. It's a chance for total redemption Max," said Himmler, sitting back, satisfied, enjoying himself immensely. How he loved being alone in the company of Major von Seeckt.

Max sat in silence as he digested what Himmler had just told him. Against all odds, he had been given another shot at the gold and just as importantly, redemption for him and his loyal band of Brandenburgers.

"Mein Reich Fuhrer, I'm deeply honored. I will not let you or the Fuhrer down. What can you tell me about the operation? I'm fascinated."

"Excellent Major, we knew you would relish a chance at a second bite of the apple. Because of the absolute secrecy required for you to succeed, the Fuhrer has ordered that you will work directly under my supervision. Everything you need to know is here in this file," said Himmler tapping the file in front of him. Then he continued, "So I will just give you a brief outline for now. You, along with Lieutenant Hott and a dozen of your finest men will be taken to Anglesey by U-boat. You will be met there by the Irish who will have the correct assets in place. You will work together with the IRA as a team to seize the gold. Then it will be smuggled back to Dublin, along with your men, using the same cattle trucks and organization that were to be deployed originally during Operation Gwilym.

Now as far as the IRA is concerned, once in Ireland the gold will be picked up at Dingle Bay, by two specially modified U-boats that have been stripped bare and redesigned to haul cargo, not sink ships. The U-boats will be loaded with arms and ammunition that we will exchange for the IRA's portion of the gold. You personally will return alone by a different U-boat to Lorient and then fly directly to Berlin," Himmler paused.

"I'm curious, why would I not return to Dublin with my men and oversee the transfer of the gold? Herr Reich Fuhrer, I'd like to be..." Max didn't get to finish his sentence before Himmler again cut him off.

"That's because you will have another separate task Max, even more important than getting the gold," answered Himmler.

"Another task? Reich Fuhrer, what could be more important than getting the British gold?" asked Max.

"Yes, another task Max. You mentioned earlier that the British would likely collapse if they knew Churchill had deserted them. We have a plan to do just that, to let the world know that Churchill is planning to bail out of England before the going gets too tough. How do you think that will go over with the already distressed British?" asked Himmler.

"I don't understand how that is possible? But there is no doubt it would have a devastating effect on British morale," answered Max. His mind was clocking smoothly into overdrive as he tried to fathom where Himmler was going.

"The Fuhrer feels that if exploited correctly, that it could potentially unravel the British war effort leading to an unconditional surrender! It's that big of a deal Max," said Himmler.

"The Fuhrer has an ability to see things that others don't. But I'm not sure how we would go about exploiting the fact that Churchill was getting ready to flee with the country's treasure. How could that be done?" asked Max.

"Yes, the Fuhrer sees all things clearer than any man in the Reich. Our job in the SS is to do his will, to put our enemies to the sword and to advance our doctrine. If we are to exploit a situation, we leave that to those who practice that line of work, and who would that be?" asked Himmler.

Max pondered Himmler's question for a moment then said, "Dr. Goebbels, the Minister of Propaganda! Nobody is better at exploiting a situation."

"Correct, I have to admit that when it comes to exploitation, Dr. Goebbels is in a class of his own. While I dislike him personally, the man has no morals, his contribution to the Reich has been gigantic. The SS will always be indebted to him for his efforts. Our ranks have swelled to enormous numbers. Young, fit German men have watched warriors like you, Max at their local cinemas crush the Poles and the French. Our recruitment is at an all-time high," said Himmler, beaming at the success of his beloved SS.

"That's excellent news to hear that recruitment is up. We need many more warriors if we are to expand the Reich. So, how exactly does Dr. Goebbels fit into a raid on Anglesey to steal the British gold? I'm still not entirely clear on that part," asked Max.

"Don't worry, Max. We won't have Herr Goebbels and his dancing girls going on the operation with you. But we will, however, send two of his cameramen along with their equipment to film you taking the gold from under the British's nose. Once they have filmed the event, they will give you the film canister and you will be personally responsible for getting it back to the Fuhrer by the fastest means possible. Hence, you will link up with the same U-boat that puts you and your men ashore which will bring you directly back to Germany by the safest and quickest means possible. The cameramen will return along with your team on the Irish ferry to Dublin. The IRA also have access to a high-powered radio transmitter on Anglesey so communication will not be an issue," said Himmler.

"I see," said Max, clearly not happy about the prospect of having two cameramen to babysit on a gold heist well behind enemy lines. However, the more he thought about the propaganda value of such a film, the more the decision made sense to him. Besides, it was of no significance to him, the decision was already made all the way up to the top. All he really cared about was that a shot at redemption had fallen in his lap. If he had to lug along two of Goebbels' cameramen, then so be it. He would have Hott tuck them directly under his wing, problem solved.

"Do you believe in fate Max?" asked Himmler, his beady eyes returning to their interrogation look.

"Yes, Reich Fuhrer, I do, very much so," said Max.

"Good, so do I. The hand of fate has dealt you a Royal Flush, Max. You suffered two setbacks in Norway and now you have the chance to land two crushing blows on the British. You need to make the most out of this. When you return home victorious with the film, and once Dr. Goebbels works his magic, you could be the most famous warrior in Germany, Max. Think of the glory you could bring to the Brandenburgers!" said Himmler as he watched his words sink in.

"I'm honored, Reich Fuhrer and thank you!" said Max, then he continued, "You said earlier, as far as the Irish are concerned the gold will go on the ferry to Dublin. What did you mean by that?"

"Very good, Major. You were paying attention," said Himmler with a grin.

"Always, Mein Reich Fuhrer," replied Max.

"That's because the ferry will not go to Dublin. The Brandenburgers will take over the ferry and bring all 50 tons of gold back to the Fatherland!" said Himmler with a look of supreme confidence.

"We are double crossing the Irish?" asked Max.

"Yes, I suppose you could call it that. Either way, that part is not your concern. Lieutenant Hott will be handling that end. It is vitally important that no one else knows about the double cross as you call it. Hott will keep his side arm and we will have Fritz the Beast, back him up. The Captain will fold like a cheap suit. There will not be a problem. You will lead the team to carry out the gold heist up until they board the Dublin Ferry. Then Hott will take over. Your main task is to rendezvous with U38 and get that film back here double time. Understood?" asked Himmler.

"Understood Reich Fuhrer," answered Max.

"Good, but it's particularly important that you stay grounded. It is easy to get led astray in Goebbels' fantasy world. Let us just say there are way too many distractions and I need your focus on the Brandenburgers where it belongs. Do I make myself clear Major?" said Himmler. A look of pure evil mixed with a hint of anger that Max had not seen before flashed briefly across Himmler's face.

"Perfectly clear, Reich Fuhrer," replied Max, holding Himmler's gaze, unflinching. Max had been to hell and back in his pursuit of the Norwegian gold. He had already killed many times and often at close quarters. While he had great respect for Himmler and his rank, he was never intimidated by him. No man on earth would ever intimidate Major Max von Seeckt.

"Good, then it's settled!" said Himmler as he rose to his feet and extended his hand.

"Thank you again, Reich Fuhrer," said Max as he took Himmler's hand and shook it firmly. Then as he went to loosen his grip, Himmler held on tight, pulling Max towards him. The same sinister look behind his spectacles, "Don't disappoint me or the Fuhrer, Major. Remember, we cannot accept another failure at this level. There will be no more chances at redemption for you." Then he lightly ran his finger across the old scar on Max's cheek and got as close as possible to his face, close enough for Max to smell his fetid breath. "This is your destiny, Major. Tell me you understand?"

Max nodded and said, "I won't fail again, Herr Reich Fuhrer". Knowing the meeting was now over, he flashed the Nazi salute, clicked his heels, placed his cap back on, picked up his briefcase along with the file and left the office.

Himmler watched him leave, then sat back in his oversized chair. A sardonic smile crept across his thin lips. He had always been in awe of von Seeckt. Max was the ultimate Nazi, a true Brandenburger warrior, a perfect Germanic specimen. He was the epitome of what he perceived the master race of the future would look like. Major Max von Seeckt was everything that Himmler had always wanted to be.

Himmler was secure in his knowledge that von Seeckt and his Brandenburgers would be representing the SS in what would surely go down as the greatest gold heist in history, along with a brilliant propaganda coup that could change the very trajectory of the war. This operation could well be the highlight of the former failed chicken farmer's career.

Now, Himmler was quite elated at the thought of cheating the Irish out of their share, to capture all the gold for future generations of Nazis. He could see his dreams beginning to come true. How dare those cow herders and pretend soldiers quibble with the Fuhrer. Things were moving along simply fine. It was good to be in control. He leaned forward, adjusted his cuffs, pushed his glasses further up his nose, and picked up his phone. A moment later Hedwig Potthast entered his office and locked the door. Himmler stood up and unbuckled his tunic belt as she smiled seductively and walked towards him.

Chapter 42

OPERATION FLOUR GRINDER

The Berghof, Bavaria

August 1940

The motorcycle escort came to a stop just past the famous Berghof steps. The SS guards killed the BMW's purring motors and dismounted as the black open top Mercedes they were escorting cruised effortlessly to a halt behind them. The duty guards sprang to attention having been alerted by the entrance guard that Reich Marshall Hermann Goering, head of the Luftwaffe was on his way.

An SS guard stepped forward and opened the rear door. The massive frame of Hermann Goering, clad in his current favorite sky-blue dress uniform, exited and stood upright on the stone pavement. He glanced up at the clear blue sky, a perfect day for flying. However, sadly, that would not be the case today. The Fuhrer had requested his presence. Therefore, his real passion, the one he seemed to be able to indulge less and less these days namely, flying, would have to wait, yet again.

His driver appeared with his gold tipped cane and briefcase and handed them to him, as the familiar figure of Martin Bormann trotted down the Berghof steps to meet him.

"My apologies, Reich Marshall, I was on my way to welcome you when an urgent phone call from Berlin arrived that I had to deal with," said Bormann as the two men shook hands.

"No problem, Martin. I spend my life on the phone these days and ninety percent of the time it's Berlin. Even when I am in Berlin, I still get calls from Berlin! As the saying goes, you may leave Berlin, but Berlin will never leave you!" replied the Luftwaffe Chief, as they turned towards the steps.

"Perhaps you should have gone flying as you had planned earlier this morning when we talked. Last I checked they haven't been able to fit our planes with a red telephone yet!" quipped Bormann.

"Yes, I was just thinking that. Look how clear the sky is. Blue sky with no red telephone, now that's the life," lamented Goering. They climbed the steps towards the oversized, heavily guarded entry doors.

"I hear you," said Bormann. "Well at least you traveled with the roof down on your Mercedes on this beautiful day, that's something I suppose."

"Yes, I enjoyed that. The simple pleasures of life, Martin are few and far between these days. Just to feel the wind in your face for once is a small victory," groaned Goering.

"Well, let us hope the weather holds. Then you can enjoy your return trip as well. Please, follow me. I am not too sure of where the Fuhrer is at the moment. He has had a very busy morning and is not at his best health wise either, just a heads up," replied Bormann.

"Don't worry, Martin. The thought of me taking over will revive him, it always does," joked Goering. Bormann made no comment as both men walked through the entrance door where an SS guard told him the Fuhrer was now in his sitting room. The two men headed down the long corridor to the sitting room. Goering's jackboots echoed off the stone floor as he rhythmically tapped his cane against his pant leg. When they arrived at the sitting room, the door was open. Still, Bormann knocked and announced, "Reich Marshall Goering is here to see you, Mein Fuhrer."

The Fuhrer was sitting on his favorite couch, legs folded, studying a file from the stack in front of him on the coffee table. "Good, that will be all, Martin. Please close the door when you leave." Bormann nodded, frowned at Goering and closed the door behind him as he left. Nothing irritated Bormann more than being excluded from his leaders meetings, especially one with as powerful a figure as Goering. Dejected, he headed to his small office.

Hitler closed the file he was reading and placed it back on the stack. Then he removed his glasses and placed them next to the files. He rose from the couch, turned and smiled, then shook Goering by the hand saying, "Good to see you my old friend. Please take a seat."

"Good to be here, Herr Fuhrer. Martin tells me that you are not feeling too well, what is wrong?"

"Nothing to worry about, the usual gut ache. I put it down to being surrounded by idiots who think they understand Germany better than I do. I will be fine. How are you? Looks like you've added a few pounds since we last met, judging by how tight that uniform seems to be. What on earth are you thinking with that color? Have you lost your mind?" the Fuhrer commented as he looked at the strain on the buttons of Goering's jacket. He loved to tease Goering about his girth, much to the annoyance of the Reich Marshall.

"Me?" countered Goering, "You look like you need to put some weight on! Try eating a good steak once in a while. I need to lose some weight and you need to gain some, a fine pair eh? Besides, I like this color. It reminds me of the open sky and days gone by," said Goering.

Hitler gave him a polite laugh. He still enjoyed sparing with his old friend even though Goering rubbed him the wrong way more than anyone else in his inner circle. The two had a long history together. Sparring over each other's weight went back a long way.

"You know Herman, I give you free reign to run the Luftwaffe any way you see fit. In the last war when I was suffering in the blood and mud and filth in the trenches, you were flying overhead in comfort! It seems things have not changed a lot. I still feel like I'm back in the mud sometimes and you are flying free over my head!" said Hitler waving his finger in circles above his head.

"I wish that was the case Mein Fuhrer, but those occasions are very few and far between these days. I seem to spend my days doing just that!" he said, pointing at the mound of paperwork on the coffee table.

"Ah, yes the paperwork. Nothing happens in the Third Reich without paperwork. We have come a long way together, you and me. Now I am your Fuhrer and you get flown wherever you want by your own personal pilot, but we still cannot get away from the paperwork," said the Fuhrer.

"Yes, Mein Fuhrer. That is sadly true, but you haven't brought me here to swap reminiscences. What can I help you with my leader?" replied Goering, anxious to find out why the Fuhrer had asked to see him.

"Don't be so impatient my old friend. I need to pick your brain a little, nothing major. But as you asked, tell me what you know about the IRA?"

"You mean the Irish Republican Army? Next to nothing, I'm afraid, and if I started to find out about them, Canaris would think I was plotting against him and come running to see you!" said Goering.

"Ah! Your friend Admiral Canaris! Do not forget he gets paid to know about such things. Now, tell me how you decide which targets you will attack in Britain?" asked Hitler.

"Why do you ask? And what has it got to do with the Irish? Oh! No! Don't tell me we have bombed Dublin by mistake!" groaned Goering, his puffy hands briefly covering his eyes.

Hitler laughed, "No, nothing quite like that. I want to know why you decided to bomb London as opposed to say Manchester?"

"Because you ordered me to do so, as you were livid that the RAF had bombed Berlin, as I recall. That and it is a lot further north. It is good for the British to know that we can hit their northern cities. They need to understand that the Luftwaffe has a long reach," said Goering, relieved that his air crews had not inadvertently dragged neutral Ireland into the war.

"Yes, I remember but also I remember you telling me that Berlin would never be bombed, and it was," retorted Hitler, giving Goering a quick jab.

Sensing his Leader's growing sensitivity, Goering knew from past experience that he needed to get the conversation back on track.

"May I ask what all this has to do with the IRA? I understand they have their own special bombing techniques, if half of what I read and hear about them is true."

"I'll get to that in a moment Herman. Now tell me, why have you been bombing Merseyside lately instead of London?" asked Hitler.

"Well, it's somewhat complicated but basically the Luftwaffe has teams that work on what we do in the day and the night over Great Britain. Liverpool and the Merseyside area are high on our priority list because it is where the vast majority of all supplies coming from Roosevelt and the Americans end up. It's their so called lend lease program.

If we destroy the docks where their unloading berths are, knock out the cranes and warehouses, smash the railway lines, generally destroy their infrastructure, then we do the job that others have failed to do," said Goering, taking a swipe at the Kriegsmarine for failing to sink more merchant ships as they made the dangerous Atlantic crossing.

He continued, "In Birkenhead, there are also large shipyard facilities at Cammell-Laird that build warships for the Royal Navy, so that would get special attention by the best pilots that we have. I was told that Cammell-Laird is producing a ship about every three weeks. Obviously, we need to put a stop to that or at the very least slow down their production. We have our differences with the Navy, but my planners like to think that the Luftwaffe can help the U-boats in their epic battle, and it is good for everyone's morale. At the end of the day, we are all on the same team, to loyally serve you, Mein Fuhrer," said Goering, attempting to smooth down the Fuhrer's heckles.

"Excellent, that is what I like to hear. Now, let me explain the IRA involvement." Hitler removed an aerial photograph from the file at the top of the pile and handed it to Goering, then he continued, "Do you remember when the IRA, not the Irish government, declared war on Great Britain? It was generally regarded as somewhat of a joke, but we decided to back them through the Abwehr, and they have supplied us with useful information which has proved to be exceptionally reliable.

Apparently, the IRA has a strong presence in Liverpool. Recently, through Canaris they told us that the mills owned by Spillers in Wallasey that run alongside the docks, now produce more flour and cereals than all the rest of England's mills put together. The grain ships from America that survive the U-boats, birth alongside the mills and the grain is unloaded into giant silos until it is turned into flour for distribution throughout the country.

The IRA told us that if those mills were destroyed by your bombers, the British would face a massive bread and cereal shortage, causing starvation and panic. So, what do you think about that?" asked Hitler, as the large man opposite him frowned as he examined the photograph.

"I can't believe that we missed such a vital piece of information that could help us starve the stubborn British into submission. The IRA have just gone up quite a few notches in my opinion. It would appear that we may have missed the obvious, but sometimes it takes someone not directly involved in the issue to put two and two together, as in this case," replied Goering.

Hitler studied him for a moment. Reasonably satisfied with Goering's response, he asked his follow up question, "So, what will you do now, Hermann?"

"Rest assured, my Fuhrer, I will get my planners to work immediately to target those mills and get our best bomber crews to bomb the hell out of this entire area as soon as possible. We may need to up the power of our ordinance. Those are some huge buildings. They look well- constructed. It will take a lot to bring them down. We might have to use a few of the new parachute mines. May I use one of your phones?" asked Goering.

Goering arose from the straining armchair and picked up the telephone indicated by the Fuhrer. He waited a few seconds and heard the duty operator ask for the number.

"This is Goering, please get me the Chief of Operations at Luftwaffe headquarters. Let him know I am currently meeting with the Fuhrer and ring me back on this telephone when you have him on the line. Thank you."

Listening to the Luftwaffe Chief giving out his orders to his own personal staff reminded Hitler of their early days together in the 1930's. Goering had an exemplary record as an Ace fighter pilot in the last war, along with his huge physical bearing, meant he wasn't a man to be trifled with.

The telephone rang almost immediately, and Goering picked it up, "Goering here, Ah Hans! Listen carefully. I want you to draw up a schedule to bomb a specific area in Merseyside where the flour and cereal mills are situated along the Wallasey side of the Birkenhead docks. Allocate the best crews we have. Arm them with whatever is necessary to blow those buildings off the map. The Fuhrer no longer wants to see them! Have the details on my desk by tomorrow afternoon or sooner. As this is a special operation ordered by the Fuhrer give it the code name…" Goering paused and thought for a moment. Then he smiled at the Fuhrer, who was listening intently, "Operation Flour Grinder…yes, stop laughing, that is what I said, Flour Grinder. Now get on with it or else I will put you through the grinder! Goodbye." Goering placed the phone down and turning back to his beaming Fuhrer said, "There! How is that for Luftwaffe service?"

"Excellent!" laughed the Fuhrer. "But I cannot promote you any further as you already have a title that no one else has. So, instead your reward will be to join me for a spot of tea and a little cake perhaps," said Hitler as he playfully pressed Goering's ample gut.

"There go my tunic buttons!" laughed Goering. Hitler roared. Suddenly, he was feeling much better as the two veterans left the sitting room to take tea outside on the spacious deck with its breathtaking surroundings. Neither bothered to cast a glance at the sulking Martin Bormann alone, glaring at Goering from his office window.

Seventy-two hours later, the first wave of 160 Luftwaffe bombers armed to the teeth with heavy ordinance unleashed hell on Liverpool, Wallasey and Birkenhead.

Chapter 43

BEWARE OF THE IRA

The War Room, Whitehall, London
August 1940

Winston Churchill placed the empty, cut crystal glass down on his desk and savored the last sip of Brandy. It had been a long brutal day. He reached for the matching decanter to pour himself another, then stopped, as his secretary announced through his intercom, "The Deputy Prime Minister, Clement Atlee is here to see you, Sir."

"Good bring him in," replied Churchill, leaning back in his revolving leather chair. He had been in the War Room all day.

The door opened, "Deputy Prime Minister Atlee, Sir," announced his secretary. Clement Atlee walked through the door. He took off his trilby hat and coat and hung them up on Churchill's antler hat stand in the process. The secretary quietly closed the door behind her as she left.

"Good evening Winston," said Atlee, as he headed towards Churchill's modest desk.

"Sit down, Clem. Take the weight off and fill your pipe, unless you have smoked your entire ration already!" beamed Churchill, pouring himself another shot from the almost empty decanter. "Shall I pour you one?" He noted the meager amount left at the bottom of the decanter. Surely, I have not polished off that whole thing already, he mused to himself.

"No thank you, Prime Minister. I'm fine with a puff of my pipe. How's your day going so far?" asked Atlee. He pulled out his pipe and tobacco pouch and expertly worked a small amount of tobacco into the perfect consistency. Then he skillfully filled his bowl and put the stem between his nicotine stained teeth and lit up.

Churchill hesitated for a second, then muttered, "Sod it," under his breath and poured out the remainder of the brandy, filling his glass right to the brim.

"Good and bad, a bit of both really. You know what I like about these private meetings between you and I? Although we are on different sides of the political fence, we agree on what we need to do to win this bloody war. When you bring in a problem, you generally have a solution. Whereas nine out of ten people that walk through that door just leave the problems with me as if I have a magic wand," said Churchill while he pointed to the overflowing wire basket marked "IN" on his desk. "See what I mean!" he said before taking a good slug of his brandy.

"Ah, the magic wand! If you have one, tell me where I can buy one. I shall put it down on my expenses," said a laughing Atlee, blowing clouds of blue smoke towards the reinforced concrete ceiling.

Churchill and Atlee genuinely liked each other, despite being poles apart politically. Both were Army veterans from the First World War. Atlee too, had fought in the disastrous campaign of Gallipoli, and had eventually risen to the rank of Major. While Gallipoli was clearly a black eye for Churchill, Atlee felt that Gallipoli was an extremely bold strategy that had been poorly executed. It had catastrophic results, but he still admired Churchill as a military strategist. The two men were in absolute unison on one clear fact, they must defeat Adolph Hitler and his Nazis by any means necessary.

"So, what brings you here late in the evening?" asked Churchill.

Atlee took his billowing pipe from his mouth, tampering down the smoldering tobacco with his index finger and responded, "Do you remember last week when we talked about why Goering had changed from bombing London to hammering Merseyside instead? We concluded it was due to Liverpool being the main entrance port for American supplies, with an added bonus of hitting the Cammell- Laird shipyard in Birkenhead?"

"I do indeed," replied Churchill, taking a sip and returning to his seat.

"Well, yesterday one of my Members of Parliament with very strong Irish connections, having been born in a little village outside of Dublin, met one of his cousins at a funeral. It was as they say, a classic Irish wake. The Guinness flowed freely and after a few pints, the talk eventually turned to the IRA. This cousin told him that the reason why the bombing was switched to Merseyside was to not only destroy the dock facilities and Cammell-Laird shipyards, but to destroy the Wallasey and Birkenhead grain mills in the area. When my MP pushed him to get a little more information, he simply said that it was the IRA that had informed the Germans of this fact. He went on to say that if the U-boats could not stop the supplies of grain, then the Luftwaffe would do the job instead. That's as much as I know," said Atlee.

"Very interesting," Churchill remarked, taking another sip of brandy. "Your MP should cultivate this contact, for we know next to nothing about the IRA connections to Mister Hitler and we should. Perhaps we could try to turn him to work for us. The IRA hate us as much as Hitler does, maybe even more. If Germany ever made a deal with them to help them unite Ireland in exchange for using the Emerald Isle as a staging ground to invade us, we would be in a world of hurt, Clem. We would be wise to consider such a threat. Our focus is right across the channel but perish the thought that they could just as easily come across the Irish Sea. That would be bad Clem, very bad," said Churchill, his furrowed brow indicating to Atlee that Churchill was seriously concerned.

"I will see what we can do," said Atlee. He smoked the last of his bowl before tapping the ash into Churchill's ashtray that was filled with cigar butts.

"Can you stay for a bit of supper?" asked Churchill, hoping Atlee would be able to stay for a while.

"No thank you, I will be off. I have a meeting in Glasgow tomorrow and need to catch the overnight train, but I thought you would be interested in this snippet about the IRA to add to our knowledge of what we are up against. I will leave what to do about it with you. Perhaps we need to consider strengthening our air defenses around Merseyside to make it harder for Mr. Goering to hit the mills?"

"Good, leave it with me. You are off to Glasgow you said? Is it anything special?" queried Churchill.

"No just routine but the Scots like to see one of us now and again to keep them in the picture. However, if you feel like a trip up north, I'd be happy to step aside," replied Atlee with a smile.

"Lord no. I'm up to my eyeballs here. However, I do have a good friend who is extremely high up at the Johnny Walker distillery. The distillers in Scotland are concerned that if the war drags on, they will be hard pushed to acquire enough grain to produce their whiskey. This would be disastrous, I'm sure you agree," said Churchill, genuinely concerned.

"Yes, agreed. I did not think of that, but you certainly can't make whiskey without grain, that's for sure. Another reason to protect those Merseyside grain mills," replied Atlee.

"Quite, perhaps Hitler is smarter than we thought. Anyway, I assured him I would bring it up with the Minister of Agriculture to see what could be done. He was most grateful and has generously put aside a special bottle of Scotch for me from a small experimental batch they had made. Apparently, it is very smooth. I wonder if I made a phone call whether you could have one of your men pick it up for me while you're there?" asked Churchill, casting a melancholy look towards the empty decanter.

"Of course, Prime Minister. I'll take care of it, anything else?" asked Atlee as he stood up from his chair. "No, thank you, that would be splendid," said Churchill. He flicked through his Rolodex on his desk and pulled out a business card that he handed to Atlee. "Good, then off you go. Have a safe trip and I will see you at the next cabinet meeting, which is shaping up to be rather a three-ring circus, shall we say," said Churchill as he too stood up and extended his hand.

"Good night, Winston," said Atlee. He glanced at the business card before placing it in his wallet, gathered his coat and hat and made his exit. "Good night, Clem," replied Churchill.

Now alone, Churchill clipped the tip off another cigar and pushed the button on his intercom. "Yes, Prime Minister," replied his secretary.

"Yes, get me Johnny Walker's distillery in Scotland, Bill McLaren please," said Churchill.

"Right away, Sir," she responded. Churchill twirled the cigar tip between his lips and pulled the top file from his IN box, opened it, took a slug of his brandy and despite being desperately tired, he began to read.

Chapter 44

THE GOLD HEIST IS ON

Graystones, Ireland
August 1940

S ean O'Reilly was a perfectionist. He liked all things around
him to be neat and orderly. He stretched his arms to their full
extent to straighten the framed painting, that was hanging slightly
crooked on the luxurious wallpaper of his capacious lounge. The
oil painting was one of O'Reilly's favorites. It was a rendition of the
green Irish hills that surrounded the O'Reilly mansion located in
the picturesque village of Graystones on the rugged Irish coast just
south of Dublin. The painting had a small bronze plaque running
along the bottom of it that contained the words:

> 'Oh! here's to Adolph Hitler,
> Who made the Britons squeal,
> Sure, before the fight is ended,
> They will dance an Irish Reel'

Sean smiled at this latest gift that he had received from the Irish
Republican Army. It was for his generous donations of hundreds of
thousands of pounds that he had secretly given to their cause during
the troubled 1930's. A shrewd businessman and third generation
cattle baron, he had risen to the highest echelons of the outlawed
army. With the British being distracted by the Germans, the activity
level had picked up dramatically. Consequently, the demand for
black market arms, and the dollars to buy them was at an all-time
high. The door opened and his faithful butler, Thomas saw him
looking at the picture and asked, "Can I be of any help, Sir?"

"No, thank you Thomas. I was just straightening this picture as it reminded me of what my Mum used to say, that a crooked picture or mirror was a sign that someone we know would die soon. So, perish the thought, I'd better straighten it out, eh Thomas? Our visitor is due to arrive any moment. I expect he may be in a diplomatic car, so I will go out front to welcome him. It is an important meeting, Thomas. So, I want everything to be perfect, which includes this picture being straight. There, much better, don't you think?" he asked Thomas, as he stepped back to inspect the slight adjustment he had made.

"Perfect, Sir," said Thomas. "Is there anything special you wish to arrange for him?"

"No, I can see that you have laid out the small table in my office with light refreshments, so that will do for now. I have no idea how long he will stay," answered O'Reilly. "I'm just glad that someone is actually…" he stopped in mid-sentence as the sound of a vehicle approaching caused both men to peer out of the lounge window.

"Ah! Speak of the Devil," said O'Reilly. The two men left the lounge and walked across the spacious entryway to the massive double oak entry doors. Thomas scurried ahead to open the left door in time for his master to step through and watch as a black taxi rounded the circular gravel driveway and pull up to a stop in front of the entry.

Thomas bolted forward and opened the taxi's rear door. A tall blond gentleman in a black overcoat stepped out, reached through the window, and paid the driver. "This way please, Sir," said Thomas, as he gestured towards the house. "May I present Mr. Sean O'Reilly, Sir." O'Reilly had already walked down his front steps and was on the driveway, extending out his hand.

"Welcome, I was expecting you to arrive in a diplomatic car, but welcome nevertheless." The visitor enthusiastically shook the outstretched hand saying, "Thank you, my name is Hans Haag and I am the military adviser to the Ambassador. I'm afraid that diplomatic cars are followed these days, so I use taxis whenever I can."

"Of course, we know for sure that MI5 have a few operatives in Dublin. You cannot be too careful, that is for sure. Anyway, I am glad you've arrived, so let us go inside," replied Sean. Both men entered the house and followed Thomas through the entryway and lounge, into an impressively stocked library that led to a door marked private. This was the entrance to the personal office of Sean O'Reilly. Thomas opened the door and the three men entered.

"Please," said Thomas, gesturing to the single vacant chair sitting across the desk from the plush tan leather chair that O'Reilly slipped into.

"I can't tell you how anxious we have been. It has been over two weeks now and nothing but silence. It is very concerning, as you can imagine. I was scheduled to meet with Seamus Kelly, the IRA Chief of Staff but the meeting was postponed not once but twice. And then I received a phone call to say that you would be coming instead to explain everything. We have been left hanging so to speak. It's good to finally meet you. So welcome, I am anxious to hear what you have to say. Thomas here, will take your coat if you like," said a clearly relieved O'Reilly.

"Yes, that would be good," said Haag. He took off his coat and handed it to Thomas.

"May I offer you a drink? Tea? Coffee? A drop of the finest Irish Whiskey?" asked O'Reilly.

"I wish! But a little early for me I'm afraid. Coffee, black would be fine, thank you," replied Haag.

"Aye, I hear you, me too. Coffee it is then, and I will have tea. Thank you, Thomas," said O'Reilly.

"Very good, Sir," said Thomas, as he turned and left, closing the door behind him.

"First of all, I apologize for the postponements, but such a meeting is now no longer possible. Mr. Kelly was basically treated as an ambassador in Berlin, and he was able to meet with all the top brass. He had various meetings with the Abwehr, the Wehrmacht top generals, Ribbentrop, Bormann, even a brief meeting with the Reich Fuhrer. He was very much in the loop, but he was forbidden to take notes as all was very top-secret. Everything had to be committed to memory. In view of the importance attached to what we mutually agreed upon, arrangements were made for a U-boat to take him directly to Ireland. A landing party was to meet him at Dingle Bay and bring him straight to you to begin the operation immediately, but as you know he never showed," said Haag.

"No, kidding," replied O'Reilly. "So, where is he?" Haag shuffled nervously for a moment, then looking directly at O'Reilly said, "I'm sorry to inform you but he is deceased."

"Mother of Mary!" said O'Reilly, as he subconsciously made the sign of the cross on his chest. "What the hell happened to him?" he asked, a genuine concern in his voice.

"Incredibly, onboard one of our U-boats on his return to Ireland, he contracted a severe illness and despite the best efforts of the U-boat's crew, he died within a few hours. Fearing that the illness might be contagious, the Captain taking a great risk, surfaced at night and the Chief of Staff was buried at sea, about a 100 miles off the coast of Galway with full naval honors as could be afforded in the circumstances. A sad end to one of the IRA's finest. May he rest in peace," said Haag, as he slowly bowed his head.

"My God, what an end. Seamus Kelly was a true warrior. May he rest in peace," replied a stunned O'Reilly.

"Things were further complicated because of the importance of your Chief of Staff and the actual operation itself. The U-boat was under strict orders to maintain radio silence. Due to security, the Captain had no idea who your man was, or the significance of the information he was bringing to you. Once he had been buried, the Captain went about his business of sinking ships. It was two weeks before he returned to his base in Wilhelmshaven, and then my embassy was informed of what had happened. I contacted Berlin and they replied with specific information that I was to bring to you immediately. Thus, finally my presence here this morning," said Haag. He reached into his briefcase and pulled out a small white envelope and handed it to O'Reilly.

"Well, it certainly explains the delay," replied O'Reilly, as he accepted the letter from Haag. Still reeling from the news of Kelly's untimely death, he opened his desk drawer and removed a small, antique, silver sword letter opener and slipped it inside the envelope, running it smoothly up the seam. Then, he retrieved a neatly folded three-page typed document that he unfolded and proceeded to read carefully.

Haag sat silently and watched O'Reilly's expression as he absorbed every word in front of him. Finally, after a couple of minutes, O'Reilly laid the letter on the desk in front of him, brushed it flat with the edge of his hand and looked up at Haag. "Well, Hans it looks like the IRA and the Brandenburgers are going to be doing a little business together in Anglesey! This is great news!" said O'Reilly.

"Yes, it appears that Mr. Kelly was remarkably successful in selling your proposal to those that matter within the Reich. The Fuhrer himself was intrigued by it and has personally signed off on the operation. It received absolute priority. Apparently, the Reich is in desperate need of gold. War is not waged on the cheap, I'm afraid. The men who will carry out the raid have been handpicked from the Brandenburgers by none other than Himmler himself. They will be led by a brilliant and daring young Major, one of the Fuhrer's favorites. They propose landing the team by U-boat at 2400 hours on 16th of August at Red Wharf Bay, the next full moon. Are you still good with that Mr. O'Reilly?" asked Haag, raising his blond eyebrow.

"Absolutely, we have been locked and loaded for weeks. My men are more than ready, Mr. Haag. It is essential that we move right away. The British might decide to move the gold at any time. We strike now, while the iron is hot!" replied a beaming O'Reilly.

"Excellent!" said Haag. "Are there any questions or areas of concern that you have? Please let me know now if you would be so kind," asked Haag.

O'Reilly looked back down at the document in front of him and turning to the second page, without looking up he said, "The part about the film crew, now that's a new twist. I am not quite sure why that's necessary. Enlighten me on that if you would please."

"Ah, yes. Apparently when Mr. Kelly explained his proposal, somehow Dr. Goebbels, the Minister of Propaganda got involved. He believes it is a unique propaganda opportunity that can be used to our advantage. The cameras are very advanced these days. Two members of the team are fully trained in their operation. They have been instructed to avoid at all costs revealing anything that would compromise the IRA. It is mainly about the Major who will lead the team. Apparently, he is quite the Nazi poster boy. The Reich has high hopes for him. Propaganda is not my field I'm afraid, but do you have a problem with that?" asked Haag.

"No, not at all, as long as you keep the O'Reilly Meats out of it. That kind of publicity would be very bad for business," answered O'Reilly with a chuckle.

Just then there was a knock and the door opened. Thomas entered with a silver tray, which he carefully placed on a small round coffee table. He proceeded to pour the black coffee into a large china cup initialed 'SOR' in gold, which he handed to Haag.

"Thank you," said Haag. He then poured his master's tea in a smaller china cup, with the same set of gold initials. Both men sipped their drinks and continued with their conversation.

Admiring his cup, Haag ran his fingers over the perfect gold leaf lettering. "I can see some of the benefits of being a millionaire, Mister O'Reilly." He turned the cup gently in his hands, "And this is one of them, what a beautiful piece," he said with a smile. "Please, call me Sean, and as a millionaire, I think I can spare that one cup if you wish to keep it as a souvenir of your visit here," said O'Reilly.

"No thank you, my life is complicated enough without having to explain why my initials have changed!" Both men laughed simultaneously and knew the business was now basically concluded. O'Reilly rang the small bell on his desk. Within seconds, Thomas appeared.

"Thomas, bring the Bentley up front. You will be taking Mr. Haag back to the German Embassy. Then on your way back, pick up Richard. I have a job for him. I'll call him to let him know to expect you," said O'Reilly.

"Very good, Sir," replied Thomas, as he exited.

Haag finished up his coffee and rose to his feet and said, "Well Sean, I suppose that wraps up our business today." O'Reilly picked up the letter and re-folded it. Then he carefully placed it back in the envelope. He picked up his cigarette lighter and lit the corner of the envelope. As the yellow flames began to lick their way around it, he dropped it into the ornate fireplace behind his chair. Both men watched in silence for a moment. It flared up briefly before petering out, leaving a wispy smoldering gray shell.

Turning with a smile, O'Reilly said, "Now that concludes our business Hans! It has truly been a pleasure to meet you." O'Reilly extended his hand and said, "As gentlemen, let us go ahead and shake on the deal, as is. I can appreciate that nothing can ever be documented. This alliance between the Brandenburgers and the IRA will remain top-secret, as both of us and our superiors require. Please assure your poster boy Major, my men will be there to welcome him and his team at midnight at Red Wharf Bay on the 16th of August. You can count on it, one hundred percent!" The two men shook hands while maintaining eye contact, then Haag said, "Excellent, you remembered the date and time. A good memory is an invaluable asset, that's for sure."

O'Reilly laughed, "Not really, the 16th of August is my birthday. So, I won't forget it!"

Haag smiled. "I doubt we will meet again. It's very difficult for me to travel unobserved. Because our telephones are being monitored by MI5, if anything changes, I will send a courier with the information. As an added precaution, anyone I send will ask you for a gold monogrammed cup!" said Haag with a smile."

Very pragmatic, you don't miss a trick," replied O'Reilly.

"In my line of business, you miss a trick only once. You don't get a second chance. You end up with a tombstone over your head," replied Haag.

"Perish the thought. Rather you than me, I'll stick to raising cattle!" said O'Reilly.

"An honor, Sir," responded Haag, as the two men left the office and walked back out to the front entryway where Thomas waited in the bright sunshine alongside a dark green Bentley, its engine humming perfectly.

"So, I've been around a lot of diplomats in my time and you seem pretty young to be one. What did you do before all this malarkey started?" asked Sean, as they walked towards the car.

"Ha! Very observant. You are right. I am on special assignment to the embassy here in Ireland, but if and when I ever return to Germany, I will revert to my day job, namely being a Colonel in the Das Reich SS Panzer Division," replied Haag.

"Ah! I knew it, now that fits with your appearance a lot better than a diplomat!" said Sean as they reached the car.

Thomas opened the rear door of the Bentley for Haag, who turned and gave a final wave to his host before slipping into the back seat. Once his passenger was safely seated, Thomas closed the car door and walked around the car checking each tire as he did so. Then he got into the driver's seat and slipped the car into gear. It quietly gathered speed on its way down O'Reilly's driveway. O'Reilly watched the Bentley go out through the gates. He looked up at the clear blue sky, turned and whistling his favorite Irish folk tune, skipped up the steps and vanished through the front door.

Sean O'Reilly was a pragmatic and wise man. However, in his eagerness to finally make a deal to steal the British gold, he had missed a critical weakness in the Nazi proposal. The IRA had left themselves with an exposed glass jaw, that Reich Fuhrer Heinrich Himmler would be more than willing to take a swing at.

Chapter 45

PAYING OFF THE DOCKERS

Dublin, Ireland

August 1940

"Top of the morning to you, Sir!" said Richard Tully, as he passed the two uniformed Customs officers standing outside of the Customs House enjoying the unusual sunshine.

"Aye, same to you Laddie," replied one of the officers. The other gestured back at him with a quick tap of his peaked cap.

Richard smiled at the irony, "If only you two clowns knew what I had in my pocket," he whispered to himself, subconsciously tapping the bulge in his inside jacket pocket.

It was a rare, beautiful day in Dublin. The sun shone brightly in a cloudless sky and his beloved River Liffey sparkled like a million tiny jewels. The ebb tide gave way to the flow tide as it had done for eternity. It was a short walk from the O'Reilly Dublin office to O'Connell street where he made a righthand turn at the massive statue of James O'Connell and headed towards Murray's Pub to meet with his contact.

He stopped at the paperboy who was always on the corner of James and O'Connell and purchased a copy of the Irish Times. At the same time, he casually looked behind him to make sure no one was on his tail. After glancing at the headline, he took the fat manila envelope out of his jacket pocket and without missing a step, slipped it inside the Times, folded it over and tucked it tightly under his arm.

Murray's Pub was dimly lit and reeked of stale cigarettes and booze. An elderly man was on the small stage playing his flute. There were a few locals standing at the bar and a small group of men sat off in the corner playing dominoes. Richard recognized the tall figure in a long heavy black trench coat with his back towards him standing alone at the far end of the bar.

"Danny," said Richard.

"Richard," said Danny without looking up from his nearly empty pint. A cigarette burned in the ash tray next to it.

"Beautiful day out there today," said Richard.

"Aye," replied Danny, still not making eye contact as he picked up his pint and downed the last inch.

"Two Guinness, please," said Richard to the bar man who had moved over to where they stood.

"Two Guinness, coming right up," replied the bar man as he grabbed two pint glasses and began to pour.

"What have you got for me?" asked Danny finally turning to face him.

Danny Finney was a hard man. One look at his gnarled face and crooked nose was enough to tell you that he had come up the hard way and had been in more than his fair share of street fights. Danny was the main man at the port of Dublin. He had been a docker for almost twenty years. In his youthful days, he had crushed anyone who challenged him. He ruled with an iron fist over the illegal contraband that flowed in and out of Dublin. While Danny was sympathetic to the IRA's cause, his only real motivation was money, a fact that Sean O'Reilly had figured out a decade ago. They had added him to the O'Reilly payroll a long time ago.

While Danny had benefited well from the arrangement, O'Reilly was the big winner. Controlling Danny gave him the ability to move millions of pounds worth of banned items into the British mainland without missing a beat. His business had skyrocketed with the outbreak of war. The shipping route between Dublin and Holyhead had become the yellow brick road for Sean O'Reilly. Danny's reputation as a hard man worked equally well with his Welsh brothers who worked the Holyhead docks on the Anglesey end, enabling O'Reilly to import all sorts of items from Britain that were in high demand in Ireland. O'Reilly was quite literally making money, both coming and going.

"Mr. O'Reilly has a very special shipment of grain coming in that he wants to make sure gets the first-class treatment, and I mean first class Danny, all the way."

"How many?"

"Twelve lorries total."

"When?"

"This Monday, 0430 ferry, the very first one out of Holyhead, nice and quiet."

"Shouldn't be a problem. There's very few people or vehicles that take the early one. It is usually pretty much empty."

The bar man arrived and placed two perfectly poured pints of Guinness in front of them.

"Good, that's why we chose it, cheers!" said Richard as he lifted his pint.

"Aye," said Danny as he took a long drag off his cigarette before extinguishing it in the ash tray.

"Danny, Mr. O'Reilly wanted you to clearly understand that the owners of the special grain shipment are immensely powerful men. Any screw ups will be catastrophic for all concerned on both sides of the Irish Sea. You with me Danny?"

"Shouldn't be a problem."

"Danny, shouldn't is not a good word to use with Mr. O'Reilly. He's looking for won't, Danny, as in, it won't be a problem."

Danny turned and glared at Richard, his dark brown eyes burned with anger. Danny moved a little closer towards Richard's face. Danny Finney was a terrifying figure, but Richard stood his ground. While Danny was the enforcer at the docks, Richard was O'Reilly's main man. Both men knew that at the end of the day Richard had the ultimate clout. "Easy Danny, easy. Let's not draw attention to ourselves on such a beautiful day," Richard said calmly.

Danny held his steely gaze on Richard for a second and then relaxed.

"Fine, so tell me Richard, what's Mr. O'Reilly's powerful friends willing to do to make sure that very special grain arrives safely in Dublin?" Danny asked. A thin smile cracked across his lips before he reached for his pint and gulped half of it down.

Richard slid the folded newspaper across the bar towards him.

"Here is a list of the lorries' license plates. There will be twelve in a convoy, all ship together, no gaps. There is five hundred pounds in small bills, you get another five hundred once all twelve clear the Dublin customs."

"Holy Jesus! That must be some really special grain his friends are dealing in," said Danny as he raised his eyebrows. This would easily be his biggest pay day to date.

"I've no idea Danny and I don't care. I'm just doing my job and I suggest you do the same. Keep things nice and simple, you know what I mean?"

Danny lifted his glass again and drained it. He wiped the frothy Guinness from his moustache with the back of his hand. Then he picked up the newspaper, pulled his cap down over his eyes, and looked menacingly out from under its peak, "Tell Mr. O'Reilly it won't be a problem."

"That's good Danny, I'll be sure to let him know. You enjoy your day now." Richard was relieved the meeting was over.

With that, Danny gathered up his cigarettes, and without another word, turned and left. As he opened the door, the bright sunlight streamed briefly through the blue cigarette smoke and across the bar room floor. "Arsehole!" muttered Richard. He leaned back to enjoy his pint and the haunting sounds of the Irish flute. With Danny paid off there would be no problems getting the gold laden lorries back into Dublin. It was time to go to work. An hour later he was aboard the Dublin ferry the Irish Larch heading back over to Holyhead. He would check on the preparations that were underway to welcome the Nazis, led by Major Max von Seeckt, when they landed at midnight at Red Wharf Bay.

Chapter 46

THE LANCASTRIA CATASTROPHE

Saint Nazaire, France
August 1940

When France fell not all the retreating British and allied troops ended up at Dunkirk. Many, including a large contingent of RAF personnel were instructed to head to ports on the west coast of France to be evacuated. Churchill authorized another rescue operation. Operation Ariel was launched to evacuate the troops scattered in ports from Cherbourg down to Saint-Jean-De-Luz close to the Spanish border. It was during Operation Ariel that the British suffered a horrendous loss of life.

Tragically it involved Peter's favorite liner, the SS Lancastria. This was the vessel that the Legh family had enjoyed long holidays aboard cruising the sunny ports of the Mediterranean, as well as numerous Atlantic crossings they made from Liverpool to New York. The Lancastria had three levels of class. The Legh's always traveled first class and as frequent passengers of the Cunard Line they enjoyed the absolute best that the SS Lancastria had to offer.

Lancastria had been in the Bahamas when war was declared. Its Captain, Rudolph Sharp left the sleepy port of Nassau and headed to New York at full speed. The Lancastria had been requisitioned by the British government and was to be retrofitted to become a troop carrier. SS Lancastria, the once luxurious liner was repainted an ominous battleship gray, her portholes blacked out, and methodically stripped of all her luxurious features. She now sported a menacing 4-inch gun and was recommissioned to be the HMT Lancastria.

Two weeks after the success of Dunkirk, Operation Ariel was launched. Lancastria was sent along with a flotilla of ships to various evacuation points on the western coast of France to rescue more of the exhausted retreating British troops along with Royal Air Force personnel and civilians desperately trying to get out of France. Lancastria was anchored about five miles off the coast of Saint-Nazaire in the Loire estuary.

In peace time, Lancastria carried 1,300 passengers and 300 crew. After her retrofit in New York to troop carrier configuration, she could carry 2,180 troops with a crew of 330. In April, Lancastria had participated in Operation Alphabet. She was part of a large flotilla of ships sent to the port of Narvik in Norway to evacuate British troops.

Captain Sharp and his crew performed admirably during Alphabet. On the return journey, the Lancastria narrowly avoided being bombed by the Luftwaffe as she raced for the safety of Greenock, Scotland with her valuable cargo of 2,653 incredibly grateful troops. A week later the Royal Navy was in the far northern port of Tromso. Here, they snatched King Haakon VII of Norway along with his government officials and the country's entire gold reserves from the pursuing Brandenburgers and their leader Major Max von Seeckt.

Shortly after dawn broke on the morning of the 17th June, three officers from the Royal Navy boarded Lancastria to advise Sharp of the deteriorating situation on shore. The Lancastria had been accompanied by another Cunard liner also converted into a troop carrier, the HMT Franconia. But on the voyage to Saint Nazaire, several near misses from Luftwaffe bombs had done enough damage to force the Franconia to immediately return to Liverpool for repairs, leaving Lancastria to continue the perilous trip to Saint Nazaire alone.

The Navy Officers ordered Sharp to take as many people as possible on board, without the usual regards to limits placed by international law. Captain Sharp, knowing how desperate the situation had become with the loss of Franconia, courageously agreed to the order. A flotilla of small boats and destroyers frantically began the desperate task of rescuing as many souls as possible, ferrying them from land to the Lancastria in a round trip that was painfully slow and took close to two hours.

With multiple crafts arriving alongside the Lancastria simultaneously to deliver their disheveled but grateful human cargo, the head count soon became muddled. Thousands of desperate men climbed up nets, ropes and ladders, any way they could to get safely aboard the ship. Frantically, they found their way into the rapidly filling cargo holds, cabins and corridors, anywhere they could find to collapse and stake their claim. The Lancastria cabin crew still dressed in their white waiter uniforms did their utmost to make the exhausted troops feel welcome. The first lucky arrivals were even served bangers and mash with hot tea.

One officer overseeing the loading, estimated that over 7,000 people were taken aboard. The exact number would sadly never be known. In the early afternoon, the Luftwaffe launched another attack, this time scoring a direct hit with a bomb on the bridge of another nearby troop ship, the 20,000-ton Orient Liner Oronsay, killing several crew members and injuring the Captain.

Captain Sharp watched as smoke poured out of the Oronsay's bridge while his own valiant crew continued to pull a final wave of evacuees on board. A British destroyer HMS Havelock advised Sharp to leave the area, but he declined as it meant he would be traveling back to Britain alone without an escort in the U-boat infested ocean. Knowing that the trapped British soldiers and airmen would be doomed if he left, Sharp bravely decided to stay and wait to see what happened to the stricken Oronsay and its crew. They too might need help.

It was a fateful decision. The Luftwaffe returned and this time its bombs found the Lancastria. She took several direct hits, two of them tragically in her holds that were packed with RAF personnel. One bomb reportedly went straight down her funnel. Another exploded close enough to her port side to rupture her fuel tanks spilling thousands of gallons of fuel into the water.

The ship immediately began to list to starboard. In a desperate attempt to counter the list, the order was given to the thousands of terrified men on her decks to move to the port side. Miraculously, the ship began to list back to port side but this time the list was too great. The massive liner rolled over, pitching thousands of terrified men into the cold water and burning oil.

In less than twenty minutes, the Lancastria slipped below the waves taking thousands of trapped souls to their doom. The loss of life aboard the overloaded liner was catastrophic. The breakdown in counting those who scrambled aboard, meant that the exact number that perished would never be known. Estimates of the loss of life ranged from 3,000 to over 6,000. It dwarfed the tragedies of both the Titanic and Lusitania, combined. It was the worst maritime disaster in British naval history.

The loss of life was so great that in the interest of national security, Prime Minister Churchill used the D Notice system to suppress any news of the tragedy leaking to an already jittery population. Although the sinking was announced that very night on the radio by Germany's Lord Haw Haw, little credence was given to his traitorous claims by a skeptical British public. It was at least five weeks later before Peter and the other members of the 92nd Squadron read the reports of the monumental loss in the press. It was a massive blow to the country but particularly painful for the Royal Air Force who had lost so many of their fellow airmen in the catastrophe. The reports were sketchy to say the least. Under the Official Secrets Act, the government sealed all records of the tragedy for 100 years. They will remain sealed until the year 2040.

The Battle of Britain was now well underway and the 92nd was right at the epicenter. They did their best to endure the strain of almost constant aerial combat with the Luftwaffe over the rolling green countryside of southern England. It was beginning to take its toll on the exhausted young fighter pilots. Finally, Peter who had been recently promoted to Flight Lieutenant got a welcome relief when he was granted a long overdue 72-hour leave. It would be his first time away from the RAF and the grizzly conflict since volunteering well over a year ago.

He already knew exactly what he was going to do with his precious leave time. He would head back home to Addington Abbey and take his new MG for a road trip. He would go as far away from the bloody war as possible at least for a couple of days. He decided to drive to Anglesey, the idyllic island off the coast of North Wales. He had never visited the island before. He intended to find a peaceful little Welsh village in the middle of nowhere and enjoy a quiet pint of local ale, while counting sheep. Perfect.

It was getting close to midnight when Peter's train finally arrived at Addington Station and he was delighted to see the smiling face of Giles waiting for him. It was a short ride to Addington Abbey. Exhausted, he asked Giles for an early wake up and went straight to his old bedroom. Everything was exactly as he had left it before enlisting in the RAF. He walked over to his desk and gently picked up the model of the SS Lancastria. It had been a gift from Captain Sharp on Peter's first Mediterranean cruise. His heart was filled with sadness at how cruel the hand of fate could be. How could such a beautiful liner built for transporting passengers in style to anywhere in the world become a death trap for so many?

All those young lives, all those futures and dreams tragically snuffed out in about twenty minutes. It was a brutal war with a ruthless enemy that would not be over any time soon. He returned the model to its stand, said a silent prayer for all those who had perished aboard her and gave thanks for the simple blessing of being home, safe in his warm bedroom. He turned around and collapsed face down on his bed. The time on his alarm clock was exactly midnight.

Chapter 47

ANCHORS AWAY

Liverpool Bay, England
August 1940

By stark contrast, it was bitterly cold just outside of the Liverpool Bay where the Mersey Lightvessel Crosby rode gently up and down on the steady swells of the cold Irish Sea. Since the outbreak of war with Germany, the Crosby had become by far the most popular vessel on the seven seas. The Crosby was constantly manned by a crew of ten and permanently anchored here to warn ships away from the massive sand bank, known as the Mersey Bar, that obstructed the entrance to the River Mersey.

It was a tedious assignment, so the men were relieved once a month. Theirs was an important and dangerous duty with ships continually passing by their vessel twenty-four hours a day. The crew often endured appalling sea conditions for days on end, and considering the meager pay each man received, they went about their business in a professional manner. They had a work ethic that was equivalent to any of the crews on the mighty ships of His Majesty's Royal Navy.

In peace time, Crosby was always a welcome sight for Mariners returning to Liverpool from all over the globe. Now with all-out war and Hitler's lethal U-boats prowling the Atlantic, the lights of the Crosby after a perilous Atlantic crossing, meant the exhausted brave men of the Merchant Navy had survived to live another day. They were finally just hours away from Liverpool's friendly harbors and even friendlier pubs.

Tonight, the crew on watch huddled in their navy duffle coats against the bitingly cold wind blowing across the Irish Sea. They had no way of knowing that they were watching $1.7 billion worth of gold secretly leave their homeland for Canada. As they leaned on the ship's rail, they watched the mighty HMS Emerald flash an "Anchors Away-God be with us all" signal to its escort. The convoy of five Royal Navy ships slipped silently into the blackness of the Irish Sea to begin its hazardous long journey to Canada, avoiding the U-boats that lurked below the surface. It was a deadly nautical game of cat and mouse. The most perilous phase of Operation Fish had just begun. What had also just begun was the ticking clock of destiny, as it started a 48-hour countdown to Major Max von Seeckt and the Brandenburgers pulling off the greatest gold heist in history.

BOOK II

— ◆ —

Forty-eight Hours on Anglesey

Chapter 48

THE FLASHING LIGHTS

Red Wharf Bay, Anglesey
August 17, 1940

The Irish Sea was like a mill pond when the ominous black cylindrical shape of German U-boat Type IX, U38 broke the surface and finally came to a complete stop. As the cold sea water poured off her superstructure, the conning tower hatch was flung open and a bearded sailor emerged. He quickly turned around 360 degrees to make sure the coast was clear before disappearing back down the hatch. A short while later, Captain Heinrich Liebe of the Kriegsmarine and holder of the Iron Cross appeared. He was followed by three uniformed figures, one of whom carried a signaling lamp.

One of the men handed Liebe his Zeiss binoculars that he lifted to his tired eyes and surveyed the shoreline. It was pitch black. The full moon was obscured by heavy clouds. Liebe could just about make out the silhouette of distant hills against the dark sky, but none of the landmarks that he and his navigating officer expected to see were visible. The landscape was devoid of any lights. The people who lived on Anglesey were diligent in adhering to the country's strict black out laws.

Liebe checked his watch. It was exactly midnight. He was right on time. He turned to the men behind him gathered in the conning tower, "Keep a keen eye out now boys. These are hostile waters." Then he turned back to his other side to the signaller next to him, nodded at him and pointed to the barely visible dip in the distant black hills and commanded, "There in the dip. Three times. Commence now!"

"Aye, aye, Sir!" replied the signaller. Lifting up his lamp, he flashed three blasts of bright light. It was accompanied by the audible thwack of metal on metal, one after the other to announce U38's arrival along with its very special visitors from Heinrich Himmler's dreaded SS.

Liebe waited for a return signal as his eyes strained into the blackness. There was an eery silence broken only by the gentle slopping of the sea up against the thick hull of the submarine. Liebe continued to wait silently counting the seconds. He got to eleven when to his relief, back from the blackness came a dim but discernible flash of light repeated three times. "Excellent!" said Liebe, "Confirm!" The signaller returned three more flashes and then quickly followed Liebe down the vertical steel ladder back into the stifling U-boat.

Miles away from the submarine and high on top of the cliff road that followed the coast, Police Constable Kenneth Cooper was returning from a visit to his ailing mother's house. He had been stopped dead in his tracks when he noticed the three clear signals flashing out in the darkness of Red Wharf Bay. Cooper was mortified. He knew there was a nighttime curfew on all fishing and boating activity, so for someone to be out in the bay blatantly signalling was far from ordinary. Then to his amazement, he saw three more bright flashes.

Inside the stuffy U-boat at the base of the conning tower, Major Max von Seeckt was waiting along with his trusty second in command, Lieutenant Hott. Surrounding them in a circle, now emerging from the shadows with their faces blackened were twelve handpicked crack members of the Brandenburgers. Along with them were two very nervous camera operators, who strained forward to gulp in the cool fresh sea air cascading down upon them through the open hatch.

"We are good, Herr Major. Your friends on shore are ready for your visit. We all know the drill. Ready?"

"Excellent! Thank you, Captain. We are more than ready!" replied Max.

Liebe ordered his landing party up the ladder to prepare the three black inflatable rafts to take von Seeckt, his team and their equipment safely ashore. He then followed them up the ladder to join his two crewmen on watch. Liebe hated these types of operations. His boat and crew were sitting ducks out here in Red Wharf Bay. Every second they were above water was a second too long in Liebe's opinion. U-boats should never be used for these types of SS top-secret missions. This was the second time Liebe had used his submarine to put Nazis on foreign soil. He had recently put a German Abwehr agent ashore on Ireland without incident at a secluded spot called Dingle Bay.

As far as Liebe was concerned, a U-boat was specifically designed to operate under water not on the surface. It made no sense to him as to what there could possibly be on the Isle of Anglesey that was worth tying up a U-boat for days like this. And why was he to pick up von Seeckt alone and rush him back to France? How would the rest of the Brandenburgers get back? There was a lot that Liebe didn't know, but he was also smart enough to know that it was better that way. At the end of the day orders were orders and his were simple. Once his landing party was back onboard, he was to submerge, then resurface at 0500 to receive a transmission from von Seeckt that the operation was a go.

Then Liebe was to relay the information back to Berlin. He would go back to his normal patrol, looking for easy targets heading into Liverpool. After 48 hours he was to return to the same location at 0530 on the 19th. His orders were to surface and wait for a second von Seeckt transmission. If all had gone according to plan, he would send another party ashore once it was dark to pick up a lone von Seeckt and return with him at full speed to Lorient. Liebe was a realist. He knew that simple operations often had a habit of going horribly wrong. Right now, his main concern was getting von Seeckt and his men ashore and getting the hell out of Red Wharf Bay to the relative safety of the open sea.

His thoughts were interrupted when a sailor appeared out of the darkness at the base of the conning tower and shouted, "Ready to board the boats, Captain!" Liebe acknowledged him and bent down to the hatch and yelled, "Let's go!"

Hott, with the Beast standing next to him, called the Brandenburgers to attention, "This is it men! Let's form a chain and get those boxes of gear up top. When your name is shouted out, ascend the steel ladder up to the top of the conning tower and get into the raft allocated to you. Be careful of the steel deck as it will be wet and slippery. Let's move!"

The men sprang into action as Max climbed the ladder and joined Liebe. The slight breeze felt good on his face. The journey on the U-boat had been von Seeckt's first time in a submarine. Although the sub was much larger, it was similar to being in a Panzer tank which he had experienced in his training. Both were claustrophobic, cramped, and stank of sweat and diesel. The only difference was being submerged under hundreds of feet of icy sea water. Max would take his chances in a Panzer on dry land any day.

In what seemed like an eternity to Liebe, the Brandenburgers and their equipment were finally aboard the rafts and ready to go. Max turned to Liebe and thanked him for his hospitality and also the friendship shown by his crew towards von Seeckt's men. Cramming sixteen more sweaty bodies on top of a full ship's compliment of men into the bowels of an operational U-boat was inevitably going to be difficult. The men shook hands and Max boarded the last raft as they quietly paddled their way into the blackness towards the shore.

High up on the cliffs, PC Cooper had waited long enough. When no further signals were forthcoming, he was convinced that whoever was out in the bay was up to no good. Cooper decided his best option would be to contact his Sergeant immediately and report the incident.

A single thread on the complicated quilt called Operation Goldilocks had just been snagged, and the slow but potential unravelling of the meticulously planned gold heist had already started.

Chapter 49

JACKBOOTS ON ANGLESEY

Red Wharf Bay, Anglesey
August 17, 1940

Richard Tully had spent the entire day with Hugh Moran,
O'Reilly's trusted eyes and ears on the Island of Anglesey.
Hugh lived alone in a small caravan on O'Reilly's secluded property
located at Rhosybol. Hugh had been recruited into the IRA as a
teenager from the hard streets of Belfast and had been a fearless
and loyal foot soldier. Wanted by the British for the murder of one
of their soldiers, he had fled Ireland and found refuge on Anglesey
in the tiny hamlet of Rhosybol. Here he efficiently ran O'Reilly's
vehicle maintenance division. It was the perfect arrangement for
the outlaw and for O'Reilly.

Now, he lay flat on the sand bluffs that overlooked Red Wharf
Bay alongside Richard. The moon was still obscured by clouds.
Through his binoculars, Richard could just about make out the
dark outline of the U-boat but no more than that. Hugh was
getting increasingly more nervous as he peered into the black void
of Red Wharf Bay.

"Jesus Richard, how long does it take? It's only three rafts, right?
Can you see anything? Where the bloody hell are they?" he asked.

"Yup, three is what we were told," replied Richard in a calm
voice.

"Well, do you see any?" continued Hugh.

"No, not yet. While the moon is covered like this, I can't see a
bloody thing," answered Richard.

"Jesus Christ! What the hell are they doing? What's taking them
so long? Can you see anything? Anything at all?" whined Hugh.

"It's dark out there, Hugh. Relax my son, they will be here soon," said Richard as he scanned the blackness looking for any shapes that might be a raft.

"Can you still see the U-boat? Is it still there?" asked Hugh. He looked up at the sky, hoping for a break in the clouds.

"Well, of course the bloody U-boat is still there. How the hell do you think the landing crew are supposed to get back on board if it dives? You need to settle down my son. It takes a while to load three rafts full of men and equipment," replied Richard.

"Jesus Christ. Where are they? Can you..." he was cut off by Richard.

"Wait! Wait! There to the left! I can see them. Right there!" said a relieved Richard as he handed the binoculars to Hugh.

"Where? Where?" asked Hugh as he adjusted the focus.

"To the left of the submarine. Do you see them?" asked Richard as he pointed in the direction for Hugh to look.

"Yes, I see them. There they are!" yelled Hugh.

"See, I told you so my son. You need to have a little faith," said Richard, smiling to himself.

"Wait! I can only see two, there are supposed to be three!" cried Hugh, now sitting up on the bluff. His eyes strained at the barely visible small craft out in the dark cold waters of Red Wharf Bay.

"There will be a third. Keep looking my son, keep looking," said Richard, still dead calm as he lit himself a cigarette and sat back to wait.

"Wait! I see him, there he is at the back. I see all three now. They are drifting a little too far west!" reported Hugh. He handed the binoculars back to Richard.

"Give them another quick flash so they know where we are," said Richard.

"Yes, Sir!" said Hugh. He pointed his torch in the direction of the rafts.

The lead raft picked up Hugh's signal and adjusted course, followed by the other two rafts. Five minutes later, Richard and Hugh stood amongst the washed-up flotsam as the first raft ground itself on the beach. The two sailors stowed their paddles and then jumped from the raft, grabbing the loops of the safety rope which ran all around the perimeter. They guided the raft further onto the soft sandy beach until it ground to a halt.

At that moment, the clouds finally cleared. The tall commanding figure of Major Max von Seeckt, illuminated by the dazzling full moon, stepped ashore. His jackboots sank slightly in the wet sand. Those footprints in the soft Welsh sand made him the first enemy commander in 874 years to successfully land his force on British soil. The last one was William the Conqueror in 1066. Max von Seeckt had finally fulfilled his prophecy from Operation Gwilym. With a broad smile he said in perfect English, "Good morning, gentlemen. I am Major Max von Seeckt of the Brandenburgers. I understand you have some gold that you might like to trade."

"I'm Richard Tully," said Richard in a thick Irish accent as he stepped out of the shadows and extended his hand to the Major. "And this is my deputy, Hugh Moran. On behalf of the Irish Republican Army, welcome to Wales. We would love to do a trade! Please, be good enough to follow us. We have transportation a little way up the path." He gestured away from the beach towards the cliffs.

With Hugh in the lead, the men followed in single file trudging their way through the sand dunes with Max and Richard bringing up the rear. They finally reached the rough path where they picked up the pace a little. The Brandenburgers kept close together in the darkness and followed the outline of a hedgerow as they continued to ascend upwards and away from the beach. Finally, they reached the road where they could see two lorries parked. The drivers were sitting in their cabs with their engines idling.

With all three rafts now safely back on board, a relieved Captain Liebe gave the order to dive. Within seconds, U-38 vanished from sight and after a few minutes the Irish Sea returned to its rare mill pond like condition. The incoming tide would erase all traces of the Brandenburgers ever landing at Red Wharf Bay.

The men loaded their equipment into the back of the first lorry and the two cameramen and Hott jumped in the back. Von Seeckt and the twelve Brandenburgers climbed into the second lorry. Richard and Hugh each jumped into the passenger seat. Quietly, the vehicles moved away for the drive to O'Reilly's secret IRA headquarters located in the secluded rolling hills of Rhosybol. This would be their base for the next 48 hours.

Chapter 50

IRA HEADQUARTERS

Rhosybol, Anglesey
August 17, 1940

It was about a thirty-minute drive from Red Wharf Bay to Rhosybol. The clouds had cleared for now and the moon was bright. They did not encounter any other vehicles. Finally, the lorries pulled off the road and followed a country lane for at least a mile. There were two well-worn tire tracks on either side of a grassy mound that ran down the middle of the lane. The lorries rocked back and forth as the suspension squealed up and down. Thick hedgerows lined both sides making it impossible to know what was on the other side. As Max suspected, it was more of the same, lush green fields, and the obligatory Welsh sheep.

Finally, the country lane gave way to a well-maintained gravel road that eventually led to a cattle gate with a battered sign that read, TRESPASSERS WILL BE SHOT. Max smiled as Hugh got out, unlocked the padlock and chain, and opened the gate for the lorries to pass. Then he closed it, locked it again and jumped back into the cab.

The gravel road lasted less than a quarter mile and ended in a huge circle. The lorries ran halfway around and then stopped in front of a massive barn. Hugh sounded the horn twice. After a short delay, the light that was visible under the barn door went out. Then, a small door within the sliding barn door opened. Two men stepped out and walked to the edge of the barn door, lifting the massive latch. Both pushed the door to the side and Hugh, followed by the other lorry drove inside. The two men closed the door behind them and turned on the lights.

The floor was concrete. The walls were all corrugated iron and there were no windows. Max could see a series of double wooden bunk beds off to the left. There was a small kitchen with a stove, sink, and a wood burning stove. He also saw what looked to be a well-stocked larder and a large butcher block table that had loaves of bread, several crates of Guinness beer, and a wheel of cheese on it.

Against the right wall was a roughly constructed wooden stage with two easels on top. One displayed a large map of Anglesey and the other a black board with chalk. There was also a small wooden desk and chair. Next to the stage was an impressive array of welding equipment, flood lights, dollies, generators, and lifts. A wooden work bench with a vice, and every conceivable tool was mounted on the wall behind it. There was a large table with piles of old clothes, jackets, caps, and trousers.

Several men had congregated in the kitchen area smoking and playing cards. Two others were lifting weights, another shadow boxed with a sandbag suspended from a rope thrown over the old wooden beam. Others just laid on their bunks, some reading. There was also a dart board that looked like it had seen better days.

Richard again welcomed Max and turned him over to Hugh. Then he excused himself from the group to make several phone calls, the first to Sean O'Reilly, before turning in for the night. Hugh would be accompanying Max on his reconnaissance mission to Parys Mountain and into the town of Menai to test that the radio transmitter on top of the bridge could successfully make contact with U38.

Hott assembled the men in single file, then Hugh whistled and said, "Let's be having you, Lads!" The men instantly stopped what they were doing and gathered to attention. "Gentlemen!" said Hugh, addressing the line of Brandenburgers and hardcore IRA soldiers in front of him.

"I understand you all speak fluent English. Hopefully by the end of Sunday night you will be able to speak a little O' the Irish too!" The men all laughed. "Welcome to Wales! This will be your home for the next 48 hours. You will be working in teams of two, one Irish and one German per team.

Lieutenant Hott and I will be going over the mission with you in great detail tomorrow, and then its practice, practice, practice. It's important that you stay in this building at all times. RAF Valley is close by and their Catalinas often pass overhead at low level on their way to patrolling the coast. I'm sure you're all hungry and tired. We will have some breakfast here for you in the morning. Meanwhile, get to know one other and enjoy some Welsh soda bread, cheese and Guinness beer, and I'll see you all in the morning!" The men instantly made a beeline for the Guinness. The Beast naturally was first to tear into the bread and grab himself a couple of bottles of Guinness. No one challenged him.

"Gentlemen, if you'd like to come with me," said Hugh, turning to Max and Hott. "I'm sure you would like to check out the modified vehicles."

"Very much so," said Max as they stepped out the back door, leaving the men behind to get acquainted. They walked along a small path that took them to another larger barn. Unlike the first one, it was open, and Max could make out the outline of a dozen identical lorries plus a black sedan.

"Here they are," said Hugh proudly, shining his torch back and forth on the fleet.

"Excellent!" said Max.

"All modified to the agreed specifications," Hugh added.

"Impressive," said Max. He ran his hand over the painted fender. The vehicles were new and in excellent condition.

"Yes, we do all the work in house here. When Mr. O'Reilly bought the place in 1935 it had a working foundry. So, he kept it running and then added a machine shop to it. This way we can do all the maintenance and repair on the fleet right here. He has over thirty Bedford's in his fleet. The twelve we will be using are long wheelbase models, so more room to spread the load. We added extra leaf springs and cross bracing to the chassis support rails. Would you care to take a look?" asked Hugh. He offered Max a torch, but he declined. Clearly, the IRA was running a tight ship.

Hugh continued, "We have just a minute or so before we set off to Parys Mountain. Would you like to see the forge?"

"Yes, I'd like to. Please proceed," said Max, indicating for Hugh to lead the way.

Hugh walked by the line of lorries to another smaller barn that had a new building attached to its rear. The men entered the barn, a blast of hot air greeted them.

"Welcome to the forge! "said Hugh. "It gets a little hot in here as you can tell."

The forge had two furnaces that were both in operation. A young man was working the bellows as the bladesmith reached into the flames with a long pair of tongs. Then he pulled out a white-hot billet of steel and walked over to an ancient anvil. He began to pummel it with a massive hammer, sparks flying. It began to take shape one blow at a time. He then examined his work, the billet was already starting to turn red. He hammered it a few more times and shoved it back into the furnace.

The bladesmith walked over to a grinding wheel and went back to work shaping what looked like a long bowie knife. Max had always been fascinated by the forging process. Man's ability to create something functional by pounding a lump of molten metal into any shape he wanted was mesmerizing. While attending Eton, he had often spent his summers in Swansea working in the smelting factories owned by his family. There was something about white hot metal that intrigued him. If time had allowed, he would have loved nothing better than to watch the bladesmith forge a new blade from the billet. It was a process that had basically remained unchanged for thousands of years.

"Very impressive," said Max. Having seen enough, the three men left the forge. Hott went back to the first barn to rejoin the men and hopefully enjoy a bottle of Guinness. Max followed Hugh to the Ford car that was lined up alongside the lorries and climbed into the passenger seat for the short ride to Parys Mountain.

Chapter 51

RECON AT PARYS MOUNTAIN

Parys Mountain, Anglesey

August 17, 1940

Hugh drove for about ten minutes before he pulled the car off in a layby and parked it under an overhanging oak tree. "If you stay on this road for another couple of miles, you will hit the British roadblock. No point in ruffling any feathers tonight. We'll go on foot from here," said Hugh as he retrieved a small rucksack from the back seat.

There was a little gap in the stone wall where the pair stepped through. They began to hike across the first of many rolling open pastures, now clearly lit by the Anglesey summer moon. It had finally developed into a perfect night, warm with a little wind. The stars were simply incredible.

"I've never seen so many stars in my entire life," said Max, gazing up at the clear night sky. "Aye," said Hugh. "That's Anglesey for you, you're so far away from civilization here. I guess the air is just purer, and with no big city lights you can literally see forever." Max thought about that for a moment. Hugh had a point. He decided that after the war was won, he would spend more time in the countryside. Who knows, perhaps he would take up blade making with his very own forge out in the middle of nowhere.

After they had been moving at a good speed for close to an hour, Hugh finally stopped at an old, ruined stone shed. Several pieces of rusted ancient farm equipment were randomly scattered around it. He dug in his rucksack and pulled out a canteen of water, "Drink?" he asked, handing Max the canteen.

"Thank you," said Max. The water was cool and refreshing. Hugh then pulled out a set of binoculars and exchanged them for the canteen.

"The next field we cross will have a stone wall that we will follow to the right. Then we'll go up to the crest of the hill. At that point, we will be able to see the Army check point where they will be within ear shot, so we must be careful. From there, we will head out to the windmill." He took a good swig from the canteen and returned it to his rucksack. "You good?" he asked.

"Let's go," answered Max.

When they got to the crest, they carefully peered over the top of the wall. The check point was about 100 yards away. Through the binoculars, Max could clearly make out the outline of the small guard hut and the roadblock.

"I can't see any guards," he whispered, without taking his eyes off the hut's door.

"Aye, you won't. At this hour, they are either asleep or playing cards. This is the only entrance into Parys Mountain. Hardly any traffic comes this way during the day, let alone in the dead of night. Trust me, there are four armed guards at all times. Poor sods, you want to talk about boredom, especially when it rains. There's absolutely nothing out here. You can only play so much poker. I'd go completely nuts! Do you see the railroad tracks?"

"Yes," said Max. He could make out the parallel shiny rails.

"OK, they go all the way up to the windmill. Tomorrow, when you get past the check point, you will follow them. Do you see the dirt road to the right of the tracks?" asked Hugh.

"Yes, I can just about make it out," replied Max.

"Good that's the way you will get in and out. It's a gradual climb for about a half mile maybe, then it becomes shale, gravel, and rocks. It zig zags all the way to the top. It's plenty wide for the lorries, just avoid the very edge. It's a one-way ticket if you go over the rim. Tonight, we are going to join it a little further up, but tomorrow this is where you will enter and leave from. Then it's a straight shot back to the barn. You just make a left on the road where the roadblock is. Cross over the railroad tracks and that will take you right back to Rhosybol. You good?" asked Hugh.

"Yes," said Max, and he handed Hugh the binoculars back.

"Ok, follow me. It's quite a hike, all uphill I'm afraid. Let's go!" said Hugh and the two men ducked back behind the wall and set off for the windmill. They had only crossed a couple of fields when Max felt them beginning to climb and the lush green grass under foot gave way to harsh shale and gravel.

Max was in excellent shape, but he had worked up a full sweat by the time they arrived at the summit and he finally got his first look at the ruined stone tower. It had always been referred to simply as the windmill. He knew now why no one came to Parys Mountain. It was a dry barren wasteland. There was absolutely nothing out here. The British seem to have found the perfect hiding place for their 50 tons of gold.

Hugh interrupted his thoughts, "There's barbed wire across the road up here. You will have wire cutters to clear it completely tomorrow night. Tonight, there's a small drainage ditch that runs alongside the road. We cleared out some of the rocks already, so we can duck under the wire there and get right up to the windmill. You ready?"

"After you," said Max, impressed with the sinewy Irishman's stamina.

Hugh walked further towards the barbed wire then left the shale road and climbed into the ditch, ducking down. He shined his torch on the barbed wire for a minute, then wriggling along on his belly, he slid under the wire with ease. Then he held it up for Max to follow him. The two men climbed out of the ditch and finally walked up to the windmill. Max made a beeline to the door, his jackboots crunching on the gravel and shale. He felt the steel and ran his hands slowly over the surface.

"Here," said Hugh, handing him the torch. Max took it and began to shine it over the entire surface. "It's in several layers, all welded together," said Hugh. "The plates total about a foot thick."

"I see," said Max, continuing to examine the door. It was very rough in its raw state, already showing signs of rust. To Max, it seemed almost medieval.

"The Brits had all sorts of problems, the biggest being the arch shape at the top. There's not a secure safe door in the land that they could pilfer that's got an arched top to it. So, they had to build one here on site. The challenge was the weight. Once they had it constructed, it was impossible to get it hinged properly into the frame. The old stone walls are not exactly what you would call square and plumb. In the end they abandoned that idea. They decided instead to anchor the door directly into the stone using these custom anchors," said Hugh, pointing at what appeared to be four steel boxes, two either side, positioned where the hinge would normally be.

"If you imagine a giant steel H," continued Hugh, making a U shape with his thumb and index finger, "They wrapped half of the H around the stone wall and anchored it directly into the stone using huge steel construction bolts. The other half was wrapped around the door. Then they lifted the door into place, lined up the two U shapes and welded everything together. Then they welded these plates on top of the face for good measure. They weren't bothered about aesthetics or getting in and out. As far as the Brits were concerned, the gold would remain hidden until the War was won. Then they could come back out, pick it up and return it to the Bank of England vault."

"That's amazing. How could you possibly know what is behind these plates?" asked Max, lightly tapping the plate with the torch.

"We had a mole who was perfectly placed. The Royal Engineers took great delight in showing him exactly how they did it. Lucky for us," smiled Hugh.

"The luck of the Irish, perhaps?" replied Max.

"Aye, you could say that. Hopefully, it will continue for us tomorrow night," said Hugh.

"I think we might need more than Irish luck, Hugh. So how do you propose to get through this thing?" asked Max, kicking the steel door with his jackboot.

"We're not," replied Hugh with an impish grin.

"Pardon?" asked Max

"We go through here." Hugh slapped his palm on the steel plate covering the bottom H that he had just described to Max.

"Really?" asked Max, now genuinely intrigued.

"Yes, the Brits have an Achilles heel so to speak. We just burn through these plates. Behind them are the anchor bolts. We cut through them and...Bob's your Uncle!" Hugh brought one palm down slapping squarely on the other, indicating the door falling out of its opening. "She'll come right out!"

"Really?" repeated Max. He continued, "That can't be easy. It would take a highly skilled welder to even get through to the bolt, and the space to work in there has to be limited."

"Aye, it would, but we don't have a skilled welder...we have the very best! And we have two of them!" boasted Hugh.

"The very best? That's quite a claim," countered Max.

"You'll see tomorrow night. You're familiar with Cammell Laird?" asked Hugh.

"The ship builder in Birkenhead?"

"Correct. We have two twin brothers, the Murphy boys. They are both certified Master Welders from Cammell Laird. They don't come any better. Nobody has cut through more steel than those boys. They are super competitive. They've egged each other on their whole professional career and now they work for us. Rumor is they built the HMS Rodney between them! They did all the suspension and extra bracing on the lorries too. You'll be impressed," said Hugh. "Seen enough?"

"Yes, I'm glad we came," replied Max. "You have clearly done your homework. Thank you, Hugh."

"OK, we will need to put on a bit of a trot on the way back. It's all downhill, stay away from the edges. If you go over, I'm not stopping to get you. We need to get to the bridge while it's still early and no one is around so you can check out the radio. You ready?" asked Hugh.

"After you!" answered Max.

The two men left the windmill and began the long hike back to the car. The very first faint traces of daylight began to break across the eastern sky.

Chapter 52

The Menai Bridge

Menai, Anglesey
August 17, 1940

M ax was mightily impressed with the Menai Bridge. To
say it was an engineering marvel was an understatement.
Now that he was up close, he could get an idea of the scale of the
rebuilding work that was underway. The project had been started
before the war broke out and was finally nearing completion after
a frantic final push. Hugh stopped the car and parked on Telford
Road.

"Ok, so it's the nearest tower to us. Take the construction lift to
the top platform where the crane is mounted. The British radio hut
is located there. Here, you'll need this," said Hugh, as he handed
Max a key on a small ring.

"They keep the hut locked at all times and this is the key.
Sometimes they padlock the gate on the lift. It's hit and miss I'm
afraid. If it's locked, you will need to take the ladder up. I hope
you've got a good head for heights. Just don't look down and you'll
be fine!" said Hugh with an impish smile that lit up his rugged face.

"How did you get the key?" asked Max.

"Let's just say it fell off the back of a lorry. One of our boys used
to be a locksmith. We can make anything at our shop," answered
Hugh nonchalantly.

"That helps," replied Max.

"And best if you take this also. You shouldn't run into anyone
at this hour, but you can never be too careful." Hugh reached over
into the back seat and pulled out a worn brown leather satchel

with the initial's WM painted on it. He also handed him a black work jacket with leather patches on the shoulders and elbows.

"Unfortunately, we don't have any control on the bridge. There are too many out of towners nosing around. So, we put together a new identity for you to use whenever you need to make contact with your U-boat. Your cover is that you work for the Ministry of Transport as a Quality Inspector. Your name is Billy Muskett and you're here to do a routine inspection on the rivets. There are enough measuring devices in this satchel to pass any inspection. There are also several fake documents to bolster your cover if you get stopped by anyone. Oh! and this…" he said, reaching over into the back seat again. "It's a set of plans of the bridge, and of course, the cap." He handed Max a rolled-up set of blueprints and a black tweed cap that matched the jacket.

"Thank you!" said Max. "No pipe?" The two men laughed.

"Come back here when you're done. If I'm not here when you get back, don't panic. I know a great little bakery in town here. They open really early. I'll pick us up some breakfast, that is unless you're not hungry," joked Hugh.

"After our little hike to the windmill, I'm starving, thanks," said Max, as he climbed out of the car. He slipped into the jacket and pulled on the cap. Then he put the satchel over his shoulder and tucked the set of plans under his arm.

"How do I look?" he asked Hugh.

"Like a know it all Engineer, straight out of bloody Oxford!" laughed Hugh.

"Splendid, Old Boy," said Max in his perfect English accent, and with a tip of his cap, he took off for the bridge. He was impressed that the Irish seemed to have covered all the bases.

Chapter 53

FATEFUL ENCOUNTER

Menai Bridge, Anglesey
August 17, 1940

Max checked his watch and was right on time. It was now daylight but the town of Menai was still completely deserted. Max walked the short distance from Telford Road to the bridge, then set off across the span to the north tower. At the base of the tower was the entry to the construction lift that ferried workers up to the top platform. Mounted on the platform was a massive crane that was used to pull the gigantic steel cables across from the south tower. This was also where the British had installed their high-powered radio transmitter that Max was to use to communicate with U38. It was housed in the small construction hut which was the highest point on the island.

The lift had a padlock on it, but it was unlocked. Max opened it, slipped the small chain off the safety gate, and stepped into the tiny lift. He pushed the lever mounted on the wall to the UP position. The lift came to life with a sudden jolt and slowly took him up to the construction platform. He briefly admired the stunning view from the top as he nervously crossed the catwalk to get onto the construction platform. He could see the Menai Straits hundreds of feet below him, as they crashed angrily over the rocks at the base of the bridge tower. The small hut was right ahead of him. He pulled out the key, unlocked the door and stepped inside to attempt to make contact with U38.

The signal was perfect. He reached U38 the first time, confirmed that Operation Goldilocks was a go and set the next rendezvous time for 0530 on Monday. By the time he had shut down the radio and locked the hut, the information had already been relayed back to headquarters by Captain Liebe. It was then immediately rushed by an aide to an anxiously waiting Heinrich Himmler at the SS headquarters in Berlin. Operation Goldilocks was finally a go.

The injection of wealth that the Fuhrer's Reich so desperately needed to wage war on the British, and Communists, would soon be on its way. Satisfied, Max got into the lift and descended back down to the roadway. It stopped with a jolt. He pulled back the gate and stepped out, relieved that everything was going exactly according to plan...until he turned to leave.

Unexpectedly, he bumped into a young, tall blond lady with a ridiculous looking hound dog on a lead. Clearly, she had been watching him as he closed the lift gate. Max was taken aback for a second. He had been caught daydreaming about the adulation that would surely come his way from Himmler when he received confirmation that the Irish intelligence had been rock solid. And now...he was busted cold by a blond at the base of the Menai Bridge tower. The words of Himmler, "Stay focused Max" suddenly replayed in his head.

"What are you doing?" she asked, as the dog's hackles went up and it began to growl.

"I'm sorry?" said Max, buying time to get his story straight.

"What are you doing on the bridge?" she repeated. Max was instantly struck by her incredible beauty. She had the most stunning blue eyes. Also, he could see that she was alone. A quick glance left and right told him that no one else was visible on the span at this early hour. If he wanted, he could pitch her and the dog over the rail to a certain death. Her body would be swept out to the Irish Sea before anyone even missed her. He regained his composure. The threat was minimal.

"Billy Muskett, Mam," said Max, smoothly switching to his alias and politely removing his cap, revealing his thick blond hair. "I'm a government inspector," he extended his hand, "And you are?"

"Err...Taryn Thomas," answered the lady. "...but why are..." she didn't finish her sentence before Max cut her off.

"Taryn, that's a pretty Welsh name and what a beautiful dog," said Max instantly switching to fluent Welsh and extending his hand. Caught off guard by his perfect Welsh, she limply shook his outstretched hand, regretting the move immediately and chastising herself for stupidly telling the stranger her name.

"Thank you," said the lady, not aware that she had taken his bait. "She's a Bassett Hound."

"Yes, a Bassett," said Max playing along. He reached down to pet the dog who growled again, and this time it flashed a glimpse of its gleaming white canines. Max thought better of it and backed up.

"Shelby, no!" said the lady, pulling on the lead. Then she bravely went back to her initial question. "So, that's nice that you can speak Welsh. But what are you doing on the bridge?" she asked again.

"My mother's side of the family is Welsh. I'm here inspecting rivets, all jolly boring really," said Max surprised at her persistence. He was admiring the woman's perfect curves. Even under the bulky sweater, he could see that she had perfect breasts, it had been way too long. "On a Saturday morning, at this hour?" she continued. She caught him lustfully eyeing her up and down and suddenly felt quite uncomfortable. "Exactly," said Max. "That's when I do my work. I would be in the way otherwise. Plus, it's rather hard to inspect a rivet that's red hot," he said trying a little humor. Her blond hair was blowing in the breeze. She was an absolute beauty, no denying that. Those perfect blue eyes. Then Max's nostrils flared as he picked up the slightest scent of her perfume, Jasmine... perhaps?

"I've never seen you here before," said the lady, boldly continuing her inquiry.

"That's because it's the first time I've been on this project," said Max. Suddenly, he reached for her left hand, grabbed it and seeing no wedding ring he quizzed her, "Not married, eh?" His grip was iron like. She saw a look of pure evil in his cold blue eyes.

"That's none of your business!" she shot back at him pulling her hand away. She looked behind her, but there was no one else anywhere to be seen. She suddenly felt very alone and for the first time quite vulnerable. Max saw the look of fear, the one he had been waiting for. He caught another whiff of her perfume. His predatory instinct kicked in. "That's a no!" he snorted back. "Would you like to take a quick ride in the lift with me? It's a wonderful view," he said, moving in towards her even closer and then deliberately grabbed his crotch.

"Oh! You're disgusting!" she snapped at him and turned away, quickly running across the road, the Bassett Hound in tow. "You don't know what you're missing!" yelled Max, as she quickened her pace. She was anxious to put as much distance as possible between her and the obnoxious inspector called Billy Muskett. Max chuckled to himself and watched her run out of sight, before heading back to Telford Road where Hugh was waiting in the Ford with the engine running. Max opened the rear door and put the plans, jacket, cap, and satchel on the back seat. Then he got in the front next to Hugh.

"Everything good?" asked Hugh, handing him a thick bacon sandwich.

"Perfect. The signal could not have been better. Straight through, first time. We are good to go, my friend. I'll be back here in a couple of days to book my ticket home, if all goes according to plan." He bit into the sandwich. As Hugh pulled away, Max's mind wandered. How would the beautiful blond Welsh lady, Taryn Thomas look naked. She was lucky he was on a mission and had a schedule to meet. Otherwise, he would have had her, right there in the lift. As he savored the bacon sandwich, he had no clue that the brief chance encounter on the bridge would later come back to haunt him...in a way he could not even begin to imagine.

Chapter 54

EXECUTIVE DIGS

Menai, Anglesey

August 17, 1940

"Ok Major, we need to hit one more spot on the way back to Rhosybol. We've set you up in your very own executive digs, courtesy of the Irish Republican Army. While you stay on our beautiful island, my boss figured you might need some peace and quiet so that you can think for a while. So, this little place will definitely give you that," said Hugh with a chuckle. As he drove out of the deserted town, he took an unmarked side lane, barely wide enough to get the car down. The unkempt bramble bushes scraped at the sides of the Ford as they drove down the narrow path. Max could feel the weeds scrape against the bottom of the car.

Eventually, they came across the crumbled remains of an ancient cottage. "Relax, this isn't it!" joked Hugh.

"That's a relief," replied Max.

Attached to the cottage wall was an old, rusted gate, barely hanging on its hinges. It was closed across the path. Hugh got out and dragged it off to the side. Then fighting his way past the nettles and brambles, he squeezed back into the driver's seat and drove a little further down the path. On the left was an old briar. Hugh pulled the Ford in and shut off the engine. "We'll walk down the hill to the cottage. It can get too muddy at the bottom and the last thing we need is to get stuck, follow me." And with that, Hugh took off down the steep path.

It was a short walk down to the tiny cottage. There was a smell of cow manure on the breeze that blew in from the west. Hugh showed Max around in less than a minute. There was not a lot to show. It was a tiny two-bedroom stone cottage. It was secluded, yet as close to the bridge and the radio that Hugh could find, given the surge of visitors in town for the bridge reopening. Max felt the bed, it was firm enough, and the sheets were clean. After the sweaty bunk beds of the U-boat, he could easily get a good night's sleep here. That was all that really mattered to him.

"Tell your boss I appreciate his consideration," said Max.

"It's the least we could do. Your people took good care of our late Chief of Staff when he was in Berlin. May he rest in peace. We wanted to return the favor. I'm afraid Menai is not exactly Berlin as far as the nightlife goes. We have a couple of good little pubs within walking distance, should Billy Muskett decide to go out for a pint," said Hugh, with a knowing wink. "Perfect!" replied Max.

The tour was complete and the two men returned to the Ford and headed back to the IRA headquarters at Rhosybol. It was time to meticulously go over the gold heist with the group of men that would be pulling it off the following night.

Chapter 55

ADDINGTON ABBEY

Cheshire, England
August 17, 1940

Peter Legh glanced at his Rolex, he was right on time. The dawn was beginning to break over the unusually clear Cheshire sky. A few cumulonimbus clouds caught the first orange glow of what promised to be the perfect summer day. The air was crisp, and a fine mist hugged the ground for a foot or so. It gave the lush green lawns of Addington Abbey a ghostly, yet tranquil and mystical appearance.

Peter had slept like a log in his old bed. Now he put his small overnight case into the trunk of his MG and climbed in. He pulled his leather driving gloves out of the glove box. His loaded Enfield MK1.38 service revolver now became the sole occupant of the little space. The gloves fit him perfectly and were a welcome improvement over the cold steering wheel and gear stick.

Peter fired the ignition, the engine roared to life. He tucked his old Eton scarf into his RAF leather flying jacket and pulled up his sheepskin collar. Slipping the MG into first gear, he gunned it. A shower of loose gravel flew out from beneath the chassis, causing a slight skid as the tires fought to gain traction. Peter grinned as he easily corrected it, dropped briefly into second and then quickly locked it into third gear. He roared past the gate house and out onto the narrow twisting lanes of the Cheshire countryside.

For a young fighter pilot who had now danced with death on numerous occasions against the Luftwaffe, the next best thrill for him was the open-air driving of his MG convertible. And for a man now used to danger and the accompanying adrenaline rush, it was the only thing that came anywhere close to the cramped fume-filled cockpit of an RAF Spitfire.

"Tally Ho!!" he yelled at the top of his lungs while he screamed around the first S curve. At that moment, in his speeding MG on those winding Cheshire country roads, with the wind in his hair, Peter Legh had never felt more alive. The prospect of freedom for a few days, away from the rigid discipline of the RAF was truly just the therapy he needed.

He looked forward to two days alone to explore some of the great ancient battle sites of Anglesey. Who knew what else he'd find there? Perhaps a nice quiet pub where he could blend in with the locals. Maybe even meet a sweet Welsh lass with a passion for a dashing young fighter pilot, currently living dangerously close to the edge.

As Peter raced towards Anglesey, the hand of fate may as well have already taken the wheel. He would soon face off with a long-forgotten adversary from his days at Eton. An epic countdown to an inevitable rematch between the two men had now begun. The stakes could not be any higher. Indeed, they could have a profound effect on the very outcome of the Second World War.

Chapter 56

THE MILK RUN

London, England
August 17, 1940

"Bloody hell! I'm getting too old for this crap," moaned Ashley, as he hung up the phone and glanced at his alarm clock, which read 0600. The call from HQ sounded urgent. Ashley pondered what the latest emergency could possibly be. He and his fellow agents had been chasing ghosts from Land's End to John O' Groats for months. Since war had been declared on Germany, the reports of alleged Nazi spies operating from the homeland had skyrocketed. A jittery and paranoid population began to view anyone behaving peculiar as a potential German spy.

At thirty-one, John Ashley was the oldest active agent at MI5. Born into a wealthy family whose fortune had been made in the textile industry long ago, he had attended the prestigious Charterhouse School in Surrey before going on to Oxford. While at Oxford, he had been recruited into MI5 by a brilliant academic who also shared Ashley's passion for rowing. A gifted natural athlete with a perfect physique, he excelled in all sports, especially rugby.

It was at Oxford that he discovered rowing, which quickly became his favorite sport. While rowing lacked the physical contact of rugby, it was the synchronicity required on a rowing team that appealed to him. His rowing team was perfectly balanced. They always moved in flawless unison to achieve a specific mutual goal, namely to beat Cambridge at the annual boat race. Unmarried and without children, becoming an Oxford Blue had so far been the proudest moment of John Ashley's life.

His time at MI5 had been a whirlwind to say the least. He had surpassed all expectations through training and at survival school.

His perfect 20/20 vision and calm demeanor made him a first-class marksman. He had spent much of his time at MI5 serving overseas, extensively in Hong Kong, Egypt, Algeria, Greece, and Spain. He had narrowly escaped death in an ambush by fascists loyal to Franco. His shooting skills were proven when he killed all six of the Spanish ambushers, allowing him and his team to escape safely over the Pyrenees and into France.

His last mission was in occupied France. With the aid of the French resistance, he had successfully penetrated the security perimeter of the massive construction project underway at Lorient. He had easily picked the lock of the main construction trailer and taken pictures of blueprints. These showed details of the proposed construction of numerous additional U-boat pens, along with fuel storage depots and defensive capabilities. This was the exact kind of information that the Royal Navy and the War Department desperately needed.

He had also witnessed firsthand the appalling brutality of the Nazis against the French people. He knew it was evil beyond belief and he was extremely relieved to be safely back in England with the English Channel and the mighty Royal Navy between him and Hitler's murderous SS.

As he washed, shaved, and dressed, he wondered again what had come up so urgently that required him to meet with David Petrie, the Director General of MI5. The call from HQ lacked information as usual. Ashley was told to pack his kit and report directly to the Director General at HQ at 0700 sharp. Ashley checked his weapon, slipped it into its holster and then into his briefcase. He glanced at his appearance in the mirror. He straightened his tie, smoothed down his hair and was content with what he saw. He pulled on his jacket, picked up his overcoat, small overnight case, and briefcase, and headed out into a gray, overcast, London summer day.

It was a twenty-minute bus ride to MI5 headquarters and Ashley was grateful to get a seat on the upper deck. He lit up and enjoyed his first cigarette of the day. The bus continued to fill up at every station, mainly with office workers heading to another dreary day behind the desk in the financial district. He also noticed the usual scattering of young men in uniform, from all branches of the British military. The sky was still gloomy as Ashley got off at his stop and walked the short distance to the intimidating main gate of His Majesty's Prison, Wormwood Scrubs. The Victorian prison was being used as a temporary headquarters to house the rapidly expanding agency whose numbers had skyrocketed since the outbreak of the war.

He was surprised to see the Director General of M15, David Petrie waiting for him directly outside the massive prison gate. He had no idea that Petrie had been up most of the night. Upon further investigation, the mysterious flashing lights that had been initially reported off the coast of North Wales, were in fact spotted off the coast of the Island of Anglesey. This seemingly irrelevant piece of information had set off alarm bells ringing in Petrie's brain. To anyone else in the department this would seem like a minor difference. After all, North Wales and Anglesey were not even on the radar in terms of priority when defending the homeland.

But Petrie, along with his trusted assistant Colonel Withers knew different. Anglesey was where Churchill had 50 tons of gold bullion secretly hidden in an abandoned windmill. The small circle of people privy to the secret were under strict instructions that any unusual activity reported even close to Anglesey must be immediately investigated. Churchill was not about to take any chances. Petrie was still figuring out his best strategy of breaking the latest news to the Prime Minister and he was hoping that Ashley might just be the ace up his sleeve that he needed.

"Ah! Ashley! Good man!" he said checking his wristwatch. It was 0655. "Sorry to interrupt your beauty sleep but something has cropped up that we need you to look into. We can talk in the car," he said, as a black sedan pulled up slowly outside the prison gate.

"Ah, here he is now. Chop! chop!" he said to Ashley. The Director General's driver, Geoffrey Green was already out of the vehicle and holding the rear door open for Petrie. "Morning Sir!" he said as Petrie and Ashley slipped into the rear of the car. "Morning Green," responded Petrie. Green closed the door behind them, put Ashley's cases in the trunk and climbed back into the driver's seat. "Where to Sir?" asked Green.

"Number 10, at the double!" said Petrie. "Very good, Sir. Number 10 Downing Street, on our way, Sir!" Then he reached back and slid the glass partition between them closed and pulled smoothly out into the London commute traffic.

"How have you been, Ashley?" asked Petrie.

"Fine, Sir. Thank you," replied Ashley.

Petrie had only been in the position of Director General of MI5 since April, when he was appointed by Winston Churchill to replace the legendary Vernon Kell. This had been a bold effort by Churchill to shake up the department. Petrie, as head of MI5 was fully aware of Operation Minnow. He was a proud Scotsman with high morals and standards. He was a terrific athlete in his day and he still followed a vigorous exercise routine. Although, it was getting ever more difficult to make the time these days since war had broken out.

Petrie had made a point of meeting as many of his field agents face to face as possible. Theirs was a deadly business and Petrie felt an enormous sense of responsibility for his people. They were actively engaged with the enemy on a regular basis. They often found themselves in incredibly perilous situations where one wrong move could lead to their capture, torture, and certain death at the hands of Heinrich Himmler's brutal Gestapo.

Ashley had stood out from an impressive field of agents. Petrie was a huge rowing fan and had not missed the annual Oxford v Cambridge boat race in years. Once he discovered Ashley was an Oxford Blue, the deal was sealed. Petrie knew that when a unique individual was required for a particularly dangerous mission, without a doubt, John Ashley was his best bet.

His intuition had already paid off. The U-boat menace was currently the biggest threat to the very survival of the British Isles. The Admiralty desperately needed to get an accurate threat assessment. The one missing link was what was hidden underneath the massive camouflage nets at the Port of Lorient in occupied France.

Churchill, as a last resort had summoned Petrie to discuss the possibility of getting an MI5 agent into Lorient. Petrie had examined the aerial photographs taken over Lorient by the RAF. The camouflage nets were colossal, bigger than a football pitch. They covered acres of land that was surrounded by fencing and clearly patrolled by armed guards. Petrie knew the mission was incredibly difficult to pull off, almost suicidal. But the Royal Navy desperately needed to know what was happening there. They needed to develop an effective strategy to deal with the U-boat threat. When Churchill requested Petrie's finest agent, Petrie knew that Ashley would be the man chosen. He would parachute into France during darkness, organize a team with the resistance and get the bloody job done.

"I haven't seen you since your little visit to Lorient. Great job, Ashley! The Admiralty was delighted with your findings. Jolly good show," said Petrie, as he grinned at Ashley and offered him a thumbs up. "Piece of cake, Sir," replied Ashley. "The French were more than helpful, a very brave bunch of lads, Sir."

"Good," said Petrie. That is what he liked about Ashley. He was humble, always giving the credit to the team and never taking any for himself. But then, what would one expect from an Oxford Blue? He continued, "This next operation is nowhere near as hair raising. The Prime Minister has a bee in his bonnet. He is very adamant that we get to the bottom of something that's cropped up here on our own shores, so to speak."

"Yes Sir," said Ashley, as he stared out of the car window watching London awakening. The streets were packed with people scurrying about their business, doggedly coming to terms with war time England-sandbags, men in uniform, gas masks, the Red Cross, antiaircraft guns, searchlights, bombed out buildings. For a moment, Ashley imagined how different it would look if the Germans invaded. Unlike all those on the other side of the glass who scurried about their business this overcast workday, Ashley was one of a very few who had seen up close, the terror that the Nazis unleashed on their enemies. He had seen life under their jackboot. It wasn't pretty. These poor souls, they simply had no idea of the pure evil that lurked just across the English Channel.

"There is a report about some flashing lights out at sea, just off the coast of Anglesey with no reasonable explanation. For a reason that will remain classified, both Churchill and Atlee want it investigated immediately. It is probably another wild goose chase, but we are very shorthanded right now. I need to get this off my desk before the Prime Minister blows his top. He is running on a very short fuse these days, as you can imagine. And quite frankly

Ashley, after Lorient you've earned a nice milk run." said Petrie, as he casually checked his watch.

"I see, Sir. Anglesey, I think I can handle that," replied Ashley, with a genuine but wry smile. "Yes, I'm sure you can Ashley. Anyway, the Prime Minister requested my presence and asked that the field agent assigned to the Lorient operation accompany me, so here we are. Let's do our best to kill two birds with one stone, shall we?" retorted Petrie, as the sedan pulled into Downing Street and stopped outside number 10. "Hopefully, this will be short and sweet. I'll do the talking…you nod and smile. We don't have a lot of time. Your train leaves in a couple of hours. Ready?" he asked.

"Yes, Sir!" replied Ashley. The driver opened the door and Ashley followed the Director General of Military Intelligence out of the car. They climbed up the steps lined by walls of sandbags and went through the black door that magically swung open into 10 Downing Street to meet Winston Churchill, the Prime Minister of Great Britain.

Chapter 57

TO WHOM IT MAY CONCERN

10 Downing Street, London, England
August 17, 1940

Churchill was dressed in his favorite navy-blue boiler suit. He was sitting behind his desk in his smoke-filled office as Petrie and Ashley were announced by his secretary.

"Director General of MI5 Petrie and Special Agent Ashley, Sir," she said, as the two men followed her in. Churchill rose from his seat and extended his hand, "Mr. Director General, always a pleasure," he said as he shook Petrie's hand.

"Likewise, Prime Minister," replied Petrie. "May I introduce Agent John Ashley, Sir," said Petrie as he motioned towards Ashley, who had kept a respectful distance behind Petrie waiting for his introduction. "Ah, so this is the chap who got into Lorient and back?!" boomed Churchill, extending his hand while giving Ashley a rare but genuine smile. "A pleasure, Sir," replied Ashley. He shook Churchill's hand and was pleasantly surprised by the firmness of his grip.

"Bloody good job, Agent Ashley. The Admiralty was well pleased with your report. If you do nothing else during this war, know that you have already done more than your fair share and that of a thousand others of your generation, I might add. Thank you, Ashley! Please gentlemen, be seated," said Churchill.

The Prime Minister returned to his side of the desk and sat back down as the men from MI5 sat in the two green leather chairs opposite him. Churchill quickly got down to business. "There's a reason I asked you to accompany the Director General here this morning, Ashley. In the early hours of this morning, we received a report of flashing lights somewhere off the coast of North Wales.

There are legitimate reasons of national security as to why I am concerned about the sighting. I need someone, someone we can count on to go up there and get to the bottom of it right away.

Hopefully, there is nothing to this whole business. I need someone who knows how to look under every rock, shake the bushes, so to speak. I need you to find out who or what was out there in the Irish Sea in the middle of the night flashing signal lights. At the same time, you need to be as discreet as possible. The absolute last thing this government needs at this time is the bright light of curiosity to be shone on this particular part of the Kingdom. Am I clear, Ashley?" asked Churchill.

"Absolutely, crystal clear, Sir," replied Ashley.

"Good, things have been moving quite rapidly on many fronts. Do we have any additional information for Agent Ashley before he departs, David?" asked Churchill.

Petrie had been bracing for the question. He took a deep breath and began to speak in a deliberate, almost matter of fact manner, "Only the location, Sir. We made some follow up calls after some initial miscommunication. Apparently, the lights were spotted off a place called Red Wharf Bay, which is on the Island of Anglesey. It is technically North Wales, which is what the initial report had stated, Sir," replied Petrie.

"Anglesey! Anglesey! Good Lord! That is even worse! Isn't it, Director General?" asked Churchill. He glared at Petrie over the top of his reading glasses. His demeanor immediately changed as did his complexion. "Yes sir, I agree with your point," replied Petrie.

"I hope I'm wrong, but we need to get on this tout de bloody suite! As in right now!" yelled Churchill, who Ashley noted was clearly even more agitated at the very mention of Anglesey.

"Quite sir! We have Agent Ashley booked on the 10:00 AM out of Euston Station to Crewe, then Crewe to Holyhead, Sir. It's our next stop this morning after we are done here," answered Petrie. Ashley remained quiet while his mind raced. He was trying to figure out what was so significant about the sleepy Island of Anglesey that could possibly get Churchill's hackles up so quickly.

"Good! Then with the location now pinpointed to Anglesey, let me clear any obstacles, any obstacles at all, that may pop up in your way, shall I? In view of the importance of your mission, I need to make sure that you don't get tangled up anywhere in red tape so to speak," said Churchill with a wave of his cigar. He reached into his desk drawer and rummaged around while muttering quietly to himself. Finally, he pulled out a white envelope.

He opened it, took out a single typed page, signed and dated the bottom before hitting it with his ink blotter. He refolded it and put it back in the envelope. Then he wrote, To Whom it May Concern on the outside and handed it to Ashley. "Here you go!" he said, "This will get you out of any potential bother. It is my full authorization for you to do whatever may be necessary to complete your given task, and to remove anyone who may stand in your way. It also gives you authority to use whatever means you may deem necessary up to and including deadly force. Now, good luck to you, Agent Ashley. Don't miss that bloody train!" said Churchill as he checked his pocket watch and extended his hand to both men. They thanked him, turned and left his office.

"Euston Station! At the double!" barked Petrie to his driver. "We'll have just enough time."

"Euston Station it is, Sir!" replied Green, as he floored the accelerator and squealed his tires, causing the car to lurch forward. "Well, that wasn't too bad after all," said Petrie.

"No sir, not too bad at all," replied Ashley, as he checked his inside pocket to feel the envelope Churchill had given him. He still could not fathom why the Prime Minister would be so concerned about flashing lights off the coast of Anglesey. It made no sense. Anglesey was so far away from the south coast where the invasion would surely come. Then he reminded himself of a line in one of his favorite poems by Tennyson, 'His was not to reason why, his was but to do, or die.'

For now, he was grateful for the milk run Petrie had assigned to him. He had cheated death by too narrow a margin on his mission to Lorient. It was a long train ride up to Holyhead, Anglesey. It was also the perfect tonic for a tired MI5 agent.

Chapter 58

EUSTON STATION

Euston Station, London
August 17, 1940

E uston Station was a mad house as usual. Thousands of
civilians and men from every branch of the British military all
seemed to be moving in no particular direction. Ashley was about
to plunge into a true sea of humanity, if ever there was one.

Green expertly pulled up to the curb and opened the rear door.
Petrie exited first and Ashley followed. The loudspeaker was
blaring a message, totally inaudible to all those below who strained
and pushed to get to their correct platforms and finally, board their
trains. "Alright Ashley, off you go. Here is what we have on the
flashing lights. It's not much, I'm afraid," said Petrie as he handed
Ashley a non-descript file. "Thank you, Sir," said Ashley as he
placed it in his briefcase. "Oh, and this is just a little something
to read on the train. Consider it a small token of my appreciation
for the job you did in Lorient. I'm glad you made it back, Ashley."
He handed Ashley a small parcel wrapped neatly in brown paper
and secured with twine. "Thank you, Sir," repeated Ashley. "Very
much appreciated."

He shook Petrie's hand, lit himself a cigarette, nodded at Petrie
one last time, gathered his cases and vanished into the crowd.
Petrie watched him for a while then turned around and climbed
back into the car. "Back to the Scrubs," Petrie said to Green as
the door closed behind him. The quiet interior of the car provided
an instant welcome sanctuary from the racket outside that was
Euston Station. Petrie sat back and relaxed. For once he felt good
about sending an agent on a mission. After all, what could possibly
be going on of any consequence on the sleepy Island of Anglesey.

Petrie loosened his tie. His furrowed brow was the only indication that he feared deep down something might already be amiss on Anglesey. The thought of bad actors potentially stumbling on to the windmill and its contents of 50 tons of solid gold bars caused him to briefly shiver. He was glad that Ashley was his man and he was confident that his best agent would get to the bottom of things, one way or the other. Petrie's first task when he returned to headquarters was to let his assistant, Colonel Withers know of the updates on the location of the flashing lights. The Colonel would be the point man for Ashley to contact if he found any issues, any at all on Anglesey.

Unfortunately, the Colonel was "indisposed" as the young Army secretary had so delicately informed him with a roll of her eyes and a slight blush. Petrie was aware that Withers was in some digestive discomfort. He had regularly observed him visiting the men's toilet on a consistent basis. Petrie, always the perfect gentleman was dreadfully embarrassed for the young secretary and instinctively told her, "Not to worry. I'll chat with him later."

As he beat a hasty retreat, he made a mental note to try to catch up with Withers later that same day to let him know that the lights were spotted off Anglesey and not North Wales. That would naturally raise the threat level, but they had Agent Ashley on his way to investigate. Then he went on with his jam-packed chaotic day. Unfortunately, he never did get together with Withers to give him an update. Colonel Withers, through no fault of his own was already behind the eight ball.

Chapter 59

UNEXPLODED BOMB

Somewhere in Rural England

August 17, 1940

Despite the human melee that was Euston Station on any busy workday, Ashley found his platform and boarded the train. He walked down several of the carriages before he found a cabin with a couple of vacant seats. He slid open the door and stepped inside. An elderly couple sat together opposite the vacant seats and four men in identical sailors' uniforms, one with fire red hair, occupied the double seats next to the window. On the small table between them was a game of blackjack well under way, with cigarettes used as gambling chips.

Ashley acknowledged the couple with a smile and removal of his trilby hat. The sailors were completely absorbed in the card game and did not even notice his arrival. Ashley removed his coat and placed it with his suitcase in the overhead luggage rack. He unbuttoned his jacket and sat down with his briefcase on his lap. He checked his watch and all being well they should be departing at any moment. The old lady opposite him was busy knitting. She smiled at Ashley as they made eye contact, "Are you going to Stafford too?' she asked.

"No, I'm going on to Holyhead," answered Ashley.

"Oh, that's a long way! How exciting for you," she replied. "We are going to Stafford to see our new granddaughter!" she continued, beaming with pride.

"Very nice," said Ashley.

"I'm knitting her a new bonnet!" said the lady, showing her work in progress at the end of her long knitting needles. "She's getting christened on Sunday. We are so looking forward to it, aren't we George?" she said as she nudged her husband who was carefully reading The Times.

"Yes Dear," replied her husband. He glanced over the top of his newspaper, made eye contact with Ashley, winked and then returned his attention to The Times.

"It's at Saint Albans Church, do you know it?" continued the lady.

"No, I'm afraid I don't. I've never been to Stafford before," replied Ashley.

"Oh, Saint Albans is beautiful. There will be over twenty people there, coming from all over, including relatives that we haven't seen in a long time. It will be so nice to see everybody. With this awful war going on, you never know when you will be able to celebrate together again. Everything seems to depend on what that scoundrel Hitler decides he wants to do and how Mr. Churchill responds. I say perhaps we give him a bloody good hiding!" she said, raising her voice an octave or two and waving her knitting needle as if it were a cutlass, at the very mention of Hitler's name.

"Yes, these are uncertain times. It's good that you can get together with your family to celebrate, especially to welcome a new arrival," said Ashley. He loved the lady's fighting spirit. He had no doubt that if push came to shove, and the Nazis did invade, she like everyone else would give her all.

"Helen," said the Lady.

"I'm sorry?" asked Ashley.

"Helen, her name is Helen Clare," replied the lady with a smile.

"Oh, I see. That's a pretty name," replied Ashley.

"Do you have any children?" asked the Lady.

Her husband answered before Ashley could reply, "Come on now Love, let the gentleman be. I'm sure he doesn't need to be bothered with children and christenings and the like."

"It's not a bother. No, I'm not married. I am afraid Mr. Hitler has caused a lot of people's plans to be put on hold. As I said, these are uncertain times. I trust Mr. Churchill and I know that God will guide him," said Ashley. Figuring this would be a good time to go to the dining car to see what, if anything there was to eat, he added, "Would you mind watching my seat? I'm just going to the dining car."

"It'll still be here when you get back," said the man looking up from his paper and giving Ashley a nod. "Thanks," said Ashley as he stood up and placed his Trilby on his seat. "Do you need anything?" he asked, looking at the lady.

"No, thank you. We are good. We have a flask of tea and a sandwich already packed," she answered. She indicated with her knitting needles towards the small wicker hamper, nestled neatly alongside the suitcase in the luggage rack over her head.

"Thank you," said Ashley, clutching his briefcase and nodding at her husband. He left the cabin to find the dining car.

Four cars later he arrived at the diner. It was packed, and the air was thick with cigarette smoke and the unique smell of bacon. A large man in an army uniform seemed to be the last man in the queue. Ashley stood behind him and waited his turn straining to look over the man's shoulder to see what was offered on the black board behind the counter. It listed four sandwiches to choose from, Egg and Cress, Bacon, Cheese and Onion, or Sausage. "Excellent," muttered Ashley to himself. A bacon sandwich with a cup of tea would be perfect.

The line seemed to be moving painfully slow. It was at least ten minutes before Ashley finally arrived at the stainless-steel service counter. Unfortunately, he had not been the only one who had sights set on the bacon sandwich. The sailor before the large Army man in front of Ashley ordered the last one. A portly man in a white chef's hat and apron came out from the small galley and promptly wiped Bacon and Sausage from the chalkboard before returning to his post without a word of explanation. Ashley settled for the egg and cress sandwich and a cup of tea. He found a seat by the window and sat down to eat.

There was a loud whistle from the front of the train. Ashley watched the flurry of activity as someone yelled, "All Aboard!" and the whistle blew. People exchanged final hugs and goodbyes before the massive engine let out a huge cloud of steam. The dining car lurched once and then the train slowly pulled out of Euston Station. It was on its way to Crewe. There, as planned Ashley would change trains and continue on to Holyhead. "Piece of cake," reasoned Ashley. He much preferred the smoky dining car as it rumbled its way North, compared to the cold belly of an RAF bomber with a parachute on his back, heading South to a pitch-black occupied France. This was indeed a milk run and he was grateful for that.

Some two hundred and fifty miles to the northwest, a veteran railway maintenance man conducting a routine track inspection froze in sheer terror. He had discovered a massive unexploded German bomb. The bomb's nose was buried in the soft ground no more than three feet away from the railway tracks.

He could barely get his words out as he finally made it to the telephone at the local railway station, "That's right! Unexploded bomb! Right next to the track! Its bloody huge! Stop all traffic on the Crewe to Holyhead line immediately until the bomb squad can clear it!" With that he hung up the phone and collapsed in a chair exhausted. His fluke discovery would set off a chain of events that would ultimately effect Ashley's milk run in a way that Agent Ashley could never have imagined.

Refreshed, Ashley headed back to his cabin and was delighted to see his Trilby still on guard. The pile of cigarettes had grown considerably as the sailors gambled on. The old lady was still knitting and the bonnet had grown by at least an inch since Ashley had left.

She smiled at Ashley but did not speak, which he was grateful for. Her husband seemed to have nodded off and did not react at all. Ashley sat down and retrieved the package that Petrie had given him. He unwrapped the paper to reveal a brand-new novel, For Whom the Bell Tolls by Ernest Hemmingway. He flipped open the first page and written in the unmistakably slanted script of Petrie was a message:

> To John Ashley,
>> Unsung Hero, Patriot, Warrior.
>> Oxford Blue!
>> This is your time, Ashley.
>> May you continue to shine!
>> Many Thanks. "Regnum Defende."
> David Petrie, 1940.

Ashley smiled. Regnum Defende was the MI5 motto. It was Latin for Defend the Realm. It was nice to be appreciated, especially by the boss. Ashley had heard about the book and as a veteran of the Spanish Civil War, he had intended to buy a copy anyway. Now Petrie had beaten him to it. He turned the page and began to read. After a while, despite his best efforts to resist, the rhythmic sound of the tracks worked its almost hypnotic magic. He fell asleep, not even making it halfway through the first chapter.

Chapter 60

THE ISLAND OF ANGLESEY

Anglesey, Wales
August 17, 1940

With a brief stop at the ancient city of Conway, Peter made excellent time in the MG. He pressed on along the coast road. Shortly after passing through the city of Bangor, he finally got his first view of the majestic Menai Bridge. He was not sure if it was the bridge itself or the picturesque Menai Straits with the Island of Anglesey as a backdrop but the whole scene had a magical fairy tale like appearance. He could not wait to set foot on the island.

The closer he got, the more impressive the bridge looked. It had awesome stonework and the massive steel cables had a bluish green color to them. It was almost reflective of the rolling blue waters of the straits themselves. He could see the workmen clearly now. They were antlike, crawling all over the structure as they worked to complete the huge rebuilding project.

As he drove across the bridge, the wind picked up and the smell of the Irish Sea filled his nostrils. The convertible allowed him to get the full panoramic view. He was in awe of the immense height of the structure as he passed underneath the mainland or south tower. As he approached the Anglesey or north tower, he could see workmen way up on top where two colossal cranes were mounted. Slowly, they weaved the steel cables back and forth. A workman perched on a cat's cradle high above the roadway waved his cap at him and Peter waved enthusiastically back.

He passed under the Anglesey tower and then finally he was on the Island of Anglesey.

"Tally Ho!" he yelled again as he entered the town of Menai Bridge or simply Menai as the locals referred to it. He suddenly felt quite energized. The horror of months of continual aerial combat was temporarily swept from his mind. He was almost euphoric. It was good to feel freedom again, even if it was for only a couple of days. He stopped and asked a lady for directions to Beaumaris. Then he headed straight to the prestigious Bulkeley Hotel.

"I'm sorry Sir, we are completely booked this weekend. There are several large parties in town making final preparations for the completion of the bridge work. The BBC crews are here as well. I am afraid all the local hotels are booked solid. How long did you plan on staying on our island?" said the day manager at the Bulkeley Hotel in a heavy Welsh accent. She looked at Peter over her wire rimmed glasses and a thin apologetic smile appeared on her slightly wrinkled face. "Have you come very far?" she asked sympathetically.

"I drove here from Cheshire," Peter replied as he cursed himself for not calling ahead. His father had recommended the Bulkeley and he had mistakenly just assumed there would be vacancies. He had not figured on the amount of additional people coming to Anglesey to see the completion of the bridge work.

"I'm so sorry," she repeated. "Do you have friends or family you can stay with on Anglesey?"

"No, I'm afraid not. It is my first time on Anglesey. It's my fault, I should have called ahead. Well, thank you anyway," he said with a look of dejection as he turned away from the front desk. "Wait! Just a minute," she said, looking left and then right to make sure no one was within ear shot. "If you drive back to Menai, you can go to Ye Olde Village Shop on Telford Road and ask for Gwen. Let her know that Laurie from the Bulkeley Hotel sent you because she is booked up solid. She might be able to help you. That is where all the local rentals are posted. It won't be anything fancy like ours, but it will be a roof over your head at least," she continued. Then she wrote down the address for him on a small notepad, ripped it off with a flick of her wrist and handed it to him with a wink and a smile. "Thank you so much!" said Peter extending his hand. "That's very kind of you." She shook his hand and the dozen or so cheap bracelets she wore rattled in unison. "You're very welcome," she said. "Enjoy your stay on beautiful Anglesey!"

Peter turned around and left, taking in the awesome view of Beaumaris Castle located across the street. Two castles in one day. "Good show," he said to himself as he jumped in the MG and headed back to the town of Menai.

Chapter 61

THE MILK RUN TURNS SOUR

Crewe, England
August 17, 1940

The train suddenly started braking and came to an unexpected stop, jolting Ashley to his senses. He quickly looked around to get his bearings and could see the elderly couple still in front of him. The lady's knitting was now replaced with a sandwich sitting on grease proof paper. Her husband was busy enjoying a small pork pie. The wicker basket was now on his lap.

The sailors were still in the same positions. The one with fire red hair was clearly the better gambler judging by the pile of cigarettes in front of him. Now their attention switched from the game to the view out of the window, which consisted of green rolling pastures, divided by hedgerows. It was typical of anywhere in rural England. Ashley checked that his briefcase was still tucked behind his calves and took a look at his watch. He had been snoozing for almost an hour.

"Where are we?" asked one of the sailors.

"Timbuktu!" answered the man next to him who looked way too young to be sporting the uniform of a seaman in His Majesty's Royal Navy. His acne spotted face told Ashley that he was still in his teens. "Nah, those are cows, not bloody camels!" added the one with fire red hair as he playfully rustled the younger man's hair. All four laughed out loud.

Ashley opened his book again and stared at the pages. He did not really feel like reading but it was the perfect defense against having to make any further small talk. It was not unusual these days for trains in and out of London to get delayed. Ashley had a good hour or so cushion built in timewise. Consequently, he was not worried that the train was sitting somewhere in the English countryside and apparently for now, going nowhere.

An hour later, with still no movement, he was a little more concerned. One of the sailors had gone to investigate and had been told by a conductor that they were holding at a red light until cleared to proceed. Another man in a railroad uniform waited by the call box at the light, casually smoking his pipe and apparently waiting for some explanation or instruction.

The sun had finally come out and the carriage was rapidly becoming quite stuffy. If the train did not start moving soon, he would miss his connecting train from Crewe to Holyhead. This would not be good as that train was the last one that left England to get to Holyhead in time for the midnight ferry to Dublin. There was not another one until 4:30 AM the next morning. He would be stranded overnight in Crewe. Not good for a mission that Churchill himself had deemed absolutely essential.

Finally, the young sailor who had the best view of the man waiting by the call box chimed in excitedly. "Eh up. Looks like he answered the phone." Everyone turned their attention to the window as the youngster gave out a running commentary. "He's talking to someone," he reported. "What's he saying?" asked his mate sitting opposite. "Wait. He's hanging up and…ok! He just gave the train driver the thumbs up. Looks like we might be finally moving." As the words left his lips, they heard a giant blast of steam followed by the train's whistle. The carriage lurched again and finally they were moving slowly but they were moving. A loud cheer rang out that went from one end of the train to the other. Ashley smiled. It was good to know that the British people had not lost their great sense of humor. He was mightily relieved to be moving again. As long as they didn't have any more delays, he should still be able to catch his train to Holyhead.

His relief was short lived when a clearly frustrated conductor entered their cabin and made an announcement. "Could I have your attention for a minute please?" he asked. "I have an announcement to make. An unexploded bomb has been discovered on the tracks outside of Wrexham. This has caused closure of the main line to Holyhead until further notice. Passengers with a final destination of Dublin should change at Crewe. You should get off at Liverpool

Lime Street and take the Liverpool to Dublin ferry. Due to the considerable disruption this has caused, please expect delays and slow going from here to Crewe. That is all the information I have currently. I will update you if anything changes. Thank you!" and with that he was gone.

Ashley slumped back in his seat. The milk run had just turned sour. His mind whirled as he immediately began to formulate a backup plan. He was scheduled to pick up a government car at Holyhead to enable him to quickly cover the island. He was aware that there were no field offices in Crewe and that the nearest one of any consequence was in Chester. After that there were none to his knowledge in North Wales. He knew getting to Liverpool would be much easier than getting to Chester. When he reached Crewe, he would call HQ and see if the chaps at Chester could get a car to Lime Street for him. Then he would simply drive directly from Liverpool to Anglesey. That should be a piece of cake.

The conductor was right, it was indeed slow going all the way to Crewe. When they finally pulled into Crewe Station, Ashley had just enough time to contact HQ to let them know his predicament and ask them to do whatever they could to get him a vehicle to Lime Street. He deliberately dropped Director Petrie's name to make sure his message did not end up sitting in a wire IN box.

Ashley made casual conversation with a couple of soldiers and several civilians. All shared similar stories of woe. The closure of the Holyhead line had a ripple effect that disrupted all trains moving into the North of England. The trip up to Liverpool turned into a long torturous ordeal, stopping and starting the entire journey.

Chapter 62

YE OLDE VILLAGE SHOP

Menai, Anglesey
August 17, 1940

The small bell jingled over the shop door as Peter entered the cramped space. The air was thick with blue cigarette smoke. Behind the old wooden counter was a petite middle-aged lady with sharp features and shoulder length dyed brown hair. She quickly eyed him up and down.

"Well good afternoon handsome, and what can I do for you?" she asked, a cigarette hanging off her lower lip moving rhythmically up and down. The ash fell onto the glass countertop and she immediately wafted it away with her hand.

"Are you Gwen?" asked Peter.

"Well, yes I am!" she said, straightening up and taking a last draw from the cigarette before stubbing it out in the overflowing ash tray. "And you are?"

"Legh, Peter Legh," he said walking forward and extending his hand.

"Gwen Dillon, it's a pleasure to meet you." She gently squeezed his hand. Her skin was soft and her nails were manicured and painted dark red. She reeked of cigarettes.

"What can I do for you, Mr. Legh?" she asked.

"Laurie, over at the Bulkeley Hotel referred me to you. I'm afraid the Bulkeley is booked solid, along with all of the other hotels. I was hoping you might be able to help me out."

"Oh no, it's been quite a problem. We are a tiny island here and just don't have the capacity for all the bridge folks. I will be so glad when they are done and life returns to normal. Are you with the BBC?" she asked, rooting in her purse for her pack of Woodbines.

"No, I'm just here for a couple of days, purely sightseeing. I just never considered the impact of the bridge retrofit. I should have called ahead, my fault."

"Smoke?" she asked showing him the Woodbine box.

"No, thank you."

She lit up and exhaled another blue cloud. "Good for you, it stunts your growth!" she laughed. "Well, your timing is horrible. All of the rental cottages are let out."

"Oh, no!" said Peter, slapping his forehead with his palm, emphasizing his dilemma.

"However…" she smiled her head tilting to one side, "It just so happens that we have one little flat still available. It's over Vaughn's Fish and Chip shop. As long as you are okay with the smell of chips, then…Bob's your Uncle!"

"Oh, yes. I'll take it. Good show Gwen. Jolly good show!"

"We aim to please," she said. "It will be two shillings a night, so four shillings total, please."

"Perfect," he said and pulled out his coins.

"Let me get the key." She turned around, deliberately flicked her hair at him and went through a small door behind her marked PRIVATE.

"Excellent," said Peter. He would go to the flat, freshen up and then head to the nearest pub to sample the local brew. Knowing that he had secured his lodging for the night was a big relief. He began to feel the tensions of the last several weeks subside. He recalled the words of his father when he had recommended a trip to the island, "There's something magical about that place. As soon as you go over the Menai Bridge, all your troubles will seem to magically just fade away."

At that moment, Gwen returned with his key. "Here you go, Peter. Let me know if you need anything else. If it's after hours, I'll be over at The Bull later if you need anything," she said with a smile, flirting shamelessly.

"Thanks so much," said Peter as he paid her. He turned and left the warm shop.

The flat was perfect, small but clean and dry. It was all he needed. He quickly unpacked a few items, washed his face, and brushed his teeth. Then, sensing rain, he pulled up the canvas roof and headed out for a pint at The Bull. It was a charming old Tudor pub that he had spotted when he first came through Menai. To say that he was looking forward to this perfect getaway from the war and the RAF, would be an understatement to say the least.

Chapter 63

THE BEAUTIFUL BLOND

Menai, Anglesey
August 17, 1940

Like many pubs in Britain, The Bull had two distinct areas for customers to drink, the Lounge and the Bar. The Lounge is plusher and more comfortable and generally preferred by the ladies and couples. The Bar is usually sparsely furnished and generally preferred by working men. Since they are separate areas, each has their own entrance. Each area is often served by the same two-sided bar, which acts as a divide between the two areas.

Peter chose The Bull lounge which was dimly lit and very loud. The air was thick with cigarette and pipe smoke, and the unmistakable smell of booze. It's what you would expect from a public house that had served beer and spirits to thirsty travelers for over four centuries.

Peter started to push his way towards the bar. It was mainly filled with bridge workers and several RAF lads from nearby RAF Valley or Mona enjoying a darts game. Peter was glad he had left his flying jacket in the MG. The last thing he needed was to be drawn into shop talk. With his white knitted Aron sweater and scarf, he looked more like a local lad out for a quiet pint. The centuries old ceiling had massive oak beams that were now grotesquely twisted and the plaster ceiling was stained brown from nicotine. It all reminded him of the Legh Arms back at home in Addington, the local pub that proudly boasts his family's name.

Nailed to every beam was an impressive collection of old horse brasses that had been buffed almost smooth over the decades by hard working Welsh hands. Several old scenic paintings of the Menai Straits adorned the walls. He also noticed a much newer framed picture of Winston Churchill hung prominently over the mantel piece. To the right of the fireplace was an ancient Welsh spinning wheel long since motionless and several reconditioned mining lamps completed the décor.

He waited for what seemed an eternity to get served, but the wait at the bar was already two rows deep with thirsty men. Looking over the bar to the other side, he could see the more sparsely furnished Bar area. Then he saw her. Standing alone at the corner of the bar was the most stunningly beautiful blond haired woman he had ever seen. Right at that moment she looked up from reading her newspaper and their eyes met. She smiled at him, he smiled back. There was a moment of magic. Then the barman moved between them to unload a tray full of used glasses.

Peter immediately made a bee line for the lounge door and exited into the now pouring rain. He made a right turn, walked a dozen feet and stepped through a large black oak door with a glass panel in it with the word BAR etched in the glass. As expected, compared to the lounge, the bar was meagerly decorated. The well-worn floor was covered in sawdust. On the left wall was a built-in bench with an old table in front of it and two small tables with stools made up the only seating arrangements. Several locals had taken the bench spot and were engaged in a game of Dominoes. An older man and lady with a border collie asleep at their feet sat next to the small fireplace. The man was happily puffing away on his pipe as she knitted what appeared to be a long scarf.

The beautiful blond woman stood in the corner close to one of the locals who had his back to her as he talked to his mate. Peter pushed behind him and said, "May I?" to the blond as he stepped into the small space. "Oh, of course," she replied making eye contact. She smiled and put down her copy of The Bangor Times newspaper.

"Thank you so much! It's a pleasure to meet you, my name is Peter Legh."

"Is that L-E-E or L-E-A or L-E-I-G-H? For I have met all three Lee's!!" she responded as she met his hand with a firm grip that both surprised and delighted Peter.

He flashed a broad smile at her. She immediately noticed his even white teeth, something not often seen in these parts.

"Neither!" he laughed.

"It's Legh, L-E-G-H, there is no I!!"

"That's unusual," she replied, gently releasing his grip while maintaining eye contact and revealing an equally impressive set of teeth, outlined by the most perfect set of red lips that he had ever seen.

"I'm a Legh of Addington, an ancient family in Cheshire. We go back an awful long way."

"Never heard of it or the Legh's without an I," she laughed while simultaneously tossing her long blond hair over her shoulder. She tapped her chin twice with her left index finger while puckering her perfect lips as if deep in thought.

"So, what brings Peter Legh, without an I to Menai with an I?" she asked, the alluring smile flashing at him again. Peter glanced at her left hand and to his delight he saw no wedding band.

"Pleasure and relaxation, as much as I can possibly get while on 48 hours leave. My father recommended it and I have always wanted to see Anglesey, so as they say, live for the day! Why not?"

"Why not indeed!" she replied. "So then, this is your first time?" she asked with a smile.

"Err, on Anglesey, yes," he responded, she caught the mischievous look in his eye, and the two simultaneously laughed.

"Please, may I buy you a drink?...err...I'm sorry, I didn't get your name."

"That's because I didn't tell you!" she replied with a chuckle, then continued, "I'm Taryn, Taryn Thomas of Menai!"

"Karen?"

"No, Taryn!" she laughed. Nothing new here, her whole life people had struggled with her first name, Karen being the usual mistake. "Try Karen but with a T," she said.

"Oh, Carrot?"

Taryn couldn't contain herself. She burst out in laughter and covered her mouth, her shoulders heaving up and down as she laughed. "No, Silly, Taryn T-A-R-Y-N Taryn!"

"Oh, I'm so sorry...Taryn! What a beautiful name."

"Why, thank you Peter Legh. I've been spelling it for people my whole life but I've never been called a Carrot before."

Their eyes met and locked for the first time. Peter felt a wave of pleasure roll from his shoulders down his spine. He had never felt that feeling before, but he knew he liked it. He knew he wanted more.

"So, Taryn with a T, may I have the honor of buying you a drink?"

"Yes, that would be nice. I'll have a glass of cider, thank you." Taryn suddenly felt terrific. Finally, a good-looking man with manners had graced the bar of The Bull. This was a rare occurrence and she planned on finding out more, much more about Peter Legh of Addington.

"Barman, a glass of your finest cider and a pint of your best bitter please," yelled Peter towards the barman.

"Certainly, Sir," said the barman, having loaded the stack of glasses into the sink to be washed. Peter smiled, he had a feeling that moving from the packed lounge to the bar was a good move, one of the best moves of his life.

"So, are you a local?" asked Peter, anxious to find out as much as possible about the beautiful woman next to him. "Yes, you could say that. I've been here my whole life, waiting for Mr. Wonderful to come and rescue me!" she laughed.

"Sorry it took me a while, but there is a war on and I'm sure we can more than make up for lost time," he replied, and they both laughed. The local man next to him moved a little farther down the bar allowing Peter to now stand squarely at the bar next to her.

"Busy little place," said Peter.

"Yeah, it's nearly all bridge related. The lounge is always packed. Between the bridge workers and the RAF boys, it has been like this for almost two years. That is why the locals who are smart drink on this side. If you are in a hurry, you do not want to be in the lounge. Right here in the bar is the only way to go," she said with a smile. Clearly, she had the place figured out. Just then the barman arrived with their drinks, "That's one and six please, Sir," he said.

"Snudge, this is my new friend, Peter Legh," said Taryn. She continued, "Peter Legh, meet Snudge, quite possibly the best barman on Anglesey."

"Nice to meet you, Snudge," said Peter, extending his hand. Snudge wiped his wet hand on his apron and gave Peter a firm handshake.

"Nice to meet you Peter, and incidentally I AM the best barman on Anglesey," said Snudge.

"Thank you and have one yourself," said Peter, as he handed over the cash.

"Cheers!" said Snudge, turning to face the thirsty, noisey men waiting anxiously on the opposite side of the bar.

"Well, here's to meeting you Taryn. Cheers!" said Peter as they knocked their glasses together. Each took a sip while looking straight into each other eyes. Peter Legh was already smitten.

"Yes, I'm glad we met Peter. To your health!" she said, and each took another drink before returning their glasses to the bar towel Snudge had neatly laid out before them.

"So, you said you are on leave. Are you in the Army?" asked Taryn.

"Lord no. I'm in the RAF!" he laughed.

"Oh my. I'm glad I didn't say anything bad about your mates over there," she said indicating with a nod towards the crowd of young RAF lads. They were all anxiously vying for Snudge's attention.

"They are not my mates, and I'm one hundred percent on leave. The last thing I need is RAF company," said Peter.

"The RAF boys aren't bad. For the most part they are good lads, missing home and Mum most of them. But some of the men that work on the bridge are just pigs, dirty old men most of them. Trust me," she laughed, momentarily recalling her meeting with the obscene Billy Muskett earlier that morning on the bridge. Then she dismissed it from her thoughts and focused instead on the good-looking man in front of her with the perfect smile and took another sip of her cider.

At that moment Peter knew that for the first time in his life he had just found someone very special. Something told him that this was going to be a memorable little trip to Anglesey.

"So, what do you do in the RAF?"

"I'm a fighter pilot, Spitfires."

"No! Spitfires! You're a pilot? Oh! God, please tell me you have a white horse tied up outside." They both laughed.

"No sorry, but how about a white MG?"

"Oh, that will work!" they both laughed, and she subconsciously moved a little closer to him.

"So, what do you do here in Menai?" asked Peter.

"Not too much these days, I retired early." They both laughed again.

"Seriously," he smiled, "what do you do?"

"Ok, I'm not fully retired. These days I take a lot of fat old men out on the straits so they can drool over the bridge. I don't see what all the fuss is about. It's just a silly bridge."

"What does that mean, take them out on the straits?" he asked.

"The Menai Straits silly, the water you drove across in your white MG to come and rescue me," she laughed.

"You sail?" asked Peter, starting to lose himself again in her aqua blue eyes.

"No, not a sailboat. You know a boat with...what's that noisy oily thing called? Err...an engine!" They laughed together again. By now both had stopped facing the bar and were now standing facing each other. The rest of the pub had simply ceased to exist. They were both focused intensely on each other.

"Oh, a motorboat, very nice Captain Taryn!" Peter snapped to attention and gave her a salute.

She giggled, "You're funny. At ease, Sailor. I'm one hundred percent off duty!" she said. Peter laughed, delighted that she seemed to have the same wacky sense of humor as his own.

"I grew up on the water here and know the straits like the back of my hand. My earliest memories are of being out on the boat with my dad, that and looking for mussels along the shoreline when the tide goes out. We still have a small boat business," said Taryn.

"Mmmm, mussels. I love mussels, all shellfish as a matter of fact," said Peter. "Gosh. Thinking about it, I did not realize how hungry I was. Lunch was hours ago. So, where is the best place in town to get some of these Menai mussels?" asked Peter.

"Oh, that's easy, the Victoria Hotel, the best! They have a huge conservatory with a restaurant that looks across the straits. It is just beautiful, but you would never get a table there. They are booked solid with all the big wig bridge boys. Come back next week. Hopefully, they will have all left by then," she laughed.

"Dang!" said Peter. Taryn could see the disappointment on his face.

"Peter, you don't listen. I said YOU would never get a table. I however, well…let's just say I know a few people in this little town," she laughed.

"You tease!" he said, "Ok I'll let you help me out this time, but on one condition."

"Oh, really. What's that?" she asked in a playful tone, her whole face lighting up, hoping.

"That you join me for dinner?" he asked.

"Ha!" she said. "I thought you'd never ask. I'm starving too!"

"Splendid!" At that moment, there was no happier man on the Island of Anglesey, or the entire Kingdom for that matter, than Peter Legh.

"But I too have a condition," she teased.

"And that is?" asked Peter.

"A ride on that white horse of yours, sorry MG…and with the roof down," she replied, her whole face lighting up.

"Done! But it's pouring down out there," replied Peter.

"Then I'll take a rain check Mr. Legh, until it's a sunny day," she laughed.

"Absolutely! I propose a toast," he said as they raised their glasses.

"To mussels and MG's."

"To mussels and MG's, cheers!" They made eye contact again, laughed and drained their glasses.

"Snudge!" she yelled across the bar. Snudge shot across to her.

"May I use your telephone please?" she asked cocking her head innocently to one side.

"Absolutely, come on through," replied Snudge and in a smooth movement he lifted up a small section of the bar that Taryn walked through and disappeared into a tiny office to the right.

After a couple of minutes, she reemerged smiling and giving him the thumbs up. "We're on, but we need to head over there now. He won't hold the table for long."

"Jolly good show!" said Peter. He helped her with her jacket and looked around for an umbrella. "Did you bring an umbrella?" he asked.

"No umbrella, unfortunately. It was not raining when I left, how about you? You only have a jumper on." She smiled at him.

"I have my flying jacket in the car. I didn't wear it in here because I didn't want to talk a lot of boring war stories with the boys. Here, please take this. He took off his scarf and gently wrapped it around her neck folding it neatly in front of her. Then he smoothed it down with his hand and gently stroked her cheek. She smiled, blushed slightly again and said, "Thank you Peter, mmmm nice scarf. I like the colors."

"Oh, jolly good! It's my old school scarf," he said, again tumbling into her sparkling blue eyes.

"What school did you go to?" she asked.

"Eton," he answered with a smile.

"Eton! Well of course. I knew you were a gentleman," she laughed.

"Quite!" said Peter. "Shall we?"

She took his arm and the two headed for the door. Peter acknowledged Snudge's wink out of the corner of his eye as they left the bar. They opened the door and ran laughing into the rain to the MG.

Snudge leaned over to collect their empty glasses. The red lipstick mark was still visible at the top of Taryn's empty cider glass. Snudge shook his head. For over two years now, as the bridge work had been underway, he had watched scores of men try to impress Taryn Thomas. Very few even got the time of day from her. Even fewer got to buy her a drink. But Peter Legh, well, he was clearly someone very special.

Chapter 64

THE VICTORIA HOTEL

Menai, Anglesey

August 17, 1940

They ran together the short distance to where Peter had parked his MG. The rain was pelting down at an angle from the cold wind blowing in from the Irish Sea. Taryn held on tightly to Peter's arm to avoid slipping on the wet cobblestones of the Menai street. He opened the passenger door for her, reached in and retrieved his leather flying jacket from the seat and she jumped in.

"Here you go, put this on your lap. It will help keep you warm," said Peter.

"Such a gentlemen Peter, thanks!" The sheepskin lining felt good on her knees.

"Quite!" he replied as he ran around to the driver's side and climbed in. He slammed the door bringing an instant calm to the cramped interior of the MG. The rain pummeled on the canvas top making it seem heavier than it actually was. But it was dry and cozy inside and that was what mattered. He fired up the engine and pulled slowly out into the street.

"Ok, I believe you said the Victoria Hotel, Madam. Directions, if you please," said Peter pretending to be her chauffeur. She loved it. What fun this was, she felt quite invigorated in the company of this incredibly handsome Spitfire pilot.

"Quite Charles. Go about a half mile, then left at Ye Olde Village Shop and then head on up Telford Road until I instruct you to do otherwise," she said with a smile, framed by those perfect red lips.

"Yes Mam. Tally Ho!" he laughed. He punched the accelerator and skidded the tires on the wet road much to Taryn's delight.

"Tally Ho!" she yelled back at him as he raced through the MG's gears with precision. Taryn Thomas, sitting in the passenger seat of the tiny MG, felt happier than she could ever remember. She was so glad that Peter Legh had just stepped right into her life.

The Victoria Hotel was, without a doubt the best restaurant in town and anyone who was anyone connected with the Menai Bridge project wanted to be seen there. It was known for its legendary fresh sea food and incredible panoramic view of the Menai Straits. The Victoria Hotel was the place to be on Anglesey.

Taryn knew the owners well. She knew their son Glyn a lot better. They had gone to school together and had always been good friends. Glyn had finally recovered from being unable to volunteer for the armed services due to his poor eyesight and flat feet. He was the Manager there and when Taryn called him excited about her new friend and requested a table with a view, he knew that her new friend must be someone special.

Glyn made a quick adjustment to the seating arrangements. The two executives from the BBC who had planned on enjoying the sweeping views of the straits while enjoying their fish and chips, instead found themselves on the opposite side of the dining room. Their view was reduced to watching a man laboriously stack empty crates of beer bottles against an outside wall.

Peter pulled the MG in front of the main entrance. The windshield wipers danced in perfect harmony as the rain continued to fall. "We may as well do this right. Stay where you are." He jumped out of the car and ran around to her side. He opened the door and took the flying jacket off her lap to hold up like a canopy. "Go! Go! Go!" he yelled as she bolted out of the car and the two of them ran to the main entrance. Laughing together in the rain, they splashed through the puddles.

Peter grabbed the shiny brass door handle and pulled open the door. The noise from the packed lounge was incredible. The air was thick with cigarette smoke and the damp smell of wet coats, scarfs, hats and hair. "You wait here, and I'll go and park the car!" he yelled into her ear. He hung the jacket over his shoulders and ran back out into the rain.

"So sweet," she said to herself.

Peter parked the MG and quickly sprinted back to the Victoria Hotel. Taryn was waiting where he had left her and gave him a big smile when he returned. "Oh, you're soaked," she said looking at his wet brown hair. "Piece of cake," he responded. To his delight she reached down and grabbed his hand, "Follow me!" she shouted in his ear.

"Anywhere," he replied, as she pushed her way through the crowded lounge to a set of double doors with the word Restaurant painted on the wall above them. Peter opened the door to the restaurant for her and the two of them walked inside. The volume of noise decreased significantly. It gave the restaurant an aura of calmness after the mayhem of the lounge. A well-dressed hostess stood behind a small lectern with a large guest book open on top of it.

"Good evening," she said. "Do you have a reservation?"

"Yes, it's under Thomas," replied Taryn.

The hostess checked the guest book and then looked back up at the couple. "Please come with me," she said with a genuine smile. She was followed by the pair still holding hands into the massive glass conservatory.

Peter was immediately reminded of the conservatory back at Addington, but this was on a much larger scale. It had a huge variety of palms and ferns. As a young boy growing up at Addington Abbey, he had always loved being in the conservatory. It was one of his favorite places to play, mainly because it was warm inside even on the dullest of days. This place was terrific. He loved the palm trees and could identify most of them as they walked by them on their way to a table for two. They would be seated next to the window with an unobstructed view.

He had that exact same warm comforting feeling when they had moved out to California. The family winery in Clayton had many of the same types of palms. Now he was being led by the hand by a beautiful woman and he had that same warm feeling all over again and loved it.

"Here we are," said the hostess, as she pulled back the chair for Taryn. Taryn released Peter's hand, but not before giving it a little squeeze first.

Peter was fascinated as he looked out at the view. Even with the overcast sky and the rain streaked glass, he was simply in awe at the splendor of the Menai Straits. The fast flowing deep blue water was beginning to show white caps as the wind picked up in strength.

The crown jewel and centerpiece was Telford's legendary Menai suspension bridge. It was unusual because it was a suspension bridge, and it had majestic supporting arches. Somehow the bridge added to the majesty of the place. It's massive size, the color of the stone, the arch ways, and the magnificent cable suspension system with its bluish green coppery finish left him at a loss for words. He simply said, "Good Lord".

"Peter?" she asked. "Is everything all right?"

"Oh, I'm so sorry," he said, lightly stroking the blond hair on her shoulder and then looking back out of the enormous picture window that framed the masterpiece before him. "It's the view, it's absolutely magnificent. I had no idea just how beautiful this place was," he said continuing to marvel at the view. He could hardly believe that he was about to dine here, in such a perfect setting with the most beautiful woman he had ever met. This unique magical place was such a welcome relief from what he had been doing on a daily basis now for months. His usual day included engaging in high stakes dog fights against the determined Luftwaffe over the rolling green hills of Kent. Anglesey was quite simply a whole different world.

"I'm delighted that you like my little town Peter," she said flashing him the perfect smile.

"I do, very much so. I'm so glad I came out here," he replied as he sat back down.

"How on earth did you get this table?" he asked her, looking around at the packed restaurant.

She smiled at him and lightly tapped the side of her nose, "On Anglesey, it's not what you know, it's who you know," she said.

"Quite," he replied making the same gesture. They both laughed and instinctively reached for each other's hands across the table at the exact same time. Both felt very much alive and acutely aware of just how much they already enjoyed each other's company.

"Hi Taryn!" interrupted a man wearing an immaculate tuxedo who had arrived at their table. She reached out her hand, which he gently kissed.

"Hello Glyn, thank you so much for helping us out. This is my friend, Peter Legh."

"Pleasure to meet you, Sir!" said Glyn, giving Peter a firm handshake.

"The pleasure is mine, Sir. Thank you for your help. What a beautiful restaurant you have here."

"Thank you, it certainly is. We also have twelve hotel rooms over the pub. They have been sold out for months. You could say business is booming," said Glyn. He quickly went over the menu and both opted for the house special, Victoria Mussels.

It was a magical dinner. The mussels were excellent. The conversation was even better. Taryn was fascinated by Peter's stories of his time in California, how he had learned to fly the Stearman crop duster, and how he had returned to Britain to volunteer to fight with the RAF. That had sealed the deal for Taryn Thomas. Peter Legh was as close as she was going to get to her knight in shining armor. He had given up his safety and freedom, to come back and fight for her. She could not be happier.

For his part, Peter learned about life on the Island of Anglesey. More importantly, he learned more about the stunning beauty opposite him. She was an only child and both of her parents had passed away. She was a cautious person and chose her friends carefully. Glyn and Snudge were clearly two of her favorites along with another older chap called Edward Thomas Riggs who went by his initials ETR.

ETR was a tough veteran of World War I and the Local Defense Volunteer Captain for the town of Menai. Peter could tell that ETR had helped fulfill the void left after her father had passed away. ETR wore a lot of hats. In addition to being the church caretaker and the LDV Captain, he also assumed the role of the local village Bobby. There was no Police presence in the village of Menai. The closest official law enforcement was on the mainland in the City of Bangor. In an emergency, there was the Port Police at Holyhead and Amlwch. The truth was there was very little crime on the island. The locals pretty much policed themselves.

ETR was well respected in Menai and all the locals were more than happy to have him act as judge and jury when it came to the occasional disagreement. ETR it seemed was her 'go to' guy and she was anxious for Peter to meet him. Checking her watch, she knew that they still had plenty of time to be able to catch up with ETR back at The Bull later. He usually stopped there for last orders. They both wanted to find out more about each other and neither wanted to lose the momentum they had built together so far.

They thanked Glyn for a wonderful dinner. Peter paid their bill and left an enormous tip. They left the Victoria and headed back over to The Bull. The rain had now stopped so they decided to take a walk the long way. They took the walking path that followed along the banks of the picturesque Menai Straits. It was the perfect setting. As the long summer day began to come to a close, Peter Legh couldn't have been happier with his decision to visit Anglesey.

Chapter 65

ONE LAST PINT

Menai, Anglesey
August 17, 1940

It was close to 8:30 PM when Max finally returned to his "executive digs", as Hugh had called the cottage. It was also known by its Welsh name, Tyddyn Ben. That was the name on the rusted metal sign attached to the gate. Max lay on the small bed and it was surprisingly comfortable. Perhaps Hugh's assessment was not too far off the mark, given that the alternative was bunking in the barn at Rhosybol with thirty or more loud, sweaty men. It was at least quiet, and Max appreciated that.

The executive digs were strategically picked by Richard to give Max easy access to the British high-powered radio set. It was also the only place in Menai that Hugh was able to rent due to the bridge rebuild. But as far as Max was concerned, its best feature other than the bed was that it was close enough to walk downtown to the inviting pub called The Bull, that Hugh had driven past earlier in the day.

It had been years since he had been on British soil. He was supremely confident that he could easily blend in. This was no different than he had done during his senior years at Eton. He wanted to take the pulse of the locals to see how their morale was and listen to their conversations. He especially wanted to hear from the RAF. He understood enough about the propaganda part of his mission to know that Dr. Goebbels would salivate over any additional information that he might be able to glean to put himself one rung further up the ladder of Nazi hierarchy.

If his role as poster boy put him closer to the Fuhrer, then he was on board. He had by now tasted plenty of action in Poland,

Norway, and France. He had seen death and violence close-up and knew that he was living dangerously. Having earned an Iron Cross so early in his career, he should now begin to set his sights higher within the Nazi organization.

He saw both Goebbels and Himmler as conduits to the fastest way possible to get closer to the one man that really mattered, Adolph Hitler. He knew that once he made it back to Germany with the film, followed by the gold, his life would change drastically. At twenty-eight, he was ready to embrace whatever came next so long as it served the Fuhrer and the needs of the Nazi party.

The bed creaked when he swung his legs off to the side and sat up. His jackboots made a thud on the old wooden floorboards. He reached down and instinctively felt the edge of the top of his left boot and there it was. He could easily feel it through his trousers, the outline of the custom gold pin that Himmler had presented to him in a private ceremony before he left for Norway. It was a custom piece that he wore with pride. He had not removed it since Himmler's batman had pierced his boot and attached it for him while the leader of the SS had looked on in sheer delight.

Max knew it was a gesture from Himmler to help ensure his loyalty to the Brandenburgers and the SS and not to be seduced into Goebbels world of propaganda, movies, bright lights and girls. It was good to be wanted. On the eve of the greatest gold heist in history, Max von Seeckt felt on top of the world. He decided he was going to celebrate, so he headed out to The Bull.

It took less than fifteen minutes before he opened the door of The Bull, and he instantly assumed the persona of Billy Muskett, Government Inspector. He headed towards the busy bar. Much to his delight, the place was full of RAF lads and bridge workers. Many were older men in cloth caps out for a pint. There were several ladies sitting in the corner around a small table. Unfortunately, none of them were the stunning blond named Taryn Thomas that he had bumped into at the bridge earlier that morning. He made his way to the bar and was able to catch the barman's eye, "A pint of Guinness please," said Max, amusing himself at his selection of a stout made in Dublin. "Certainly, Sir," replied the barman as he pulled on the hand pump directly in front of Max. "Busy tonight, eh?" asked Max.

"Not really. This is about normal for a Saturday night. You watch, in a while you won't be able to move in here. They all like to come in for last orders. It's just the way things work around here. Of course, the best pint on the entire island might also play a small role," joked the barman.

"Oh, I see. Good, then I picked the right spot," said Max, as he watched the black frothy liquid being expertly poured into the glass.

"Are you working on the bridge?" asked the barman, without looking up from the hand pump.

"Yes, just for a couple of days. Then I head back to London, back to the Blitz I'm sorry to say," replied Max.

"Oh, that's a shame. Awful business bombing innocent civilians like that," replied the barman.

"Yes, it is awful. Hopefully, it will end soon, but it's nice to go out for a pint without my gas mask," laughed Max. He watched the barman put his pint down for a moment to allow it to settle.

"Yeah, it's pretty safe here on the island. It's almost as if we're not at war. We hear the bombers going over, but they are heading to Liverpool, not Menai. I doubt we are on Goering's hit list. All we have is bloody sheep. Are you staying in Beaumaris?" asked the barman.

"Yes, you're probably right. No, I'm staying here in Menai in a little cottage. It's about a fifteen-minute walk from here, so it works out fine," answered Max.

"Good for you," said the barman as he topped off Max's pint and pushed it towards him. "I'm Snudge by the way. Let me know if you need anything else."

"I'm Billy, Billy Muskett," replied Max, "Just the pint for now, thanks Snudge," he continued as he handed Snudge a half crown. "Please have one for yourself also," said Max, familiar with the best way to tip a good barman in Britain.

"Thank you, Sir!" said Snudge as he rang up the till. He handed Max his change after dropping a three-penny bit into the staff's glass tip jar located next to the till.

Max nodded his approval and picked up his pint of Guinness. An elderly couple got up to leave their small table next to the fireplace. He made his way over to it as it gave him a great view of the whole lounge. Max took a seat and satisfied that his pint had settled sufficiently, he took several large gulps. It was good. It had been many years since he had enjoyed a good pint of Guinness. He lit himself a cigarette and sat back in the chair as a large group of men wearing blue RAF tunics entered and headed straight to the bar.

The men were noisy, boisterous, and incredibly young looking to Max. None of them looked older than 20. If these were the men charged with the safety of RAF Valley or RAF Mona, then Max and his men would have had no problem capturing the airfields as he had laid out in his original invasion plan.

Max smiled as he considered the irony and how much things had changed. Instead of getting ready to go into battle against the young British airmen, he was getting ready to rob them of their gold, and even better, rub their nose in it! He simply could not wait for Goebbels to release his masterpiece film that included himself, Major Max von Seeckt of The Brandenburgers in the starring role. He took another long drink from his Guinness, counted his blessings, and listened intently to the conversation between the boys from the RAF as they jostled for Snudge's attention.

Interestingly there seemed to be little talk of war, mostly they seemed to be taking the piss out of one of their officers. Max reasoned that it was no different really than the banter enjoyed by enlisted German boys of the same age.

Max finished up his pint, waited for all the RAF lads to get served and returned to the bar. He caught Snudge's eye. "Same again, Billy?" asked Snudge. "Absolutely. That was an excellent pint of Guinness," replied Max. Snudge poured him another perfect pint which he promptly paid for, tipped Snudge again, then headed back to his seat.

The second pint seemed even better than the first. He was glad that he had made the decision to walk down to The Bull and have a drink. It had been years since he had sat by himself, without Hott or the Beast, with just his own thoughts and enjoyed a great pint. Anglesey almost seemed to be an alternate universe. While the citizens were diligent about observing the blackout and rationing rules, there was really no indication that a war was even going on.

People, at least here, seemed to be getting by just fine. He was sure that life was completely different a hundred miles or so from here in the rough streets of Liverpool. They were made even rougher lately by the deadly incendiary bombs that Hermann Goering's Luftwaffe rained down upon them from the air on an almost nightly basis.

The door opened again and two more workman came in. They were followed by a single lady, probably in her forties and a little overweight. She was not bad looking, at least in the dimly lit lounge. She followed the two men towards the bar but then went to the other side of the group of RAF lads gathered in the middle, indicating that she was alone. He watched her as she immediately got Snudge's attention and ordered herself a drink. Max decided to make a move. He downed his pint, got up from the table and squeezed himself between the RAF group and the woman, arriving at the bar next to her just as Snudge appeared with a gin and tonic.

"Same again, please Snudge!" said Max. "And may I buy this beautiful young lady her drink?" he continued, as he flashed her a warm smile and touched the peak of his cap in a polite salute. "I'm Billy, Billy Muskett," he said as he held out his hand. "Why yes, thank you, that's very nice of you. Nice to meet you, Mr. Muskett. My name is Anwen Bennion," she replied as she took his hand and smiled. "Busy little place," said Max as more RAF boys came through the door. Anwen looked at her watch, "It's always busy but especially as it gets closer to closing time. That is why I get in and out before the madness starts," she laughed. "Of course," replied Max as he noticed her perfectly manicured red fingernails.

She reached in her purse and pulled out her cigarettes. He watched her as she fumbled to get one out of the box. As soon as it was between her lips, Max was there with his lighter. She lightly touched his hand as he lit it. Her skin was soft. They made eye contact and smiled at each other. Anwen blushed ever so slightly as she exhaled.

Snudge arrived with his pint. Max paid him and turned his attention to his new companion. "Cheers, Anwen," he said. "Cheers!" replied Anwen. The door opened again and at least a half a dozen more RAF men came in. Evidently, they were friends with the crowd that was already at the bar. "I see what you mean," said Max as he moved away from the bar to allow others to get served. He stayed in close proximity to Anwen, who now turned her back towards the bar so that she could focus entirely on the good-looking gentleman with the piercing blue eyes and thick blond hair. He had just made her day.

In less than fifteen minutes, Max knew everything he needed to know about Anwen Bennion. When he offered to walk her home to the little house in the village where she lived alone, she could not say "Yes!" fast enough. They finished their drinks and cigarettes and left the lounge. The racket of a sing along by the RAF lads echoed in Anwen's ears as the nice man named Billy Muskett slipped his arm around her waist and the two quickly vanished down one of the back streets of Menai.

An hour later, well satisfied, Max von Seeckt left an exhausted Anwen Bennion in her bed and began heading back towards his cottage. It had been a perfect night. He had worked up a good sweat servicing Miss Bennion and was suddenly quite thirsty. He took a quick look at his watch and saw that there was still time to catch last orders at The Bull for one very last pint of their superb Guinness if he picked up his pace. He began to trot.

Perhaps the influence of three pints of Guinness and the easy conquest of Anwen Bennion had blurred his finely tuned instincts. It was a casual spur of the moment decision, made by a man who generally planned things out meticulously. That decision would trigger an incredible sequence of events that would have a profound effect on the outcome of Adolph Hitler's gold heist.

Chapter 66

LAST ORDERS AT THE BULL

Menai, Anglesey
August 17, 1940

The bar at The Bull was quite full but a big improvement over the packed Victoria and the bedlam of The Bull lounge. Peter and Taryn were able to clearly see over to the other side of the bar. Taryn had made a bee line for the far corner of the bar where they had first met.

She checked with Snudge about ETR, but he had already been and gone. Disappointed, she ordered another round and she and Peter talked and laughed like a couple who had been together for years. Each was eager to learn more about the other. Peter was delighted with her offer to show him more of Anglesey the next day. Neither wanted the evening to end, but Snudge had other plans.

"Last Orders!" yelled Snudge as he rang the old brass ship bell hanging on the wall next to the cash register. The RAF lads immediately went into a frenzy gulping down what they had in their glasses to make way for last call.

"Would you like another drink?" Peter asked Taryn, gently stroking her long hair.

"No, thank you Peter. I think I've had enough for tonight. It's been such a wonderful evening and we have a big day tomorrow!" she said as she realized how happy she was to be in this man's company. Peter Legh was such a change from the usual bridge worker riff raff, and now she would get to spend tomorrow with him. She felt energized and very much alive. But she wasn't done with this evening yet.

"Yes, I couldn't agree more. This has been the best evening that I have had in a long, long time. We should drink up and get going. You know I just realized that I don't even know where you live? Is it far?" he asked.

"No, it's about a ten-minute walk that way," she said pointing her thumb over her shoulder. "And about two minutes in your little MG," she laughed.

"Absolutely, bottoms up!" he replied and they both had another couple of gulps, as the traffic at the bar increased by a few more locals for last orders. One had a young Staffordshire Terrier with him. The RAF lads were all trying to outdo each other for Snudge's attention. Snudge, totally unfazed continued to pull pints as if they simply did not exist.

Then, Peter noticed Taryn's face. In an instant, her expression had gone from one of delight and happiness to a look of anger and fear. She glared across the bar past Snudge and into the lounge.

"Taryn, what's the matter?" he asked her.

"Oh, Peter please don't look now. But there is that awful blond-haired man I ran into this morning on the bridge. He is with the government and his name is Billy Muskett. He is some sort of big wig inspector on the bridge. Anyway, I saw him coming down from the bridge tower earlier this morning when I was out walking Shelby. I asked him what he was doing, and he said he was testing the tolerances on some of the rivets or something like that. He said he did not work for the bridge contractor but worked for the government and could basically do whatever he pleased.

He was arrogant, talking down to me, which is a real pet hate of mine. He really annoyed me. He hit on me in the crassest manner. He disgusted me, I couldn't get away from him fast enough, a real creep." Peter couldn't help but smile. One thing that he had already learned and loved about this woman was that she had plenty of spunk. No man was going to push Taryn Thomas around, that was abundantly clear.

"And what did he say to that?" asked Peter.

"Augh. He got me so mad. Anyway, that is him over there in the lounge. He's the tall man with the blond hair. He's turned around now so you can look at him," she said looking across the bar into the lounge area.

Peter turned around and looked into the lounge but Snudge and an RAF lad were blocking his view. He could see the top of the man's blond hair but not his features.

"Do you see him?" she asked.

"Yes, but only from the back. I can see his blond hair," answered Peter.

"See, how creepy is that? Men don't have blond hair, only women!" she laughed.

Peter continued to try to get a better look through the crowded bar, but the blond man still faced away from him. The crowd at the bar had grown bigger because of Snudge's final bell. Then the blond man turned slightly to his left and Peter could finally see more of his profile. Then he froze. "It couldn't be," he muttered under his breath. He strained to get a better view. He was fairly sure that the man he was looking at, who went by the name of Billy Muskett was none other than his old nemesis from Eton, Max von Seeckt!

Then Snudge moved over and blocked Peter's view so all he could see was the top of the man's head, "Dammit!" he cursed.

"Peter? What's wrong?" asked Taryn.

"Dammit, I lost sight of him. Snudge is blocking my view," said Peter standing on his tip toes to get a better look. Then two of the locals pushed in front of him to get to the bar. "Excuse me, Mate," one of them said, now further blocking Peter's view.

"Oh, forget him. He's a total idiot! Please forget I even told you," said Taryn.

"You don't understand, I think I know him," said Peter, a stone-cold look now on his face. He tried desperately to get a better look across the sea of heads and the thick haze of smoke.

"How could you know him? Peter, what's the matter? Please forget it, please Peter!" She pulled him closer to her. A look of concern was now visible in her blue eyes.

"Please Taryn, listen to me. If it is who I think it is, I went to Eton with him and there is something bad afoot," he said to her as he strained to get a better look.

"Snudge!" he yelled to get his attention. But it was lost in the racket that had now overwhelmed both sides of Snudge's crowded bar. Realizing it was futile, he turned to a now concerned Taryn and said, "I need you to stay here. I have to go and see if that is who I think it is. I'll be right back, stay here!" he said directly into her ear over the din.

"Peter, no. Please don't go. He's not worth it. Please!"

"Stay here," he said. "I'll be back. I will not make a scene, I promise. I just need to be certain." With that he kissed her gently on the cheek and spun around to leave. Unfortunately, he had not noticed the keen-eyed Staffordshire that had somehow spotted a small piece of bread crust on the floor. At that exact moment, it made a bee line for the unexpected treat.

Peter had no idea what happened. All he knew was that both of his feet had been taken out from under him and that he was tumbling headfirst into one of the bar's small round tables. Unfortunately, two full pints, an overflowing ash tray and three towers of empty pint glasses were stacked up on the same table.

The crash was terrific. Beer flew through the air and glass shattered as the table went over. Peter went careening over the top and landed on his back with a thud on the floor. People scrambled left and right in the crowded space to try to avoid the melee. A huge "Hooray!!!" erupted from the RAF contingent in the lounge at the sound of the breaking glass.

"Peter! Peter!" Taryn cried as she rushed to his aid. The bar briefly lapsed into chaos as the revelers checked to make sure everybody was ok.

"What happened?" he asked as she helped him to his feet.

"Are you ok? You poor thing!" she said dusting him off. "You tripped over Koda, she said pointing to the young Staffordshire wagging its tail.

"Good Lord! I'm terribly sorry!" he said to the two locals who had been sitting at the table. "Please let me get you another drink."

Just then Gladys, The Bull's cleaning lady arrived with a mop and bucket. "Let's be having you," she said as she ushered Peter and the two locals out of the way. She righted the table in one swift move and began to sweep up the broken glass.

Peter pulled a pound note out of his wallet and yelled, "Take care of these two gentlemen for me please and tell Snudge I'll cover any damage!" With that he kissed Taryn again and rushed out of the door. He quickly ran to the lounge door and opened it to a barrage of noise and a mass of RAF blue greatcoats and jackets. Everyone was yelling at the top of their lungs to be heard.

Peter pushed his way towards the bar. He was straining to see over the mass of heads but there was no sign of the man with the blond hair. He finally made it to the bar and with a last "Excuse me!" he stood on the brass foot rail to get a better vantage point. He scanned the entire lounge, but it was fruitless. The only blond in The Bull that night was the one standing on the opposite side of the bar, watching him with a look of bewilderment on her face.

"Dammit!" he cursed. Then he saw a sign on the far wall with an arrow below it that said Toilets. Realizing this was his only remaining shot, he turned around to give Taryn a wave to indicate he was coming back around to the bar. He pushed his way through to the toilets. Several RAF chaps were standing in the corridor drinking and sharing an apparently hilarious story. "Excuse me," said Peter again, as he pushed his way to the door marked GENTS.

He shoved open the door. There were several locals and an RAF lad using the urinal trough, none of whom had blond hair. The stall door that was closed had the word "Engaged" showing in red on the brass dial above the door handle. Peter felt his heart rate increase. The blond man had to be behind the stall door. He stood opposite the closed door and waited.

He checked his watch. It was now past 10:30. The pub would be emptying out fast. More men came in to use the urinal, adding to the loud drunken conversations all echoing off the white subway tiled walls.

"Dammit!" he cursed to himself again. The irony was not lost on him that he was standing in a Gentlemen's toilet listening to utter nonsense, waiting for a stall door to open. If the man he suspected of being behind that door turns out to be Max von Seeckt, then all hell would break loose. It would make the incident that just took place in the bar look like tidily winks. All this, while the girl of his dreams waited alone on the other side of the bar.

Unable to contain himself any longer, Peter moved forward to knock on the door. It suddenly swung open and an old man in a shabby donkey jacket and an old cloth cap came shuffling out.

"No!" yelled Peter. He realized his mistake and he bolted for the door. He then headed back into the now clearing lounge. No sign of anyone with blond hair.

Peter left the lounge and ran out into the wet cobbled stone street, frantically looking left and right. There was no one even close to von Seeckt's profile. All he saw was a group of locals weaving their way home and two RAF boys supporting their legless friend. All seemed typical for a Saturday night in Menai.

Disappointed, he walked towards the bar door, gathering his thoughts as he did. Really? Max von Seeckt, here in Menai? It made no sense. He had heard through the Eton Old Boy's network that von Seeckt had not only joined the Nazis but that he had won the coveted Iron Cross. He could not possibly be here on the Island of Anglesey. Plus, he knew that he had consumed more than his fair share of alcohol. The whole thing was likely to be one big misunderstanding. One thing he did know was that he wanted to get back to Taryn to clear up the mess he had made.

By the time he got back into the bar things had calmed down. Gladys had done a marvelous job of cleaning up the broken glass and had now cleared all the empties from the remaining tables. She was beginning to sweep up the rest of the sawdust from the floor. The two locals who had lost their pints when Peter knocked over their table gave him the thumbs up. They were more than happy with the replacement pints and a Scotch to help with their loss. Koda the dog sat quietly by his owner, slowly wagging its tail.

Taryn stood at the bar and smiled as he approached her, "Well, was it him?" she asked.

"No, I don't think so. He was not there by the time I got over to that side of the bar. In retrospect, it could not have possibly been him. It wouldn't make any sense," he said giving her a reassuring hug. "I see you got our friends taken care of. Was Snudge ok?"

"Yes, no problem. He knows it was an accident. He said not to worry about it, so we are all set," she said looking into his eyes. She extended her arm and said, "Now, shall we?"

"Quite," he replied. He kissed her perfect lips again and melted into her blue eyes. Then, arm in arm they left The Bull.

Chapter 67

THE COZY COTTAGE

Menai, Anglesey
August 17, 1940

It was a short walk back to the Victoria to pick up the MG. Then they drove the brief distance to Taryn's little Welsh cottage. Peter pulled up in front and killed the engine. The sky had finally cleared, the rain had stopped, and a new moon was now shining brightly. He stepped out of the car with his perfect 20/20 vision he could clearly see the small cottage. Without saying a word, he went around the back of the MG and opened the passenger door for her.

"Home Mam," he joked resorting back to his chauffer role.

"Quite Charles," she said holding out her downturned hand for Peter to help her out. "Shall we?" A huge smile spread across her face.

"Absolutely!" he replied closing the car door.

Taryn opened the little wrought iron gate and ushered him through. They walked down the slate stone path to the small front door. The cottage was classic Wales. It had whitewashed walls and a slate roof. The small casement windows were painted black with diamond shaped leaded glass. As they got closer to the front door, Peter became aware of a booming bark coming from the other side of the door. The noise increased in intensity. By the time they reached the front doorstep, it had reached a crescendo and now was beginning to turn into a low howl.

"Shelby, no!" Taryn yelled at the front door as she fumbled in her bag to retrieve her key. She opened the door and before she could say anything, Shelby came bolting out. The hound stopped briefly to wag at Taryn then went straight to Peter's shoes. The barking stopped for a second, just long enough for Shelby to inhale the stranger's new odor. Her brain instantly registered that he posed no threat. The booming bark then continued while she raced around excitedly in tight circles between the two of them. The white tip of her tail was just a blur.

"I think she likes you," laughed Taryn.

"Rather. She's a beautiful Bassett," replied Peter.

"Oh good, not everyone likes dogs. Shelby here, is definitely part of the package."

"Oh, I love them," he responded. "We breed Mastiff's at Addington. We have for centuries. Our pet one is called Sam, he's huge. But Shelby has a much deeper bark, it's quite extraordinary," he laughed as Shelby bolted back into the house. She turned around to make sure they had followed, firing off a couple more barks.

"Do come in Peter," Taryn said, taking his hand and entering the living room. Shelby was ecstatic. The barking continued.

"Welcome to my cozy cottage," said Taryn as she let go of his hand. She closed the door, turned on the light and did a little twirl in the middle of the room. Her arms were extended out and her head tilted back. Her long blond hair flowed down her back and her blue eyes were on fire. Shelby ran around the couch twice before stopping and looking at Peter. She gave him another ear full, just for good measure.

"Shelby, no!" yelled Taryn above the commotion. Shelby immediately stopped and came over to Taryn for a reassuring pet before sitting down. Her tail wafted across the oak floorboards and her eyes locked squarely on Peter.

"My word, you're right. This is a cozy little cottage, I love it," he said taking stock of the tastefully decorated room. There was a large fireplace off to the left that had a massive old oak mantle. It looked to have bent over time and ran the width of the fireplace. There was a nice pile of logs ready to light.

There was an oil painting over the mantel piece of the sunset over the Menai Bridge. A small velvet couch faced the fireplace and an oval coffee table was in front of it. In the corner was a radio on a small rustic wooden table. A wicker dog basket sat by the fireplace. There was a set of stairs on the far wall that led upstairs and the hall on the right led to the kitchen.

"Would you like a cup of tea, Peter?" she asked as she slipped off her coat and hung it on the coat stand next to the door. She deliberately left Peter's Eton scarf around her neck.

"Yes please, that would be smashing," he replied.

"Ok, I'll put the kettle on, come on Shelby!" Like a rocket, Shelby dashed into the kitchen, followed by Taryn and Peter.

The kitchen was small but well equipped. It had a split farmhouse style door that led to the back garden. Taryn filled the kettle and put the whistle on the spout. She placed it on the stove and lit the burner. Shelby sat on the floor, gazing up at a small tin on the counter. It had the word SHELBY painted on it in pink letters.

"Oh, you poor thing. Are you hungry Shelby?" she asked. The tail wagging accelerated.

"Would you like a treat?" That was it. Shelby let off a volley of loud barks and stared at the tin. Taryn reached in and took out a small strip of dried rawhide. Shelby focused intensely on it and gently took it from Taryn's hand. Then she shot off to her basket with her tail wagging to enjoy her treat. Taryn reached into a cupboard and pulled out a small silver tray. She placed two cups and saucers, a small milk jug, and a sugar bowl on it. Peter watched her as she moved about the tiny kitchen. He could watch her for hours. The way she moved, her hair, everything about her, he already idolized.

"I'd offer you a biscuit but I'm out I'm afraid. This rationing is such a pain," she said, snapping him out of his trance.

"Oh, I'm more than stuffed after that great meal, thank you," replied Peter.

"Let's go back into the living room, shall we? The kettle will be boiled in a few minutes," she said as she picked up the tray and headed back into the front room with Peter right behind her admiring her perfect buttocks.

Shelby was in her basket totally focused on the rawhide that she now held between her huge paws. The two sat on the couch together, Taryn placing his arm around her shoulder. She gently played with his fingers.

"I had such fun with you tonight Peter. It's been a long time since I went to dinner with a gentleman. Other than your acrobatics in The Bull, it was a wonderful night. Thank you."

"Oh, that!" he laughed. "It must have looked hilarious I suppose."

"It did!" she laughed. "I wanted to laugh but I wasn't sure if you were hurt. I'm glad you're ok. I'm sorry I said anything at all about that silly Billy Muskett."

"I'm fine, it was just a case of mistaken identity I suppose."

"When you thought he was from Eton, what was it about him that got you so upset? You said something bad might be happening. What did you mean exactly?"

"Oh, it's nothing. No need to worry, it wasn't him."

"Peter? You're holding out on me, what did you mean?"

"Really, it's nothing."

"Peter?"

Realizing that she wasn't going to stop, Peter reluctantly began to speak. "Ok, I thought the man might be Max von Seeckt. He was in my class at Eton. We hated each other with a passion. As you might guess by his name, he is of German heritage. Before the war broke out, I heard through the Eton Old Boy's that he had already joined the Nazis. Then once the fighting started, he was evidently at the forefront. The last rumor we heard was that he was already a Major and that he had won the Iron Cross. Apparently, Hitler himself had presented it to him. There was film footage of the ceremony. Which is why it's ridiculous for me to think he was in The Bull. It was the blond hair and the jaw line that were the image of him. I just couldn't be sure. I had to go and confirm it, but we know how that worked out," he laughed, remembering the scene again and Taryn did the same.

The kettle began to whistle. Taryn got up and went into the kitchen to make the tea. Shelby stopped chewing, dropped the rawhide in her basket and followed Taryn. Peter could hear the tea being made while she talked softly to Shelby. Soon she reappeared with a small china tea pot which she placed on the tray. Shelby returned to her basket and continued to happily work on the rawhide.

"Do you take sugar?" she asked.

"Please, one sugar is fine."

Taryn leaned forward and poured the tea, handing him a small china cup and saucer that matched the teapot. Then laughing she said, "I wish you had told me all that in the first place. I could have saved you a whole lot of trouble."

"I don't understand?" replied Peter, a look of confusion on his face.

"Well, if you had told me that this Max chap was German, I would have been able to tell you that he was not your man," she said with a broad smile.

"Really? How is that?" he asked as he stirred his tea, then took a sip.

"Well, that's easy. The conversation that I told you we had on the bridge this morning..."

"Yes?"

"He spoke fluent Welsh to me the whole time. He even pronounced my name right the first time. Unlike someone I know," she laughed.

Peter froze. He was aware that von Seeckt's mother had deep Welsh connections and that he spoke fluent Welsh. Now he knew. Something deep inside told him that Max von Seeckt was on Anglesey and he was definitely up to no good. He also knew for sure that he must find him or at least report what he knew to the local authorities.

"Oh, then it was all a mistake," he said, his mind whirling. "Mmmm, good tea thanks!"

They drank their tea and talked for a while longer until the clock on Taryn's wall chimed once, indicating it was 11:30. Peter looked at his watch to confirm the time.

"Lord, it's getting late. What a day! I hate to leave but I should probably get going. What time should we meet tomorrow morning?"

"Oh, I don't want you to leave Peter. We've had such a good time. I'm so glad we met," she said looking into his eyes. He gently put his hand on the back of her neck and pulled her towards him and their lips met again. They kissed slowly and softly at first and then more intensely and passionately. Slowly, she laid back on the couch, pulling him on top of her. Shelby looked up and wagged her tail. She curled up and went to sleep, secure that all was well in the tiny, cozy cottage.

On the other side of town, less than a couple of miles away, Max von Seeckt lay on his small bed wide awake. He was content with a belly full of Guinness, thinking of the stacks of gold bars hidden in the old windmill that soon he would be seizing for the Third Reich.

Despite the comfortable mattress, Max hardly slept at all. He was up at first light. His mind had replayed the events of the last 24 hours again and again. He methodically went through every planned detail of the heist. He was totally wired. With nothing to do in the cottage, he dressed, climbed into the Ford and drove out to Rhosybol. The island seemed deserted. He did not see another sole. He could see the genius of Churchill selecting Parys Mountain to hide the gold. Max doubted whether there was a more sparsely populated area in Britain. As he drove the deserted country roads, he smiled at the irony. Too bad for Churchill that Sean O'Reilly had put together a first-class IRA Headquarters on the same island for the exact same reason...total seclusion.

In the first light of dawn, Max was impressed by the size of the IRA base. The property consisted of several acres located in the green rolling hills that covered the island. There were many different buildings of all shapes and sizes. In addition to the dozen lorries that had been modified to accommodate the weight of the gold, Max counted at least another twenty more. All had the name O'Reilly Dublin painted on their sides. There was a massive junk yard that was piled high with rusting vehicles of every type and age. In addition to the forge that he and Hott had toured the night before, there were two fully functioning garages. Everything the IRA needed to steal the gold was right here at Rhosybol. The Nazis had wisely chosen their new partner. He shut off the engine and headed to the main barn where the men would still be sleeping. That was until he smashed his steel heeled jackboots repeatedly against the corrugated iron walls. Time to get up. It was going to be a long hot day, and an even longer night.

Chapter 68

LIME STREET STATION

Liverpool, England
August 18, 1940

When an exhausted Ashley finally arrived at Lime Street, the first rays of a new English summer day were already breaking over the great city of Liverpool. The train ride had been a nightmare and he had only managed a couple of hours of sleep at the most.

Ashley gratefully climbed down from the train car and walked towards the exit with his drained fellow travelers. Then thankfully he saw his name, written in large black letters on a piece of cardboard. "You're a sight for sore eyes," said Ashley to the older man who held up the sign. The man was wearing a threadbare dark blue railway porter uniform. "Mr. Ashley?" said the man. "Yes, John Ashley. It's nice to meet you," said Ashley as he extended his hand.

"Nice to meet you too, Sir. Please follow me. Do you have any bags?"

"No, just this," said Ashley, holding up his suitcase as he followed the man through the crowd. They headed to the tall spiked black bars of the exit gate. "Long trip?" asked the man.

"Yes, you could say that," answered Ashley with a smile.

Once through the gate, the man turned to Ashley and said, "We are over here in the transportation building." He pointed to the small building situated in the corner surrounded by a chain link fence. "My name is Paul Kinnear. I'm in charge of shipping and receiving here at Lime Street. Some of your men came by and left some items for you and said that we were to assist you in any way necessary."

"Excellent, thank you Paul," said Ashley. He was relieved that the department had come through for him. All things now being well, he would soon be driving the beautiful coast road on his way to Anglesey.

Paul opened the gate and ushered Ashley into a large yard that contained a variety of crates, boxes, and equipment. There were pallets full of the day's newly arrived newspapers that would soon be distributed throughout the city. "Follow me," said Paul as he walked towards the office. "Here you go," he said, pointing proudly at Ashley's new transportation. "And there's a package for you in the office too," he said as he gestured towards the office. "We were about to make a brew. You are welcome to join us if you like," he said with a smile.

"Wait! This is what they sent? A motorbike?" asked an incredulous Ashley. He looked in disbelief at the green Army Matchless motorbike sitting menacingly in the yard. "Yes sir! That's what they said you would be picking up. Is there a problem?" asked a concerned Paul.

"Well, I just presumed that they would have provided me with a car. I never even considered a motorbike," replied Ashley as he checked out the Matchless. He noticed that it was relatively new, no rust, and the tires were good. "But everything is fine, just fine, thank you," he checked the tank and it was full. It had been a while since Ashley had ridden a motorbike, but he was a more than capable rider.

A glance outside at the bright blue sky told him it looked like a nice summer day. It could be the perfect day to take a motorbike ride from Liverpool to Anglesey.

Better yet, it would be all on the company dime. The milk run was back on. The more he thought about it, the more he warmed up to the Matchless. He grinned as he patted the tank and followed Paul into the office for a welcome cup of tea.

Paul handed him a large cardboard box that the boys from the Chester office had left for him. It contained a green Army greatcoat, gloves, goggles, binoculars, petrol coupons, a hotel reservation and a detailed road map of North Wales and Anglesey.

Satisfied, Ashley studied the map for a moment, memorizing the main route to Anglesey. Then he packed his gear into the side bags of the Matchless and thanked Paul for the tea and hospitality. He mounted the motorbike and was relieved that it started with his first kick. He slipped the goggles on and pulled out of Lime Street Station. He was impressed with the roar the Matchless made as he accelerated towards the Mersey Tunnel on the way to his first stop, the little town of Parkgate.

Chapter 69

LLANDDONA BEACH

Anglesey, Wales
August 18, 1940

I t promised to be another spectacular, long sunny summer day on Anglesey. Although the forecast had also called for a severe storm front to move onto the island later in the day. It was Sunday and Taryn was free for the day. Determined to enjoy the best of the weather after she cooked them both breakfast, Peter folded the car roof down and the happy young couple took off to explore the island.

The coast road from Menai to Beaumaris was built for the MG. Taryn squealed with delight as Peter raced through the gears getting dangerously close to the cliff edge several times. Her long blond hair blew wildly in the wind.

"Oh, Peter look. It's a sea plane!" she yelled as they entered a jagged outcrop on the island known as Gallows Point.

"Yes, it's called a Catalina," he answered.

"Could you fly that?" she asked.

"Absolutely. The principles are still the same. It would be a little slow and cumbersome after flying a Spitfire, but then again try landing a Spitfire on the Menai Straits," he joked.

"Oh, Peter you are such a ham!" she said as she playfully slapped his thigh. The MG raced into the town of Beaumaris where they made a sharp left turn up a narrow street named Ratting Row, heading to the tiny village of Llanddona.

The road to Llanddona was a classic Welsh country road, perfect to test the limits of an MG. It was narrow and twisty, with ancient stone walls and hedgerows bordering both sides. On some stretches, the trees either side had formed a canopy over the road. The shadows they cast emphasized their speed as the MG flew through the shady green tunnels.

Llanddona was a tiny village with a small village shop that also doubled as the local post office. There was a solitary pub that was closed on Sunday, called The Owain Glyndwr. It was named after the last native Welshman to have the title of Prince of Wales. Owain Glyndwr was still considered a legend in these parts.

Peter parked the MG and they walked down a long path that took them to a very secluded Llanddona Beach. The weather was perfect, and the breeze was refreshing as it blew in from the pristine Irish Sea. They walked along the sand hand in hand, carrying their shoes. They looked forward to paddling at the water's edge. The sand felt soft beneath their feet. Other than the occasional seagulls that periodically flew overhead, there was no one else around as far as they could see. It was as though the two had been marooned on an island. The war, for now, seemed a long, long way away.

Looking out across the vast sands of Red Wharf Bay on the opposite side, Peter could see what looked like a little hotel right on the edge of the quay. "That looks like a nice spot, do you know what it's called?" he asked Taryn.

"Yes, it's The Ship Inn. Why do you ask?" They stopped and looked across at the inviting row of white buildings nestled alongside the shoreline.

"Because I was hoping that you might want to join me for dinner there tonight," he said, as he put his arm around her shoulder, and she slipped hers around his waist.

"I thought you'd never ask!" she laughed, and they kissed again as the cold waves washed over their bare feet. Her long blond hair engulfed them both in the breeze.

They walked for several miles on the sand. They shared their hopes and dreams, along with their fears and their mutual hatred for the Nazis and the war. They both knew that this would be their last evening together for a while. Peter was well aware that he would have no more leave until he and his mates had fully disposed of the Luftwaffe. They promised to write to each other every day, and as soon as the Luftwaffe stopped their bombing raids, she would get the train down South to be with him. He promised to pick her up in the MG with the top down, rain or shine.

Chapter 70

THE LIGHTS OF PARK GATE

Parkgate, England
August 18, 1940

Ashley hit heavy traffic in Birkenhead due to road closures from the previous night's air raid by the Luftwaffe. It was lunchtime when he finally arrived at Parkgate. The weather was perfect, a light breeze was blowing across the River Dee from the mountains of North Wales. Other than a few high scattered clouds, the sky was a beautiful deep blue.

It was Ashley's first time in Parkgate. He knew right away that he liked it. There was a vast open space of what appeared to be marshland. Centuries of silt had now all but clogged up the once mighty River Dee. Parkgate was the polar opposite of London where Ashley lived with its noise and congestion.

In Roman times, the River Dee was the main river and transportation route into the ancient city of Chester. Thousands of years later it had finally silted up, spawning the River Mersey on the east side of the land peninsula known as The Wirral as an alternate waterway. It ultimately led to the birth of the port of Liverpool.

Ashley drove slowly along the promenade. The Matchless got the nod of approval from the local postman as he passed by. He pulled up in front of an inviting looking pub called The Red Lion and killed the engine. He was about to dismount when he noticed two men coming back in from the marshes carrying a large toolbox between them. He wondered what the men could be doing out in the marsh with tools. He climbed off the Matchless and removed his greatcoat which he neatly folded and placed in the saddlebag along with his fly spattered goggles. He ran his hands gently back over his hair, straightened out his tie and headed towards the pub.

"Nice motorbike you have there, Mate," called out one of the men.

"Why, thank you," said Ashley as he turned around to face them. He immediately noticed that the two men had identical arm bands with LDV proudly displayed in black letters on a white background. The letters stood for Local Defense Volunteer.

"You picked a perfect day for it," the other man chimed in. "The weather I mean," continued the man, pointing to the cloudless sky. "It's the perfect day to be driving around on that little baby!!" Both men laughed.

"Did you drive far?" asked the first man as he held his hand close to the engine. He could feel the heat radiate out from it, "She's a beauty."

"Yes," laughed Ashley. "I just drove from Liverpool. It wasn't really that far but you could say I've been putting the old girl through her paces, the last couple of miles. And I have to ask you two, what is the LDV's finest doing out there in the marsh, catching shrimp for the war effort?" All three men laughed.

"And who wants to know?" asked the second man, lightly tapping the side of his nose.

"I'm sorry, John Ashley, Military Intelligence," said Ashley extending his hand to the second man.

"Military Intelligence, eh?" replied the first man. "It's a pleasure to meet you Mate!" Warmly, he shook Ashley's hand.

"I am Freddy Pritchard and this is Nigel Gilbert."

"A pleasure to meet you both," said Ashley. "And I certainly didn't mean to pry. You can't be too careful these days."

"No problem, Mate," said Nigel. "We are all on the same team here. We all do whatever we can to beat Jerry. We stick together, that's how we will beat him. Plus, we know what Jerry understands, isn't that right, Freddy boy?"

Freddy nodded back smiling. He knew the old routine.

"I'm curious," began Ashley, sensing a set up. "So, tell me. What does Jerry understand?" he asked.

"Let me tell you something, my son. There's only one thing Jerry understands, isn't that right Freddy?" asked Nigel, knowing exactly how Freddy was about to respond.

"That's right, steel! Cold bloody steel, Mate! That's the only thing Jerry understands!" yelled Freddy. He thrust his fist out in front of him, slashing the air wildly as if clenching a sabre, to the sheer delight of Nigel.

"I see," laughed Ashley. "I couldn't agree more. Cold steel will get their attention for sure."

"You bet your arse it will get their attention, and what kind of steel does Jerry understand best? Eh, Freddy?" asked Nigel again. Setting up Freddy for part two of their well-rehearsed routine.

"What kind of steel? The only steel there is! Sheffield steel! That's what Jerry understands. Sheffield bloody steel!" yelled Freddy, running forward towards a nonexistent foe, as he slashed and jabbed away with the imaginary sabre.

When he was done, he turned around, pretended to wipe off his blade then pretended to slide it back into a scabbard and bowed to polite applause from Ashley and Nigel. Ashley and his newfound friends continued the banter for quite a while. It turned out both men had fought together against the Germans in the bloody battle of the Somme. And years later, the wounds had still not healed. There was still no love lost between these hardened old warriors and their interminable foe, Jerry.

They had immediately volunteered for the LDV when the call went out for all men that were not engaged in current military service. Any man between the ages of 17 and 65 could volunteer to help fight off the expected invasion. The response had been overwhelming. Over a quarter of a million men joined up in just the first week. Many were proud veterans of the Great War and were more than ready to fight to the death to defend their family, homes, and neighbors. They wore their Local Defense Volunteer arm bands with enormous pride.

Ashley also discovered the nature of the men's business out on the marsh. The LDV, following orders from the Ministry of Defense, were involved in a clever decoy project. They placed many small lights way out in the marsh of the River Dee. With the entire area under the black out, it was hoped that Luftwaffe pilots would see the lights and drop their bombs there, assuming it was a populated area. The bombs would fall harmlessly into the thick, muddy marsh of the River Dee instead of the heavily populated towns of The Wirral, such as Wallasey, Birkenhead and of course the big prize across the River Mersey, Liverpool.

Ashley was fascinated by what the men had to say. Here, by remarkable coincidence, two men had just explained to him why someone might see lights off the coast at night. He had asked the two LDV men if they were aware of any other areas of the coastline that had similar activity. Neither man knew the answer. Ashley made a mental note to file it in his report. There might be a similar decoy program at work in Red Wharf Bay. If that were the case, he could have the flashing light mystery wrapped up today, which would be welcome news to Churchill.

Checking his watch, Ashley realized that he needed to get going. He reluctantly bid his newfound friends farewell and headed to The Red Lion pub for lunch. He was determined to enjoy some of Parkgate's legendary brown shrimp. Ashley sat outside on a small wooden bench and enjoyed the splendor of the Welsh Mountains as he ate. The shrimp were excellent. He chose the ready peeled option. He splashed them with a little salt and malt vinegar and enjoyed them right out of the Liverpool Daily Post newspaper cone. He also had a side of Hovis bread and another cup of tea to finish it up.

Refreshed, Ashley checked his map. Next up was Queensferry. Shortly after that he would leave England and cross the unmarked border into Wales and then take the coast road to Conway. Then it was on to Bangor. At that point, he should be able to get his first glimpse of Anglesey and the Menai Bridge. The traffic was light in his direction but there were several traffic jams going the opposite way. It seemed to be due to large lorries coming in from the Port of Holyhead.

He flew through the towns of Prestatyn, Rhyl, Colwyn Bay, Conway and finally after passing through the city of Bangor he caught his first view of the Menai Bridge. He slowed down and just before he got to the bridge, he saw the sign he was looking for on the left, The Antelope Hotel. He pulled slowly into the car park, killed the Matchless, unpacked the side bags and briefly took in the incredible panoramic view. Then he mounted the stone steps that led to the lobby of the hotel. It would be his home for the next night or possibly two if he could stretch it.

Chapter 71

THE ANTELOPE HOTEL

Bangor, Wales
August 18, 1940

T
he clear Irish Sea air was blowing through the Menai Straits
and was a stark contrast to the welcoming smell of burned
oak, beer and tobacco that greeted Ashley when he walked into
the lobby of The Antelope Hotel. Inside to the left was a small
bar proudly displaying its name, "The Snug". Its antiquated brass
name plate was placed over a pair of crossed brass hunting horns
above the entrance. The Snug was currently empty but mounted on
the bar, Ashley could see three hand pumps that proudly offered
their wares. There were two local beers that he was not familiar
with and Guinness. They also had a nice selection of whiskies, all
of which were enough to elicit an "Excellent" from him. Across
the lobby was a reception window with a shiny brass bell. It had
a small sign above it that read, Ring for Assistance, which he
dutifully did.

Promptly, a chicly dressed lady appeared wearing a tartan
plaid skirt and a white blouse under a light gray shawl. A pair
of well-placed eyeglasses perfectly fit her image of a friendly
gatekeeper. Her thick graying hair was fixed in a ponytail behind
her impressively long neck. Ashley figured she was in her forties,
but her near perfectly proportioned facial features instantly told
him she had been a real clock stopper in her day. She had an air of
self-confidence about her and a smile that melted Ashley.

She looked at the tall figure standing before her focusing squarely
on his forehead, "What on earth does he have on his head?" she
asked herself. Ashley watched her gaze and immediately realized
he had not yet removed his goggles. They had been pushed up over

his forehead as soon as he had dismounted the Matchless to take in the breathtaking views of the Menai Bridge. His thick brown hair was now pushed up in a coif by the goggles and combined with two bright red cheeks, gave him a somewhat comical appearance.

"Yes?" she asked, continuing to smile sweetly at him with her bright red lips.

"Sorry Mam," said Ashley as he removed the goggles from the top of his head, simultaneously attempting to smooth down his hair. "I rode here on a motorcycle."

"No kidding, I would have never guessed," she dryly replied. Both laughed instantaneously.

"John Ashley," he said extending his hand.

"Becky Forbes," she said, lightly clasping his hand between hers in return.

"I believe you have a reservation for me?" he replied digging into his inside jacket pocket for an envelope.

"We do indeed. Go ahead and sign in and I'll get your key. You will be in room number 8 upstairs. Your office also requested that you give them a call as soon as you check in. There is a private office in the back where you can use the phone," she said, nodding to her right. She handed him the thick leather-bound register to sign in. Then she disappeared to fetch his key. A slight smile was still on her face at Ashley's clownish facade.

"Thank you," said Ashley as he noted the office door she pointed to. It was painted black and had a sign hung in the center that simply said PRIVATE. Becky soon returned with his key.

"Just go up the stairs and make a left turn. You are the fourth door on the right. It's got a great view of the bridge. I'm sure you will like it." She smiled again and handed him the key.

"Thank you, very much," repeated Ashley, as he gathered up his belongings and headed towards the staircase.

"Anytime, Mr. Ashley," she said, playfully tapping her forehead for an imaginary pair of goggles and with that, she was gone.

Chapter 72

BACK IN THE SADDLE

Bangor, Wales
August 18, 1940

Room number 8 was small, clean and cozy, with the slightest smell of fresh lavender. However, the contents and ambience seemed almost irrelevant compared to the spectacular view of the bridge. It was framed perfectly by the double hung window in the center of the room. Ashley walked over to it, unlocked the worn brass hardware, and pushed up the lower sash. The room was instantly filled with cool fresh air.

He was in awe not only at the majesty of the bridge but at the size of the colossal cranes mounted to each end of the bridge towers. They had slowly weaved the massive steel cables back and forth for over a year now. He could clearly see the bridge workers at the top of the towers. They seemed so incredibly small compared to the bridge and immune to the certain death they faced if they put a single foot wrong or lost their grip. Ashley figured that it must be at least a two-hundred-foot plunge from the top to the icy blue waters below. "Rather you than me, Mate," muttered Ashley to himself. He shuddered slightly and instinctively pulled the sash back down. The worn pulleys squealed as it bumped to a close on the sill.

Ashley pulled out the folded road map, spread it on the bed and looked at the Island of Anglesey. He quickly realized just how rural Anglesey was. With the exception of the main road, the A55 that ran from Menai directly out to the port of Holyhead, there were relatively few roads. With his index finger he traced the coastal road, the A545 from Menai to Beaumaris where he could get a good look at the opening of the Menai Straits. From Beaumaris, he would head north past the tiny village of Llanddona, then on to Red Wharf Bay on the A5025. That would take him all the way to the fishing port of Amlwch. There, he would interview a Sergeant Lewis with the Port Police who had filed the original report. After the interview he would return by the shortest route on the B5111. It cut across the middle of the island through the village of Llangefni and back to Menai. Satisfied, he refolded the map and put it in his coat pocket. Then he went downstairs to contact HQ as requested by the ever so charming, Miss Forbes.

Ashley found the small private office, switched on the light, and he immediately detected a slight scent of perfume. It was the same scent he had noticed on Becky Forbes. The office was windowless but had enough room for a tiny desk and a filing cabinet. He closed the door, picked up the black receiver and dialed. It rang several times before a receptionist with a strong cockney accent answered.

"Operations, how may I direct your call?"

"Extension 137, please," responded Ashley.

"Certainly, connecting, please stay on the line," chirped the receptionist and with a click she was gone.

Ashley waited for a few seconds then the silence was replaced with a ring tone and immediately the sound of a receiver being lifted from its cradle.

"Colonel Withers office," announced the thick Scottish accent.

"Ashley, reporting in as requested," retorted Ashley. He knew the voice on the other end well by now. Brian Ferguson had been the Colonel's assistant and gate keeper for years. He annoyed Ashley immensely with his ridiculous attempts at humor that seemed to always seep into their conversations. But overall, he was harmless and a lot easier to deal with than some of his more cantankerous counterparts.

"Ashley! Old boy, how's your arse?" Ferguson could not contain his merriment at what he perceived to be his best one liner in years.

"Very funny Ferguson," said Ashley, rolling his eyes.

"Sorry old boy, it was the only transportation we could lay on at such short notice. After all, there is a war on you know," chuckled Ferguson.

"Yes Ferguson, very funny," Ashley repeated. "Now, do you have anything new for me?"

"You're a good sport, Ashley! So, just for you I will actually get up from my chair and check your box to see, just a moment…"

Ashley heard the receiver being laid down on the desk and waited. He could hear a shuffling of papers, and within a few seconds Ferguson was back on the line. "Nothing for you, Ashley. The cupboard is bare."

"Excellent," replied Ashley.

"Well, carry on then as ordered Ashley. Your next requested check-in is at 20:00."

"Roger, 20:00. Thank you, Ferguson," droned Ashley as he hung up the phone.

"Yes, get back in the saddle as the US Cavalry would say!" blurted out Ferguson laughing at his own meek attempt at a joke, "Ashley? Are you there? Ashley…" The merriment vanished as he realized that Ashley had avoided his parting shot. He returned the phone to its cradle and resumed his mundane desk duties. Ashley left the office and headed down the dim hallway, then he stepped outside into the bright afternoon sunshine and the awaiting Matchless. It was time to go to work.

Chapter 73

Beef and Liberty

Amlwch, Anglesey

August 18, 1940

With the town of Menai rapidly fading in his rearview mirror, Ashley focused on the Matchless rumbling between his legs. He opened up the throttle on the twisting coast road and followed the straits as they rolled by on his right. The cragged coastline had been hammered by thousands of years of erosion and the narrow coast road that followed it produced an exhilarating ride with some breathtaking curves. Ashley pressed his chest tightly against the petrol tank as he left the last of the curves and entered a straight portion of roadway. He opened the throttle a little further. The Matchless roared louder, and Ashley thrilled, held on tighter. He was intrigued at how much power the Matchless had left in it, but the road ahead was now starting to curve again. Ashley backed off, the Matchless responded, and the roar gave way to the low rumbling once more. Then ahead he could see a nice straightaway and the outskirts of a town.

A few minutes later, he arrived in Beaumaris. He rode down Main street keeping the Matchless in check. He resisted the temptation to find out just how loud the motorbike would be if he opened it up on the narrow cobblestone street. It was a Sunday after all. Tudor style buildings lined either side. Ashley took a right turn that brought him on to the deserted promenade.

Coming up on his left was a very prestigious looking hotel, with its grand entrance facing the sea. A line of impressive cars extended to the front entrance. The sign out front read The Bulkeley Hotel. Ashley grinned again. He was not one for pomp and circumstance.

He was glad that he was staying at the Antelope. It was cozy and quiet, much more to his liking.

Further down on his right, Ashley spotted what he was looking for, the old pier. He parked the bike and shut down the engine. He dismounted, hung his goggles on the mirror and took in the spectacular view in front of him. The straits seemed to reflect the clear blue sky above them. Ashley lit a cigarette, flattened down his hair and undid his greatcoat. He retrieved his binoculars and set off down the pier.

Off in the distance, Ashley could see about a half dozen small fishing boats. Once he arrived at the end of the pier, he focused his binoculars on the boats. They varied by size and number of crew, but they all seemed to be operating from the same play book. Ashley figured they were fishing for Mackerel and judging by the way they were hauling in nets full of fish, he knew that they had been doing it the exact same way for centuries.

Ashley watched them for about ten minutes. Seeing nothing unusual, he made a mental note of the number of boats and the time. For the first time he noticed dark gray storm clouds way off on the horizon. He needed to get out to Amlwch as quickly as possible and then back to the Antelope. Hopefully, he would have the pleasure of the charming company of Becky Forbes and a quiet evening. The narrow twisting roads of Anglesey could be terrifying during dry conditions. Even Ashley, with his nerves of steel did not want to find out what kind of handicap a slick wet road surface might add.

He placed his binoculars back in the carrier bag, mounted the Matchless and easily kicked started it first time. He pushed it off its stand and headed out to Llanddona. Then he would pass Benllech, Pentraeth, and the vast Red Wharf Bay. The roads were virtually deserted except for a small convoy of vehicles on their way to RAF Valley. Ashley took great delight in passing them at full throttle. The jeers of the RAF lads riding at the back of the open lorries rang in his ears as he shot by them. The obligatory V sign was flashed at him when they saw the bike's green Army colors.

Ashley was impressed with the size of Red Wharf Bay as he blew by it at a high speed on a nice stretch of open road. He also realized that there were no marshes on which to lay out decoy lights as he had seen at Parkgate. Any lights out on Red Wharf Bay would have to be from a manned vessel. This put to rest any chance of solving the mystery early. Perhaps he could enjoy a couple of nights at The Antelope Hotel after all.

Finally, he arrived at the Port of Amlwch. Dating all the way back to Viking times, Amlwch had been a bustling seaport and ship building region in its heyday. It still had a small but active fishing fleet.

At the entrance to the small dock was an old brick building that housed several offices, including one bearing a weathered blue sign that said Police Station in white letters. Ashley pulled up in front of it and killed the engine. Dismounting, he skipped up the two well-worn steps and entered the police station. It consisted of a small office with a long wooden counter that ran its entire width. The wall had various posters and announcements pinned on it. One large poster warned, Loose Lips Sink Ships!

An elderly officer with a large frame and an impressive gray handlebar mustache sat typing behind an oak desk. His stripes indicated the rank of Sergeant. A wooden pipe perched on the edge of an ashtray sent spirals of deep blue smoke slowly upwards to the peeling and damp stained ceiling. A large portrait of King George VI stared down upon the scene from the wood paneled wall behind the Sergeant's desk. The Sergeant acknowledged Ashley's presence by holding up his index finger and booming, "One second, young man!" Without taking his eyes off the typewriter keys, he continued to tap away at his report at a painfully slow pace.

Sergeant Bryn Lewis no doubt, thought Ashley to himself. Finally completing the task, the Sergeant yanked out the sheet of paper. He briefly looked it over before dropping it into a wire basket marked OUT. Then he finally turned his gaze squarely on Ashley.

"Yes?" he asked, retrieving his pipe from the ashtray and inhaling deeply.

"Ashley, MI5," said Ashley, holding up his ID.

The Sergeant's demeanor changed instantly. He exhaled a thick cloud of smoke and rose to his feet. He pulled his black uniform jacket down, emphasizing the round profile of a large well-fed belly. His hands instinctively ran quickly over his lapels, then onto his tie knot which he tightened slightly. When satisfied, he turned to face the agent from MI5.

"Ashley, yes, welcome to Amlwch. I've been expecting you, please come on around," he said.

"Thank you," said Ashley. He went behind the counter and extended his hand. "John Ashley."

"Sergeant Bryn Lewis, nice to meet you Agent Ashley," replied the Sergeant shaking Ashley's hand.

"Likewise," said Ashley. The Sergeant indicated that Ashley take a seat on the opposite side of his desk. "Can I offer you a spot of tea, Ashley?" asked the Sergeant. "Cooper here has just brewed a pot, haven't you Officer Cooper?" Cooper, who had been at the rear of the office, barely visible over the rows of filing cabinets, responded immediately, "Yes Sir, Sergeant Lewis, Sir. Just brewed, Sir. Right away, Sir!" And with that he disappeared through a small doorway into what was presumably a little kitchen.

Ashley removed his greatcoat, draped it across the back of the chair and sat down. He purposely loosened his tie and took out his pack of cigarettes, offering one to the Sergeant, "Smoke?" asked Ashley.

"No, thank you. I just enjoy a pipe these days. It helps me think." A broad smile was barely visible beneath the bushy gray moustache that cracked the wrinkled face.

"Splendid, and yes on the tea please," said Ashley.

"Sugar?" asked the Sergeant.

"Real sugar or Saccharine?" queried Ashley. It was always a crapshoot these days.

"Nothing but the finest for our brothers in MI5," grinned the Sergeant. "Officer Cooper, sugar for our guest!" he bellowed.

"Yes Sir! Coming up, Sir!" yelled Cooper from the kitchen.

"They didn't waste any time getting you up here. When did you leave the Smoke?" asked Lewis as he puffed on his pipe.

"I left London yesterday by train but got diverted to Liverpool Lime Street because of an unexploded bomb somewhere on the track near Wrexham. I was supposed to come all the way through to Holyhead which would have been a piece of cake. I guess Goering had a different plan for me," responded Ashley. He subconsciously tapped his cigarette at both ends on the cigarette box, put it between his lips and felt his trouser pockets for his lighter. Lewis beat him to it and shoved a box of Swan Vestas across the desk towards him.

"Oh, you got caught in that back up. What a mess. Things are still not caught up. All sorts of people missed their connections to the Dublin ferry. A right mess," said the Sergeant shaking his head sympathetically.

"Thanks," said Ashley, noting that the swan on the matchbox had been neatly colored in with blue ink. "Helps me think," repeated Lewis, noting Ashley's quick examination of his handy work.

"Hey, whatever works," replied Ashley as he lit his cigarette and pushed the match box back to Lewis. "Ex-Army?" asked Ashley.

"Welsh Guards, I did ten years." Ashley noticed that Lewis instinctively puffed out his chest.

"Good show, and police work?" asked Ashley.

"It will be fifteen years this November," answered Lewis proudly.

"Excellent, all here at Amlwch?" continued Ashley.

"Lord no! I was at the Port of Holyhead for twelve years. When this position came up, I took it a couple of years ago."

"I see, a lot quieter I suppose?"

"Absolutely, Amlwch is a tiny port. It's pretty much all local fishing boats these days. I know most of the fisherman by their first names. Never a problem. It's a dream job compared to Holyhead." He puffed on his pipe again several times producing bellows of blue smoke before resting it in the ashtray.

"Oh, why's that? asked Ashley, genuinely interested. He watched the blue haze of pipe smoke dance in the sunlight that poured through the windows located high on the wall behind the Sergeant's desk.

"Holyhead is a zoo at the best of times. It has way too much shipping business for such a small port. It is nonstop 24 hours a day that place, both coming and going. It was always busy with the Dublin business alone but once the war broke out the amount of trade with Ireland has just exploded. Like I said it was never built to handle that type of traffic but as they say, there is a war on you know."

"Yes, I suppose you're right. I never really thought about that," said Ashley. He was eager to learn as much as possible about the maritime activity.

"They have plans to expand it but like everything else, there are priorities. You just do the best you can. These days all we can do is make random checks and searches, but there are very few incidents," said Lewis. He retrieved his pipe and managed to get one more tug out of the bowl before tapping out the black ash into the ashtray and propping it on the rim.

"What's the main type of cargo that goes back and forth?" asked Ashley.

"That's easy, cattle. Cattle comes in, beef mainly. Then grain goes back. That's probably 75 percent of it."

"Really?" asked Ashley.

"Yes, that's the bulk of it. The good news is that most of the shipping is done between two companies. You have O'Reilly in Dublin, he is the cattle king. He sends the cattle in. It's taken by lorry to Liverpool to get slaughtered and butchered and then shipped all over England.

O'Reilly's lorries then go back to Birkenhead to Spillers Mills to pick up sacks of grain and take it back to Dublin. The Guinness plant there takes the entire shipment. What makes it easy is that you only have two sets of paperwork and the same lorries go back and forth. Beef in and grain out. All the dockers call it the Beef Guinness run!" The Sergeant laughed again. He'd always thought that was a great name. Everyone at the docks in Dublin and Holyhead referred to it as the Beef Guinness run which made it easier to know what was coming and going on the lorries.

"I see," said Ashley. His thoughts suddenly drifted to his favorite restaurant, Hodrien's Chop House in Piccadilly. Beef and Liberty was proudly engraved in the huge plate glass window. He imagined sitting at his favorite table enjoying a Ribeye, bone in, medium rare with a glass of fine Claret. He was getting hungry. Perhaps Becky Forbes could pull a few strings for him back at the Antelope. Worst case scenario he would settle for some Welsh lambchops…maybe she could join him. He focused back on Lewis. "Don't you miss all the action?" he asked.

"Actually no, I still get as much as I want," answered Lewis. A look of satisfaction flashed across his round face. He was dying for Ashley to ask his next question.

"Oh, how so?" asked Ashley.

Delighted, the Sergeant shifted his weight from one buttock to the other, checked that there was no sign of Cooper, and leaned forward towards Ashley. Ashley played along instinctively and leaned in also. In a low voice he said, "I've got my own police car." And then he sat back, grinning like a Cheshire cat.

"Good show!" said Ashley continuing to play along.

"Yes, I know," continued Lewis. "It's a Morris! All fitted out. It has a siren, a loudspeaker, and a spotlight. It turned out that one of the Port Authority big wigs decided that Amlwch was too small for a fulltime force, especially with the uptick in the Dublin business. So, they combined it with Holyhead. They figured it would be more economical and save on manpower. Naturally, they needed a vehicle that could go back and forth between Amlwch and Holyhead, so they provided a car. The best part is I get to take it home with me!

I live in the village of Bodedern. It is almost midway between the two ports. My wife thinks I'm a genius, especially as the petrol is all covered. So, I spend time at each port depending on the volume coming through Holyhead. When the madness gets too much, I come out here to Amlwch to decompress and catch up on my paperwork, if you will," said Lewis pointing at his In and Out trays.

"Good show," repeated Ashley. He could see that having the use of a motor car was a big deal for the Sergeant and he was glad that it had worked out for him. Ashley took a couple of deep drags, crossed his legs, checked his watch and said, "Well I suppose we had better get down to business. So, what can you tell me about those mysterious lights spotted out yonder?" he jerked his head in the general direction of the Irish Sea.

"Of course," said Lewis. He pulled the neatly stacked pile of manila files in front of him a little closer and thumbed through the first couple of them. He handed one to Ashley. "Not much to say really. There were lights clearly visible that flashed in a sequence. It happened twice, with a gap of a few minutes in between. Either way, whoever it was had no business being out there after the curfew. We sent in the report, and apparently your branch thought it important enough to send you all the way out here."

Ashley was analyzing the short and simple typed report. The information was identical to what Petrie had handed him.

Cooper arrived with two mugs of hot tea.

"And the actual eyewitness, is he available for me to talk to?" asked Ashley. Focusing on the steaming mug.

"Oh, no problem there. It's Muggins here!" snorted Lewis, nodding towards Cooper while rolling his dark gray eyes. Ashley noted that Lewis was not Cooper's biggest fan. He also noted the name of the witness in the report Kenneth Cooper, and below that was his occupation, Police Constable.

Chapter 74

THE WITNESS

Amlwch, Anglesey

August 18, 1940

"Of course...Constable Cooper," said Ashley as he stood up, accepted the mug of tea and reached out his hand. "John Ashley, nice to meet you," he continued, seemingly oblivious to the cigarette still between his lips.

"Cooper...err...Police Constable Kenneth Cooper...Sir. Nice to meet you too," stammered the middle aged awkward looking man in front of him. He handed the other mug to a now frowning Sergeant Lewis.

"Excellent, grab a chair here Constable. Let's have a chat," said Ashley. He watched Lewis become increasingly agitated as Cooper pulled up a chair next to Ashley. Ashley took another drag on his cigarette and placed it on Lewis's ashtray. He took a gulp of his tea. It was strong, hot, and sweet. "Thanks," he said raising his cup to Cooper.

"Yes Sir, my pleasure," replied Cooper.

"Now tell me Constable, exactly what did you see?" asked Ashley.

"Yes, Sir." Cooper sat upright and had a serious look on his face. "I was on my way back from my mum's house in Benllech. I stopped by to make sure she was safely tucked in for the night. That is when I saw the lights for the first time. There were three distinct flashes. They were way out there but you could not miss them. I thought it was very unusual, so I kept watching. Then it happened again, three more flashes in the exact same spot. It looked like a clear signal to me. I waited for it to happen again, but it never did. In total, I saw six independent flashes, two sets of three."

"Your mother lives in Benllech you said?" asked Ashley.

"Yes," interrupted Lewis, before Cooper could answer. "But the lights themselves would have…" Ashley cut him off by raising his palm in front of the Sergeant's round face.

"I'd like to hear it directly from Constable Cooper…thank you!" His icy blue eyes were fixed onto Lewis. Instantly, the old Sergeant knew he was outranked and outgunned by Ashley. He immediately knew he needed to be respectful of the man sitting in front of him from MI5.

"Yes Sir, Benllech Bay. My mum was born and raised there. She's only ever been to the mainland about six times," answered Cooper. He was delighted that Ashley had put Lewis in his place, a rare occurrence in these parts.

"So, she's very much a local lass," joked Ashley.

"Yes Sir, you could say that," agreed Cooper.

"So, the report says the lights were about due South off the coast of Benllech, which puts them closer to Red Wharf Bay, correct?" asked Ashley as he glanced over the report.

"Yes Sir, Red Wharf Bay is the next bay down from Benllech. Those lights would be about three quarters of a mile or so out at sea, no more than a mile at the very most," answered Cooper.

"And you are reasonably sure because…" inquired Ashley.

"I grew up there, Sir. I know that part of the coast like the back of my hand. My mum lives at the top of the bluffs. From there you can see both Benllech and Red Wharf Bay. I've spent my whole life playing on those cliffs. I know the lay of the land and sea. Whoever it was, they were off Red Wharf Bay for sure," answered a confident Cooper.

"Excellent," said Ashley, glancing back to the report that confirmed exactly what Cooper had told him. He took another drink of tea and read a little more, then said, "So tell me what you can about the actual lights themselves. Were they big? Small? Bright? From a torch? Anything at all would be helpful," asked Ashley.

"Yes, Sir. I know they were from a signalers lamp for sure. Before the war, I was in the Boy Scouts. We used to meet in Beaumaris. I took my signalers badge and will never forget it. Our Skipper was a Navy veteran named Mike Haggstrom. He had an old Royal Navy signalers lamp. He showed us how it worked with all the movable parts. We took the whole thing apart and cleaned it. Then we had to reassemble it. It was a real challenge. As part of our final test, the Skipper sailed out to sea at night far enough so we could not see him. Then he flashed a message to those of us waiting back on the pier. We had to get it right to pass the test."

"And did you?" smiled Ashley, taking another drag off his cigarette.

"Yes, Sir. I can even remember the message he sent," answered Cooper.

"Good show. What was it?" asked Ashley.

"The Boy Scout motto sir. Be Prepared!" replied a beaming Cooper.

"Quite, sound advice wouldn't you agree, Sergeant?" asked Ashley, bringing the old Sergeant back into the conversation.

"Absolutely," chimed in Lewis, relieved to be included in the discussion again. He was still fuming inside that the damn rookie had spotted the lights instead of himself. Something was a foot. For the brass down in London to send an agent all this way to Amlwch was intriguing. It aggravated him immensely that the bumbling Constable was now center stage. He subconsciously stroked his moustache and tried to think of anything he could add, anything at all.

"So, you feel pretty confident that the source was from a navy signalers lamp?" asked Ashley.

"Yes, Sir. I'm one hundred percent confident in that," answered Cooper.

"That would indicate a naval vessel then. I am pretty sure that your average fishing trawler does not carry a signalers lamp. Would you agree, Sergeant?" asked Ashley looking directly now at Lewis.

"Agreed. And I have personally checked with every registered vessel here and at Benllech and Red Wharf Bay, none were out at sea. We also followed up with the Royal Navy HQ in Liverpool and they have no record of any of their ships being anywhere close to Anglesey. It's all there in the report," replied Lewis.

"Yes, I see that. Thank you. What time did you see the first set of signals?" asked Ashley, turning his gaze back to Constable Cooper.

"At exactly midnight, Sir. I checked my watch. It has illuminous fingers on the face, see?" He pulled back his blue shirt cuff to reveal his watch. Ashley smiled, "Nice, and how long before you saw the second set?" asked Ashley.

"Less than a minute," answered Cooper.

"And what did you do then?" continued Ashley.

"I notified the Sergeant and he relayed the information to the LDV Captain at Menai. In turn, I assume he passed it on to your chaps?" he looked at Lewis for assurance. Lewis immediately chimed in, "That's correct. According to the report, per protocol, we notified Captain Riggs of the LDV at Menai at 12:50 PM."

Ashley made a mental note. He looked forward to chatting with Captain Riggs on his return to the Antelope, hopefully over a pint. He scanned the report into his mind one more time before closing it.

"Good, very good," said Ashley. "Is there anything else you can think of that may be of help?" Ashley rubbed his chin. He needed a shave badly.

"No Sir, I'm sorry. That's everything I know," said Cooper.

"Ok, good job Constable Cooper. You have been very helpful. That will be all," said Ashley, wrapping up the meeting.

"Thank you, Sir!" said Cooper as he stood up. He saluted crisply, ignored the scowls of Lewis, and vanished from sight back behind the wall of gray filing cabinets.

"So, what do you think?" asked Lewis, tapping out the ash from his pipe bowl.

"Hard to say. He is a good witness, but unless we have a vessel or individual who was out there, we may never know. Unfortunately, you have no other reports. There's nothing else suspicious or anything at all that might be connected?" asked Ashley. He handed the file back to Lewis, finished his tea, and took a final drag on his cigarette.

"No, I'm sorry. Amlwch is a pretty quiet place as is the whole island. Other than the occasional drunk, not much of anything ever happens here," lamented Lewis.

"You've been very helpful," said Ashley as he stood up and put his greatcoat back on.

"Good luck, Ashley," said the old Sergeant. "Where's your next stop?"

"I'll head back to Menai and try to check in with Captain Riggs. Maybe he can shed some...ahem...light on the situation, so to speak," Ashley grinned at his own subliminal joke.

It went right over Lewis's head. "Riggs goes by ETR, his initials. You will probably find him in The Bull by the time you get back to Menai," said Lewis checking his watch.

Ashley smiled, "The Bull, got it." It also reaffirmed to him, that even out here in rural Wales, the local pub played a critical role in everyday life. It truly was the best place to gather any type of ground intelligence. It was the hub, the center of activity and gossip in most villages.

With nearly all the young men actively serving in the military, the pub also acted as the source for locating different tradesman. If you needed a plumber, bricklayer or electrician, you simply went to the pub and asked. Inevitably, someone who knew someone, would connect you. Payment was often done by barter. Petrol coupons currently had more value than cash. This was especially true here on the island. He slipped on his goggles, kick started the Matchless, offered Lewis a crisp salute and was gone.

Lewis watched him until he was out of sight. It was only after he heard the Matchless roar away, that he realized he should have told Ashley about the road closure on the direct route back to Menai. The shortest route was on the B5111 road, which cut directly across the island. But the road was now closed to all traffic at Parys Mountain. It was also a fair distance before he would hit the roadblock. Then he would have to double all the way back to Amlwch and take the coastal road back to Menai, meaning that he would probably miss his meeting with ETR. Dammit he thought to himself. He had missed a chance to finally score some points with Agent Ashley and MI5. He shrugged his shoulders. What difference did it make now? Nothing would ever become of the mysterious flashing lights of Red Wharf Bay. He was sure of that. Consequently, he figured that he would never see the agent from MI5 again. He could not have been more mistaken.

Chapter 75

ROAD CLOSED

Parys Mountain, Anglesey
August 18, 1940

Ashley screamed out of Amlwch and away from the dark clouds off to the west. Just as Lewis had feared, Ashley took the road to Llangefni. It was the shorter route back to Menai that he had memorized, unaware that it was closed to all traffic at Parys Mountain.

Ashley was lying flat down on the petrol tank doing around 70 mph. By now, Ashley had bonded with the Matchless. He was delighted by its performance and no longer regretted not getting a car from HQ. He blew by the first ROAD CLOSED AHEAD sign as it registered in his brain. He quickly backed off the throttle and sat upright as the engine moaned its way back down through the gears. Then he passed another sign that said SLOW followed about 50 yards later by another ROAD CLOSED AHEAD warning.

Ahead, about a half mile up the hill he could see a small hut and some figures in the road. Ashley dropped down to around 30 mph. As he got closer, he could make out a red and white striped barrier across the road. Standing in front of it were two uniformed men. One had his left hand raised, palm forward indicating for Ashley to stop. Ashley pulled up slowly in front of the men, who he could now see wore their full Army field uniform. All were armed. A glance at the badge on the guard's beret told him they were with the Royal Welsh Fusiliers.

"Halt! The road is closed!" yelled the man in a thick Welsh accent still holding his arm out.

Ashley killed the engine and dismounted the Matchless. He pushed his goggles up and raised up both of his hands in a peaceful gesture. "Road Closed?" he asked genuinely puzzled.

"Yes Sir, I'm afraid so. No traffic is allowed beyond this point," said the guardsman.

"Bloody Hell!" cursed Ashley. "What's the problem?" he asked straining to look beyond the barrier at the perfectly intact road.

"The ground is contaminated all around Parys Mountain. There was a pump failure and the contaminated ground water from the copper mine has saturated the ground for miles. No one is permitted to go through the area until it can be cleaned up. Government orders, sorry," said the second guard walking towards the Matchless.

"Strewth," said Ashley. "I've never heard of such a thing before. Contaminated?"

"Join the club," said the first guard who had been holding his rifle pointed towards Ashley. Ashley raised an eyebrow and looked at the rifle. The guard in turn looked at his mate, who nodded at him to stand at ease. Then satisfied, he slowly lowered the rifle.

"Yeah, we hadn't either. But if you had seen how many dead sheep and birds we have hauled out of here, you would understand. It is not where you want to be. This place is the arsehole of the world at the best of times. Throw in the stink of dead sheep, now you're talking eh, Taffy?" laughed the second guard.

"Yeah, and don't forget the dead badger! Cor Blimey, what a smell that was!" replied the man known as Taffy.

"Whoa yeah, the badger was nasty, the worst so far," said the second guard.

"What's worse than Marty's underpants?" quipped Taffy.

"No, not that bad!" laughed the second guard looking at the third guard who was sitting on top of the sandbags stacked around the entrance to the hut, smoking a cigarette. Looking through the guard hut's open door, Ashley could make out the shape of a fourth guard, who appeared to be sleeping on the lower level of a wooden bunk bed.

"Very funny," said the third guard who Ashley determined to be Marty, as he climbed down from his perch on top of the sandbags.

"Is that a Matchless?" He asked looking at Ashley's motorcycle. Ashley noticed the Corporal stripe on his arm.

"Yes Sir," answered Ashley.

"Nice! I'm Martin, Marty for short" he said as he puffed on the cigarette between his lips.

All three guards, sure that Ashley was not a problem now turned their attention to the motorcycle. Its scorching motor was ticking loudly as the metal began to cool.

"Are you Army then?" asked Taffy looking at the paint job and license plate.

"I'm with Military Intelligence. I'm Ashley," said Ashley pulling out his pack of cigarettes. "Smoke?" he said. He offered his pack to the two guards who both accepted with a "Cheers mate." Marty pulled out his lighter. Ashley noticed it was a miniature green Guinness bottle that when he twisted off the bottom, revealed a small petrol lighter. He flipped the tiny wheel that sparked the flint. The wick instantly caught fire and he expertly lit all three cigarettes. He screwed the lighter back into the tiny bottle and slipped it back into his pocket.

"I'm Fergus," said the last remaining unidentified member of the trio.

"Fergus," Ashley nodded.

"How long is it going to be closed?" asked Ashley.

"No idea, Mate. It could be days, weeks, months, no idea. I just know that this is the only way in or out, and no one gets to pass. Our Sergeant said it comes down from the very top. No one gets through until further orders. As you know, once the War Department gets involved it could go on forever," answered Marty.

"MI5, eh? I thought you blokes were supposed to be behind enemy lines. What the bloody hell are you doing out in this neck of the woods?" asked Taffy. He ran his hand slowly over the petrol tank before bending down to take a good look at the engine.

"That's a good question," replied Ashley. "I'd tell you...but then I'd have to kill you!" All four men roared with laughter. "So, there's absolutely no way through here to Llangefni?" he asked again.

"No sorry. You will have to go around the coast road. It will be a fantastic ride on this little beast," said Fergus as he imitated Taffy by also running his hand slowly across the petrol tank.

"Trust me, it is," replied Ashley between draws on his cigarette. "I came out here that way, through Beaumaris and Red Wharf Bay. It was a fabulous ride, but I wanted to save some time heading back to Menai by cutting across the island. I guess that's not going to happen now is it?" he opined.

"Not unless you want to end up like the old badger!" laughed Taffy.

"Thanks," said Ashley. "I think I'll pass." He took another drag on his cigarette, pulled down his goggles and climbed back on the Matchless. "I'd love to stay and chat but some of us have work to do. You chaps stay out of trouble now," he said as he kickstarted the hot engine. The Matchless roared to life. Ashley dropped it into first, yelled "Ich Dien!" It meant, "I Serve," the Welsh Fusiliers motto. He could see the surprise on the three guards' faces.

"Ich Dien!!" they shouted together back at him. Ashley took a last drag on his cigarette before tossing it to the roadway where it disintegrated in a cascade of sparks. He let out the clutch and with a growl the Matchless shot forward. The rear tire sent a shower of dust and pebbles all over the dodging Taffy. His two mates howled with laughter, and with that he was gone. He headed back towards Amlwch to take the coast road back to Menai. A smile crept across his lips as he blew by rows of crumbling ancient gray stone walls. He knew that he had just dazzled the three guards. Imagine a chap from MI5 who actually knew the Fusiliers motto! There was hope yet.

The guards watched him fade out of sight. They were delighted at having turned away their first motorist in days. All the locals knew the area was off limits. With strict petrol rationing, the amount of people passing by Parys Mountain was virtually nil. All four Fusiliers thought the posting was a ridiculous waste of everyone's time, but orders were orders. They smoked their cigarettes and horsed around with each other as they watched Ashley and his Matchless fade from sight. Then they returned to the mundane task of manning an isolated roadblock in one of the most desolate areas on planet earth.

The sun was finally beginning to get a little lower in the western sky and would soon inevitably disappear behind the black storm clouds now stalled menacingly off the coast. As the guards fooled around to pass the time on that long summer day, none of them had a clue that they would not live to see it rise over their beloved Island of Anglesey, ever again.

Less than ten miles away at the secret IRA Headquarters, under the watchful eye of Lieutenant Hott and Richard Tully, the ruthless killing machine known as The Brandenburgers had meshed seamlessly with their counterparts from the Irish Republican Army. Satisfied with the progress that everyone had made and that all the bases had been covered, Max headed back to his executive digs at Menai to get some sleep. He knew it would be a long night out on Parys Mountain.

Hugh drove Richard back to Holyhead to catch the ferry back to Dublin. Here he would get some sleep and wait for the first ferry in on Monday morning. It would be carrying the Brandenburgers and the stolen gold for him to escort safely to Dingle Bay for the exchange of guns, ammunition and explosives for gold. Finally, the IRA would have the weapons it needed to give the British a real bloody nose.

Chapter 76

RETURN TO MENAI

Menai, Anglesey
August 18, 1940

Peter and Taryn finally pulled in front of Taryn's cottage in Menai, a little before six o' clock. They planned to drive out to The Ship Inn for dinner as they had agreed earlier in the day. Its location on the banks of Red Wharf Bay made it perfect for a dinner date that would be a totally different atmosphere to the one they had enjoyed so much last night. Taryn had told him that its out of the way location, meant that you could still enjoy a quiet evening without being surrounded by drunken bridge workers and boisterous RAF lads. It was the perfect place for dinner for a young couple who were absolutely mesmerized by each other.

Shelby was delighted when the couple returned. She greeted them with her loudest barking yet. Peter got an extra fuss. It was clear that he was her new favorite. Sufficiently pleased with her welcoming reception, Shelby shot back into the little kitchen and sat on the floor. Her tail wagged as she gazed intensely once again at the little container on the counter that held the rawhide.

After a quick cup of tea, Peter left. He had just enough time to go to The Bull to try to locate ETR to relay his story of Max von Seeckt. Then he needed to stop by his flat and quickly change clothes before picking Taryn up for dinner. He parked outside The Bull and after a brief conversation with a couple of elderly bridge workers about the MG's performance, he entered the scene of his calamity from the night before.

Chapter 77

CAPTAIN RIGGS AKA ETR

Menai, Anglesey

August 18, 1940

Sure enough, ETR stood at the bar in The Bull dressed exactly the way Taryn said he would, cloth cap, scarf, Woodbines, and bicycle clip set neatly on the bar next to him.

"Captain Riggs?" asked Peter, flashing him a perfect smile.

"Who wants to know?" responded ETR dragging on his Woodbine. His calloused nicotine stained fingers indicated it was not his first or last cigarette of the day. He continued to look down at the head on his freshly poured pint that Snudge the barman had just pushed in front of him.

"Peter Legh," said Peter extending a hand. ETR turned to face him, his gray eyes locked firmly on to Peter's who knew in an instant that this was a hard man. ETR never flinched as he too studied Peter's eyes. In a millisecond both men knew they liked each other.

While maintaining eye contact, ETR took Peter's outstretched hand in his. Peter was immediately aware of the roughness of ETR's skin and the strength of his grip. Like anyone born into privilege, Peter was well versed in the art of the handshake. Men always look for a firm handshake and good eye contact. ETR took firm to a whole new level. His grip was unbelievable, and it continued to get tighter. Peter responded in kind squeezing back as hard as he could which brought a smile to ETR's weathered face. ETR increased his grip again causing Peter to visibly squirm. At that point, ETR immediately released his hand and smiled.

"Nice to meet you, Mate, please call me ETR," said ETR, delighted that Peter shook his crushed hand a couple of times in an effort to dispel the pain.

"Nice to meet you too ETR, that's quite a grip, Sir," said Peter returning ETR's smile.

"Is that right, Mate? I've never been told that before," replied ETR.

"Oh, what happened there?" asked Peter pointing to the back of ETR's hand which he noticed had an unusual lump covering the center three metacarpals.

"I was a bombardier with His Majesty's Royal Artillery. I picked this up in France when our gun misfired. I got hit by its breach and it shattered my whole bloody hand. There was no one around to reset it, so my mate bandaged me up the best he could. By the time we finally returned from the front it had already knitted itself back up, just like this. Funny thing is that it increased my grip strength," he grinned at Peter. "The callouses are courtesy of working at Spillers Mill at the Birkenhead docks. I spent donkey's years stacking sacks of grain, day in and day out before we moved out to Anglesey because of my health. I got gassed at the Somme and I only have one lung that works now. The air quality out here is so much better than in Birkenhead. I can actually breathe out here!" said ETR.

He grinned to himself at the irony of what he had just said as he dragged again on the Woodbine. Peter seemed to sense what ETR was thinking and looking at the ash tray full of cigarette butts and the plume of smoke that ETR exhaled, he simply replied, "Quite." Both men made eye contact again and laughed simultaneously at the irony of what had just transpired.

"Not quite France," said Peter holding up his right hand which revealed a bent middle knuckle with a jagged scar. "The Wall, at Eton College, and it did nothing to strengthen my grip." Both men laughed again.

"Eton? You're a Toffeenose?"

"No, not exactly. I'm from Addington in Cheshire. Most of the boys at Eton are..."

ETR cut him short. "If you went to Eton, then you're a Toffeenose. Are you in the Army?"

"No, I'm in the RAF," replied Peter.

"The RAF! Eton! You're definitely a Toffeenose!" laughed ETR.

"Quite. Well I'm a Toffeenose who is delighted to meet you ETR." Both men smiled at each other.

ETR raised his glass and in a few huge gulps emptied it and returned it to the bar. He wiped the foam off his top lip with the back of his hand, then wiped his hand on the back of his pants. He took another drag of his cigarette and looked at Peter again.

"What do you do in the RAF?" asked ETR.

"I'm a pilot, I fly Spitfires," replied Peter.

"Spitfires! Oh. Good on you, Mate! You boys have been kicking Jerry's arse according to the BBC. Let me buy you a pint! Bitter?"

"Quite. Thank you," said Peter, with a nod and a smile.

"Snudge! Two pints of bitter please and put it on the slate," barked ETR.

"Coming up, ETR," said Snudge.

"What's the slate?" asked Peter.

"Lord save me, what did they teach you at Eton? Never mind that now son. So, who gave you my name? And what can I possibly do for an RAF Toff from Eton or Addington or wherever the bloody hell you came from?" he grinned again.

"A lovely lady I met, Taryn Thomas told me you are the LDV Captain for Menai."

"Captain, that's a laugh. I'm an army of one more like it. I'm a squaddie, chief cook and bottle washer, church caretaker too. Yup, that's me along with being the backup village bobby. You never know when these bridge workers might get out of hand," laughed ETR. He nodded towards the busy lounge across from the bar. "There are no local police here in Menai. The nearest real police station is on the mainland in Bangor. As far as the law goes in this town, I'm about it. Taryn Thomas, eh? Look at you!" he said as he looked Peter up and down teasing him with a quiet wolf whistle. "She's the finest woman on Anglesey lad, bar none, other than my wife Fanny of course. I've come to her aid more than once in here. Some of these out of town bridge workers need to learn some respect, especially when they've had a few pints." He paused as Snudge delivered two perfect pints of bitter. The frothy head slowly settled from the bottom up.

"I haven't seen much of her lately. She's been busy taking boatloads of suits for tours underneath the bridge. Now they are almost ready to reopen. Everyone wants to be on the scene, you know how politics works," lamented ETR.

He took another long drag on his cigarette and blew out a perfect smoke ring that floated slowly before breaking apart. He pulled out his pocket watch and checked the time. He would need to get going soon.

"Cheers!" They both said it in unison and began to drink.

"Anyway, how do you know Taryn and what exactly is it that I can help you with?" asked ETR as he tapped his ash into the shiny black Johnny Walker Whisky ash tray.

"I just met Taryn in here yesterday, right in this spot actually. She told me this was where you always stopped after work. You are right, she is quite a lady. We got on like a house on fire. In fact, we are going out to The Ship Inn at Red Wharf Bay for dinner tonight. This is my first time on Anglesey. I had a couple of days of leave so meeting her was purely by chance, but I am really glad I did. Then she inadvertently gave me some information that really bothered me, which is why I wanted to talk to you," said Peter giving ETR a knowing wink that the old bombardier understood. He instinctively looked over his shoulder as he moved in a little closer to his newfound Toffeenose friend.

"What kind of information?" asked ETR.

"It's rather a long story. Do you have time right now?" asked Peter.

"As long as you are buying, I'm listening!" said ETR, grinning at Peter while gulping down his pint.

Peter took another sip and relayed the entire story, including the fight at Eton. He described the L shaped scar on Max's cheek, and he ended with the incident last night in The Bull. ETR stood and listened intensely. That was until he sprayed a mouthful of beer on the bar when Peter told him he thought that the man called Billy Muskett was in fact Major Max von Seeckt, an Iron Cross holding Nazi in the SS.

Suddenly, the reports of mysterious flashing lights that he had received in the early hours of the morning from his old pal at the Port Police Sergeant Lewis, had a whole new significance. ETR was sound asleep when the phone call from Lewis woke him up to report the sighting. He had done his due diligence and cycled out to Red Wharf Bay at first light. The tide was out. There was nothing unusual about the beach. He had checked the bluffs that lead from the beach up to the cliff road and again, saw nothing unusual. Per orders, he then combined his own report with Lewis's and relayed it on to MI5 Headquarters at Wormwood Scrubs. Now with the report of a possible Nazi sighting right here in his pub, perhaps something was unfolding, something deadly serious.

The old man turned over the facts in his mind as he rubbed the white stubble on his chin. Finally, he spoke, "Well, stone the bloody crows. That's quite a story, young man." He struggled to unbutton his back trouser pocket and finally retrieved a small leather notebook. Ironically, it was a Christmas gift from their mutual friend, Taryn Thomas. He thumbed it open, whipped the pencil out that was lodged on top of his ear, and wetted the lead with his tongue. He thought carefully for a moment and then slowly, deliberately wrote down, 'Billy Muskett. On bridge, early hours spotted by Taryn Thomas'. Then he paused again and added two tiny lightning bolts, the mark of the SS next to Billy Muskett. Peter read it and smiled.

Then ETR stopped and pushed the notebook to Peter and handed him the pencil. "Here, I don't speak or write German, never have, never will. It's a personal thing. I'm sure you understand." He grinned at Peter. "Write down his name and put yours in there too. Also, add a phone number for me to reach you after I get through with my investigation." Peter picked up the pencil and to ETR's delight wrote in the most perfect script handwriting that he had ever seen, the name Max von Seeckt. Then below it he added his own name, Peter Legh and handed it back to him.

"I'm sorry, there is no phone at the flat I'm staying in and I leave tomorrow. How long do you think it might take?" asked Peter.

"I see. Not long if he's on this island. Trust me, I'll track him down. Give me a few hours. Can we meet back here later tonight for last orders?" replied ETR with a grin.

"Quite, that would be perfect," said Peter, as ETR polished off the rest of his pint. Snudge acknowledged ETR's nod towards him, indicating that the session was over.

"Do you have any idea where he is staying?' asked ETR.

"No, I'm sorry, I don't know. I do know that places to stay here in Menai are somewhat scarce because of all the bridge workers. I got a tip from a lady at the Village Store, she was very helpful. She might be a good place to start. I believe her name was Gwen Dillon," said Peter.

ETR grinned and winked. "Very good, Lad. I know Gwen very well. I'll stop by and see what she knows. Now I need to get going. My Fanny has cooked me a Shepherd's Pie for my dinner and if I'm late, it won't be the Nazis you will have to worry about. Fanny and her rolling pin would put any Panzer tank in reverse real quick!" he said, pulling hard on his cigarette. "If he's anywhere close to here, I'll track him down. And if he's got an L shaped scar on his cheek...he's dead." ETR grinned. His white whiskers framed his perfect square chin while he exhaled a massive cloud of smoke.

"Be careful, ETR. He's a dirty fighter," warned Peter.

"Nah, he's a Toffeenose," scoffed ETR.

"Ok, great! Thank you, I really appreciate this. So, I will be with Taryn tonight. We will see you here later for last orders. I'll look forward to it," said Peter. He was relieved that he had been able to share the burden that he had been carrying since last night's incident at that very spot.

"As a backup plan, once I get his address I'll stop by here and give it to Snudge. That way if there's any problem, at least you will know where to send the cavalry if I don't show up!" said ETR with a laugh. He took a last drag on his Woodbine before stubbing it out in the newly cleaned ash tray. He put the pencil back on top of his ear and reviewed his notes. He marveled at the tale he would be able to tell Fanny when he showed her the perfect script handwriting by his new mate, Peter Legh, the RAF Spitfire pilot that went to Eton. He returned the notebook to his back pocket, put on his cap, and pulled it down over his eyes. He checked his pocket watch again, 6:20. He was right on schedule.

"Snudge!" he yelled with authority.

Snudge on queue appeared in front of the two men.

"My mate Toffee here is picking up the tab," he said jerking his thumb at Peter.

"Quite, my pleasure," said Peter reaching for his pocket to get his wallet out.

"Ok Lad, see you around ten thirty right here at the bar. Mums the word!" he tapped the side of his nose.

"Mums the word," replied Peter as he repeated the gesture. The two men smiled at each other and ETR stepped out into the early evening sun. His mind was not on his wife's freshly baked Shepherd's Pie but on a Nazi whose name was Max von Seeckt, here in his town. He knew it. He could feel it. He could smell it. That Bastard was here in Menai and he was going to get him. Make no doubt about it, he was going to get him because that was just the way it had to be. It was the way it had always been. The only good Nazi was a dead Nazi.

Chapter 78

ETR GOES ON THE HUNT

Menai, Anglesey
August 18, 1940

ETR's connections in Menai were second to none. Within ten minutes, he not only had the address from Gwen Dillon at the Village Shop, but also the duplicate front door key to where the mysterious Billy Muskett was staying. The location was a small farmhouse called Tyddyn Ben on the outskirts of town. It was less than ten minutes for him to cycle out there and the same to get back. Plus, who knows how much of a fight this character might put up. He smiled to himself, no problem there mate.

The biggest problem he had was not how to sort out Max von Seeckt, that was easy, but what excuse would he use to leave his house after he was done eating? Fanny knew he was a creature of habit. After eating his dinner, he would always retire to his favorite rocking chair next to the fireplace to smoke a few more Woody's and drink tea out of his favorite royal blue and white Everton Football Club mug. Then he would listen to the BBC News until nodding off. He would always wake up around 9:30 to have a quick shave and put a clean collar on his shirt before popping down to The Bull for last orders. It was the same routine every night, like clockwork.

Then it came to him, the ladder. He had borrowed the church's eight-foot ladder to paint the gutters of his house. It was still on the side of the house and he did need to get it back to the church. The Vicar had asked him to clean the stained-glass windows. The ladder would be his ticket. A grin crept across the old, weathered face as his peddling picked up in intensity.

Chapter 79

KING OF THE NORTH

The ride back to Menai was largely uneventful, other than a long delay as he entered Menai. Ashley got stuck in a traffic jam behind a shepherd moving a large herd of sheep from one pasture to another. Several sheep had broken away from the flock and despite the best efforts of a young sheepdog, were causing havoc by running into people's yards and trashing their victory gardens. He finally passed the herd and noticed a gleaming white MG waiting to go the other direction. The equally frustrated driver offered a courtesy wave as Ashley sped by on the Matchless.

He stopped at the first petrol station in Menai and topped off his thirsty machine. The young man who worked there gave him easy directions to The Bull. It was a little past six thirty as Ashley approached the pub. He slipped the Matchless into a parking spot directly out front. He cut the engine, dismounted, and checked his face in the mirror. He noted again how badly he needed a shave and headed into the bar.

Ashley made his way to the bar taking note of the customers and looking for any sign of an LDV armband. He quickly realized that except for a few chaps clad in RAF blue, all the others were locals or bridge workers.

Snudge gave him a welcome nod, "Yes Sir?" he asked while pouring out a Scotch.

"Yes, I'm looking for Captain Riggs, is he here by any chance?" asked Ashley.

"You mean ETR. Sorry mate, you just missed him," said Snudge. "A shilling," he said to the recipient of the Scotch.

"Dammit!" said Ashley. "Does he own an MG?"

Snudge laughed, "Hardly! He owns a bicycle."

"I see," replied Ashley.

"Drink?" asked Snudge.

"Yes, a pint of bitter, please," Ashley pulled out his cigarettes and lit up. Damn that roadblock and the herd of sheep. He had hoped to wrap up his investigation by interviewing ETR. Then he would be free for the evening.

"Don't worry, Mate. He will be back again for last orders I can give him a message if you like," said Snudge.

"Thanks, that's ok. I will come back later. I have plenty to do," said Ashley with a smile. He knew that other than checking in with HQ, there was nothing on his agenda but a hot bath, a shave, and some well needed sleep. He could be back here later for last orders a new man. What a milk run this was turning out to be after all.

The bitter was excellent, so he had another before leaving. The wind had picked up considerably since he got back to Menai. The ride back over the bridge's open span to the Antelope Hotel was particularly bad. Ashley had to lay flat against the tank again, this time not for speed, but for fear of being blown off. He resolved that it would be wiser to leave the bike at the hotel and walk across the bridge when he returned to meet with ETR.

Back at the Antelope, he was delighted to see Becky working behind the small bar. There was a decent size crowd for a Sunday night. He climbed the stairs and made his way down the hall to his room. She made brief eye contact with him as he went by, long enough for him to pretend to remove an imaginary pair of goggles from his forehead. She immediately got the joke and winked back at him, the red lips forming an inviting smile.

He figured he would have a shave before checking in with HQ. Once he had interviewed ETR about any possible activity related to the lights, he would have covered all his bases. He was sure that ETR would have little to add to Constable Cooper's report, but the Prime Minister could not have been any clearer. His orders were still ringing in Ashley's ears, "Leave no stone unturned Ashley, I mean none!" ETR would certainly be considered a stone in the Prime Minister's assessment.

Ashley flung his greatcoat on the bed, removed his jacket and shirt, and filled the tiny wash basin in his room with hot water. He removed his shaving kit from his small kit bag and began to scrape away at his beard. At exactly eight o'clock, a smooth faced Ashley leaned into the Snug, this time pretending to be talking on a telephone. Becky loved it and understood what he was asking. She pointed him back to the little office marked PRIVATE, indicating it was clear for him to make a phone call. This time it was Ashley who winked.

"Operations, how may I direct your call?" asked a female voice through the crackling phone line.

"Extension 137 please," answered Ashley.

"Thank you, one moment," replied the voice. Then she was gone and replaced by a ring tone.

"Colonel Withers office," answered Ferguson.

"It's Ashley," replied Ashley.

"Ah! Ashley, King of the North!" laughed Ferguson.

"Yes Ferguson, King of the North, reporting in," said Ashley mundanely.

Ashley proceeded to brief Ferguson on his findings, which were slim. Nothing Ashley had discovered added anything to the report he had been given originally. However, given the priority put on the mission by Churchill, Ashley included every detail of his day. He included what he had learned about the decoy lights set out in the marshes at Parkgate. He mentioned that the same decoy lights could not be used out at Red Wharf Bay because there was no marshland. He let Ferguson know that he still had one remaining interview with the elusive LDV Captain Riggs. He hoped to complete it within the next few hours. As an afterthought and to cover his tracks he also reported that an unexpected road closure at Parys Mountain due to ground contamination had added an additional 40 miles to his estimated mileage. Ferguson dutifully jotted down the information in shorthand. He would type it up later in the proper format and give it to the Colonel.

Ashley was relieved that Ferguson did not try any more of his feeble attempts at humor. He rightly deduced that the annoying assistant must be buried in paperwork. Touché Ferguson thought Ashley. He hung up the phone and headed back upstairs to run his long-awaited bath.

Chapter 80

HEART OF OAK

Menai, Anglesey

August 18, 1940

The long day of training at Rhosybol went well. All the
Brandenburgers spoke good English and worked well with
their counter parts. Confident that things were well under control
and knowing that it would be a long time before he would be able
to get some sleep, Max left Hott in charge and headed back to the
executive digs. He would catch up on some sleep before returning
to Rhosybol to lead the gold heist later that night.

Max parked in the briar and headed to the cottage. It was hot
and stuffy inside. He left the door ajar and went into the bedroom
to open the one small window. A nice cross breeze immediately
came through the cottage, instantly lowering the temperature. He
took off his jackboots and stripped down to his underwear. The
bed creaked as he sat on it and he laid back and closed his eyes.
Unlike the previous night, within ten minutes he was sound asleep.

On the other side of town ETR woofed down his Shepherd's Pie
and washed it down with a mug of hot tea. He kissed his beloved
Fanny on the cheek and said, "I have to go up to the church, love.
I need to take their ladder back. I've got a ton of things to get done
up there before it gets dark."

"Ok Pet," she replied. Pet was the nickname she had given him
decades ago when they were young newlyweds, before he had set
off to war from Liverpool. She had stood on the cold wet platform
at Liverpool's Lime Street Station with thousands of other wives.
The band played Rule Britannia and Heart of Oak as Britain's
young warriors headed off to the war that would end all wars.

"And I suppose you will be stopping by The Bull for a swifty on your way home," she said as she brushed the dandruff off the shoulders of his jacket.

"I might if I get done in time. Either way, I'll be late. Don't bother waiting up for me love," he said with a smile.

"Oh, don't you worry about that. I will just do the dishes and finish up a bit of knitting and then hit the sack. My hips are bothering me again," she replied as she rubbed her arthritic hips.

ETR plucked his cloth cap off the hat stand by the tiny front door. He tucked his scarf into his jacket and then pulled on his heavy raincoat. He tightened his coat belt and gave Fanny a gentle hug. "Right, I'll be off to the church then."

He closed the door behind him and looking up was delighted to see the threatening rain had not yet started. Off in the distant western sky, he could see the ominous black storm clouds slowly moving in his direction. The evening storm that had been predicted was beginning to materialize. The weather pattern was typical for Anglesey at this time of year. There would often be a series of storm fronts that would blow in from the Irish Sea to batter the island. Following this would be periods of beautiful calm sunny clear days. That could change back to howling wind and rain in an instant.

ETR went around the side of the house, fired up another Woodbine and retrieved the ladder. Although the large wooden ladder was extremely heavy, ETR propped it on his shoulder with incredible ease as though it was made of balsa wood. Then in one smooth motion defying his years, he cocked his leg over the bicycle's seat, pushed himself off and cycled down the road to St. Mary's.

It was a short ride to the church. ETR parked his bike, lifted the ladder off his shoulder and rested it against the old maintenance shed that was located behind the church. He fished in his coat pocket and pulled out an enormous key ring with a vast assortment of keys. Several of them had their own smaller key rings attached with various initials punched on them. Since he was the unofficial law in town, many of the local merchants relied on ETR to keep a spare key for their business in case of emergency.

He unlocked the door and quickly stashed the ladder inside the shed. Then he locked it and popped the heavy keyring back into his pocket and mounted his bike. Both hands now firmly on the handlebars, he set off in a steady, almost robotic pace. His gray eyes focused intensely as he rode down the church path past the rows of ancient moss-covered tombstones and out through the iron entry gates.

The first drops of rain began to arrive at Menai. He quickly cycled back to The Bull and handed Snudge the address written on a piece of paper from his notebook. "If I'm not here for last orders, give this note to the Toffeenose Peter Legh from the RAF when he shows up," he said and left the bar. Snudge folded it over and stuffed it into his shirt pocket without another thought. The ride out to Tyddyn Ben was uneventful. To lift his spirits, he sang the words from his favorite song, Heart of Oak.

Heart of Oak are our ships,
Jolly Tars are our men,
We always are ready,
Steady Boys! Steady!
We'll fight and we'll conquer!
Again, and again.

For a man his age, ETR made good time. He finally saw the whitewashed walls of Tyddyn Ben. His first objective was to peddle to the old, abandoned briar at the edge of the property. The rain was falling heavier now, and he was grateful that he had worn his raincoat.

Once he arrived at the small path that ran downhill to Tyddyn Ben, he dismounted and leaned the bicycle against the ruins of what had once been a wall. He was careful to avoid the nasty stinging nettles that grew in abundance at this time of the year.

Peering into the briar he could see a car parked just inside. It was a fairly new Ford that he had not seen before. He tried the door, but it was locked. A quick glance through the window showed him that the car was empty except for a roll of plans laid across the rear seat. Who was this mysterious man described to him by Peter Legh?

Now quietly by himself, he took a moment to consider the ramifications if Legh was right and a Nazi was here on his island.

What if there were more of them? What if this was the beginning of an invasion? Was the man staying in the cottage in any way connected to the flashing lights out in Red Wharf Bay?

Then as soon as he had let the nightmare thoughts begin, he snapped out of it. "Get yourself together lad! Not here, not my town," he told himself. Besides, everybody knew the boys in the RAF wouldn't let them down. The RAF, that's who's going to stop those bastards. Peter Legh and his mates in their Spitfires, they would give them what for.

He stepped into the dusty briar and removed his heavy raincoat. He folded it neatly and laid it on the ground. He removed the large key ring from his jacket pocket and put it into the smaller pocket of his waist coat. The large brass ring barely fit in. He took off his jacket and placed it on top of the raincoat, then unbuttoned his cuffs and rolled up his shirt sleeves.

Lastly, he reached into his other waist coat pocket and took out his most prized possession. It was the gold pocket watch that Spillers had presented to him in Birkenhead when he had retired. He disconnected the silver chain attached to it from his waistcoat buttonhole, checked the time and then turned over the watch to reveal his initials ETR engraved on the back. He gently put it on the neatly stacked clothing.

Then the old fighter stepped into the center of the briar, rolled his head clockwise then counterclockwise and rotated his shoulders several times. He assumed the fighting stance that he had done hundreds of times before and began to shadow box with a dexterity that defied his age.

Sufficiently warmed up, he left the briar and hugged the old stone wall with its wild hedgerow. It provided him with a perfect cover as he got nearer and nearer to the small rusty garden gate. It was open. He passed through and made it quietly to the front door which he noticed was slightly ajar. He stopped and listened, but no sound could be heard from within. Next, he moved silently to his right and poked his head around the front room window. No one could be seen inside. He followed the white wall around to the tiny kitchen window and peered in. The kitchen was empty and still, so he proceeded around the corner ducking under an empty clothesline. He hugged the wall and made a left turn at the back of the house where one of two small bedrooms were located. One of the windows was open.

Reaching it he peeked in and there he was, asleep on the small single bed in his underwear laying on his back. ETR shot back quickly and waited a moment before taking a second look. The man had not moved. ETR stood transfixed for a couple of minutes. Then, convinced the man was asleep, he returned to the front door. He stood for a few seconds, his heart pounding, listening acutely. Hearing no sign of life, he slowly pushed on the door which to his massive relief opened without a sound. He was also relieved that he did not have to use the key after all. For a moment, he stood in the entryway and waited again. When he was quite sure that the man had not heard him, he silently entered the tiny cottage.

Chapter 81

BATH TIME

Bangor, Wales

August 18, 1940

Ashley smiled as he finally had a private moment to read the letter that Churchill had given him at their meeting at 10 Downing Street. It was a powerful ticket that could get him anywhere in the Kingdom. Too bad, it was only good for 48 hours. He put it back in the envelope and then slipped the envelope back into his jacket pocket. Then he stripped naked and finally ran the bathtub. Ashley lay on the bed, it was firm and to his liking. After he had filled his belly and enjoyed a couple of pints, he would sleep like a log tonight.

When the tub was ready, he fetched his cigarettes, lighter, and gun and put them all on the small table that held an extra towel and soap alongside the tub. Ashley concluded that there are few sensations that can match the pleasure of stepping into a hot bath when you are dirty and tired. As he slipped into the warm water of the claw foot bathtub, he placed the large loofah behind his head and totally relaxed for the first time in days. In less than a few minutes he fell fast asleep.

Downstairs, business in the Snug was brisk. It was an unusually busy night and one of the locals had brought in his accordion and started a sing along. The beer flowed, it was noisy, and the patrons were having fun. Becky was the perfect hostess. It was hard to even imagine that there was a war going on at all. It all seemed so far away from this picturesque place. Yet at that very moment the Luftwaffe was busy loading its bombers with tons of incendiary bombs. They were getting ready for yet another nighttime bombing raid, designed to turn the dock yards and homes of Merseyside into a blazing inferno.

Chapter 82

First Blood

Menai, Anglesey

August 18, 1940

Catlike, ETR walked across the small front room to the bedroom. Reaching the open door, he stopped in the doorway, dead still. His eyes were transfixed on the man lying motionless in front of him on the small bed. ETR quickly surveyed the room. Other than the bed, there was a tiny table lamp with a battered shade on a small nightstand. He also saw a water jug and an empty ashtray. A single wooden wardrobe sat against the wall. Two white lamb skin rugs lay on the floor, one by the side of bed and one at the foot.

Then he saw them. Two black jackboots stood together, rigid, at attention next to the nightstand. On one of them he could see a Nazi Swastika below an eagle in gold! ETR felt a cold chill move down his spine. In an instant he knew that the Toffeenose was right. The enemy was here, right here in this bedroom, in Menai. Here! The bloody Nazis are here! He fought to calm himself as he crept slowly around the bed. ETR looked again at the jackboots with the gold Swastika clearly visible. Then as he got closer, he saw three initials below the Swastika, MvS...Max von Seeckt. ETR had found his man.

Almost as if he had a new sense of purpose, ETR ever so slowly walked closer to the bed, one foot carefully in front of the other, closer, now just a couple of feet from the bed. Just a couple of more steps, he moved closer, easy does it. Just one more thing he wanted to check. Now at the bedside, growing in confidence as his adrenalin kicked in, ETR leaned over the statue-like man. Just a little closer, just a little closer to see if there was a scar. And there it was on the side of his right eye, exactly the way Peter Legh had described it, the perfect L.

ETR smiled. The bloody Toffee was right. Major Max von Seeckt of Hitler's crack SS was lying in front of him, sleeping like a baby, right here on Anglesey. ETR checked him out again, scanning him from head to toe. He was built like an ox. The thick blond hair, the square jaw, ETR was impressed.

Then, suddenly, Max opened his eyes. Their eyes met. Before he could react, ETR was on top of him, full mount, his deformed right hand grabbed Max's throat and clamped down hard. Max, still in shock, grabbed ETR's wrist and tried to pry him loose, while bucking his body to throw the old man off. ETR anticipated his effort and gripped his legs together tight, his work boots digging into the back of Max's huge thighs. Max gasped for air. The grip on his windpipe was phenomenal. Max had been in more of his fair share of fist fights with fellow Nazis. Brawling was encouraged in the ultra-machismo culture of the Third Reich. But he had never been in this predicament before.

He was staggered by the strength of the old man looking down on him with a dark hatred burning in his gray eyes, the like of which Max had never seen before. He knew without a doubt that this man was here to kill him. He continued to try to pry ETR's hand from his grip when a tremendous left hay maker rained down and smashed into his nose. Max had never been hit so hard in his life. He was stunned and in serious, serious trouble. He continued to try to buck ETR off of him. The old bed was creaking and banging as the two men thrashed around on top of it. Max could barely breathe. ETR continued to squeeze his windpipe. The blood was pouring out of Max's nose and going back down his throat. This was bad, very bad.

Wham! Another hay maker right into his left eye. ETR stared down at him. His face was contorted due to the effort he was putting in to stay mounted and to choke this bastard out. Max tried to scream but could not breathe. He gasped for air, but none came.

Wham! Again! It was the same intensity, right into his right cheek bone. Realizing he could not pry away ETR's grip and knowing that he was in a deadly fight for his life, he desperately started to claw at ETR's face. He scratched at his mouth and cheeks. ETR leaned his head back to protect his eyes. He screamed as Max's fingers found the inside of his cheek. ETR squeezed tighter on his windpipe. Max began to feel the first effects of the lack of oxygen getting into his lungs and brain. He continued to scratch and claw at ETR's mouth. He was beginning to fade. He knew he had to do something and do something fast.

For a millisecond, he was able to gather his wits and looking down at his assailant's torso he saw it, the large metal key ring hanging from ETR's waist coat pocket. He was close to blacking out, this was it. He had one last shot. In a flash, he grabbed the key ring and pulling back his arm in one all mighty blow he smashed it into ETR's temple. Blood shot across the bedroom from the deep gash that immediately opened up. The death grip was finally released on Max's windpipe as ETR fell stunned, sideways off the bed.

Max gasped. He tried desperately to suck in air. Then he spit out a frothy bloody wad. He gasped again. Air, he needed air. ETR started to slowly get to his feet. Blood was pouring down the side of his face and soaking into his well-worn shirt, blurring the vision in his left eye.

Max saw his chance and jumped off the bed onto ETR as he was standing up. Both men crashed into the plaster wall which cracked and split under their combined weight. In a cloud of plaster dust Max pinned ETR to the wall and using his body weight held him there. Max was still gasping, trying to compose himself, trying not to suffer any more damage, as the blood poured out of his nose. "Who was this man? What the hell just happened?" Max thought.

A crunching bony knee to the rib cage interrupted Max's thought process. The blow caused him to lean too far to the left, losing his center of gravity. ETR summoned all his strength and used his momentum to push him a little further to the left, giving him enough room to get off the wall. ETR then spun a half turn to face his foe and adopted his classic fighting stance, blood pouring from the deep gash in his temple.

"Come on, Jerry. You want some? Come on, Jerry!" he snarled. His fists were tightly clenched, making small slow circular motions in the air. "Come on! Come on, tough guy. What you got, eh? Tough guy, eh. What you got, Jerry!" His adrenaline was peaking now. He was loving it. This was what he wanted, one more crack at Jerry. Since leaving France and his long road to recovery, he had always lamented that he had not done more, had not killed more Jerrys, had not done enough to avenge all his mates, the ones who had not come home and they never would.

And now here, in this dim, sparse tiny bedroom, in a little Welsh cottage on the island of Anglesey, his tormented decades of silent prayer had finally been answered. ETR had been given one last shot. Max said nothing. He too took a fighting stance and weighed up his opponent. Astonished at the strength and shear toughness of the old man before him, he processed the situation at hand. He would utilize every advantage. The key ring!

With lightning speed Max launched his attack. He was too fast for ETR, who saw him make his move. But the reactions of the old fighter were not as sharp as they were in his youth. Max caught him square on the jaw with the heavy brass key ring that acted as the perfect knuckle duster. ETR felt what were left of his own teeth shatter and a searing pain that started in his jaw and shot up into his brain. He fell backwards and landed heavily on his back against the old plank floor.

Like a cat, Max was on him. ETR tried to mount a guard against the Nazi, but Max was too fast. The second blow landed square on his nose breaking the bone into pieces. Blood sprayed all over the two of them. The third strike was right between the eyes. The impact smashed the back of his head into the floorboards. ETR groaned, his eyes were streaming from the blow to his nose. Now it was he that could not breathe. He could just about see the next blow coming as it hit him again in the nose. Then the next one shattered his eye socket.

Max, now in the full mount position continued to pummel ETR's face. He was amazed that the old man was still fighting. He had never seen such courage. Max knew there was no turning back, he had to finish this. He continued to smash the key ring again and again into ETR's bloody face. How could this old bastard still be fighting?

ETR tried to block the assault as best as he could, but now he was no match for Max. The blood-soaked keyring continued to rain down onto his mangled face. ETR knew that he was done. He was exhausted, unable to see or breathe. The old Bombardier knew he had finally fired his last salvo. He stopped blocking. There would be no more defense. But the blows did not stop, they just kept coming.

He was fading now. It was over. He could not feel anything. He began to float somewhere over misty fields. Poppy fields. Flanders. Then there was just a dull pounding of unimaginable power that he needed to stop. But it just kept coming and coming. Would someone please stop the pounding? Anyone? Please? Then he saw his Fanny. She was standing on the platform at Liverpool's Lime Street Station in her long blue dress. She had her favorite hat on. She was holding her gloves and a bouquet of flowers that he had given her. She waved goodbye. She was young and beautiful, and the band played Heart of Oak, and then it was finally over.

Exhausted and finally convinced that ETR was dead, Max stopped the pummeling. He looked down at ETR's unrecognizable face. The bloody mess that was his nose and mouth no longer gurgled after ETR drew his last breath. Max climbed off ETR's limp body and slumped against the bed. He dropped the bloody key ring to the floor next to him and sat there breathing rapidly. The blood continued to drip out of his nose. He didn't care, he just needed to breathe, to gather his thoughts. Who was this old man who had fought like a tiger? And why did he just try to kill me? Did he know about the planned gold heist?

After a few minutes, he pulled himself to his feet. He winced at the pain in his ribs from the knee ETR had driven home. He stood looking down at the lifeless body, shaking his head. He pinched the bridge of his nose to try to stop the blood flow and staggered into the small bathroom. Then he filled the tiny sink with water. His reflection in the mirror shocked him. His nose was bloody and possibly broken. His left eye was badly bruised and already swelling up and he had a good size gash on his cheek bone that was bleeding. He shook his head again. Still in shock, he was trying to fathom how this old man knew who he was and cursing himself for not locking the front door.

Taking the small white towel from the brass towel hook, he soaked it in the cold water and gently placed it on his eye and nose. He grimaced in pain as his adrenaline level began to taper off. He was exhausted. He sat on the side of the old claw bathtub to gather his thoughts. For now, he was just grateful to breathe in the cool Anglesey air that came through the small open window.

Chapter 83

THE NOTEBOOK

Menai, Anglesey
August 18, 1940

It took Max well over five minutes of sitting still to gather his thoughts. He was bewildered by what had transpired. It certainly was not part of the meticulously planned Operation Goldilocks. He knew nothing about the old man lying dead on the other side of the thin plaster wall. The man knew that he was a Nazi. Max had an excellent memory and he would remember if he had met this man. He simply had not. Who the hell was he? To his mechanically tuned precision mind, for the first time in his life, nothing made any sense.

Slowly, he got to his feet and looked again into the tiny mirror. Other than a trickle still coming out of the split in his cheek, the bleeding had mostly stopped. His eye was badly swollen but not closed shut and to his pleasant surprise his vision was still a perfect 20/20. His ribs were badly bruised, but he concluded that they were not broken. Although he had taken a beating, there was nothing that would prevent him from going ahead with the gold heist.

He had just been in hand to hand combat with another man in a brutal fight to the death, and he was acutely aware that without the old man's keys, he would have been a goner. Nevertheless, he had been victorious. The good news, he reckoned, if there was any, was that the old man had come alone, and the vicious fight was contained here in this isolated farmhouse. There was no one even close to within ear shot that would have heard the screams emanating from the small bedroom. Realizing that he had completely lost track of time, he had no idea how long he had been asleep before he was attacked by the old man. He needed to get to Rhosybol. He straightened up and made his way back into the bedroom.

Even for the battle-hardened Nazi, the scene was particularly gruesome. ETR had lost a tremendous amount of blood. The white lambskin rug next to the bed where the final pounding had taken place was drenched in it. The floorboards around ETR's battered skull were in similar shape. The blood spatter from the keys covered the plaster ceiling, the caved in wall and the bed. Max pulled himself together and refocused all his attention back on the mission. It was time to find out all he could about the old man that was dead at his feet. Then he needed to get the hell out of the gruesome cottage.

He checked ETR's pockets and found them all to be empty. He rolled him over and checked his rear pocket. Immediately he felt something solid. He pulled out a worn leather wallet and a small leather notebook. He looked at the notebook for a second, then sat on the bed and flipped it open. On the inside cover he read:

To ETR,
Merry Christmas 1939.
Your pal,
Taryn Thomas.

Taryn Thomas? That was the name of the little blond bitch that was questioning him at the bridge. And somehow, she must have said something to this ETR fellow, whoever he was. The first piece of the puzzle fell neatly into place. Anxious, he flicked through the dog-eared pages that contained a jumble of phone numbers, names, vague notes, shopping lists, nothing out of the ordinary. When he flipped to the last page, his square jaw literally dropped. There was the name Billy Muskett and drawn alongside it the twin lightning bolts of the SS. Below, in perfect script was written Max von Seeckt, and then he was flabbergasted when he saw the name of his old nemesis from Eton, Peter Legh.

"Peter Legh," he said. "Well, well, well! I'll be dammed! Peter Legh...I'll be dammed!" His brain rapidly sorted the pieces of the puzzle. Legh and the Welsh tart must be somehow connected to the man he had just killed who went by the initials ETR. Then he opened the wallet and pulled out an identification card that told him that the dead man was Edward Thomas Riggs, a Captain in the LDV. That would explain something at least. Perhaps the blond had reported him to the Captain for being on the bridge. How he had tracked him down he had no idea. Only the Irish knew he was here. Then there was Peter Legh, his involvement left Max baffled. Either way, the answer would not be found here in the bloody bedroom, miles from anywhere. He needed to get back to Rhosybol to make sure the whole plot had not been foiled. He tossed the wallet and notebook onto the bloody sheepskin.

He returned to the bathroom and cleaned up his bloody face as best he could. At least his nose and the gash on his face had now stopped bleeding. He would have a shiner tomorrow for sure. He quickly wiped the blood off his arms and torso, dressed, and then returned to the bedroom. Using the wet towel, he wiped the blood spatter off his beloved jackboots and pulled them on. Then he straightened up, turned around to face ETR's motionless body and gave him an almighty kick right in the rib cage. There was a sickening thud and the cracking of bone as the jackboot found its mark.

"See you in Hell ETR!" Max spat on the lifeless body and walked out of the bedroom, through the front room and out the front door without stopping to close it. He walked quickly up the garden path, through the gate and up the hill to the briar. At the top he saw the old man's bicycle parked against the wall where he had left it. He picked it up with ease and tossed it over the stone wall, he heard it land with a thud. Then looking into the briar, he saw ETR's pile of clothes and his few belongings.

He picked up the jacket and overcoat. Finding nothing in the pockets, he bent down and picked up the watch. Turning it over he sneered at the old man's initials, ETR engraved on the back. Deliberately, he dropped it onto the concrete floor of the briar, shattering the glass. Then he raised his right foot and stamped the metal heel of his jackboot squarely on top of it. The watch shattered into pieces all over the cold concrete. Then he climbed into the car and left the so-called executive digs to head back to the Irish Headquarters at Rhosybol.

Chapter 84

CONNECTING THE DOTS

HM Prison, Wormwood Scrubs, England
August 18, 1940

Colonel Withers sat back in his chair and watched the rain fall softly on the narrow arch shaped window complete with black prison bars that formed the backdrop of his small, dingey office. It was warm and slightly stuffy inside and the air stank of stale cigarette smoke. He seriously wondered how much longer he would be able to carry on in his current capacity. The sheer amount of intelligence that was being gathered and then processed from MI5 agents in the theater was daunting to say the least. He had been meaning to talk to Petrie about some relief, but the time they spent together was getting less and less every day. In fact, he had not even seen Petrie all day.

There was a constant game of cat and mouse to figure out when or where Hitler would invade. The game had become all consuming. He felt quite overwhelmed and could see no light at the end of the tunnel. The irony that he was spending his life mentally toiling behind the prison bars of one of the most notorious Victorian era prisons in the country, Wormwood Scrubs simply added to his misery. Not quite the golden years that he had been expecting.

Lately, Withers' stomach was constantly tied in knots and he had not slept for more than a few hours in weeks. He often got a sharp pain in his left arm that he could not explain, and his appetite was poor. His pants needed to be taken in, yet again. He made a mental note to have Ferguson book an appointment with his tailor. He reached down to the bottom drawer on the left side of his battered oak desk and retrieved the dark blue bottle of Milk of Magnesia. He took three huge gulps of the white, creamy liquid.

The days of measuring it out by the recommended teaspoon full had long since passed.

He continued to watch the rain flow down the grimy glass as he ran his tongue around his gums and teeth, making a sucking sound to make sure he got every precious drop. Then he swallowed again. He put the bottle back in its place and closed the drawer, quickly wiping his lips with his handkerchief. "This bloody war," he cursed to himself. He turned away from the window and looked at the piles of papers strewn across his desk.

Withers was about to tackle one of the papers at the top of the biggest pile when he noticed more new files in his previously empty "In Box". They must have been placed there without him noticing by the ever-efficient Ferguson. He was vaguely aware of Ferguson entering and exiting his office for most of the day. He glanced at the file on top and looked at the cover and read the agent's name, John Ashley.

"Ashley," he whispered out loud. "Give me some good news Ashley. Lord knows I need it." He picked up the file and opened it. His stomach growled again but he resisted the urge to run to the toilet. It would have been the fifth time that day. The file contained a single report typed by Ferguson. Colonel Withers put on his glasses and scanned it quickly. He thought for a second that it was odd that Ashley was evidently back in the field again and that Petrie had not notified him.

He read the highlights out loud to himself as he skimmed through it. He had no idea that the LDV of Parkgate had been putting lights out in the marshes of the River Dee to confuse the Luftwaffe. What a brilliant idea, he thought. Then his frustration began to mount as he could not pronounce some of the names in the report that followed, such as Amlwch. Perhaps Ferguson had committed a typing error.

Colonel Basil Archibald Withers had been educated at Harrow and Oxford where he had excelled at Mathematics before heading to Sandhurst and the Army. Withers had survived the sweeping changes at MI5 ever since Churchill had taken over. He was delighted to have formed an excellent relationship with David Petrie, the new Head of MI5. Withers was also a former Oxford Blue. Petrie had introduced Withers to Ashley and the three now enjoyed a good friendship. They even got together occasionally for a quiet pint to reminisce about the good old days.

Withers had never been to Wales, let alone the Island of Anglesey. He thought of the Welsh as nothing shy of a bunch of sheep farmers and coal miners who had simply bastardized the English language. Who on earth would combine A-M-L-W-C-H to name a town? And how was one supposed to pronounce it? The whole thing seemed backwards. It just seemed so uncivilized to Withers who had never ventured further west than Bristol.

Then he saw something that interested him. Clearly, Ashley had already been dispatched to North Wales. That would explain some of the spelling. Some flashing lights had been reported off the coast at a place called Red Wharf Bay. He kept on talking quietly to himself, still frustrated at the pronunciation. Then as he read the report, he realized that Red Wharf Bay was actually on Anglesey. Anglesey, now that's not good. Red warning lights suddenly flashed off the paper as he now began to rapidly scan the report.

He continued to talk to himself, "Road closure at...Parys Mountain. Due to ground contamination. Guarded by the Welsh Fusiliers...No! Not Parys Mountain!! It can't be so. Say it can't be so!" His tired mind whirled away as the pieces began to fall rapidly into place. "Parys Mountain! Anglesey! Jesus Christ! The Kings Gold!! That's where they hid the bloody gold!" He sat back, took his glasses off and digested what he had just put together. It was not good news, far from it. Of all the places in the Kingdom, why in God's name was he reading anything, anything at all about Parys Mountain! This could be the beginning of a total bloody disaster!

"FERGUSON!!!!" he boomed. He shot to his feet and bolted over to the drafting table that was set against one of the office walls.

"FERGUSON!!" he bellowed again as he frantically dug through the piles of rolled up maps on the drafting table. Ferguson was already at his side by the time he finished yelling his name the second time. "Sir?" he responded, pencil and writing pad at the ready.

"I need a full-size map of Anglesey, at the bloody double!" yelled Withers.

"Yes Sir," said Ferguson. Within a few seconds Ferguson had what the Colonel so desperately wanted. "Map of Anglesey, Sir!"

snapped Ferguson. He handed him the rolled-up map that showed Anglesey and portions of the North Wales coastline.

The Colonel snatched the map out of Ferguson's hands and in one violent sweeping movement of his outstretched arm, he cleared the drafting table of every map and pile of paper. The whole mess cascaded noisily to the wooden floor. Several of the typists in the area immediately outside of his office looked up at the sound of the crash. A lady in a crisp Army uniform who was clearly in charge of the typing pool, stood up and quickly closed the Colonel's door.

"Sir?" asked Ferguson incredulously.

"Magnifying glass!" screamed Withers. Ferguson shot to his desk and retrieved it. The Colonel turned on the overhead light and spread the map out flat on the table.

"Here you go, Sir," said Ferguson as he handed the Colonel his magnifying glass. Withers grabbed it without saying a word. He peered through the glass and followed the A55 road to the city of Bangor. Then he followed the road across the Menai Bridge and along the twisting Anglesey coastline. It was the same route that agent Ashley had taken.

"Marker!" he yelled. "Sir," responded Ferguson instantly reaching back to the desk and grabbing a red crayon. "Gallows Point, Beaumaris, Llanddona...here Red Wharf Bay! Mark this!" he barked at Ferguson who drew a large circle around Red Wharf Bay above the Colonel's nicotine stained brown fingernail as it nervously tapped on the map.

"Now, where the bloody hell is Parys Mountain?" The Colonel followed the coast road to Benllech, Moelfre. Amlwch! Bull Bay... no, no...I have gone too far...Bloody Hell!" He retraced his route backwards, cursing like a trooper under his breath.

"Where the hell is Parys Mountain?" Then he saw it, slightly inland from the coast. "Here! Here! Parys Mountain!" The Colonel tapped his finger nervously again over Parys Mountain. Ferguson instantly circled it in red.

"Caliper!" he yelled. "Sir," said Ferguson, who was already retrieving it from the small toby jug on the Colonel's desk. Withers quickly noted the scale at the bottom of the map. He then set the caliper and like a skilled ship's navigator, measured out the distance from Red Wharf Bay to Parys Mountain. "Pencil and paper!" he demanded. Ferguson handed him the pad and noticed that beads of sweat had formed across the old man's forehead and the back of his neck. Withers intensely ran a calculation on the pad. "Jesus Christ!" he said to himself as he looked back at the map then back to his calculation. "Jesus Christ!" he exclaimed again. "Red Wharf Bay is less than twenty minutes away by road from Parys Mountain! That is way too close. Way too bloody close!"

"Sir?" Ferguson was truly baffled. In all the years that he had been with the Colonel as his right-hand man, he had never seen him behave like this. He had no idea what had happened. Clearly something catastrophic seemed about to unfold. But he did not get any more time to try to figure out what the problem was. "Get me Ashley, right now! On a secure line…At the bloody double!" he screamed. Ferguson was gone.

The Colonel stood gazing silently at the map of the Island of Anglesey laid out before him. How could he have possibly missed this? He suddenly felt a cold chill, despite being in a warm office and fought the urge to shiver. His gut tightened again. He began to rationalize the events in his mind. He was one of a very few military men who knew of the ultra-top-secret Operation Fish. He was also one of an even smaller group who knew what was hidden at Parys Mountain. Major General Scholes had personally assigned him to oversee the successful transfer of gold to the windmill. Once Major Hunt had reported that the gold was secured and Martins Bank had signed off, he had not given Parys Mountain a second thought…until now. It had just hit him between the eyes like a two by four.

Colonel Withers lit a cigarette and thought for a moment, how could this have happened? The initial reports had informed him that the lights were off the North Wales coast. He knew that Petrie had requested Ashley's presence for an early morning meeting with the Prime Minister, but he had not seen or heard from either man since. He had not yet been briefed that further investigation had placed the flashing lights off the Island of Anglesey. This in turn must have been known by Ashley before he was dispatched, but no one had updated him. That was odd.

The first he knew about Ashley actually being on Anglesey was when he had read the report. No one else in his office or the entire building for that matter, especially Ferguson and Ashley had any idea about the crates of solid gold bars stacked neatly floor to ceiling, row after row, inside the abandoned windmill at Parys Mountain. He shuddered at the visual now rolling through his mind, then winced at the pain in his bowels.

The Colonel tried to reassure himself. There was nothing else other than a report of some flashing lights out at sea. While this was unusual and should be investigated, Parys Mountain was off limits and secure. Ashley had confirmed that it was still sealed off by the armed Welsh guards. The gold was surely secure. Could it be that the whole thing was nothing more than a simple coincidence? Perhaps the pressure was finally getting to him, or was he just being paranoid? Was he leaping to ridiculous conclusions? The answer could be as simple as the discovery made by Ashley of the marsh lights at Parkgate. There could be a logical explanation. He needed to calm down.

Now alone in his office, the Colonel took a long drag on his cigarette. He pulled out another map of the entire British Isles. Now Anglesey looked smaller and he tried to convince himself that it was a lot less important. It was just a small island off the coast of North Wales. He took his red crayon and with the aid of his magnifying glass, he marked the spot that said Red Wharf Bay. Then next to it he made a mark on Parys Mountain. He stood back and gazed at the map. It measured about three feet by five feet when spread out. Over the last few months, he had gazed at it for literally days, but he had only focused on the south coast of England. He had concentrated on areas like Dover and Kent, and all the regions that squared off against the monster that prowled on the other side of the thin pale blue line that said, the English Channel.

He had never given the North Wales Coast or Anglesey a second glance. Now as he looked down at the map that showed the entire Kingdom, north to south, east to west, he looked at how close the two red dots were in relation to the size of the overall land mass. He looked at the vast coastline that ran all the way around the British Isles. All those hundreds and hundreds of miles of coastline and the one area with a reported sighting of suspicious flashing lights, was there, right there, at Red Wharf Bay, right next to… Parys Mountain!

He stared at the two red dots in silence, thinking intensely, until he began to squint at them. Then they started to blur, and he felt a little lightheaded. He steadied himself against the table as the dots came back into focus. One dot represented millions of pounds worth of the country's gold and the other one was the location of some strange lights seen flashing out at sea. "Too close! It's just way too bloody close!" he repeated to himself again.

His gut began to rumble. He grabbed the bottle of Milk of Magnesia again. This time he finished the bottle. Then fighting to tighten his sphincter, he made a bee line for the gentleman's toilet, unbuckling his belt as he ran. "Ferguson! Where in the hell is Ashley? I need to talk to him. I need to talk to him bloody well now!!" he yelled as he locked the door. His cigarette was left unsmoked to burn down in the ashtray.

Chapter 85

THE SHIP INN

Red Wharf Bay, Anglesey
August 18, 1940

The young couple headed out to Red Wharf Bay. At Taryn's request, they kept the roof down even though it was colder now and rain was imminent. The storm that had been forecast to hit the island by evening and had stalled off the coast, was finally beginning to come ashore. Peter gave her his Eton scarf to wear, as she huddled under his flight jacket again. During the drive he explained to Taryn that out of an abundance of caution he had already met with ETR about von Seeckt. ETR was going to see if he could find out anything and they would meet back at The Bull for last orders. Taryn thought the whole thing was a silly waste of time but did not dwell on it anymore. Instead, she chose to focus on the handsome man behind the wheel right next to her, who she simply loved to be with. The couple still had a few hours of daylight left to enjoy during the long summer evening.

"Red Wharf Bay, how do you say that in Welsh?" asked Peter as they walked hand in hand the short distance from the MG to The Ship Inn.

"Traeth Coch," she said with a smile. "It literally means Red Beach. Legend has it that it was named after a brutal battle that took place here against the Vikings in the eleventh century."

"The Vikings were here?" asked Peter, looking at the vast flat reddish sandy beach. "I had no idea, that's fascinating."

"Oh, yes. It was a long, long time ago. Believe it or not, this used to be a busy little port dating back to the eighteenth century. They used to build ships here. It is the perfect sheltered cove. Notice how the wind has already stopped?" she asked, tilting her head. Her blue eyes mesmerized him, yet again. "By Jove, you're right," he said noticing how much calmer it was on this side of the bay. The Ship Inn was nestled back into the hillside and looked like part of a row of small white painted cottages.

"Yes, they still have trading records here dating all the way back to the fifteenth century," she continued.

"Good Lord, there is so much history here. I had no idea that the Vikings landed and fought here, that is incredible. Then again, look at how flat it is. There are no rocks to get dashed on. You can just sail right up the middle and you are in. It's the perfect place for a sea born invasion," he said gesturing with his hand towards the end of the bay.

Then quite suddenly his own words resonated with him, landed…and fought…flat…no rocks…right up the middle and you are in…sea born invasion, my God! Max von Seeckt! That must be why he is on the island. They are going to invade here on Anglesey, coming in through the back way while all eyes are looking at France. Sheer panic washed over him as he grasped the enormity of what his mind was trying to conceive. It began to race as he tried to put the pieces together, nothing made any sense. Then for a terrifying moment, for the first time in his life he began to question his own sanity.

"Peter?" Taryn's voice snapped him back to reality. "Did you even hear me?"

"Yes, sweetheart," he said as his mind churned.

"Inside or outside?" she asked.

"I'm sorry?" replied Peter, he had no idea what she was talking about.

"Do you want to sit inside or outside for dinner?" she said pointing to several small tables in front of the pub outside on the small patio.

"Oh, outside. Let's enjoy the view while it's not raining," he said. He looked back at the vast swaths of flat sand. "Outside will be fine." He pulled himself together and gathered his thoughts as he rationalized the situation. First, he could not be sure if it was von Seeckt. He had met with ETR who said he would investigate. They would meet back at The Bull in a few hours and the whole thing would be wrapped up. Everyone knew that the Germans were amassed along the English Channel and that the invasion would be somewhere on the south coast. This ancient island that was the home to the woman he had now fallen hopelessly in love with, simply did not fit into the plan. It just did not make any sense. In the meantime, he needed to put Max von Seeckt out of his mind and make the most of his time with Taryn, who was now leading him by the hand through the front door of The Ship Inn. Her long blond hair blowing in the breeze coming in off the bay.

The Ship Inn was a cozy little pub. A small bar was located in the center and a brick fireplace was set off in the corner. A framed portrait of Winston Churchill with his trademark cigar and bowler hat hung over the center of the mantel piece. The pub had more than its fair share of brasses and model ships. It had an excellent variety of various brass nautical pieces that completed the tasteful décor. Best of all, and as Taryn had promised it was nice and quiet. Other than a few locals and a Bulldog that belonged to the owner, the place was deserted.

"Perfect," said Peter as he walked up to the bar.

"A pint of bitter and a glass of cider, and could I get a couple of menus, please?"

"Certainly, Sir," said the young barmaid in a thick Welsh accent as she handed him two menus. "I'll take your order whenever you're ready," she continued as she pulled on the black shiny hand pump. A quick scan of the menu resulted in the unanimous decision of two orders of fish and chips. He picked up their drinks and followed Taryn back outside. They sat at the table farthest away from the door. A young waitress arrived shortly afterwards with their silverware, napkins and a small tray with salt, pepper and malt vinegar. She placed it in the center of the table and quickly returned to the bar.

"Here's to us and Traeth Coch!" said Peter as they touched glasses.

"Cheers!" Taryn replied, and they both took a long drink. Then they smiled at each other and kissed again. Peter, looking out again at the flat beaches began to replay in his mind the nightmare of wave after wave of Nazi troops, armed to the teeth, running across the sand. He had to fight desperately hard to regain his composure and was relieved when Taryn finally spoke.

"Tell me what it's like when you are up there fighting the Luftwaffe," she inquired, putting his arm across her shoulders and moving in closer to him.

"Jolly scary!" he laughed. "The actual fighting is usually over pretty quick. Our main job is to go after the ME 109 fighters that escort their bombers. The Hurricanes go after the bombers, the ME 109's go after the Hurricanes and so we go after them. It is all very chaotic really once it starts. It happens very quickly. The actual dog fighting does not usually last for more than a few seconds. That's about it for the ME 109's before they have to return to refuel or they are out of ammunition. Then we head on back, refuel, re arm, hopefully have time for a cup of tea and wait for the next wave. The worst part is the waiting around for the signal to scramble. You just never know when it will sound. You never really get to relax.

Most of the time we have to wear our Mae West, which makes it jolly difficult to play cricket!" he laughed. He was relieved to see the sparkle in her eyes that told him that she believed his tepid version of the real terror of what he and his mates did on a regular basis over the English countryside. He did not tell her about the vomit that he had to choke down to avoid it filling his oxygen mask as red-hot shells tore through his fuselage just inches behind his seat. Or about the nightmares that occurred now with more frequency. He often saw the ghosts of Twiddle, Wilson, Shoddy and Alex, pilots of the 92nd that had been lost in the last few weeks of fighting alone.

Then there were the screams of Turner that never went away, who had burned to death in his cockpit. His Spitfire slowly corkscrewed down from 25,000 feet straight into the green fields of Kent. "Jolly scary," he repeated. He drank his bitter and squeezed her shoulder a little tighter. "Peter do be careful. Promise me you will be careful," she said as she kissed him softly on the lips. "I promise," he said, lost again in her blue eyes.

The waitress arrived with their fish and chips.

"Here we are, fish and chips twice," she said placing two identical plates of perfectly cooked fish and chips in front of them.

"Anything else?" she asked.

"No, I think we are fine, thank you," said Peter, and with that she smiled and left.

"Good show!" said Peter and they both tucked in.

After dinner, they sat outside enjoying the evening. They told each other stories from their past and shared their likes and dislikes. They were delighted at how much they had in common. The sun was now blocked by the darker storm clouds as evening fell on the island. The wind began to pick up even in the sheltered cove of Red Wharf Bay. The first white caps began to appear on the water and flocks of seagulls were already heading inland ahead of the storm that was now battering the west side of the island.

Peter paid the bill and as they headed back to the MG, the first raindrops began to fall.

"Still want the roof down, my Lady?" asked Peter as he ushered her into the passenger side.

"No, I think you can put it up now, Charles," she laughed at him.

"Yes Mam!" he said as he pulled up the canvas top and locked it down.

"Thank you, Charles."

"Home Mam?"

"Yes Charles, my Lady Shelby awaits!" she laughed. He fired up the ignition and drove off into the now steady falling rain.

They finally arrived back at Taryn's house. Shelby was delighted, again reserving her loudest bark when she discovered Peter had returned too. They enjoyed the rhubarb pie that Taryn had made specially for their dessert. Knowing that ETR would soon be back at The Bull, Peter suggested that they head over there. They agreed to drive the short distance in the MG in an attempt to stay dry.

Chapter 86

WAKE-UP CALL

Bangor, Wales
August 18, 1940

Nobody could hear the telephone ringing continually from the little office marked PRIVATE down the dimly lit hall. Least of all John Ashley, the now fast asleep MI5 agent.

Hundreds of miles away at MI5 Headquarters, secretly located in Wormwood Scrubs prison, an ailing Colonel Withers was fading fast. Ferguson had been unable to get an answer from Ashley's hotel and was now desperately trying to enlist the help of a local telephone operator in Bangor. After two failed attempts to locate businesses or residents close to the Antelope, Ferguson was praying to the almighty that someone, anyone, would answer his third and final shot, Berry's Hardware Store located less than a half mile from the Antelope Hotel. Then finally his prayers were answered by an angel with a soft Welsh accent, named Cora.

"Who on earth was that?" asked Cora's husband Kenny, as she hung up the phone.

"It was a man from the War Department. They have been trying to reach the Antelope Hotel but apparently no one was answering the phone over there. They need to talk to one of their guests, err, a Mr. Ashley, John Ashley. Evidently, it's very urgent," she said looking down at her shakily written note.

"The War Department? What the bloody hell do they want with the Antelope Hotel?" asked Kenny as he expertly flipped over the page of his newspaper.

"Not the Antelope Hotel, dear. One of their guests."

"Same thing," he said as he studied his paper. "What do they want us to do about it?"

"Apparently, we are the closest business they could find to the Antelope that has a working telephone. The young man sounded very serious. He said it was especially important that they make contact with this Mr. Ashley. He said it was of national importance," she said. She took off her slippers and put on her shoes.

"What are you doing?" he asked folding down the newspaper and peering over the top at her. His eyebrows tightened in a frown above his thick reading glasses.

"I'm going to go over to the Antelope and tell them to check their phone and see if this Ashley bloke is around," she said picking up the note and looking at it again. "It must be important. He said he was calling for a Colonel Withers, whoever he is," she slipped the note in her handbag.

"You're going now?" he said looking at his watch.

"No, tomorrow bloody morning!" she said growing frustrated. She put on a thick tartan headscarf and grabbed her raincoat. She kissed him on the head and said, "I'll be right back." Then she opened the front door and was gone.

"But it's raining out and we don't know..." he never bothered to finish his sentence. Kenny shook his head and went back to reading his newspaper.

It was less than a five-minute walk to the Antelope Hotel from Berry's Hardware Store, the family business that Cora and Kenny had operated together for close to thirty years. Cora was glad she had put on her jacket. The rain had begun to fall a little more heavily now. She started to trot but quickly ran out of breath. The hill seemed to get steeper every time she walked up it. She was almost there now just another hundred yards or so. Cora smiled when she finally began to hear the sound of old Gordy's accordion and a chorus of voices singing, "Roll out the barrel." It was Gordy's current favorite. No wonder no one was answering. They can't hear anything over that din, she surmised to herself. It was even louder when she finally opened the door and entered the hallway. She took off her headscarf and then stepped into The Snug, which tonight was living up to its name. She pushed by a few men in damp suits and made her way to the small bar, "Becky!" she yelled above the din.

"Hi Cora! Nice to see you," Becky replied with a smile, "What can I get you?"

"Nothing, thank you Love. You need to answer your phone. The War Department is trying to get hold of one of your guests, a Mr. Ashley. It sounds like it may be important, do you know him?"

"Oh Lord! Yes! We do have a guest by that name. I will get him right away, thank you! You're such a pal," she reached over and squeezed her small cold hand.

"You're welcome Love," replied Cora. She was tempted for a moment to stay and have a quick drink and maybe sing a song or two. It had been a long time since she had even been out at night. She remembered for a moment how much fun she and Kenny used to have before the war, the dances, the New Year's Eve ball, how she used to love to dance…but then the thought of having to explain it all to Kenny when she returned put an immediate damper on it. She turned and walked out.

A gust of cold wind whipped at her as she stepped out into the street. The rain was now quite relentless. At least it was downhill on the way back and she took care not to slip on the wet cobblestones. The haunting melody of Gordy's accordion was still audible to her. It almost tempted her back to The Snug, but the music began to fade as she scurried back home to the ever-curious Kenny.

Becky quickly left The Snug bar and as soon as she got to the hall, she could hear the phone ringing in the back office. "Dammit!" she swore to herself. She quickened her pace and opened the office door and picked up the handset. "Good evening, this is The Antelope Hotel, how may I assist you?"

"Oh! Thank God!" exclaimed the voice on the other end of the phone. It was an exasperated Ferguson. "Young Lady! Listen very carefully to me. My name is Officer Ferguson. I am calling on behalf of Colonel Withers for John Ashley who is a guest at your hotel. It is a matter of the utmost national importance that he come to this telephone immediately! Please tell me that you understand my request and will comply!"

"Yes, yes!" said Becky, nodding her head. "I understand."

"Then go now, tout de suite. Immediately, please! It's very important. I'll be holding the line right here!" bleated Ferguson.

"Of course," she said. Gently placing the handset on the small desk, she flew out of the office and up the stairs to Ashley's room.

"Mr. Ashley!" she shouted as she knocked on his door. "Mr. Ashley are you there?" she knocked again. No answer. "Mr. Ashley!" she yelled again. Still no reply. "Ooooh, why me?" she moaned. She made a snap decision to try the door. It was locked. She reached into her apron pocket and pulled out a ring of keys. Selecting the master key, she opened the lock and entered Ashley's room. It was empty but the bathroom door was slightly open. "Mr. Ashley?" she said again as she walked across the room and opened the bathroom door.

Ashley was already halfway out of the tub and reaching for his gun when he saw her. She screamed. Ashley immediately realized it was Becky Forbes and no threat. He quickly lowered his gun. "I'm so sorry! What? What are you doing in here?" he blurted out as he tried to get his wits about him. Then in an instant, he realized he was at The Antelope Hotel in the tub. He must have nodded off, and he was...naked! Stark naked...in front of a wide-eyed Becky Forbes.

"Oh my!" she said as she covered her mouth and turned away, but not before she had quickly admired his thick hairy chest, hard abs and well...his manhood. She instinctively grabbed the white bath towel off the hook and threw it in his direction without looking back.

"Thanks," he said as he caught it and wrapped it around his waist. She could hear the trickling of the bath water and the creaking of the old floorboards as he finished getting out of the tub.

"You have an urgent phone call from your office. They have been trying to reach you, but I was not able to hear it because of the noise in The Snug. I am terribly sorry, Mr. Ashley. I hope I didn't get you in any trouble," she said looking at the door. She wanted to turn around again and look at him, but that was not what a lady would do. She smiled to herself because the truth was she had already seen everything Mr. Ashley had to offer.

"I'm so sorry, how embarrassing. I must have fallen asleep in the tub. What time is it?"

"It's a little after ten o'clock, I think. They are still on the phone holding for you in the office, Mr. Ashley."

"Holding? Yes, quite," said Ashley as he got out of the bathroom and put his gun back in its holster. "I'm so sorry about all this," he said again, quickly slipping on his pants. "You can come out now."

Becky came out of the bathroom and they made eye contact again and smiled at each other.

"Do you always take a gun with you when you take a bath?" she asked with a smile.

"Part of my job, I'm afraid. It goes everywhere I go. I should not have fallen asleep. I was up all night on a train from London. I must have been a lot more tired than I thought. I'm so sorry."

"Please don't apologize anymore, it's our secret," she said and gave him that fabulous wink again.

"Thank you," he said. "You are very kind."

"You'd better get going. It sounded very important," she said as she passed him his shirt.

"Absolutely, thank you...perhaps I could buy you a drink later?" Ashley wasn't sure why he had asked her that, but he knew that he liked her. He also knew that he wanted to spend some time in her company under more normal circumstances.

"Yes, I'd like that very much, thank you," she said as she gathered up his shoes and socks and handed them to him.

Delighted, he grabbed them, smiled at her, and flew out of the room.

Chapter 87

DIRTY LITTLE SECRET

Bangor, Wales

August 18, 1940

Ashley ran down the stairs, rounded the corner and headed into the small office. He sat at the desk and picked up the handset. "Ashley!" he said as he fumbled with his shoes and socks.

"Jesus, Ashley! Where the hell have you been?" bleated a distressed Ferguson.

"I was taking a bath..." Ashley began to explain but Ferguson cut him off.

"Taking a bloody bath?" wailed Ferguson. "Jesus, Ashley! The old man is going cuckoo down here! We have been trying to get you for ages! Stand by, I'll patch you through..."

"Cuckoo? Over what?" asked Ashley, genuinely perplexed.

"I don't know exactly. I just know he is coming unglued. I think it is something to do with that toxic Parys Mountain in your report. Don't ask me what, now stand by!" There was a brief buzz of a dial tone, then the Colonel was on the line.

"Ashley?" he hollered.

"Sir?"

"Where in god's name have you been man!!?"

"I'm sorry, Sir. I was taking a..." he was cut short.

"Never mind that now, we don't have time!"

"Sir?" asked Ashley, still clueless about what could possibly be so important.

"Listen very carefully to me Ashley, we don't have time for any misunderstandings! Clear?"

"Yes Sir," said Ashley. He turned around to make sure the door was closed.

"Parys Mountain! Ashley, Parys Mountain! It is in your report. You were there? Correct?"

"Yes Sir."

"And it was restricted? Correct? Armed Guards? Ashley, tell me you saw the armed guards, correct?"

"Yes Sir, there were four. They were with the Welsh Fusiliers."

"Armed, they were armed Ashley? Correct?"

"Yes Sir."

"Good. And they would not let you pass, correct Ashley?" asked the Major, sounding just a little bit calmer.

"Correct, Sir. They explained to me that there was ground water contamination and that it was toxic enough to kill off some of the local sheep and wildlife. I believe a badger also, Sir. The place is truly in the middle of nowhere," said Ashley as he replayed in his mind his meeting earlier with the guards.

"What about the guards, Ashley? See anything unusual about the guards? Anything at all? Anything out of the ordinary? Everything looked ship shape? Think Ashley, this is very important," continued the Colonel.

"They seemed fine, Sir. They challenged me when I approached, but once I explained my dilemma, they were professional. We shared a smoke and then I left. I went back the way I had come and took the coast road back here…"

The Major cut him off. "Did you see the windmill Ashley?"

"Windmill, Sir?" Ashley was baffled.

"Yes, the windmill, at Parys Mountain, did you see it?"

"I didn't know there was a windmill at Parys Mountain, Sir."

"Of course there is a bloody windmill there!" snapped the Colonel. Then as soon as he had said it, he realized that the windmill might be located some distance from the guard post. That would almost certainly make it invisible from the roadblock. He needed to look at a more detailed map.

"Hold the line Ashley!" he said, as he tried to calm himself down. He reminded himself that Ashley was completely unaware of Operation Minnow and the Nations gold hidden at the old windmill at Parys Mountain.

"Yes Sir," said Ashley. He listened to the thud of the Colonel putting the handset down and then the rustle of papers. He could hear the Colonel muttering and cursing to himself before he heard him say, "Ah ha!" Then he was back on the line.

"Ashley?"

"Sir?"

"I want you to listen very, very, carefully to me," said the Colonel for the second time during their conversation. "What I am about to tell you is top-secret, known only to a few men. It is a matter of national security that you return immediately to Parys Mountain. I want you to tell the guards that they are to take you directly to the old windmill. I need you to physically inspect the door that leads inside the windmill. It should be secured. You will probably see an abundance of locks and steel I'd imagine, barbed wire even. I need you to confirm that the doorway has in no way been breached. Do you understand, Ashley?" asked the Colonel.

"Yes Sir, but what about the ground contamination. The place is off limits for a reason, Sir. I know that the Guards will not..." he was cut off again.

"Ashley, listen carefully," the colonel repeated.

"Yes Sir."

Ashley heard the Colonel take a deep breath, then he said, "There is no contamination at Parys Mountain, it's a ruse, Ashley."

Ashley was silent for a moment.

"Ruse, Sir?" asked Ashley.

"Yes Ashley, a ruse. The whole contamination thing is a cover. It is to hide what's in the windmill. There is nothing wrong with the ground or the air or the water or the bloody sheep at Parys Mountain, Ashley. It's a cover to keep people away from the windmill!"

The Colonel sat down. His right hand was trembling ever so slightly as he held the red handset to his ear. His left hand was slowly rubbing circles on his temple. He felt the beginnings of a blistering headache. He shivered again and was beginning to fade fast.

"Why do you want to keep people away from it, Sir?" queried Ashley.

"Because of what it contains," replied the Colonel, closing his eyes.

"I see," said Ashley. "And what exactly is in the windmill, Sir."

The Colonel paused for a moment. The silence on the line was ear shattering, but Ashley was not about to speak first. Finally, the Colonel totally exhausted, cracked. "Very well, Ashley." There was another long pause, Ashley waited patiently. "The gold, Ashley. The country's gold is hidden there, inside the windmill," said the Colonel, sounding utterly spent.

Now, Ashley had no problem staying silent. The enormity of what he had just learned had left him speechless. The country's gold was hidden in a windmill, at a place called Parys Mountain. It was in the middle of nowhere on a rural island off the coast of Wales. He looked around again at the closed office door, but now he stood up, and physically checked to make sure he had closed it.

"Ashley?" the Colonel's voice snapped him to.

"Sir," said Ashley, trying to focus his attention on the Colonel. His mind was awash in visions of gold bars stacked high in an old windmill. "Like I said Ashley, this is top-secret. I'm clearing you on a need to know basis. Now listen up!" The Colonel regained his composure.

"Yes Sir!" snapped Ashley.

"Good," said the Colonel, standing again and lighting another cigarette. He was glad that it was Ashley who was his point man on this. At least he only had to tell him once. He continued, "The flashing lights that you went up to investigate that were spotted off the coast of Red Wharf Bay, how long would it take one to drive from Red Wharf Bay to Parys Mountain?"

Ashley thought for a moment, "I'd say about twenty minutes or so, at the most."

"Exactly, that's about what I had calculated also," said the Colonel.

"And you think the lights may be connected to the hidden gold, Sir?"

"Well Ashley, I'm afraid this has to be a case of better safe than sorry. When I look at the country as a whole and all the miles of coastline that surrounds Britain, it just seems a little too close for comfort to me. When I think of what could be at stake, we have to be certain that there is no mischief afoot. All the information I have gathered tells me there is absolutely nothing at Red Wharf Bay or the whole bloody island for that matter, that would lure bad actors to those shores. That is unless the bad actors knew about the gold hidden at Parys Mountain.

I'm relieved that the Welsh Fusiliers were at their post but now studying the aerial photographs, it doesn't look like the guards can even see the windmill from the roadblock." The Colonel paused as he viewed the aerial photographs through his magnifying glass again.

"As an abundance of caution, I'm ordering you to go back out to Parys Mountain to physically check that the windmill and its contents are secure. You must report back to me on the double. This goes all the way to the top, Ashley and I mean all the way to the top."

Ashley froze. Up until now he simply had not thought to connect the dots between the lights off Red Wharf Bay and Parys Mountain. But now that he knew Parys Mountain's dirty little secret, the Colonel's concern became completely justified. At the same time, Ashley finally understood why he had been dispatched to such a remote area to investigate some mysterious lights. Initially, it had seemed a million miles away from defeating the Nazis who were amassed just across the English Channel ready for invasion. Now, his mind drifted back to the meeting with Petrie and the Prime Minister. He understood why Churchill reacted the way he had, at the very mention of the word Anglesey. His milk run had just changed to an active operation.

"Yes Sir! Loud and clear. I'm on my way!" replied Ashley.

"Quite! Good man. Good luck Ashley. I'll be standing by."

The line went dead. Ashley hung up and ran upstairs. Becky was coming towards him in the corridor with a smile on her face. She jangled his door key in front of his face. "Here, you will need these," she said as she handed them to him. "I locked your door after you left. One wouldn't want to leave a firearm unsecured, would one?" she smiled.

"Oh Lord, thanks again!" said Ashley.

"Don't worry, Mr. Ashley. All your secrets are safe with me! Are we still good for our drink later?" she asked with a knowing smile.

"Absolutely, but it might be late. I have to go back out again to work I'm afraid," answered Ashley.

"Oh no, it's really starting to come down out there. It feels humid enough that it might thunder," warned Becky with a note of concern in her soft voice.

"Yes, I'm afraid you're right, but I shouldn't be too long," said Ashley.

"Be careful," she said.

"I will," he replied. Their eyes met again. They both liked what they saw.

Ashley got to his room and gathered his riding gear. He checked his gun again. It was loaded. He closed and locked his door. On his way out, he poked his head into The Snug. He tried to catch Becky's eye, but she was serving a customer and didn't look up. Disappointed, he walked out of the door and headed towards the Matchless. It was soaked. He cursed as he made a vain attempt to wipe the water off the saddle with his gloved hand. He hoped that the Matchless would start in the rain. It did again, first time.

The rain continued to pour down. He could watch the sheets come down and blow across the street. Looking to the west and through the rocky straits, he could see the same black clouds that had stalled off the coast for most of the day. Now they were ominously closer and had already pummeled the west coast of Anglesey with wind driven rain. He also noticed the change in the water now racing through the straits at a faster pace. The color had changed to a much deeper blue and there were plenty of angry white caps and swirling foam.

He headed out across the span and retraced the same route he had taken earlier in the day. At least now he had a clearer purpose. He started to imagine how the conversation with his new mates, the Welsh Fusiliers might go. What would the look on their faces be like, he wondered? Would he have to pull out his letter that was signed by Winston Churchill himself? Then he thought of Becky and her soft smile and how he wished life were different. How it might be, if not for this bloody war. The wind at the middle of the span was intense. Several times it pulled him dangerously close to the guard rail. He rounded the roundabout and headed cautiously back out to Parys Mountain. This time he drove more carefully as the daylight finally began to fade. The long bright summer day on Anglesey was giving way to a dark stormy night.

Chapter 88

DEATH ON PARYS MOUNTAIN

Parys Mountain, Anglesey

August 18, 1940

Max pulled into the Irish Headquarters at Rhosybol and was relieved to see that everything looked normal. The last of the equipment was being loaded into the lorries. Then he saw Hott at the front of the queue waving him forward. Max drove slowly by the twelve identical Bedford's and stopped in front of Hott.

Then he got out and walked around to the rear of the car towards the passenger seat, trying to avoid eye contact as Hott jumped in the driver's side. Max knew what was coming.

"My God, Major! What happened to your face?" asked Hott, looking at Max's swollen eye and cut cheek as his boss climbed into the passenger seat.

"Don't even ask," answered Max.

"Oh, I see!" laughed Hott, realizing his boss had obviously been in quite a brawl. It was not the first time he had seen Max licking his wounds.

"Anything unusual happen while I was gone?" asked Max without looking at Hott, anxious to change the subject.

"No Sir, we just continued with the drill. Then each man got dressed in his best Irish farmer suit and we are locked and loaded and ready to go," replied Hott.

"Excellent!" said a relieved Max as he finally cracked a smile at his old friend.

"So, you know I have to ask. How is the other guy?" asked Hott.

"Dead," replied Max, dryly. "Now, Drive!"

"Yes, Sir!" replied Hott as he released the handbrake and slipped the Ford into first gear.

Right on time the convoy pulled out of Rhosybol slowly and headed out to Parys Mountain. Max and Hott were in the lead driving the Ford. The rain and wind had picked up and buffeted the lorries as the drivers fought to keep a tight formation. When Max was satisfied that they were close enough but still able to avoid detection, Hott pulled over and waved to the convoy to do the same. He jumped out and ran back to the first lorry and instructed the driver to follow them to the top of the next hill and then wait there. They would receive a signal from the Ford's headlights when the guards had been neutralized. Hott returned to the Ford and nodding at Max said, "Let's go and get ourselves some British gold!" He pulled out and headed towards the roadblock up ahead.

Marty was the first to see them approaching. "Hey up! Who in the bloody hell is this?" he said to his mates as the shaded headlights of the car got closer.

"How the hell would I know, they're probably lost." added Fergus, watching the approaching car.

"Who in their right mind would be out here on a night like this?" asked Taffy.

"Like I said, they must be lost." replied Fergus.

"Fergus give them a quick wave of the torch so they know we are here," said Marty.

"Roger!" Fergus replied as he jumped into the hut and quickly returned with a large torch that had a red lens. He turned it on and pointed it in the direction of the car, waving it slowly side to side. In the car, Hott checked his Lugar that was nestled between his thigh and the seat. "They've seen us," he said to Max calmly.

"Yes, slow down a little. How many can you see?" asked Max as he strained to look beyond the soaked windshield with its wipers working overtime.

"I can make out three," replied Hott.

"Affirmative," replied Max. "There should be four of them. Where is the fourth?"

The car was getting closer now as Hott backed off the accelerator. Then Max saw the fourth man coming out of the guard hut. "There's number four!" said Max.

"Excellent, party time," replied Hott.

"Here goes! Hold steady, let them come to us. Closer is better, my friend," said Max. He was as cold as ice. Hott came to a slow stop in front of the lowered barrier and saw the man waving the red torch at him. Taffy now moved forward with his hand extended out in front of him. "Halt!" he yelled. "The road is closed!" Simultaneously, the other three guards pointed their rifles directly at the car.

"I'll take the two on the right," said Hott calmly, lowering his window. Max slipped the safety off his Lugar then lowered his window at the same time. Taffy now approached Hott's side of the vehicle, shining his small torch. "Are you lost? You cannot get through here. The road is closed to all traffic," he said as he bent down towards him.

"Apparently so," replied Hott in perfect English. "We are trying to get to Holyhead. Evidently, we must have gotten lost somewhere."

"Holyhead! You are way off mate. This is Parys Mountain. You need to turn around and go back towards Bodedern," said Taffy. Then turning to his mates, he said, "Stand easy, they are lost, trying to get to Holyhead." In a fatal move, the three men relaxed their guard and slung their rifles back over their shoulders. Marty, who had already figured it was another lost soul out on a crappy night, pulled out another cigarette and his lighter. He was the first to start walking back towards the sparse comfort of the hut. "Idiots," he muttered to himself, as he put the cigarette between his lips.

"Didn't you see the sign back there that said Road Closed?" asked Taffy, wondering if perhaps their warning sign had blown over.

"Yes, actually I did see the sign," answered Hott, grinning at him as the rain blew through the open window and into the vehicle.

"Huh? Then why did you keep on going?" asked Taffy.

Max leaned over and said, "Because we don't take any notice of your piss poor road signs!"

"What?" said Taffy taken aback.

"You heard me," said Max leaning towards a shocked Taffy. "We don't take any notice of your piss poor signs on this moss covered rock that you call an island, because we don't have to!" sneered Max.

"You what? Whoa! What happened to your face?" he said as he shone his torch on Max's swollen eye and cheek for the first time. He instinctively figured that something was wrong with these two and began to go for his rifle. Before he could raise it, Hott replied, "The same as what's about to happen to yours!" and lifted his Lugar and shot Taffy in the face at point blank range. He killed him instantly, before turning the gun on Fergus who was fumbling to get his rifle cocked. Fergus was hit twice in the torso and collapsed like a rag doll.

Max shot the guard nearest him in the center of his chest, striking him in the heart. Blood pumped out of his wound as he fell to the ground. He groaned once and then fell silent. Marty, almost to the office, heard the first shot and reached for his rifle again when Max pumped three shots into his back. Marty fell on the steps screaming in pain. Still alive, he tried to crawl his way into the office, but his spine had been severed and he couldn't feel his legs. He desperately tried to pull himself up the steps. He had to sound the alarm. The remote roadblock at Parys Mountain was under an armed assault.

Max got out of the car and calmly walked towards Marty who had now dragged himself over the guard hut door threshold. Without saying a word, he pointed the Lugar to the back of Marty's head and coldly pulled the trigger. Marty collapsed with a dull thud onto the floor of the hut. The cigarette lighter fell from his dead hand next to the step.

Hott jumped out of the car and started checking the other three to confirm they were dead. Then he went to the hut and without saying a word helped Max drag Marty's lifeless body inside. They laid him out on the floor. Then they took Marty's rifle and ammunition and repeated the process with the other three until all four bodies were placed side by side in the guard hut. Hott cut the phone line. Then they exited and loaded the rifles and ammunition into the back seat, a nice little bonus for their Irish comrades.

Max walked over and raised the barrier arm for Hott to drive through. Hott made a U-turn and flashed his headlights three times. A few minutes later they could make out the shape of the first lorry heading down the hill towards them. The moon was completely covered in heavy black clouds, it was almost pitch black. The drivers would have to rely on their woefully inadequate shaded headlights. When all twelve lorries had arrived at the roadblock, Hott jumped back in the Ford and waved them to follow. Slowly, they proceeded up the wet gravel road on the long drive to the abandoned windmill that was packed to the rafters with solid gold bars.

Chapter 89

A Grisly Discovery

Parys Mountain, Anglesey
August 18, 1940

The rain now seemed to be coming in waves. It alternated between a torrential downpour that stung Ashley's face and made it difficult to see the road, to barely a sprinkle. Finally, Ashley made the left turn onto the road for Parys Mountain. He headed up the hill towards the roadblock, this time he blew right past the Road Closed signs. He was thoroughly soaked by now and glad when he could finally see the outline of the guard hut at the ridge of the hill. As he got closer, he slowed down and noticed that the barrier had been swung upwards in the vertical position. For some reason, it was not blocking the road as it should have been and even more troubling, he could see no sign of the guards.

Instinctively, he killed the Matchless and turned off the shaded head light. "Not good," he said to himself as he silently slipped by the barricade and glided the Matchless to a halt alongside the hut. Other than the sound of the rain pelting on the corrugated iron roof, the guard post was completely silent. Ashley carefully dismounted and removed his goggles and gloves. He pulled out his gun and cocked it and pressing his back against the hut, he waited, still no sound.

Slowly, ever so slowly, he felt his way to the corner of the hut. Again, he waited, nothing stirred. Ashley took a deep breath. Then with his gun pointed out ahead of him, he darted out to the front of the hut, again nothing. He slowly climbed the steps and stopped at the door, silence. Ashley carefully turned the handle and pushed the door open. It was dark inside and there were no signs of life. He pulled out his torch and turned it on.

The four guards were laid out in a neat row on the floor. A cursory glance at their wounds told him that they all had been shot at close range probably within the last hour. With his adrenaline pumping, he cautiously entered the small hut. His torch briefly illuminated the interior. Other than the bunk beds, there was a small wood stove and a tiny desk and chair. Then his beam picked up the wall mounted telephone. He slowly walked over to it and picked up the receiver. He put it to his ear but there was no sound. He tapped the cradle up and down, hoping to get a dial tone but there was nothing. He carefully replaced the receiver and waited in silence for a moment. The rain was hammering the metal roof and streaming down the tiny window.

He grimaced as he knew what he had to do next. He needed to check the Fusiliers for their weapons. One at a time, he checked them. It was Marty, Taffy, Fergus and the fourth guard that he never got to meet. All their weapons were gone. Whoever killed the four guards were now well-armed for sure. Ashley shuddered and suddenly felt very claustrophobic. He needed to get out of the grisly hut.

He backed out of the door and down the steps, gun still cocked and ready. He reasoned that there was more than one killer to be able to take out four armed guards. They had already moved on and Ashley knew exactly where to find them. The Colonel's worst nightmare was rapidly unfolding in front of him. The bad actors and the flashing lights were indeed one and the same. The gold secretly hidden in the windmill was now in serious jeopardy.

He checked the perimeter of the hut and noticed that the phone wires had been cut. The killers had done their homework. This had all the signs of a professional job for sure. Ashley considered his options. The closest help he could think of was Sergeant Lewis out at Amlwch. Ashley knew at this hour that the Sergeant would be long gone, and his station closed for the night. Other than that, his best bet would be to get back to Menai to raise the alarm and gather reinforcements. He did not know how far the old windmill was from his current position, but he did know that he needed to go out there to see if he was right. The amount of gold that the Colonel had described would take manpower and horsepower to move, and all this would take a considerable amount of time.

Briefly shining his torch, he looked at the twisting, muddy dirt road that headed off over the hill in front of him. Ashley considered jumping on his Matchless, but he feared it would be too noisey and the chances of getting a puncture were high. He needed to get close but not get discovered. He could see that there were two distinctive grooves in the fresh mud that were too wide to be made by a car. They looked like lorry tracks for sure and judging by the tire tracks in the mud Ashley determined there was more than one. He decided that his best bet was unfortunately to go on foot.

The rain was relentless again. Ashley pulled up his collar and buttoned up his greatcoat. He went back to close the door on the macabre scene inside the hut, to leave it the way he had found it. Just then, he heard an audible crack underneath his left shoe. He stopped, shone his torch on the ground and there next to the sandbags he saw the shattered remains of a tiny Guinness bottle cigarette lighter. It was the one Marty had used earlier in the day to light their cigarettes. It had been bright and warm, and they had joked and laughed and were full of life. Now they were all dead. They were dead on the cold floor of a guard hut out in the middle of nowhere.

"Bastards!" spat Ashley. He went back into the hut and gently placed the broken lighter in the pocket of Marty's blood-soaked jacket. "Ich Dien, Lads," he said again quietly. "Rest in peace." He closed the door again and cautiously went up the hill with absolutely no idea what he would do, or who he would find when he got to the windmill.

Chapter 90

TO THE WINDMILL

Parys Mountain, Anglesey

August 18, 1940

The road was steep and muddy, and the rain was relentless. Off to the west, Ashley saw the first flickers of lightening. The temperature had started to drop but he was not cold, far from it. He had worked up a good sweat while moving at a cautious pace in the darkness. He had been walking for a good half hour by now and it was hard to tell exactly where he was. He thought he could make out open moorland either side of him, but it was difficult to say. The ground under his feet had changed though. The road now felt like shale, rock and gravel. It was noisier than the muddy dirt he had come through earlier. He stopped every hundred yards or so to listen, but it was silent. Except for the wind and the rain, there was no sign of any life.

He continued on the shale road for another quarter of an hour, then the road was not as steep. The flatter moor-like terrain had given way to rocky walls either side of the road. They were gradually growing in height, and now were well over Ashley's head. He felt like he was walking down a vast outside corridor. The rain had eased up a little, but the wind seemed to howl down the corridor causing Ashley to lean forward into it as he trudged, doggedly on.

He walked on for another ten minutes or so. There was no change in the road other than it was now beginning to climb again. Ashley stopped for a moment to listen and catch his breath. He calculated that he had been walking at a brisk pace mainly uphill for a good forty-five minutes. Still there was nothing to be seen out here. Certainly, there was no windmill in sight. He may as well be on the surface of the moon. Was he even on Parys Mountain?

Had he missed something? Was there another turnoff? He began to second guess his decision. Perhaps he should have headed straight back to Menai and raised the alarm. How much longer should he continue? The thought that he may have made the wrong call sickened him. All that time and effort would have been wasted and the Colonel would be absolutely furious.

He made the decision to press on for another fifteen minutes or so. Then if there was still no sign of the windmill, he would abandon his search. He would head back to the Matchless and ride as fast as he could to Menai to call HQ and raise the alarm. Out of the corner of his eye, he caught another flicker of lightening in the distance. Thankfully, the rain had now stopped, but the wind was still blowing with a fury. Just then, there was a break between the storm fronts, and for a moment the moon came out.

As his eyes adjusted, he could see enough of the shale road to pick up his pace to a fast trot. He looked cautiously around and realized that this place was quite literally in the middle of nowhere. Worse than that though, it was a barren ugly environment. It was devoid of life. There were no trees, no bushes, no hedgerows, no grass, nothing but broken shards of rock, gravel and boulders. The entire landscape seemed to be extremely hostile. Ashley kept feeling like he was being watched. He could not put his finger on it exactly, but it was an uneasy sensation. He began to run a little faster.

At times, he could make out distant peaks in the moonlight as it shone brightly between the breaks in the clouds. It looked like a massive void between him and those peaks. There was nothing but blackness, a massive black hole. Ashley knew he had been climbing the entire way to the windmill, but he was not sure what the elevation was now. He reasoned that there was probably a fairly good drop off if he wandered off the shale road. Then his earlier fears of falling off the Menai Bridge came back to him. His mind ran terrifying scenarios of losing his footing and plunging off the edge…into the blackness. He shuddered, and not from being cold. He suddenly felt quite vulnerable. He hated this place. He needed to find this bloody windmill and get the hell out of Parys Mountain. Then the moon vanished behind a heavy black storm cloud, and to add to his misery, it began to rain again.

Ashley continued in the darkness. He recalled his field training and now that training made sense to him. He had stomped around the Lake District of England in conditions much colder and wetter than this for two days. He had managed to avoid capture by the team of soldiers who were experienced survivalists. They had attempted to hunt him down, but it had been much colder then and the conditions considerably worse. Ashley was the only one in his class who had evaded capture. Buoyed by that thought, he soldiered on. He was an Oxford Blue after all. He would get to the windmill and see what the bloody hell was going on and report back to the Colonel.

Then directly ahead in the distance, he saw another flash of lightening. Ashley began to count the seconds to the inevitable thunderclap, but none came. "That's odd," he thought as he continued trudging on the shale. Then he saw it again. This time it lasted longer, much longer. Then Ashley froze. He had seen this before earlier in the day when he had first set out across the Menai Bridge. He had watched the bright blue arc of the bridge worker's welding tools high above the roadway.

It was not lightening. It was somebody cutting or welding steel out here in the middle of nowhere. "My God!" said Ashley out loud. "They are at the windmill door!" He instinctively dropped to a crouch and waited and watched. The blue flashes had stopped now. Everything seemed quiet except for the wind. Then it started again. A second identical flash started to the left of the first one, momentarily lighting up the skyline. For the first time, Ashley could clearly see in the blue arc light, the shape of a solid stone tower. He had finally found the windmill at Parys Mountain.

Ashley moved ahead at an increased pace. The blue and white flashing arc lights continued to shine the way. After a while, Ashley could clearly see figures moving around in the lights and showers of sparks emanating from the welders' torches. Now, he could see four men and what looked like two or three lorries. He moved closer. He could just begin to hear voices, possibly an Irish accent, but the wind was blowing too hard to catch what they were saying. A little ahead to his left he could make out an identical shale road entering his. He quickly realized that the road he was on ran around the windmill, and then reentered at this point. Then the unmistakable sound of a generator starting up came from the direction of the lorries. Almost simultaneously, to Ashley's amazement the whole area was bathed in bright light from a bank of six spotlights raised up on a pole about ten feet in the air.

Ashley shuddered in disbelief at what he could now clearly see. The old windmill was lit up brightly. Ashley could see the wet gray stones that it had been built from. He could even see the green moss clinging to the partially visible east face. At the top, the stones were beginning to crumble, giving it a medieval look. It was probably fifty to seventy-five feet high and twenty-five to thirty feet across. It had a small arched window located about halfway up. The only way to get inside seemed to be through the one door. It had no sails like the windmill he had been searching for. He immediately surmised that they must have succumbed to the brutal Anglesey weather long ago. Obviously, it had been abandoned for decades.

Then Ashley gasped as he counted not three, but twelve identical lorries and a passenger car neatly lined up on the road ahead of him. He could plainly see many figures now. There were at least twenty men standing and watching the men who were busy cutting away at the windmill door. This was a gold heist on a massive scale. To his astonishment, he also saw two men operating what looked like a Hollywood movie camera. They were filming the entire event. Ashley, now on his belly slithered closer on the wet shale. He could hear the men talking and joking with each other but still could not hear what they were saying.

Finally, Ashley made it to the last lorry in the queue. All of the men seemed to be standing around the windmill watching the welders cut away at the door. Ashley could smell the burning metal and the exhaust fumes of the generator that hung heavily in the damp Welsh air. He took the time to examine the lorries. They were all identical, Bedford WLT's with solid wood sides, an open top and a drop tail gate. They also had one other thing in common, the name O'Reilly Meats, Dublin was painted on the side of each truck.

O'Reilly! Ashley instantly made the connection. It must be the same company that Sergeant Lewis had told him about. The famous Beef Guinness run. The first piece of a complicated jigsaw fell into place. Ashley climbed up the tail gate of the last truck and peered inside. It was totally empty. He climbed down and began to move closer to the windmill, using each lorry as a shield. He was soon just three lorries from the first one in the queue, directly behind the car. The rain had for the moment finally subsided.

Ashley noticed the welders had stopped now. They had removed their goggles and were conferring with a third man who appeared to be overseeing their work. "Beast! Let's go!" yelled the overseer, as he gestured towards a giant of a man in the group who removed his jacket and rolled up his sleeves. He carried a gigantic sledgehammer. Ashley could see the man's massive biceps and chest bulging beneath his shirt. After spitting in both of his palms, he began to smash away at the soot covered hinges. After several blows, the first hinge finally fell to the ground with a clatter. He repeated the exercise three more times, then he turned and nodded to the overseer. The Beast had efficiently done his job.

Another man came forward and attached a thick rope to the door, then yelled, "Clear!" Several of the men, led by the one called the Beast pulled on the rope and the steel door slowly moved. Suddenly, it made a horrible grating sound of metal on metal and fell out of the opening with a colossal crash onto the rocky shale.

One man who clearly was the leader of the group stepped forward into the windmill out of sight of Ashley. The rest of the men walked slowly forward, all peering into the windmill, blocking Ashley's view. There was a sound of something heavy being dragged across the floor followed by an almighty crash. The noise sounded like cracking lumber. Then a moment of silence was followed by an explosion of excitement as the men cheered. They jumped into the air and hugged and congratulated each other. The secret of the gold that was stashed in the old windmill at Parys Mountain was a secret no more.

Chapter 91

THE GOLD HEIST

Parys Mountain, Anglesey

August 18, 1940

Ashley moved up another lorry length and watched as the leader emerged. He was illuminated by the spotlights, and stood rigid, his shiny black jackboots set slightly apart. He was a tall man, solid build, with thick blond hair. In the spotlight, Ashley now noticed his face looked a little battered, like he had been in a recent fist fight. He was one tough cookie for sure, nothing but trouble, Ashley told himself.

The leader held out two solid gold bars that gleamed in the spotlight. "Gentleman!" he yelled over the noise of the generator in perfect English, no hint of an accent. He raised the gold bars victoriously above his head, "This is what Victory looks like!" The men roared and pumped their fists wildly in the air. A smile crept across the beaten face, "Victory for the Fatherland! Victory for our Irish Brothers in Arms! Long live the IRA! Heil to the Fuhrer, Adolph Hitler!" The men went wild. The two men with the movie camera signaled a thumbs up to the leader. He stepped closer towards the camera for the money shot, and to get a close-up of his battered face. At that moment, the victorious Nazi warrior holding two solid gold bars was more than Goebbels could have ever wished for in his wildest dreams. Major Max von Seeckt was delivering the goods.

Ashley remained frozen and was stunned at what he was witnessing. The leader continued, "Now men, the true work begins!" he looked at each of them in turn and in silence. This man knew how to captivate an audience, Ashley thought. Then he began, "We have exactly two hours, no more, to fill our lorries. Remember, under no circumstances are you to go over the maximum number of crates. If our calculations are correct, we should get the majority, if not all of it. Then we leave. The Dublin ferry leaves at 0430 hours on the dot. Everyone knows what they must do. Now let's MOVE!!" There was another roar of excitement as the leader stepped aside and the men rushed into the windmill anxious to see the booty. Ashley could hear the melee inside. The men were clearly ecstatic. The two men with the movie camera dutifully documented everything.

Ashley found a small drainage ditch that ran along the length of road where the lorries were lined up. It offered good cover. He was able to see what was happening through the gap underneath the vehicles. A man came towards him and headed to the first lorry. He climbed in and carefully moved it into position in front of the windmill entrance. He dropped the tail gate down. Then Ashley watched as the first crate of gold was wheeled out on a large dolly with thick rubber tires. Two men hopped into the back of the lorry as two more met the dolly at the tailgate and lifted the heavy crate up to them. No sooner had they loaded the crate, when another man came out of the windmill with an identical dolly and crate. The whole process was repeated like clockwork.

Ashley counted at least six different dollies. He watched the men rotate with each other, working with military precision. Everyone clearly knew their role. The leader stood and watched with his number two man, arms folded and in total command. The cameraman gently panned from the leader to the men loading the gold. Everything was bathed in the bright spotlights. As Ashley watched in disbelief, he thought it resembled a Hollywood movie set. But this was no movie, it was a heist in progress. The Nazis and the IRA were stealing the precious British gold.

Ashley was still putting the pieces together in his mind. The IRA hated the British, that he knew for sure. The considerable logistics to move such a massive amount of gold had clearly been put into place. But why had the IRA teamed up with the Nazis? The war made for strange bed fellows. He had heard and understood the saying, the enemy of my enemy is my friend. One thing was abundantly clear, this was a meticulously planned professional gold heist on an epic scale to pillage Britain's most secret treasure trove. Two of Britain's sworn enemies were working together to steal millions of pounds worth of her gold and incredibly, they were filming the entire heist.

The same lorry driver was now returning to the next lorry in line, the one directly in front of Ashley. This time, he fired it up but did not move it. He sat in the cab and waited. Ashley remained motionless. He watched as crate after crate of gold was efficiently loaded into the lorry. Ashley observed as the suspension began to groan and flatten out as the lorry's chassis sunk closer to the tires. He was surprised that the lorry could hold so much weight.

Slowly and silently he slipped out of the ditch and rolled under the truck next to him. He checked the windmill and saw that everyone was focused on moving the gold. He pulled out his torch and quickly shone it on the chassis and suspension. As he suspected, the lorry had been customized to hold the weight of the crates of gold. He could see the shiny new leaf springs that had been expertly added to the existing ones and two additional I beams had been skillfully welded to the frame rails. Ashley figured this configuration could probably double or even triple its load capacity.

Then one of the men yelled in a thick Irish accent, "That's it, she's good!" The two men climbed down and closed the tailgate. "C'mon!" he waved at the man sitting in the lorry that was idling ahead of Ashley. The man dropped his vehicle into gear and moved it cautiously forward to the same spot vacated by the gold filled first lorry. The first lorry had been driven slowly around the windmill and was then parked by the entry road. "Like bloody clockwork," Ashley whispered to himself. Having filmed the whole cycle and taken great care to avoid the O'Reilly Meat signs on the lorries sides, the two movie makers chatted for a moment. Next, one of them removed the film canister from the camera, placed it in a round metal container, and handed it to the leader. He nodded his gratitude and stuffed it carefully inside his coat.

Ashley had seen enough. He knew the driver would be back to move the lorry that he was hiding under. He slid quietly on his belly across the shale until he passed under the fourth truck. Now sure that he was out of visual range, he rolled out from under the lorry and set off down the hill. A well-timed break in the black clouds provided him enough moonlight to see the road ahead. He began to run, being smart enough to pace himself.

Ashley dug deep. As he ran, the enormity of what he was involved in hit him for the first time. He was literally on an island that was miles and miles from any help or civilization. He now understood why they had chosen this place to hide the country's gold reserves. It was, without a doubt, absolutely remote. As far as John Ashley was concerned, no one in their right mind would want to go to Parys Mountain. You didn't even need the fake, toxic contaminated ground story.

He tried to focus on the even bigger picture. Of all the things he had witnessed at the windmill, the one thing that had him totally baffled was why anyone would want to go through the effort and expense to film their own robbery? That part simply made no sense. The last thing any robbers would want would be to document their crime on film. The goal usually is to get rid of any evidence that could link the perpetrator to the crime, not create a film record of them carrying out the heist. It just did not add up.

Then the troubling question of why? Why move the country's gold out of the safety of a bank? and hide it in the first place? Clearly, the government had based their decision to move the gold to a remote hiding place on something they knew was going to happen. They had gone to great lengths to keep it a secret from the general public by creating false stories of ground contamination. The British people would be mighty ticked off at the deception being played on them by their own government, who they desperately needed to be able to trust.

The film would have an immense propaganda value if it were to get into...the wrong hands! Ashley instinctively picked up the pace again, his mind racing along with his legs. The problem was far bigger than the Nazis stealing England's gold. If the film was ever to get back to Germany, then Dr. Goebbels would have a field day. His propaganda machine would be unleashed and would have a devastating effect on the gritty British public. Ashley's thighs and calves were burning, but he pressed on. He was fueled by the terror of the consequences if the Nazis and the IRA were to succeed. They could deliver a body blow to the British people, that they might not be able to recover from. He had to figure out a way to stop them.

Finally, a soaked and exhausted John Ashley arrived back at the guard hut. The next band of the storm was beginning to unleash its wrath. The rain was the worst it had been so far, but the wind was a bigger problem. It was gusting now at near gale force as it picked up speed and screamed across the open rolling fields of Anglesey, driving the rain almost horizontally into his face.

The lightening was spectacular. Ashley had never seen such a powerful electric storm. Counting the seconds between the lightning and thunderclaps, he guessed it was probably over central Anglesey and for sure it was heading his way and towards Menai. He walked around to the far side of the hut. The Matchless was waiting faithfully. Ashley's prayers were answered when yet again she fired first time. He turned around and took a final look at Parys Mountain as a lightning bolt flashed across the sky, bathing the entire area in a brief eerie blue light. There was an almighty crash of thunder. He twisted the throttle and screamed out of what was, in his opinion, the eeriest place he had visited so far on planet earth.

Chapter 92

THE MACABRE COTTAGE

Menai, Anglesey
August 18, 1940

Peter parked outside The Bull and he and Taryn dashed through the rain to the pub. He quickly opened the bar door and they went inside. Immediately they were disappointed to see that ETR was not in his usual spot. Instead they saw a couple of older locals playing dominoes. The two locals with the dog, Koda were sitting in the same place as last night and three RAF chaps were talking quietly and sharing cigarettes.

Snudge nodded at Peter and Taryn, "Evening," he said with his customary wink. "Taryn, always a pleasure."

"Good evening, Snudge. Has ETR been in here yet?" she asked.

"No, he hasn't. I was expecting him for last orders, but he has not been back tonight. He asked me to give you this if he didn't show up by the time you got here," he told Peter, casually handing him the folded piece of paper. Snudge checked his watch and noticed it was now 10:20. He gave the bell rope a good tug and yelled, "Last orders, please!" Peter opened the note and passed it to Taryn. "Do you know where this is?" he asked her.

"Of course, it's about a five-minute drive from here, why?" she replied.

"I need to take a quick run out there. I'll order us a last round and be back in no time," he said to her. He immediately turned his attention to Snudge, "A pint of bitter and half a cider please, Snudge. How do I find this place?" he asked.

"Coming right up, Peter. Go straight down Telford Road, left at the Post Office, then head up the hill. When you get to the top, it's the road on the right. Keep going and you will arrive at Tyddyn Ben," said Snudge.

"Peter why are you going out there?" asked Taryn.

"Nothing to worry about my Sweet. You stay here, no point in getting soaked. I promise I'll be right back." He kissed her on the lips and before she could protest, he had turned around and was gone.

The rain made it even more difficult to see with the shaded headlights, but he was finally able to negotiate the narrow country lanes to Tyddyn Ben. He pulled up to the gate in front of the stone wall and killed the engine. He stopped and thought for a moment. All was quiet except for the rain pounding on the canvas roof of the MG. He took a deep breath and reaching for the glove box, he retrieved his revolver. He slipped it into his jacket pocket, then pulled up the zip as he exited the car.

He walked down the narrow lane that led to the cottage that he could see at the bottom of the hill. He noticed the front door was open, which was odd given the pouring rain. A shiver of fear ran through his body again. Something was not right, he whispered. He stood for a moment watching the cottage and seeing no sign of life, he cautiously walked down the wet path and approached the open door. He stopped again at the threshold and hearing no sound, he waited.

Finally, convinced there was no one inside, he cleared his dry throat and called out, "Hello?" No response. "Hello, is anybody there? Hello?" Again, receiving no reply, he pulled out his gun. He slowly entered the cottage. It was quiet. He could see the small kitchen and two doors ahead of him, one was open. He slowly cocked his revolver and holding it steady with both hands, he called out, "Hello?" Slowly, he entered the front room. He closed the door behind him then switched on the light. There was no sign of life in the living room, so he slowly made his way to the bedroom. He opened the door and felt for the light switch and flipped it on.

The sight of the battered face on the corpse on the bedroom floor was more than he had bargained for. He was instantly gripped by panic before vomiting uncontrollably on the slick bloody floor. He felt himself falling backwards. He grabbed the door jamb to steady himself. My God, what happened in here? There was blood everywhere, all over the walls, the ceiling, the bed, and the floor. He knew right away it was ETR on the floor and that the man who had done this had to be, Max von Seeckt.

His mind was swimming. He was sweating and felt an overwhelming urge to vomit again but he fought it. As his adrenalin kicked in, the horror and terror began to give way to anger. The Nazis were on Anglesey and they were not here for sightseeing... My God! The invasion is happening here on Anglesey, it couldn't be...not Dover, not Plymouth, not the south coast. They are indeed coming in through the back door! His earlier nightmare thoughts about the Nazis invading were coming true. It was all too much to comprehend. He began to feel woozy again.

Just then there was a massive flash of lightening that snapped him back to reality. He took several deep breaths and using every ounce of his considerable will power, he regained some control. A terrific thunderclap followed. He walked to the sink and turned on the tap. He washed the vomit from his hands and face, the cold water felt good. He regained his composure and hurried out of macabre cottage without looking back. He needed to get back to The Bull as quickly as possible to raise the alarm.

Chapter 93

THE EMPTY WINDMILL

Parys Mountain, Anglesey
August 19, 1940

At exactly the two-hour mark, Hott blew his whistle. It was more of a formality than anything else. It had been at least five minutes since the final crate of gold had been loaded securely aboard the last lorry. The men were covered in grime and sweat and were exhausted. Several of them were lying on their backs on the wet shale, their chests heaving from their efforts. They were completely and utterly spent. They were acutely aware of the fact that anything that did not get loaded by the time Hott blew his whistle, would be left behind.

They had worked at a furious pace to load the last lorry to beat the deadline. It was a remarkable physical fete by some seriously committed men. Also, it was a true testament to the unique effect that gold has had on mankind since the dawn of ages. Most of the exhausted men simply stood together, drinking from their canteens, shaking hands, and sharing cigarettes.

Max walked into the now empty windmill for a final inspection. His jackboots echoed off the steel floor. A smile crept across his bruised face as he turned around and looked at the men.

"Excellent work gentlemen. Now, back to Rhosybol where we Brandenburgers will say goodbye to our Irish brothers. Then we have a ferry to catch. Stay tight! Move out!"

Max and Hott walked to their car. It was now idling at the front of the line of lorries loaded down with wooden crates containing solid gold bars. They set off back down the long steep road. The lorries followed snake like, in perfect formation. Their suspension groaned under the weight of the stolen gold. The men were glad to be aboard, flushed with excitement at what they had just pulled off-the greatest gold heist in history.

The Brandenburgers, along with the Irish had emptied the wind-mill. They now had in their possession 50 tons of British gold. The hardest part was over. Now, they simply had to drive to Holy-head and board the first ferry out to Dublin. The first phase of Operation Goldilocks was complete. To top it off, the worst of the storm seemed to have now passed over Parys Mountain and was heading towards Anglesey's east coast and the Welsh mainland, away from their destination of Holyhead. Everything was going exactly according to plan.

After the last of the lorries had disappeared down the hill, an eerie silence returned to the windmill. Now totally still, it was a stark contrast to the hive of activity that had happened there just a short time ago. The generator continued to purr smoothly along. The crime scene still bathed in the bright spotlights. The welding equipment, oxygen tanks, petrol cans, customized dollies, water jugs, assorted tools, crowbars, and ropes all deliberately left behind to make room for the gold. The thick rusty steel door, now soundly defeated, lay face down on the shale in front of the ancient windmill. Its once top-secret contents, now gone forever.

Then, the generator coughed and sputtered, ran again for a few seconds, and stopped altogether. The spotlights immediately went out. The now empty windmill at Parys Mountain was plunged once more into total darkness and silence.

Chapter 94

TALLY HO!

Menai, Anglesey

August 19, 1940

The ride back to Menai was a disaster. Ashley finally had to remove his black out shade from his head light to even have a fighting chance. The wind had whipped a multitude of tree branches all over the road. Several times he had to dismount to clear a pathway. He couldn't afford to get a puncture.

Just outside of Beaumaris, he encountered a particularly large branch that took all his strength to drag it off to the side. He could only travel at a painfully slow speed, barely twenty miles per hour. He had to navigate the Matchless slowly around the debris that was scattered all over the slick roadway.

The storm was getting closer. Much to Ashley's relief, the next lightening flash lit up the little town of Menai about a mile ahead. It had taken Ashley well over an hour to make the perilous ride. The conditions had been appalling. He had not encountered a single sole on the roads, but he always knew that Menai offered his best bet to raise the alarm and get help. Coming in from the opposite direction, just slightly ahead of him, Peter Legh in his MG had experienced similar appalling road conditions.

The wet streets were deserted as Ashley cautiously negotiated his way around the debris that was scattered across the road on the slight hill that led into the town. Finally, he could make out The Bull and then to his surprise he saw a brief flash of light as a silhouette of a man entered the open door. As he got closer, he also noticed that it was the same MG that he had seen earlier in the day when he had passed the flock of sheep. Ashley pulled the Matchless in behind it. He killed the motor and headed to the door.

It was not locked, so he pushed it open and entered. The bar was completely empty except for Snudge the bar man who he had met earlier. He noticed that Snudge was on the customers side of the bar alongside an attractive, tall blond lady, who clearly looked scared. The only light came from a hurricane lamp sitting on the bar. Both of them looked at the drenched Ashley in utter surprise.

Ashley was first to speak, "I need to use your telephone! It's a matter of grave urgency!"

"Hey! Aren't you the one who was looking for ETR earlier?" stammered Snudge.

"Yes, but it's too late for that now. I need your telephone. This is an emergency, now where is it?" asked Ashley firmly. It was then that he heard the unmistakable click of a revolver being cocked. He felt the cold steel barrel of the Enfield pressed firmly into the back of his neck.

"Move and I'll kill you," said Peter, with a calmness that surprised even himself.

Peter had just parked the MG back outside The Bull when he caught the Matchless headlight coming up the street. He had quickly stepped into the bar and watched through the small sidelight window as the rider parked his motorcycle behind his MG and dismounted. To Snudge and Taryn's surprise, Peter put his finger to his lips in the silent gesture and remained hidden behind the door as Ashley pushed it open. Now he had at gun point the man who Snudge recognized had been in earlier also looking for ETR. Sadly, it was the same ETR that Peter had just discovered beaten to death on the bedroom floor in the tiny cottage.

"Easy," said Ashley, as he raised his wet gloved hands.

"Peter!" cried Taryn, "What on earth are you doing?"

"Not now!" snapped Peter.

"Easy," said Ashley again, "Please put the gun down."

"Tell me why you're looking for ETR?" demanded Peter.

"You need to put the gun down. Nobody needs to get hurt. I am a British Intelligence Officer with MI5. If you put the gun down, I will gladly show you my identification papers," said Ashley, dead calm.

"I don't care if you are King Farook, don't you move a muscle. Now, I'll ask you once again, why are you looking for ETR?" growled Peter.

"I'm doing a top-secret investigation. His name was on the list of people that I needed to interview. Now, please put the gun down," replied Ashley. "I'm happy to show you my identification but you need to put the gun down, please."

"No, keep your hands up!" snarled Peter, pressing the Enfield harder into Ashley's neck.

"Snudge! Check his pockets," he commanded.

"Investigate what?" asked Peter, as Snudge approached and checked Ashley's pockets.

"I can't tell you, it's top-secret, which is why I need to use the phone. I have a national emergency on my hands, and you sir are inhibiting my progress!" said Ashley, rapidly tiring of being held at gunpoint.

Snudge found Ashley's wallet in his jacket pocket. He opened it and looked at Peter, "He is who he says he is, a John Ashley and he's with MI5 alright," said Snudge, greatly impressed at the credentials he was examining.

"Very well," said Peter, as he released the gun from Ashley's neck. "I'm sorry about that old chap," he continued, "But I'm afraid the man you are looking for is already dead!"

"No!" screamed Taryn. "No! No! Not ETR! Oh Peter, say it's not true!" she wailed, dropping to her knees. Peter rushed to console her. She was absolutely devastated.

"Dead? ETR dead? How can that be? What happened?" asked Snudge, shocked by what Peter had just revealed. He handed Ashley his wallet back.

"Someone murdered him, and I know who it is," replied Peter. He pulled Taryn back to her feet and held her tightly as she continued to cry.

Snudge froze. "What? Who?" he cried at Peter.

"I believe his name is Max von Seeckt. He's a Major in the SS. He is already on the island. He's behind this, I'm sure of it," answered Peter.

Ashley had been listening and now Peter looked directly at him for the first time.

"Sorry about the gun again, Ashley, but I thought you had followed me. I thought you were with von Seeckt. I'm terribly sorry."

"It's alright," said Ashley. "And who might you be?"

"Peter Legh, RAF," he said without looking up. He was busy trying to console Taryn, who sobbed uncontrollably on the shoulder of his soaked flight jacket.

"The phone, Sir. I need the phone!" yelled Ashley to Snudge.

"I'm sorry but the line's dead. We lost all power about ten minutes ago. It is blowing like the Devil out there, probably a tree came down on the wires. I'll check again if you like," said Snudge. He went around to the other side of the bar where the telephone was and picked up the handset. He listened for a dial tone, but there was none. "Sorry," he said looking at Ashley. "It's still dead."

Ashley needed to think fast.

"This von Seeckt character, does he have blond hair?" asked Ashley.

"Yes, yes he does," replied Peter.

"Tall, close to six-foot-tall?" continued Ashley.

"Yes, he's a tall one," answered Peter. "Why? Have you seen him?" he continued.

"Yes, I believe so. You're right, he's on the island and he's not alone." Ashley's comments seemed to linger for a moment. Taryn finally stopped crying.

"What do you mean?" asked Peter.

"Wait," interrupted Snudge, "Are you really saying that there are Nazis here on Anglesey right now? That we have been invaded! My God! This can't be happening!" A look of terror appeared on the barman's face.

"Yes, I am afraid so. I don't think it's a full-scale invasion, but I do know he is not alone," said Ashley as he tried to formulate his next move. "Now, what's your connection to all this? How are you involved?" he asked, looking directly at Peter.

"It's my fault! It's all my fault!" Taryn sobbed. "If I had not said anything last night, none of this would have happened and ETR would still be alive! Oh! No! No! Tell me it's not so Peter." She burst into tears again.

"It started last night. Taryn pointed out a man in the lounge who had bothered her earlier in the day. She thought his name was Billy Muskett, but the man she pointed out to me was the spitting image of a man I know named Max von Seeckt. I needed to get a better look to be sure it was him. But I had a mishap trying to get around to that side of the bar. By the time I got there, he was gone," lamented Peter. "Snudge here witnessed the whole fiasco," he gestured towards Snudge, who nodded in agreement.

"Yes," said Snudge "but I also remember serving a man by the name of Billy Muskett last night. He seemed very normal to me. He was tall for sure and had blond hair."

"And what's your connection to him?" asked Ashley, turning again towards Peter.

"We were at Eton together," replied Peter, stroking Taryn's long blond hair. "Shhhh, shhhh," he said trying to comfort her.

"I see," said Ashley, raising an eyebrow. "So much for England's finest," he added sarcastically.

"Yes, he's such a stain. He always has been. Damn him!" conceded Peter.

And ETR, how does he fit in?" continued Ashley.

"He's in charge of the LDV here in Menai. He is the closest thing there is to law enforcement. The possible sighting of von Seeckt bothered me all day, so I reported what had happened to ETR earlier this evening. He said he would go and investigate and that he would meet us back here at closing time. He was not here when we arrived, but he obviously found out where von Seeckt was staying and left Snudge the address. It was his back-up plan in case something happened to him. Snudge gave me the address so I drove out there. That is when I found ETR. He was dead, beaten to death by the look of it. It was an awful scene.

Then I knew for sure it must be von Seeckt's work. I raced back here to raise the alarm and that is when I saw you following me. I thought you were with von Seeckt, and the rest is history," he said, without taking his gaze off Taryn.

"I see, and where did you meet him Taryn? Tell me about that if you could. It may be valuable," Ashley asked moving closer to her.

"I saw him coming down from the bridge tower. It was early in the morning. I was out walking my dog," she said between sobs. "I asked him what he was doing on the bridge and he was very short and rude to me. He said his name was Billy Muskett and that he was a government inspector who had access to anywhere on the bridge. Oh! I so wish I had never met the stupid man. ETR would still be alive now if I had not. It's all my fault!" Once again she began to sob uncontrollably.

"I see, thank you Taryn. You have been very helpful. You're not to blame for any of this," said Ashley, trying to comfort her. "Here, drink this," nodded Snudge. He had been busy pouring out four shots of brandy. He handed her a glass, then repeated the same to Peter and Ashley. "Lord knows, we need it!"

"Thanks, said Ashley. He downed it in one shot. The warm glow felt good. He briefly thought of Becky back at the Antelope and the drink that he had promised her. The chances of that happening now was zero. "Any idea why he would be on the bridge?" Ashley knew the same man, von Seeckt must be the leader of the gang he had witnessed stealing the gold out at the windmill. His battered face was surely the result of the fight to the death he had engaged in with ETR, but he still could not make the connection with the bridge.

"The only thing I can think of is the radio. He must have been after the radio or at least access to it," said Peter. "There's a radio in the hut at the top of the tower. ETR told me about it. It is the highest point on the island. There is nothing to block the signal. He must have been trying to use the radio, perhaps to communicate with others?" asked Peter, deep in thought.

Ashley looked at his watch. He had lost a lot of time. He knew the gold heist would be wrapped up by now and that the convoy of O'Reilly lorries would be well on its way to Holyhead to catch the Dublin ferry. With no way to contact the mainland, there was no hope of raising any help. He was on his own and had to make the call. The Oxford Blue would give it his all.

"How long does it take to drive from here to Holyhead?" asked Ashley.

"It takes about forty-five minutes. But in this storm, who knows. The roads could be flooded or trees may be blown down. It could take a couple of hours, but I really have no idea." replied Snudge. Right on cue there was another flash of lightening followed by another almighty thunderclap.

"How good are you with your Enfield?" asked Ashley turning to face Peter.

"Bloody good," said Peter soberly

"Excellent. How much petrol is in your MG?" asked Ashley. He knew that to risk getting to Holyhead on two wheels in this storm would be futile.

"She's about half full," Peter answered.

"Good, then I'll need you to come with me. Right now!" commanded Ashley.

"No! Peter! Don't go!" cried Taryn as he stood up. "Please don't go. No! No!" she pleaded.

Ashley had Snudge write down his headquarters phone number. He instructed him to have all possible help sent to the Port of Holyhead and to delay the sailing of the 0430 ferry to Dublin should he be able to get through on the telephone.

"Here is all the authority that you will need," said Ashley as he showed Snudge the letter Churchill had given to him. Snudge's eyes grew wide as he read the letter that ended with Churchill's signature and handed it back to Ashley with one word, "Impressive." Then Ashley handed it to Peter. Peter read it and handed it back to him as Taryn clung tightly to his jacket.

"Good Lord," said Peter, impressed by the enormity of the power given to Ashley by Churchill himself. He wanted nothing more than to take Taryn home to her cottage. To be with her, just the two of them, like last night. That was not going to happen. Peter Legh knew that years after their epic fight at Eton's Wall it was time to finally settle the score with Max von Seeckt. He also knew that for Ashley to be in possession of such a letter from Churchill must mean that the nation was indeed under threat. He would do everything in his power to assist the MI5 agent. Then looking Ashley squarely in the eye, he nodded and said, "Right then let's go. Tally Ho!"

"Tally Ho," replied Ashley with a brave smile. He knew Legh was made of the right stuff.

It took all Snudge had to hold a now hysterical Taryn back. The two men were facing impossible odds. They slipped out of the door into the still raging storm, and headed for the little MG.

Chapter 95

GUNS FOR FLOUR

Rhosybol, Anglesey
August 19, 1940

H ugh checked his watch. "Spot on time," he muttered as Max and his victorious convoy returned to Rhosybol.

"Good morning, Sir!" he said to Max as he opened the passenger door and Max stepped out. "I trust your visit to Parys Mountain was a successful one despite our wonderful Welsh weather."

"Most successful, thank you Hugh," replied Max.

"Excellent!" said Hugh. Then he noticed Max's swollen eye and cheek. "What happened there?" he asked.

"Courtesy of the Royal Welsh Fusiliers," lied Max, with a grin.

"I see, and would you by any chance be interested in trading a few items this morning? Items that your men no longer need, perhaps?" asked Hugh with a wink of his eye.

"Indeed, I am in need of some of Spiller's finest grains, fifty-pound bags preferably. Would you happen to have any lying around?" asked Max, eying the wooden pallets neatly stacked with sacks of grain.

"I do sir. But they are hard to come by. There is a war on you know. What might you have to trade if I was interested?" joked Hugh. Behind him were two separate stacks of Spiller's grain sacks on either side of the road. Each had a six-foot wooden step ladder in front of the stack.

"How about some of the Fatherland's most advanced arms, complete with thousands of rounds of ammunition?" asked Max, happy to play along with Hugh.

"Done!" said Hugh, and the men shook hands.

"And we thought you and your men might enjoy a little tipple on the ferry ride to Dublin," added Hugh as he handed Lieutenant Hott a bottle of Irish Whiskey.

"Thank you, Hugh. Much appreciated!" said Hott as he too shook the Irishman's hand.

Max nodded at Hott, who turned to the convoy and screamed "MOVE!"

The men jumped out of the lorries. The Nazis began placing their weapons and ammunition into either of two wooden crates that sat on a pair of sawhorses in the barn. Hott reached into the back of the Ford and grabbed four rifles along with their ammunition. "This is a little bonus from our friends, the Welsh Fusiliers," he said to Hugh as he deposited them into the crate. No one noticed that Hott cleverly avoided adding his own Lugar to the wooden crate. If all went according to plan, he would need it once he was onboard the ferry later that morning.

"Thank you kindly," replied Hugh with a wink.

Then in a repeat of the round robin process they had performed so well at the windmill, the men proceeded to load the sacks of grain onto the lorries. Each lorry drove slowly between the ladders, while a man on each side placed the sacks neatly on top of the crates of gold. They perfectly filled the void that had been deliberately left at the top, completely concealing the crates and their contents from view. Then they pulled a thick canvas tarp over the top of the sacks and tied it down tightly. Once the last sacks of grain were neatly loaded, the men all shook hands. The Brandenburgers climbed into the lorries and waited for the command to roll. The Irish headed to their bunk beds to get some well-earned rest.

"That looks to be about it," said Hugh, looking at the two step ladders alongside the empty pallets. "I believe so," said Max.

"Good luck then!" said Hugh, extending his hand. "It's been a pleasure doing business with you."

"Good luck to you also, Hugh," replied Max. The two men shook hands. It was a genuine, firm grip of a handshake between two men. Each had a common enemy, and both wondered if they would ever see the other again. For a brief moment Max had a hint of guilt. The Irish had been good partners. The men had worked in unison alongside the Brandenburgers and had been good hosts.

It seemed a low blow to double cross them when Hott along with the Beast would take over the ferry. Then he snapped out of it. He remembered the words of his commander Himmler, stay focused Max.

Max turned and jumped into the passenger seat of the car and the convoy pulled out slowly. They rejoined the road they had come in on and headed south to the next village of Llanerchymedd. There was still a break in the rain, which was a relief. But the wind howled across the open fields, again buffeting the lorries as they struggled to keep a tight formation. No one else was on the road. They made slow, steady progress and finally arrived at the outskirts of the tiny village of Bodedern. Now it was a straight shot out to the coast road, and then on to the Port of Holyhead.

Chapter 96

THE SLEEPY VILLAGE OF BODEDERN

Bodedern, Anglesey
August 19, 1940

I t had been a long day for Sergeant Lewis. He was convinced that he would sleep like a log after his second helping of Blodwyn's Irish stew and a smoke of his pipe. They both retired early to bed, but of course he did not sleep. All was dead quiet in the sleepy village of Bodedern where Lewis had lived for over twenty years. It was close to three o'clock and he still lay wide awake. His mind kept on playing over the events of the day. He thought about Ashley, Cooper, the lights, and not letting Ashley know that the road was closed at Parys Mountain. Somewhere, something was amiss about this whole flashing lights business. He just could not put his finger on it.

He turned his pillow over yet again and closed his eyes. The rhythmic gentle snoring of Blodwyn, his wife of forty years was the only sound in the small bedroom. But now, suddenly it was not the only sound. He could hear something else. Lewis opened his eyes, laid on his back and listened intensely. Now he could hear it for sure. It was a distant rumble that was getting louder and louder. It sounded like a lorry. It was a diesel for sure, but more than one. There might be two or three maybe? More? At this hour?

Now they were getting really close. Lewis jumped out of bed, pulled back the blackout curtain and peered down at the wet street. He was just in time to see a car followed by a convoy of lorries. All of them were going at a good speed. Lewis began to count. By the time he got to six, the small, terraced house was literally shaking from the sound of the heavy lorries. The rumble intensified as it ricocheted off the terraced houses on the other side of the street.

He was also able to see that all the trucks belonged to O'Reilly Meats. They had to be heading out to the port.

"Ten, eleven, twelve," whispered Lewis to himself, as he watched the last lorry speed by. He looked back down the street but could see no more coming. He looked at his luminous watch, three o'clock on a Sunday morning. "Something's a foot," whispered Lewis to himself. He looked over at Blodwyn who had not even moved. Being partially deaf did have some advantages.

Quietly, Lewis walked over to his wardrobe and carefully opened the door. His Policeman's uniform was hanging at the front and he carefully removed it from the hanger. Then he picked up his shirt and belt off the small chair next to it and crept downstairs to the kitchen. Quickly, he got dressed.

He knew it had finally stopped raining, so he passed on wearing his greatcoat. Besides, it covered up his Sergeant's stripes. He wasn't exactly sure why twelve of O'Reilly's trucks were speeding by his house in the early hours of a Monday morning, but his Policeman's instinct told him something was not right. He strapped on his boots, grabbed his helmet, and headed outside to his car. He would drive straight to Holyhead and get to the bottom of it. Somebody was in for the high jump for sure, for disturbing the Sergeant's sleepy village of Bodedern in the wee morning hours, at a very minimum.

Chapter 97

THE IRISH LARCH

Holyhead, Anglesey
August 19, 1940

The storm had now passed over the west coast of the island and the very first light of dawn was beginning to break on the horizon. The convoy of lorries had finally reached the Port of Holyhead. When they got within a mile of the entrance, as planned, Hott gunned the Ford and sped ahead of the first lorry. By the time Hott arrived at the guarded entry point at the port he could just about see the shaded headlights of the trailing convoy in his mirror.

The entry was guarded by two soldiers who had an Anderson shelter set up as their base that was surrounded by sandbags. The guard signaled for Hott to stop, which he did. He brought the nose of the Ford to within inches of the sign that spelled STOP in the middle of the crossing arm. Max leaned back away from the guard into the shadows to avoid having him see his beaten face. Hott lowered the window and said, "Good Morning," in impeccable English.

"Good morning," replied the guard, "What can I help you with?"

"I'm looking for the passenger drop off area for the Irish Larch. It has been a heck of a drive. It took me forever to pass the convoy of lorries behind me," said Hott calmly, while jerking his thumb over his shoulder, pointing to the convoy rapidly approaching behind him. The first lorry pulled up, as planned right behind his rear bumper. Hott could hear the engine. The guard immediately switched his attention to the lorry as the other eleven pulled up in tight formation behind it. The guard leaned back to get a better look. Immediately, he recognized the O'Reilly Meats name on the side of the truck. The smell of exhaust fumes began to fill the heavy dawn air. The guard nodded to his mate, who slowly raised the barrier.

"Go straight, then take your second right hand turn. You will see the signs. Just follow them," said the guard without even looking back into the car.

"Splendid," said Hott. He put the Ford into first gear and drove smoothly away. The guard walked to the first lorry and spoke to the driver for a moment. He took a brief cursory look at his paperwork. Satisfied, he climbed up onto the back of the tail gate, lifted the tarpaulin and briefly shone his torch underneath. He saw only stuffed brown sacks with Spiller's Grain stamped on them. Again satisfied, he climbed back down. Then he turned to his mate and yelled, "Twelve O'Reilly's coming through!" His mate gave the thumbs up and waved the first lorry through. The convoy slowly followed behind in perfect formation. The guard rhythmically waived each one by.

Hott watched in his mirror as the convoy passed uneventfully through the barricade. "All clear," he said to Max as he made the right turn and headed towards the dock. Max sat back up. After a few hundred yards, Hott saw a sign that said CARS with an arrow indicating left and LORRIES with a right arrow and EXIT straight ahead. Hott followed the CARS sign and watched as the convoy headed off to the right towards the commercial loading area.

He drove for about a quarter of a mile alongside the dock. Finally, ahead they could see the stern of the Irish Larch. The hull was painted black with huge white letters that spelled IRISH LARCH DUBLIN EIRE. He could just about make out the colors of the Irish Flag at the stern that fluttered in the wind. "There she is!" said Max. "You are almost home, my friend." He smiled at Hott, who kept his eyes firmly on the road.

Hott spotted the parking area, pulled the Ford up to the curb behind a polished black Bentley, and cut the engine. The two men got out and walked to the dock. They followed the ship down about halfway where they could now see passengers on the gang plank slowly filing on board. Beyond the gang plank, the area was fenced off with a chain link fence. Through the fence, they could see that the convoy was now neatly parked in rows of two. They waited to be loaded aboard. The drivers were out of their vehicles, each handing their paperwork to a docker standing at the base of the crane with a clip board. Then the lead driver followed him into an office that had a sign over the door that read Irish Shipping Limited. A short time later, he emerged and handed the other eleven drivers the paperwork to be placed on each dashboard. Then the twelve Brandenburgers with the two sheepish cameramen still in tow, headed up a second gang plank that was near the bow and stepped aboard.

Max and Hott watched as two huge cranes began lifting the two smaller lorries ahead of the convoy. The dockers attached the harness. Then when everyone was clear, with a whistle and a thumbs up, the cranes picked them up like toys. In less than a minute, they were securely loaded in the hold of the Irish Larch. The dockers moved up the first two lorries from the convoy and secured the harnesses. Then with the same whistle, the first crane began to lift.

Max held his breath. The crane seemed to struggle at first. Then the operator applied a little more horsepower and a cloud of black diesel smoke belched from the crane's exhaust pipe. The steel cable groaned. Then finally, the lorry was airborne. Max's jaw clenched tight as he watched the lorry rise higher and higher. Then it was swung over the Irish Larch, where it paused for a moment. Millions of pounds worth of gold was suspended in midair. Only a thick steel cable prevented a total disaster. Finally, it began to lower and then it disappeared into the hold. It was followed almost immediately by the second one.

"I was sweating that," said Hott.

"Me too, I'm glad someone did their arithmetic right," admitted Max. He watched the dockers ready lorries three and four for loading, "We should be good now. They all weigh the same," he allowed himself a small smile. Then the men watched until all twelve lorries were loaded safely on board. All the other passengers were now aboard as well as the last of the cargo. Max checked his watch. "Well my friend, that's it. It is up to you now Lieutenant, Operation Mother's Milk is all on you. The Fuhrer and all of Germany are counting on you. Don't drink too much Irish Whiskey!" The ship let out a blast on its foghorn indicating it was time to depart. "You had better be getting on board unless you want to come back with me via Captain Liebe's U-boat," he laughed.

"Yes Sir, I'll pass on the U-boat for now," said Hott. He looked at his commander, who saw a hint of sadness in his eyes now that they were parting ways after so many years spent together. Max sensed his old friend's concern and lightened the atmosphere. "The next time I see you will hopefully be over Schnapps in Berlin. Schnapps and a couple of dancing girls!"

Hott smiled at the thought, "Schnapps and dancing girls in Berlin it is!" said Hott. It was time for Lieutenant Hott to finally take command. He felt the Luger safely stuffed in his greatcoat pocket. He was ready. The two men shook hands. Hott turned and walked up the gang plank. A young sailor wearing a tricolor knitted hat collected his ticket and then he vanished inside.

The dockers pulled away the gang planks. The ship's bell sounded, and the shore crew cast off the massive mooring ropes. With the aid of two tugboats she gently left her berth. Max stood alone on the dock and watched the ship slowly slip out of the harbor and into the choppy Irish Sea. He had done it! The raid was a complete success. They had come in through Britain's unprotected back door and ripped off their gold reserves, all while they slept in their beds. Now it was up to Lieutenant Hott to pull off the ultimate double cross on the Irish.

Max lit himself a cigarette and finally allowed himself the luxury of imagining the accolades he would receive upon his triumphant return to Germany. He could envision the delight on the Fuhrer's face when he received the news that his gold heist was a success. It was, after all the Fuhrer who had personally signed off on the gold heist. The cost of waging war was enormous. Max, his fellow Brandenburgers, and their successful operation had gone a long way to ensuring the Reich's coffers would once again be flush with gold. That is gold to buy tanks and planes to smash the enemy.

Then there was the film. He had come to realize the value of the film and the importance of getting it back to Germany so it could be immediately released worldwide. The effect on British morale would be devastating. There was a very real possibility that it could drive a wedge between Churchill and the British people, which is what the Fuhrer had wanted more than anything.

Finally, there was Reich Fuhrer Himmler, the head of the SS and now undisputed commander of The Brandenburgers. It was

Himmler who had given him his chance at redemption. Max would always be in Himmler's debt for that. The success of Operation Goldilocks and Operation Mother's Milk would do much to boost Himmler's standing with the Fuhrer, in the constant battle for his attention. He took a few more drags of his cigarette before flicking it into the dark muddy water of Holyhead dock. The failure in Norway was now a distant memory. Major Max von Seeckt had finally achieved his redemption.

Max hugged his overcoat a little tighter, reassured by the cylindrical outline of the film canister up against his bruised ribs. It was safely nestled in the specially tailored pocket that was expertly sewn into the lining. Before he had left, Goebbels himself had even confirmed that the size was correct to hold the canister. Nothing had been left to chance. The planning for Operation Goldilocks had been meticulous and it had paid off for Adolph Hitler and his Third Reich big time. The gold was on its way. Shortly, Operation Mother's Milk would begin, Lieutenant Hott backed up by the giant Brandenburger strong man the Beast, would soon be forcing the Captain at gunpoint to head south to La Rochelle, France.

Himmler's brilliant double cross would completely cut out the IRA from getting their share. It was a huge windfall for the Nazis. Now, he just had to drive back to Menai, get up the bridge tower, make radio contact with U38 to confirm his pickup time and he was home and dry. The Brandenburgers had pulled off the greatest gold heist in history. He checked his watch, it was time to head back to the Menai bridge to rendezvous with Captain Liebe of U38. He would take the Ford on the shortest direct route back to Menai on the A55. It would be a welcome straight shot across the island, after the twisting back roads they had travelled on since leaving Rhosybol.

His thoughts were suddenly interrupted by the squealing of tires. He looked around to see a white MG come skidding around the corner and screech to a halt directly behind Max's Ford, perfectly boxing it in behind the Bentley. Max was already running for cover before the MG stopped. He was across the road and heading into the open barn door of one of the many old warehouses that lined the dock. "There he is!" he heard a voice shout. Then he heard, "von Seeckt, stop! Stop or I'll shoot!" He immediately recognized the perfect English accent of Peter Legh. It was followed by a shot that crashed into the door frame just above his head, showering him in splinters as he bolted inside the warehouse.

Max sprinted across the warehouse floor. There were rows of wooden crates stacked eight feet high on the left side, and various pieces of agricultural equipment on the right. There were plenty of places to hide but he dashed to a door at the end of the warehouse and quickly opened it. Then he dove back into the warehouse behind one of the crates and lay silently in the shadows. His heart was thumping as he heard the two men running through the warehouse. "This Way!" one yelled. They sprinted right by him and out the rear door.

Max jumped to his feet and ran back out the way he had just come. He was about to make a dash for the cars when a Morris with a POLICE sign on its roof came racing in and pulled up alongside the MG. It was Sergeant Lewis. He had just been told by the gate guard that an agent from MI5 in an MG had just got through the gate. The agent said that it was a national emergency and to sound the alarm!

"Then bloody well sound it!" Lewis yelled and then floored the accelerator, leaving the bewildered guard in a blue haze of burnt rubber. Now he was alongside the MG, but it was already empty. Max saw his chance. Lewis was about to turn off his engine when the passenger door burst open and Lewis was looking straight down the business end of a German Lugar.

"Drive!" said Max. He pressed the tip of the Lugar barrel firmly into Lewis's ear.

Lewis obeyed. His hand was shaking as he pushed the gear stick into first and pulled away. Another shot rang out shattering the car's rear window.

"Move!!" screamed Max, jamming the Luger even harder into his ear. Lewis punched the accelerator and followed the EXIT signs. He raced out of the Port and headed east. Ashley and Peter jumped into the MG and followed the Morris in hot pursuit. The first alarm bells began to ring on the quayside as the MG flew out of the Port exit.

The Irish Larch, now far enough away from the Port of Holyhead was released by the last tug. Deep in the ship's hold was

Lieutenant Hott, surrounded by his victorious Brandenburgers, two cameramen and the 50 tons of stolen gold. The men formed a tight circle around Hott. He cracked open the bottle of Irish Whiskey that Hugh had given them and proposed a toast, first to their Fuhrer, and then to their fearless commander, Major Max von Seeckt. As the men chugged down the whiskey, they could not imagine what their leader was up to. At that moment, he was involved in a desperate race to get back to the Menai Bridge ahead of a pursuing MI5 agent and a lifelong adversary who he had violently clashed with once before, over a decade ago, at The Wall at Eton College.

Chapter 98

RACE TO MENAI

Menai, Anglesey
August 19, 1940

M ax looked over his shoulder and could see that the MG was following him. He decided to abandon the obvious route of taking the main road directly back to Menai. He was afraid that the direct route would make it easy for the MG to overtake them or that they might try to run them off the road. "To the Menai Bridge and take the back roads!" demanded Max. Lewis did not say a word, he was petrified. He had no idea who this man with the battered face was. He did know that he was looking at pure evil. If this was not the face of the Devil himself, then Hell must be missing an Angel. Oh, how he now regretted his decision to leave his warm bed just a short time ago.

Lewis did as he was told. He took a hard left at the roundabout instead of going straight and taking the most direct and obvious route to Menai. The majority of Anglesey was made up of single lane roads that linked its tiny villages together. Except for the A55, which was the main route from Menai to Holyhead, everything else was single lane. On the rare occasion that a vehicle was coming the opposite direction, both drivers would have to slow down and inch past each other. Both vehicles usually had to brush up against the grass curbs and hedgerows to safely pass. If one of the vehicles was too wide, the smaller one would reverse backwards to the first available layby or turn off. It was common practice and all the locals knew the rules of the road.

"Faster!" demanded Max. Lewis complied, he knew the backroads of the island like the back of his hand. He handled the Morris well considering he had a gun to his head. Lewis reasoned that while he was driving this fast, there was little chance that the man next to him would pull the trigger, as they both would probably be killed. As long as nothing came the other way, he still had a chance. They soon came to his own village of Bodedern. They screamed through the main street and right by his house. Lewis knew Blodwyn was still upstairs sound asleep, blissfully unaware of the peril her beloved husband was in. He silently cursed the situation he had got himself into and began to think methodically about how he could get out of it. For now, he would remain calm. He would do whatever the man next to him with the gun jammed in his ear demanded.

Lewis noticed that Max was continually glancing over his shoulder any time there was a straight section of road. He checked his mirror but there was no sign of anyone following them. They must have lost the MG when they turned off the roundabout to take the back roads. Lewis had been pushing the Morris hard. As they sped through the little village of Bodffordd, he noticed that the temperature gauge was beginning to climb, "She's overheating," he said quietly.

Max glanced at the gauge but was unconcerned. He barked, "Just drive!" Lewis obeyed.

Max ran through his options and concluded that if he could get close enough to the bridge, he would kill the old fool. He would then make contact with U38 to inform them that the mission was a success. After that, his own successful transport off the island would depend on him simply getting to Red Wharf Bay by midnight. He knew that Legh was one of the men who shot at him. His was the only name in the notebook that he had found on the old man who attacked him at the farmhouse. He did not know who the other man was or how they came to be at the Port. Perhaps the old Police Sergeant might know.

"The men who shot at me back there, who were they?" Max asked.

"I don't know, I was just...argh!" wailed Lewis. Max jabbed the barrel of the Luger into his ear hard. A trickle of blood dripped down Lewis' ear lobe on to his white collar, staining it a bright red.

"Don't lie to me you old Bastard! Who were they?" Max yelled. He stiffened the Luger and applied more pressure to Lewis' already bloody ear. "Argh! Alright, I'll tell you. They were...Port Police!" wailed Lewis, desperately trying to formulate a story.

Clearly this crazed man with the gun did not know who Ashley was. Lewis tried to put the pieces together in his mind. Somehow this man was connected to the lights that Ashley was investigating. Also, he must somehow be connected to the Beef Guinness run. That never ran in the early hours of the morning. Something very nefarious was afoot involving O'Reilly's lorries, he knew that much. How they were related, he couldn't fathom, but he knew it was not good.

"Really? Port Police driving an MG?" asked Max. In a flash, he pistol whipped Lewis across his forehead with the butt of the Luger. "Argh!" Lewis screamed. The blood poured out of a gash that opened over his eyebrow. "You're going to kill us!" cried Lewis. He fought to stay focused on the road. He prayed that no one would be coming the other way as he rounded another blind curve. "Again, who were those men?" demanded Max.

"I swear to you, I have no idea. I swear!" cried Lewis.

Max switched tactics, "Why did you pull up like you were following the MG then?' he demanded.

"I wasn't following the MG! I was following the O'Reilly truck convoy!" said Lewis. He felt the pressure easing slightly on his throbbing ear. "And why was that?" asked Max. Now he was puzzled as to why a Police Sergeant would be following his convoy. But how could the old fool possibly know what was going on? The Irish perhaps? Taryn Thomas? Peter Legh? The old man who had attacked him in his sleep? Max was intrigued. He looked over his shoulder again, still no one was on his tail.

"Because it was a big convoy and it was taking the 0430 ferry. I knew there was some monkey business going on because O'Reilly's return lorries get the 1400 ferry. They have to come in all the way from Birkenhead. They wouldn't take the 0430 on a Monday morning, that's for sure," lamented Lewis.

"Monkey business!" laughed Max. "You could say that. Yes, monkey business!"

Baffled, Lewis kept driving. The stretch was reasonably straight but hilly. He had one eye on the rising temperature gauge. Then he saw it, in his rearview mirror, just for a second before it vanished in one of the roads dips. It was way back, but Lewis knew it was the white MG. It was Ashley from MI5. He was not on his own! Now there was a glimmer of hope. Max saw him looking in the mirror and looked back over his shoulder, but he saw nothing. By sheer luck, the MG had still not come up from the dip in the road. Lewis accelerated some more and screeched around another blind curve. Max rapidly focused again on the road ahead.

The old Sergeant was chasing his tail, reasoned Max. He was clueless. The gold was already out in the Irish Sea before he had arrived on the scene. There was nothing to be learned from him. The closer the Morris got to Menai and the coast, the worse the weather became. It had already started to rain again. They drove towards the storm that had now stalled menacingly over the Menai Straits. The slick roads and downed branches added a whole new dimension of terror. Max checked his watch. The detour of taking the back roads to Menai, even with Lewis pushing the Morris to its limit, was taking longer than he had anticipated. He was going to be cutting it close to make his agreed rendezvous time with U38.

Soon they started to see the first signs of life early on a Monday morning on Anglesey, as the Morris flew through the ancient market village of Llangefni. There was the Vicar fighting with his umbrella on the way to church and the local milk man leading his drenched horse and cart. Neither of the men even looked up at the speeding Morris. Lewis checked his mirror again and caught another glimpse of the MG before losing him around another series of curves. The temperature gauge was now pegged in the red zone, but the Lugar still pressed firmly in his ear kept him on pace.

Finally, just ahead they could see the town of Menai, with its famous back drop bridge. The sky was still dark gray and overcast. Heavy black thunder clouds hung ominously over the town. It looked like there would be one more good barrage delivered before it moved over to the Welsh mainland.

A slow-moving car appeared up ahead of them. Lewis automatically started to slow. "Don't slow down! Pass him! Pass him!" screamed Max. He simply could not afford to lose time being stuck behind a slow-moving vehicle. He slapped him again, this time with the Lugar barrel. Lewis winced but this time he did not scream. He gritted his teeth and floored the accelerator. He shot through the narrow gap between the car and the gray cobblestone wall that lined the road.

There was a smash and a shower of sparks as Lewis tore off his wing mirror on the wall. The other car blasted its horn in anger at him for his dangerous driving, but it did not matter. Lewis had made up his mind. He was done with being poked by the Luger. He had no idea where this mad man was taking him or what he would do when they got there. He figured the worst. He also knew that Agent Ashley was behind him and that Ashley would help. He just had to figure out how to survive long enough until Ashley could get to him.

As they entered the roundabout at the base of the bridge it finally happened, there was a loud bang! A gush of steam was accompanied by a horrible grinding sound. It was followed by dirty radiator water splattering the windshield. The wipers smeared it over the glass. "I can't see!!" screamed Lewis as he hit the brakes. The car started to skid wildly. Lewis over corrected and then lurched the wheel the other way. The tires squealed as they tried to get traction on the wet road. The Morris slid sideways and hit the curb of the roundabout hard, sending out a shower of sparks. Then it shot forward on the slick surface, straight towards the Anglesey Arms Pub. Max saw what was coming and had just enough time to brace himself as the Morris smashed sideways into the brick wall of the pub. The driver's side took the full impact. Max hit the windshield and dashboard hard but managed to get his arm up to protect his already battered face. When the car finally stopped, he was dazed for a moment.

The engine hissed loudly and there was a strong smell of petrol. Max looked at Lewis, he was not moving. He put the Luger in his jacket pocket. The door was jammed shut at first, but he put his shoulder to it, and it flew open. Max staggered out. He could see several people alerted by the noise of the crash running towards him. He checked the film canister and to his relief it was firmly in its place. He needed to get up that bridge tower.

Max was at the base of the bridge where the massive steel cables that support the span are anchored to colossal concrete blocks. He looked up and saw the north tower construction platform and the radio hut that he had been in yesterday morning. The tower was about two hundred yards away. Max began to run. The rain pelted down on him, especially once he ran out on to the span. The wind was howling through the straits. As he ran, he heard the sound of another car's engine racing and getting closer. He looked over his shoulder and saw the MG. It pulled up next to the wreckage of the Morris and two men jumped out. One ran to the Morris. The other man, Peter Legh, wearing a flight jacket and waiving a gun, was coming after him.

Chapter 99

DEATH ON THE BRIDGE

Menai , Anglesey
August 19, 1940

M ax swiftly reached the tower. He quickly decided to use the temporary lift as opposed to the steel ladder that ran up the outside of the stonework to the top platform. To his relief the gate was unlocked. He pushed back the gate and entered the tiny lift. He cranked the steel lever to UP and the lift shuddered to life. Slowly, it started to climb.

As it began to ascend the side of the tower, the wind and rain continued to intensify. He stepped backwards to try to get a little more shelter, but it did not make much difference. The rain was almost horizontal, and the winds howled through the little cage. There was a tremendous crack of lightening, followed by an almighty clap of thunder. Max began to worry that it might affect his radio transmission or worse still, strike the tall antenna.

He cursed the speed of the elevator as it creaked and whined its way slowly up the outside of the massive stone column of the north tower. Max could only judge how far up he was by the levels of scaffolding that he slowly passed. But the intensity of the wind told him he had to be near the top. He was looking out through the cage and saw the man in the flight jacket. He was almost up to the tower and now close enough to recognize him. For sure it was Peter Legh.

What on earth was Legh doing on the island and why was he chasing him? It was baffling. He would worry about that later. He also noticed a crowd of people had now gathered at the crash scene by the Anglesey Arms. They must have heard the crash and were now surrounding the smoking wreckage of the Morris. Two men seemed to be trying to pull a motionless body out of the crumpled wreckage. Then he recognized the blond he had encountered the previous morning at this very spot. She was looking right at him and pointing in his direction as the small cage continued its climb up the stone tower.

Suddenly the lift jolted to a halt. He had made it to the top. He pulled back the gate and left it open, knowing that the lift could not descend until it was closed. Max slowly walked across the narrow walkway that connected the lift to the base that housed the crane and the radio hut. He held onto the cable that acted as a safety rail and inched his way forward. The wooden planks that made up the walkway were now slick from the relentless rain.

Directly below him, over a hundred and fifty feet straight down, he could see the black rocks at the base of the tower. The white surf was flowing over their wet jagged surfaces as the waves relentlessly smashed into them. He was mightily relieved to make it back on to the relative safety of the wooden deck. The usual clunk of his jackboots was lost in the tempest that swirled around him as he made his way to the radio hut.

It was padlocked, Max grinned. He reached into his pocket and pulled out the duplicate key that had been given to him by Hugh. He slipped it into the padlock and entered the tiny hut. Closing the door behind him, and grateful to be out of the storm, he checked his watch. It was 0528, perfect. He began to get to work on powering up the radio. There was another massive thunderclap outside that shook the small hut. He needed to make contact with U38, and he needed to do it now.

He took out his code book and began to dial in the assigned frequency. It took longer than Max had figured for the radio to warm up. He had the headset on and his finger was at the ready to tap out his message to U38. But he couldn't pick up anything, not even static. He frantically worked the dial again, trying to make contact. He knew he was running out of time. Legh would be well on his way up the ladder by now. Cursing, and out of time, he took off the head set and left the shelter of the hut.

Peter had arrived at the tower. He had watched Max take the lift up to the top and he knew he would have to climb the wet steel ladder. He put the Enfield in his pocket, dug deep and began to cautiously climb, while the wind and rain battered the tower.

At that moment, exactly on time, three miles off the coast of Anglesey, U38 surfaced in the choppy Irish Sea. Captain Liebe cursed the SS for having him risk his boat and the entire crew again for one man. Liebe glanced at his watch, it showed 0529. Major Max von Seeckt had exactly one minute to make contact.

Max ran to the edge of the platform. He could see Peter climbing up the ladder less than twenty feet away. This was his shot. He pulled out his Luger, aimed at the top of Peter's head and without hesitating, pulled the trigger. Nothing happened. The Luger jammed. He tried to cock it again, but it was jammed solid. Max cursed himself, pistol whipping the old Sergeant had obviously taken its toll. Peter was unaware that he had just cheated death. He continued to climb, holding on to the ladder tightly. The wind and rain continued to pummel him.

Max had to change tactics fast. He would ambush him instead. He looked around for a place to hide. The massive empty wooden spools that were used to hold the steel cables were stacked neatly on the deck. They provided the perfect cover. He would be able to watch Legh as he crossed the catwalk. He stepped back into the shadows, still trying to unjam his gun and waited.

Peter finally made it up to the crane's platform. He could see the small hut where the radio must be housed. He pulled out his Enfield and walked cautiously towards the closed door. Max pulled further back into the shadows and waited as Peter moved ever closer. Max watched him pass by as he made his way towards the radio hut.

Then Peter yelled out, "von Seeckt! The game's up! Come on out of there now with your hands up!" He walked slowly towards the hut with his gun extended out in front of him. "Von Seeckt, I'm armed. Come out now or I swear to God, I'll shoot you!"

Max grinned. Peter Legh was still an idiot after all these years. Stealth and…surprise! Max picked his moment. As Peter approached the hut, Max rushed him from behind. He hit him with tremendous force between his shoulder blades. Both men fell to the wet deck. The gun flew out of Peter's hand and landed spinning on the deck. The two men wrestled for position on the soaked wooden deck.

"You never learn Legh, you just never learn!" growled Max. They rolled back and forth on the deck. Peter was holding on tight to Max's soaked coat. He tried to regain his breath, "I should have finished you at Eton, Legh. You've been living on borrowed time ever since," he continued.

Both men were trying to get a footing on the wet surface. Then they started to exchange blows. The rain and wind were relentless at the top of the bridge. Again, there was another flash of lightening. It was followed immediately by a deafening clap of thunder. The storm was now directly overhead. The wind howled and screamed through the steel cables of the crane above them.

"The game's up von Seeckt. We are on to you. There's nowhere for you to hide!" yelled Peter above the wind as they squared off. Each had their fists clenched in the classic fighter stance, waiting for the other to make a move. They circled around each other on the deck. It was a replay of the clash between them at the Eton Wall, all those years ago.

"What do you mean? You have no idea what I did," laughed Max.

"Oh, you're a big man von Seeckt. You killed a helpless old man. It fits right in with the SS code of conduct, I'm sure!"

"He should have kept his nose out of my business, that old fool," Max laughed.

Another flash of lightening seemed to highlight his whole face. At that moment, Peter Legh knew he was quite literally looking into the face of a monster. After all the missions he had flown, all the friends that he had lost in combat against the Luftwaffe, the ongoing nightmares, the battered face of ETR, the Sergeant crushed behind the wheel of the Morris, it all suddenly welled up inside him. It was more than he could stand. In that moment, Peter Francis Legh of Addington, simply went berserk.

A torrent of rage that he had never felt before exploded inside him. The source of all this terror and misery was now standing right in front of him. He let out a guttural, primitive scream as he lunged at Max, landing on top of him. Max screamed as the film canister was crushed into his bruised ribs by Peter's weight. Both men slid dangerously close to the edge of the deck. They grunted, cursed, and strained. Each tried to get the upper hand. Max was badly winded and tried to get to his feet. Peter saw his chance. He was faster scrambling to his feet, and in one massive adrenalin charged effort, he charged at Max again, this time sending the Nazi right over the edge.

At the last second, Max grabbed at Peter's soaked flight jacket sleeve as he went over the side. Peter felt Max's body weight pulling him over the edge. He dropped to the soaked deck and fought for all he was worth to hold on to the slick surface. Max's legs were swinging wildly in the air. Using his free hand, Peter tried desperately to pry Max's fingers off his jacket. There was another flash of lightening. This time it hit the crane's boom directly over their head. In a massive crash, the lightening strands travelled down the boom to the cab in milliseconds. Peter could now see the sheer terror on Max's bruised face as he dangled in the air, holding on desperately to Peter's sleeve, hundreds of feet above the churning icy waters of the Menai Straits.

"Help me! Help me!" screamed Max. He looked down at the jagged black rocks breaking through the surf below him. Peter strained against Max's weight as he clung desperately onto his flight jacket. Peter knew he just had to break Max's grip and it would be over. "The Hell with you! von Seeckt!" yelled Peter. He methodically peeled Max's fingers off his jacket one at a time, bending them back to the breaking point before Max screamed. Finally, Max released the grip on Peter's sleeve and in a frantic effort grabbed the edge of the deck in a desperate attempt to hold on to anything to prevent him from falling to his death. Then with a superhuman effort, Max began to swing from side to side until he finally hooked the heel of his jackboot onto the edge of the deck. During the fight, Max's pant leg had been pulled up to his knee and Peter could clearly see the golden eagle and Swastika badge attached to his jackboot. The sight of the Swastika gave Peter another surge of adrenalin as he kicked Max's foot off the deck with his boot. Max grunted and tried again. The metal cleat on his heel gouged into the wet wood for a second time. Again, Peter kicked him off. Max tried to swing sideways again but he just could not summon the strength to get his leg up high enough.

"Help me! Legh, for God's sake man, help me!" he wailed. His screams were almost inaudible as the rain and wind raged around them. Peter was able to get to his feet. He looked around for his revolver and saw it just a few feet away. He picked it up, cocked it, and stepped to the edge of the deck. A petrified von Seeckt was still desperately holding on to the edge. His legs were flailing away in the cold turbulent air, "Help me! Help me! Legh! Help me!" von Seeckt continued to scream.

Peter stood over him, looking into the eyes of his lifelong foe. He knew that the end was finally near. He pointed the revolver at Max's head and calmly said, "Goodbye, von Seeckt!"

"No, no, no, don't do this! I can be valuable to you! I know things! Help me!" wailed Max.

Then to his surprise Peter lowered the gun.

"Yes Legh! Help me! Help me!" A flicker of hope crossed the Nazis contorted face.

Peter held up his right hand and bent down closer to Max's face clearly showing him his deformed knuckle. "Remember this? You bastard!"

"Help me. Help me! Please, for god's sake Legh! Help me!" Max's arm muscles burned, as he desperately clung on. Peter sneered at him. "Go to hell, von Seeckt. Touché!" And with that, Peter stomped down hard on Max's fingers, crushing his knuckles between his heel and the wooden deck. Max screamed, and then he was gone, along with Goebbels' propaganda film and his gold adorned jackboots. Peter never heard him hit the water and did not bother to look over the edge.

Exhausted, he staggered back into the radio hut and slumped into the chair. The radio was still on and the dials lit up. Peter looked at it for a while, then picked up the headset and listened. There was nothing but static. He put the headset back on the desk and turned off the power.

Then he heard a familiar voice crying out his name, "Peter! Peter! Peter!" It was Taryn climbing up the ladder to the platform. He smiled as he slowly got to his feet and left the tiny hut. He walked out onto the soaked deck where he and Max had just fought. Then she appeared at the top of the ladder, "Peter, Peter! Oh! Thank God!" She ran towards him. She was soaked. Her blond hair was a wet straggly mess covering her face. "Oh! God! I thought you were dead!" she cried as they embraced. "No, I'm here, it's alright, it's alright." He gently reassured her.

She looked at him, tears streaming from her incredible eyes and down her wet cheeks. "Promise me you will never leave me again!" she said. "I promise," he answered totally lost in her blue eyes. "I'll never leave you again as long as I live. I love you, Taryn," he said. "And I love you too!" she answered as she kissed him again and they hugged each other tightly. Neither one noticed the convoy of Police and Army vehicles that were now pouring across the bridge from the Bangor side. Snudge had managed to get through to Bangor and per Ashley's command, sounded the alarm. The Cavalry had arrived.

Chapter 100

The Last Shot

Conditions were quickly getting worse out in the turbulent Irish Sea. A thick sea fog had begun to form, dramatically reducing visibility. At 32 and already wearing an Iron Cross, Captain Liebe was a rising star amongst Germany's elite U-boat Commanders. U38 was assigned to the 6th U-boat flotilla. Liebe and his crew had already seen action in Operation Weserunbung, the invasion of Norway. U38 had since been patrolling the rough seas of the Western approaches of Ireland. Since war had broken out, he had sunk an impressive 17 British or Allied ships for a total of over 76,000 tons.

But the sinking's were not without controversy. Amongst the tally were two neutral Irish flagged vessels. In September, an Irish petrol tanker, the Inverliffey at 9,456 tons was the largest ship he had sunk. Liebe reasoned that she was carrying petroleum to the British and therefore fair game. He had shelled the defenseless Inverliffey, causing her to catch fire and spill her burning fuel into the sea. The crew took to the lifeboats but were in danger of drifting into the burning petrol. Perhaps with a tinge of guilt and risking his own vessel, Liebe threw the crew's tow lines and dragged their lifeboats to safety. No action was taken against Captain Liebe.

Emboldened, six months later he sank another Irish vessel, the trawler Leukos but there would be no rescue this time. The Leukos went down with all hands. Liebe claimed the Leukos had acted as a shield for a British convoy that he was attempting to attack. While the Irish protested strongly, again no action was taken against the trigger-happy Liebe. Clearly, he was a man who preferred to ask for forgiveness, rather than to ask for permission. His escapades had given him an almost cult like following within the Kriegsmarine. His fellow Commanders had nicknamed him Captain Shamrock, an unspoken nod of approval for the ruthless manner that he conducted the Fuhrer's business at the helm of U38.

Captain Liebe was done waiting. He had already waited an additional five minutes without any signal from Major von Seeckt. He checked his watch one last time, 0535. "Dive!" he yelled to his lieutenant. "Let's get on with the business of winning this war!"

With one last torpedo left on board, U38 blew its ballast tanks and slipped silently below the waves. Liebe's navigator relayed to him the course he had already plotted to return to Lorient, a course that would take them ten miles off the Irish coast and the main entry into the port of Dublin. With plenty of open sea, who knew what targets might be found,

Less than an hour later they finally spotted a solitary merchant vessel, but the rolling seas and terrible visibility made it impossible to make an identification. After tailing the vessel for another half hour and with the conditions rapidly deteriorating, an exhausted Liebe, anxious to get home, and knowing no friendly vessels would be in this area, ordered his torpedo crew to prepare to fire. Liebe waited patiently for the ship to come back into view. It would have to be now or never. Then he finally saw her. This was his best shot.

"Fire!" screamed Liebe. U38 shuddered as the last torpedo shot out of its tube.

Meanwhile, in the hold of the Irish Larch, Lieutenant Hott was still surrounded by his victorious Brandenburgers and their adopted cameramen. They all looked on as Hott gazed at the last drop of Irish Whisky left in the bottle and raised it in a salute to his men. Now sufficiently far enough away from the Welsh mainland, it was finally time for him to make his move. "To the Brandenburgers!" yelled Hott, as he downed the last shot to the delight of the men.

They cheered, then instantaneously burst into a chorus of Deutschland! Deutschland! that reverberated off the steel hull of the ship's hold. None of them noticed Hott giving the Beast the nod as the two men slipped quietly away from the group. They stepped through the hold door and began to climb the steel stairs to the ship's bridge. Hott cocked his Luger as they climbed. The

Captain of the Irish Larch was about to get his new destination. It was no longer Dublin but now they would be heading instead for the seaport of La Rochelle, France, a location that was firmly under the Nazi jackboot.

But it all depended on how accurate Captain Liebe's last shot was. The dark gray torpedo, with its finely tuned mechanisms running perfectly, sliced through the deep blue water of the Irish Sea at an impressive speed of 30 knots.

EPILOGUE

Menai, Anglesey
Present Day

I t took Kieran McCarthy less than ten minutes to drive back home from Penmon Beach with his two dogs and the incredible find of the battered Nazi jackboot and its mysterious golden badge. He was anxious to do some historical research. He made himself a cup of tea and fired up his laptop. Five hours later after searching hundreds of different websites, Kieran finally hit paydirt.

Lady luck was now on his side. As part of the commemorations of the 80th Anniversary of the Battle of Britain, students at the University of Bangor had embarked on a research project. The Bangor News was a weekly newspaper that covered everyday life in the City of Bangor as well as its island neighbor, Anglesey. During the war it was the only paper of any note that was published in North Wales, but it had gone out of business in the early 1950's. After some painstaking research and the cooperation of the main Bangor Library, the students had posted on the university website every front page of the newspaper for the entire year of 1940. It was a novel way of looking back on the history of the region during the epic struggle.

After many hours gazing at his screen, Kieran was examining the front page of the third week of August 1940 when the main headline caught his eye.

DUBLIN FERRY THE IRISH LARCH MISSING

He quickly read the article. The Irish Shipping Company had reported that the ship, the Irish Larch had lost radio contact and not arrived in Dublin as scheduled on Monday after departing Holyhead on time. The article described that the Royal Navy was still conducting a search and rescue operation in a wide area but had found no sign of the ship, its crew, or any wreckage. Two Catalina sea planes based at RAF Valley had joined in the search. Unfortunately, the onset of bad weather conditions had severely hampered the effort. Then he looked further down the page to the next article.

TRAGIC DAY ON STORM BATTERED ANGLESEY

The article told of a major storm that had ravaged the island, damaging buildings, blowing over trees and knocking out all power for hours. The highest ever watermark was recorded at Menai. Then there were several other tragic storm related stories.

MAN KILLED BY FALLING TREE

A Captain Edward Thomas Riggs of the Menai Local Defense Volunteers was killed during the storm by a falling tree.

FOUR DEAD IN FIRE

Four soldiers, all Welsh Fusiliers were tragically killed out at Parys Mountain when their guard hut apparently caught on fire. Investigators said it looked like a wood stove may have accidentally caught fire, trapping the men in the hut. All the men were burned beyond recognition.

Then he finally found a golden nugget.

MAN DROWNS IN MENAI STRAITS

A man fell into the Menai Straits and apparently drowned following a car crash at the Menai Bridge that fatally injured a local Police Sergeant, Bryn Lewis. Police confirmed they were chasing the man who was wanted for questioning about a local robbery. Police released the man's identity as Max von Seeckt, age 28 born in Aberystwyth, Wales. No other details were released.

Kieran noted the name Max von Seeckt, and that the initials matched MvS. He had to be the owner of the jackboot. The name was German, yet the man was from Aberystwyth. Clearly, the storm that had battered the island over 80 years ago, with the highest ever water mark had played a role in preserving the jackboot. He could find no other mention of the robbery that the Police wanted to question von Seeckt about. Kieran was still baffled. He had a long way to go but he had a name, Max von Seeckt. He had found his first clue. Tomorrow he would switch his search to Aberystwyth to see what he could find out about Max von Seeckt. If von Seeckt was 28 years old when he drowned in 1940, he must have been born in 1912. Kieran had a name, date, and a place to start his search. It had been a great day. He quickly took a screen shot, then exited the website.

On that one page, cryptically were all the clues he would ever need to begin to unlock the secret of the jackboot and who knows, maybe what really happened on Anglesey all those years ago.

There are very few clues left these days. The abandoned windmill that once hid 50 tons of gold still stands out at the remote Parys Mountain. The name has been changed now, with an almost Disneyfication to The Copper Kingdom. It boasts of its own interactive exhibition center, where visitors can learn all about the grim history of Parys Mountain and travel back in time to see over 4000 years of copper mining history. It even has its own gift shop. The windmill has been given a new lease on life and is proudly featured as a line drawing on The Copper Kingdom's snappy new logo. The railway lines and spur are long gone. Tourists from all over the world, armed with a Heritage Trail leaflet can now safely follow a gravel path, stopping at vista points to take selfies, as they hike to the windmill and back. The hike would be a stark contrast to John Ashley's perilous journey on that stormy night, eighty years ago.

If Kieran ever managed to connect the dots and get as far as Martins Bank in Liverpool, here is where he might find his first real clue. Sadly, Martins Bank no longer exists. It was swallowed up by banking behemoth Barclays Bank decades ago. However, a single clue to its involvement in one of the most closely kept secrets of World War II can still be found.

Its once proud head office is now boarded up. The massive bronze doors that Eamon Dylan held open for Akroyd on a rainy day in 1940 are still standing guard. Now, along with their columns, after decades of exposure to the sea air that still blows off the River Mersey, they sport a rich patina finish. Behind them hidden from view, perfectly preserved is the massive, luxurious marble interior and spectacular ceiling of the grand banking hall.

The hum of activity that once filled the imposing hall, generating millions of banking transactions five days a week, is silent now. The structure is a Grade II listed historical building. It sits patiently waiting to write its next chapter in the ongoing story of the great City of Liverpool.

If Kieran walks up Water Street and makes a left turn on Exchange Street, he will find an opening cut into the pavement about halfway down the street on the sidewalk. The opening that led down to the bank's massive vaults was concreted over many years ago. Above the concrete patch is a granite plaque. It is one of the very few pieces of physical evidence that Operation Fish even took place. Engraved deeply into the granite, in gold letters are 34 words. They somehow seem begrudgingly vague in what they are willing to reveal, given the secret role Martins Bank played in the greatest movement of wealth out of Britain in history. Read them and you decide.

IN MAY 1940 WHEN THIS COUNTRY WAS THREATENED WITH INVASION PART OF THE NATIONS GOLD RESERVE WAS BROUGHT FROM LONDON AND LOWERED THROUGH THE HATCH FOR SAFE KEEPING IN THE VAULTS OF MARTINS BANK.

LIST OF MAIN CHARACTERS

Akroyd, Simon – Head of Security, Martins Bank
Ashley, John – MI5 Agent
Attlee, Clemence – Deputy British Prime Minister
Bormann, Martin – Hitler's Private Secretary and Gatekeeper
Canaris, Wilhelm – Chief of the Abwehr
Churchill, Winston – British Prime Minister
Dylan, Eamon – IRA Mole
Ferguson, Brian – Assistant to Major Withers
Goebbels, Joseph – Nazi Minister of Propaganda
Goering, Hermann – Chief of the Luftwaffe
Himmler, Heinrich – Chief of the SS
Hitler, Adolph – Leader of the Third Reich
Hott, Fritz – SS Brandenburgers Lieutenant
Kelly, Seamus – IRA Chief of Staff
Legh, Peter Francis – RAF Spitfire Pilot
Lewis, Bryn – Sergeant Holyhead Port Police
Liebe, Heinrich – Captain U-boat U38
Moran, Hugh – IRA Soldier
Norman, Montague – Governor of the Bank of England
O'Reilly, Sean – IRA Commander
Petrie, David – Director General of British MI5
Riggs, Edward Thomas (aka ETR) – Captain Local Defense Volunteers LDV
Snudge – Barman
Schacht, Hjalmar – President of the Reichsbank
Thomas, Taryn – Welsh lady
Tully, Richard – IRA Leader
Von Seeckt, Max (aka Billy Muskett) – SS Major Brandenburgers
Withers, Archibald – Colonel M15

Author Biographies

Peter Wells

Pete was born and raised in Wallasey, England. He grew up less than a half mile from the banks of the River Mersey, where he lived with his father Bill, mother Sybil, and sister Karen. He remembers playing in the ruins and rubble of terraced houses that still remained after being bombed by the Luftwaffe during the Blitz of World War II. At age 7, he recalls going to the Gaumont, the local cinema to see one of his favorite movies, Twelve O'clock High with Gregory Peck. It told the story of the young Americans who flew the mighty B17 Flying Fortresses from Britain to the heart of Nazi Germany. He was in awe at the courage of the crews, young men far from home willing to lay down their lives so that Britain and Europe could live in freedom. It began an early fascination with America and Americans.

Pete has led an interesting life. In his early twenties, he and two friends combined their resources to purchase a Land Rover and headed overland to see the Great Pyramids of Egypt. Along the way, he picked grapes, waited tables, worked as a photographer, and tended bar. They made it as far as Crete before finally running out of money. They returned home, sold the Land Rover and tried again the following year. This time they used planes, trains, and buses and finally made it to the Pyramids.

The following summer in 1980, Pete and one of the same two friends, filled the last two remaining seats aboard a no-frills Freddy Laker Skytrain, and flew to Los Angeles, California, With a pocket full of dreams and $120 he had finally made it to California. Pete settled in the San Francisco Bay Area where he met his wife of 36 years, Taryn. They have a son together, Britton who lives in Utah.

Pete spent close to four decades enjoying a successful career in sales and living the American dream. During a Christmas visit with his family in England in 2017, his dad, Bill shared an idea for a book that he had in his mind for over ten years but was never able to join all the dots and complete it. Intrigued, Pete agreed to partner with him to complete the novel. It began quite an odyssey. He and Taryn traveled to Ireland, Wales, England, Scotland, Holland, Belgium, Norway, France, Italy, Germany, and Austria to gather research for the Jackboot. It took almost three years of being totally immersed in 1940 and a world at war, for him to finally make Bill's dream a reality. The Jackboot is their first novel.

Now retired, he and Taryn live a quiet life on Florida's Sun Coast, where they enjoy cooking, watching movies, traveling and riding their bicycles for miles along some of the world's greatest beaches.

Bill Wells

Born a few years before the Great Depression in the 1920's, Bill Wells came up the hard way. He was the youngest of three boys growing up in war torn England. During the Nazi blitz of 1940, he watched in horror as his family home in Wallasey went up in flames. An incendiary bomb dropped by Hermann Goering's Luftwaffe had crashed through their chimney and exploded in the fireplace.

As a teenage Sea Cadet, Bill gained his sea legs with a short spell on a trawler that had been converted to a minesweeper, clearing enemy mines in the often turbulent Irish Sea. As a young seaman, he served on multiple sea going tugs. Their main task was towing in battered United States and Royal Navy ships that were casualties of the Battle of the Atlantic that had managed to limp to the safety of the Mersey Bar.

Prior to the D-Day landings, Bill participated in towing sections of the massive concrete floating harbors known as Mulberries. They were used by the Americans and their allies to land men and supplies in support of the Normandy invasion. Bill's next step was the Royal Navy, where he planned on following in the footsteps of his older brother Alf, who was already on active destroyer duty. However, His Majesty's Government and the British Army of the Rhine had other ideas. At age 18, Bill was conscripted and served as a medic in the Royal Army Medical Corps serving in a troubled Northern Ireland and Germany during the Cold War. A proud World War II veteran, he has eight medals and a veteran's badge.

In civilian life he became a National Secretary of an adult educational organization and then onto a publishing and advertising career. He ran unsuccessfully for Parliament but finished up his political career as the Mayor of Wirral, then one of the top ten largest local authorities in the UK. He was married to Sybil, his wife of 68 years, who sadly passed away in September 2020.

Now in his nineties, he lives in a small town in the UK near his daughter Karen and her family. Co-authoring The Jackboot kept him in almost daily contact with his son Peter in Florida. Bill describes The Jackboot as the big cherry on the cake of a very full life. While he gets a kick from his name being on the cover, it pales in comparison to being able to communicate with readers from all over the world via www.thejackboot.com from the comfort of his home office. For a guy who remembers once using a slate and chalk to communicate and reading his first books and comics by gaslight, he thinks we have all traveled a very long way.